To Willie.

From, Mary, with the
best of wishes for
a very happy birthday.

31/10/30.

BEN-HUR:

A TALE OF THE CHRIST

BY

LEW. WALLACE

AUTHOR OF "THE FAIR GOD"

"Learn of the philosophers always to look for natural causes in
all extraordinary events; and when such natural causes are wanting,
ecur to God."—COUNT DE GABALIS.

WARD, LOCK & CO., LIMITED
LONDON AND MELBOURNE

Printed in Great Britain by Butler & Tanner Ltd., Frome and London

BEN-HUR : A TALE OF THE CHRIST

BEN-HUR :

A TALE OF THE CHRIST

BOOK FIRST

CHAPTER I

OUT of the wady which rises at the extreme end of Mount Jebel, and, extending east of north, becomes at length the bed of the Jabbok river—a traveller passed, going to the table-lands of the desert. To this person the attention of the reader is first besought.

Judged by his appearance, he was quite forty-five years old. His beard, once of the deepest black, flowing broadly over his breast, was streaked with white. His face was brown as a parched coffee-berry, and so hidden by a red *kufiyeh* (as the kerchief of the head is at this day called by the children of the desert) as to be but in part visible. Now and then he raised his eyes, and they were large and dark. He was clad in the flowing garments so universal in the East ; but their style may not be described more particularly, for he sat under a miniature tent, and rode a great white dromedary.

When the dromedary lifted itself out of the last break of the wady, the traveller had passed the boundary of El Belka, the ancient Ammon. It was morning time. Before him was the sun, half curtained in fleecy mists ; before him also spread the desert ; not the realm of drifting sands, which was farther on, but the region where the herbage began to dwarf ; where the surface is strewn with boulders, of granite, and grey and brown stones, interspersed with

3

languishing acacias and tufts of camel-grass. The oak, bramble and arbutus lay behind, as if they had come to a line, looked over into the well-less waste, and crouched with fear.

For two hours the dromedary swung forward, keeping the trot steadily and in the line due east. In that time the traveller never changed his position, nor looked to the right or left. As one of the results of the rapid advance, the face of the landscape underwent a change. The Jebel stretched along the western horizon, like a pale-blue ribbon. A *tell*, or hummock of clay and cemented sand, arose here and there. Now and then basaltic stones lifted their round crowns, outposts of the mountain against the forces of the plain; all else, however, was sand, sometimes smooth as the beaten beach, then heaped in rolling ridges; here chopped waves, there long swells. So, too, the condition of the atmosphere changed. The sun, high risen, had drunk his fill of dew and mist, and warmed the breeze that kissed the wanderer under the awning; far and near he was tinting the earth with faint milk-whiteness, and shimmering all the sky.

Two hours more passed without rest or deviation from the course. Vegetation entirely ceased. The sand, so crusted on the surface that it broke into rattling flakes at every step, held undisputed sway. The Jebel was out of view, and there was no landmark visible. The shadow that before followed had now shifted to the north, and was keeping even race with the objects which cast it.

Exactly at noon the dromedary, of its own will, stopped, and uttered the cry or moan, peculiarly piteous, by which its kind always protest against an overload, and sometimes crave attention and rest. The master thereupon bestirred himself, waking, as it were, from sleep. He threw the curtains of the *houdah* up, looked at the sun, surveyed the country on every side long and carefully, as if to identify an appointed place. Satisfied with the inspection, he drew a deep breath and nodded, much as to say, " At last, at last ! " A moment after, he crossed his hands upon his breast, bowed his head, and prayed silently. The pious duty done, he prepared to dismount. From his throat proceeded the sound heard doubtless by the favourite camels of Job—*Ikh ! ikh !*—the signal to kneel. Slowly the animal obeyed, grunting the while. The rider then put his foot upon the slender neck, and stepped upon the sand.

The man as now revealed was of admirable proportions, not so tall as powerful. Loosening the silken rope which held the *kufiyeh* on his head, he brushed the fringed folds back until his face was bare—a strong face, almost negro in colour ; yet the low, broad forehead, aquiline nose, the outer corners of the eyes turned slightly upward, the hair profuse, straight, harsh, of metallic lustre, and falling to the shoulder in many plaits, were signs of origin impossible to disguise. So looked the Pharaohs and the later Ptolemies ; so looked Mizraim, father of the Egyptian race.

The traveller's limbs were numb, for the ride had been long and wearisome ; so he rubbed his hands and stamped his feet, and walked round the faithful servant, whose lustrous eyes were closing in calm content with the cud he had already found. Often, while making the circuit, he paused, and, shading his eyes with his hands, examined the desert to the extremest verge of vision ; and always, when the survey was ended, his face clouded with disappointment, slight, but enough to advise a shrewd spectator that he was there expecting company, if not by appointment ; at the same time, the spectator would have been conscious of a sharpening of the curiosity to learn what the business could be that required transaction in a place so far from civilized abode.

However disappointed, there could be little doubt of the stranger's confidence in the coming of the expected company. In token thereof, he went first to the litter, and, from the cot or box opposite the one he had occupied in coming, produced a sponge and a small gurglet of water, with which he washed the eyes, face and nostrils of the camel ; that done, from the same depository he drew a circular cloth, red-and-white striped, a bundle of rods, and a stout cane. The latter, after some manipulation, proved to be a cunning device of lesser joints, one within another, which, when united together, formed a centre pole higher than his head. When the pole was planted, and the rods set around it, he spread the cloth over them, and was literally at home—a home much smaller than the habitations of emir and sheik, yet their counterpart in all other respects. From the litter again he brought a carpet or square rug, and covered the floor of the tent on the side from the sun.

From a willow basket he brought forth materials for a meal : platters close-woven of the fibres of palms ; wine in small gurglets of skin ; mutton dried and smoked ; stoneless *shami*, or Syrian pomegranates ; dates of El Shelebi, wondrous rich and grown in the *nakhil*, or palm orchards, of Central Arabia ; cheese, like David's " slices of milk " ; and leavened bread from the city bakery— all which he carried and set upon the carpet under the tent.

All was now ready. He stepped out : lo ! in the east a dark speck on the face of the desert. The speck grew : became large as a hand ; at length assumed defined proportions. A little later, full into view swung a duplication of his own dromedary, tall and white, and bearing a *houdah*, the travelling litter of Hindustan. Then the Egyptian crossed his hands upon his breast, and looked to heaven.

" God only is great ! " he exclaimed, his eyes full of tears, his soul in awe.

The stranger drew nigh—at last stopped. Then he, too, seemed just waking. He beheld the kneeling camel, the tent, and the man standing prayerfully at the door. He crossed his hands, bent his head, and prayed silently ; after which, in a little while, he stepped from his camel's neck to the sand, and advanced towards the Egyptian, as did the Egyptian towards him. A moment they looked at each other ; then they embraced—that is, each threw his right arm over the other's shoulder, and the left round the side, placing his chin first upon the left, then upon the right breast.

" Peace be with thee, O servant of the true God ! " the stranger said.

" And to thee, O brother of the true faith !—to thee peace and welcome," the Egyptian replied, with fervour.

The new-comer was tall and gaunt, with lean face, sunken

eyes, white hair and beard, and a complexion between the
hue of cinnamon and bronze. He, too, was unarmed.
His costume was Hindustani ; over the skull-cap a shawl
was wound in great folds, forming a turban ; his body
garments were in the style of the Egyptian's. In place
of sandals, his feet were clad in half-slippers of red leather,
pointed at the toes. Save the slippers, the costume from
head to foot was of white linen. The air of the man was
high, stately, severe.

They looked to the north, where, already plain to view,
a third camel, of the whiteness of the others, came careening
like a ship. They waited, standing together—waited until
the new-comer arrived, dismounted, and advanced towards
them.

" Peace to you, O my brother ! " he said, while embracing
the Hindu.

And the Hindu answered, " God's will be done ! "

The last-comer was all unlike his friends ; his frame was
slighter ; his complexion white ; a mass of waving light hair
was a perfect crown for his small but beautiful head ;
the warmth of his dark-blue eyes certified a delicate mind,
and a cordial, brave nature. He was bareheaded and
unarmed. Under the folds of the Tyrian blanket which
he wore with unconscious grace appeared a tunic, short-
sleeved and low-necked, gathered to the waist by a band,
and reaching nearly to the knee ; leaving the neck, arms,
and legs bare. Sandals guarded his feet. Fifty years,
probably more, had spent themselves upon him, with no
other effect, apparently, than to tinge his demeanour with
gravity and temper his words with forethought. The
physical organization and the brightness of soul were un-
touched. No need to tell the student from what kindred
he was sprung ; if he came not himself from the groves of
Athené, his ancestry did.

When his arms fell from the Egyptian, the latter said with
a tremulous voice, " The Spirit brought me first ; wherefore I know myself chosen to be the servant of my brethren.
The tent is set, and the bread is ready for the breaking.
Let me perform my office."

Taking each by the hand, he led them within, and removed

their sandals and washed their feet, and he poured water upon their hands, and dried them with napkins.

Then, when he had laved his own hands, he said, " Let us take care of ourselves, brethren, as our service requires, and eat, that we may be strong for what remains of the day's duty. While we eat, we will each learn who the others are, and whence they come, and how they are called."

He took them to the repast, and seated them so that they faced each other. Simultaneously their heads bent forward, their hands crossed upon their breasts, and speaking together, they said aloud this simple grace :

" Father of all—God !—what we have here is of Thee ; take our thanks and bless us, that we may continue to do Thy will."

With the last word they raised their eyes, and looked at each other in wonder. Each had spoken in a language never before heard by the others ; yet each understood perfectly what was said. Their souls thrilled with divine emotion ; for by the miracle they recognized the Divine Presence.

CHAPTER II

To speak in the style of the period, the meeting just described took place in the year of Rome 747. The month was December, and winter reigned over all the regions east of the Mediterranean. Such as ride upon the desert in this season go not far until smitten with a keen appetite. The company under the little tent were not exceptions to the rule. They were hungry, and ate heartily ; and, after the wine, they talked.

" To a wayfarer in a strange land nothing is so sweet as to hear his name on the tongue of a friend," said the Egyptian, who assumed to be president of the repast. " Before us lie many days of companionship. It is time we knew each other. So if it be agreeable, he who came last shall be first to speak."

Then, slowly at first, like one watchful of himself, the Greek began :

" Far to the west of this there is a land which may never

be forgotten ; if only because the world is too much its debtor, and because the indebtedness is for things that bring to men their purest pleasures. The land I speak of is Greece. I am Gaspar, son of Cleanthes the Athenian.

"My people," he continued, "were given wholly to study, and from them I derived the same passion. It happens that two of our philosophers, the very greatest of the many, teach, one the doctrine of a Soul in every man, and its Immortality ; the other the doctrine of One God, infinitely just. From the multitude of subjects about which the schools were disputing, I separated them, as alone worth the labour of solution ; for I thought there was a relation between God and the soul as yet unknown. On this theme the mind can reason to a point, a dead, impassable wall ; arrived there, all that remains is to stand and cry aloud for help. So I did ; but no voice came to me over the wall. In despair, I tore myself from the cities and the schools."

At these words a grave smile of approval lighted the gaunt face of the Hindu.

"In the northern part of my country—in Thessaly," the Greek proceeded to say, "there is a mountain famous as the home of the gods, where Theus, whom my countrymen believe supreme, has his abode ; Olympus is its name. Thither I betook myself. I found a cave in a hill where the mountain, coming from the west, bends to the southeast ; there I dwelt, giving myself up to meditation. The door of my hermitage looks over an arm of the sea, over the Thermaic Gulf. One day I saw a man flung overboard from a ship sailing by. He swam ashore. I received and took care of him. He was a Jew, learned in the history and laws of his people ; and from him I came to know that the God of my prayers did indeed exist, and had been for ages their lawmaker, ruler and king. What was that but the Revelation I dreamed of ? My faith had not been fruitless ; God answered me !

"That was not all. The man so sent to me told me more. He said the prophets who, in the ages which followed the first revelation, walked and talked with God, declared He would come again.

" One night I sat by the door of my cave trying to get nearer the mysteries of my existence, knowing which is to know God ; suddenly, on the sea below me, or rather in the darkness that covered its face, I saw a star begin to burn ; slowly it arose and drew nigh, and stood over the hill and above my door, so that its light shone full upon me. I fell down, and slept, and in my dream I heard a voice say :

" ' O Gaspar ! thy faith hath conquered ! Blessed art thou ! With two others, come from the uttermost parts of the earth, thou shalt see Him that is promised, and be a witness for Him, and the occasion of testimony in His behalf. In the morning arise, and go meet them, and keep trust in the Spirit that shall guide thee.'

" And in the morning I awoke with the Spirit as a light within me surpassing that of the sun. I put off my hermit's garb, and dressed myself as of old. From a hiding-place I took the treasure which I had brought from the city. A ship went sailing past. I hailed it, was taken aboard, and landed at Antioch. There I bought the camel and his furniture. Through the gardens and orchards that enamel the banks of the Orontes, I journeyed to Emesa, Damascus, Bostra, and Philadelphia : thence hither. And so, O brethren, you have my story. Let me now listen to you."

The Egyptian and the Hindu looked at each other ; the former waved his hand ; the latter bowed, and began :

" Our brother has spoken well. May my words be as wise."

He broke off, reflected a moment, then resumed :

" I was born a Brahman. My life, consequently, was ordered down to its least act, its last hour. The part of a Brahman's life, called the first order, is his student life. When I was ready to enter the second order—that is to say, when I was ready to marry and become a householder—I questioned everything, even Brahm ; I was a heretic. I could not rest. Brahm had filled the world with so much wretchedness. The Sudra, or Servile caste appealed to me ; so did the countless devotees and victims. The island of Ganga Lagor lies where the

sacred waters of the Ganges disappear in the Indian
Ocean. Thither I betook myself. In the shade of the
temple built there to the sage Kapila, in a union of
prayers with the disciples whom the sanctified memory
of the holy man keeps around his house, I thought to find
rest. But twice every year came pilgrimages of Hindus
seeking the purification of the waters. Their misery
strengthened my love. Against its impulse to speak, I
clenched my jaws ; for one word against Brahm or the Triad
or the Shastras would doom me ; one act of kindness to
the outcast Brahmans who now and then dragged themselves to die on the burning sands—a blessing said, a cup of
water given—and I became one of them, lost to family,
country, privileges, caste. The love conquered ! I spoke
to the disciples in the temple ; they drove me out. I spoke
to the pilgrims ; they stoned me from the island. On the
highways I attempted to preach ; my hearers fled from
me, or sought my life. In all India, finally, there was not
a place in which I could find peace or safety—not even
among the outcasts ; for though fallen, they were still
believers in Brahm. In my extremity, I looked for a
solitude in which to hide from all but God. I followed the
Ganges to its source, far up in the Himalayas. There I
went to abide alone with God, praying, fasting, waiting
for death."

Again the voice fell, and the bony hands met in a fervent
clasp.

"One night I walked by the shores of the lake, and spoke
to the listening silence : ' When will God come and claim
His own ? Is there to be no redemption ? ' Suddenly
a light began to glow tremulously out on the water ; soon
a star arose, and moved towards me, and stood overhead.
The brightness stunned me. While I lay upon the ground,
I heard a voice of infinite sweetness say, ' Thy love hath
conquered. Blessed art thou, O son of India ! The
redemption is at hand. With two others, from far quarters
of the earth, thou shalt see the Redeemer, and be a witness
that He hath come. In the morning arise, and go meet
them ; and put all thy trust in the Spirit which shall guide
thee.'

" And from that time the light has stayed with me ; so
I knew it was the visible presence of the Spirit. In the
morning I started to the world by the way I had come. In
a cleft of the mountain I found a stone of vast worth,
which I sold in Hurdwar. By Lahore and Cabool, and
Yezd, I came to Ispahan. There I bought the camel, and
thence was led to Bagdad, not waiting for caravans. Alone
I travelled, fearless, for the Spirit was with me, and is
with me yet. What glory is ours, O brethren ! We are
to see the Redeemer—to speak to Him—to worship Him !
I am done."

CHAPTER III

THE vivacious Greek broke forth in expressions of joy and
congratulations ; after which the Egyptian said, with
characteristic gravity :

" I salute you, my brother. You have suffered much,
and I rejoice in your triumph. If you are both pleased to
hear me, I will now tell you who I am, and how I came to
be called. I am Balthasar the Egyptian."

The last words were spoken quietly, but with so much
dignity that both listeners bowed to the speaker.

" I was born at Alexandria, a prince and a priest, and
had the education usual to my class. In my country,
brethren, we have, from the day of the unfortunate Pharaoh,
always had two religions—one private, the other public ;
one of many gods, practised by the people ; the other of
one God, cherished only by the priesthood. But very early I
became discontented. If, as my teacher taught, God was
just, why was there no distinction between the good and
the bad ? At length it became clear to me, a certainty, a
corollary of the law to which I reduced pure religion, that
death was only the point of separation at which the wicked
are left or lost, and the faithful rise to a higher life—
life active, joyous, everlasting—LIFE WITH GOD ! The
discovery led to another inquiry. Why should the Truth
be longer kept a secret for the selfish solace of the priesthood ? One day, in the Brucheium, the most splendid

and crowded quarter of Alexandria, I arose and preached.
The East and West contributed to my audience. Students
going to the Library, priests from the Serapeion, idlers
from the Museum, patrons of the racecourse, countrymen
from the Rhacotis—a multitude—stopped to hear me. I
preached God, the Soul, Right and Wrong, and Heaven,
the reward of a virtuous life. You, O Melchior, were
stoned ; my auditors first wondered, then laughed. I
tried again ; they pelted me with epigrams, covered my
God with ridicule, and darkened my Heaven with mockery.
Not to linger needlessly, I fell before them."

The Hindu here drew a long sigh, as he said, " The enemy
of man is man, my brother."

Balthasar lapsed into silence.

" I gave much thought to finding the cause of my failure,
and at last succeeded," he said, upon beginning again.
" From that day, O brethren, I travelled up and down the
Nile, in the villages, and to all the tribes, preaching One
God, a righteous life, and reward in Heaven. I have done
good—it does not become me to say how much. I also
know that part of the world to be ripe for the reception
of Him we go to find."

A flush suffused the swarthy cheek of the speaker ; but
he overcame the feeling, and continued :

" The years so given, O my brothers, were troubled by
one thought—When I was gone, what would become of
the cause I had started ? Was it to end with me ? I
had dreamed many times of organization as a fitting
crown for my work. To hide nothing from you, I had
tried to effect it, and failed. Brethren, the reformer must
have a more than human sanction ; he must not merely
come in God's name, he must have the proofs subject to
his word ; he must demonstrate all he says, even God.
And who in this age can carry the faith of men to such a
point but God Himself ? To redeem the race—I do not
mean to destroy it—to *redeem* the race, He must make
Himself once more manifest ; HE MUST COME IN PERSON."

Intense emotion seized the three.

" Are we not going to find Him ? " exclaimed the Greek.

" You understand why I failed in the attempt to organize," said the Egyptian, when the spell was passed. " I had not the sanction. One night I walked beside the river. ' The world is dying. When wilt Thou come ? Why may I not see the redemption, O God ? ' so I prayed. The glassy water was sparkling with stars. One of them seemed to leave its place, and rise to the surface, where it became a brilliancy burning to the eyes. Then it moved towards me, and stood over my head, apparently in hand's reach. I fell down and hid my face. A voice, not of the earth, said, ' Thy good works have conquered. Blessed art thou, O son of Mizraim! The redemption cometh. With two others, from the remoteness of the world, thou shalt see the Saviour, and testify for Him. In the morning arise, and go meet them. And when ye have all come to the holy city of Jerusalem, ask of the people, Where is He that is born King of the Jews ? for we have seen His star in the East, and are sent to worship Him. Put all thy trust in the Spirit which will guide thee.'

" And the light became an inward illumination not to be doubted, and has stayed with me, a governor and a guide. It led me down the river to Memphis, where I made ready for the desert. I bought my camel, and came hither without rest, by way of Suez and Kufileh, and up through the lands of Moab and Ammon. God is with us, O my brethren ! "

He paused, and thereupon, with a prompting not their own, they all arose, and looked at each other.

By a simultaneous impulse the three joined hands.

There was silence, broken by sighs and sanctified with tears ; for the joy that filled them might not be stayed. It was the unspeakable joy of souls on the shores of the River of Life, resting with the Redeemed in God's presence.

Presently their hands fell apart, and together they went out of the tent. The desert was still as the sky. The sun was sinking fast. The camels slept.

A little while after, the tent was struck, and, with the remains of the repast, restored to the cot ; then the friends mounted, and set out single file, led by the Egyptian. Their course was due west, into the chilly night. The camels swung forward in steady trot, keeping the line and the intervals so exactly that those following seemed to tread in the tracks of the leader. The riders spoke not once.

By and by the moon came up. And as the three tall, white figures sped, with soundless tread, through the opalescent light, they appeared like spectres flying from hateful shadows. Suddenly, in the air before them, not farther up than a low hill-top, flared a lambent flame ; as they looked at it, the apparition contracted into a focus of dazzling lustre. Their hearts beat fast ; their souls thrilled ; and they shouted as with one voice, " The Star ! the Star ! God is with us ! "

CHAPTER IV

LET us take our stand by the Joppa Gate of Jerusalem, just out of the edge of the currents—one flowing in, the other out—and use our eyes and ears awhile.

As we watch, suddenly there is a commotion in the crowd, a parting quickly to the right and left, with exclamations sharp and decisive. Then the cause comes—a man, Hebrew in feature and dress. The mantle of snow-white linen, held to his head by cords of yellow silk, flows free over his shoulders ; his robe is richly embroidered ; a red sash with fringes of gold wraps his waist several times. His demeanour is calm ; he even smiles upon those who, with such rude haste, make room for him. A leper ? No, he is only a Samaritan. The shrinking crowd, if asked, would say he is a mongrel—an Assyrian—whose touch of the robe is pollution ; from whom, consequently, an Israelite, though dying, might not accept life. In fact, the feud is not of blood. When David set his throne here on Mount Zion, with only Judah to support him, the ten tribes betook themselves to Shechem, a city much older, and, at that date, infinitely richer in holy memories. The final union of the tribes did not settle the dispute thus begun. The Samaritans clung to their tabernacle on Gerizim, and, while maintaining its superior sanctity, laughed at the irate doctors in Jerusalem. Time brought no assuagement of

the hate. Under Herod, conversion to the faith was open
to all the world except the Samaritans ; they alone were
absolutely and for ever shut out from communion with
Jews.

As the Samaritan goes in under the arch of the gate, out
come three men so unlike all whom we have yet seen that
they fix our gaze, whether we will or not. They are of
unusual stature and immense brawn : their eyes are blue,
and so fair is their complexion that the blood shines through
the skin like blue pencilling ; their hair is light and short ;
their heads, small and round, rest squarely upon necks
columnar as the trunks of trees. Woollen tunics, open at
the breast, sleeveless and loosely girt, drape their bodies,
leaving bare arms and legs of such development that they
at once suggest the arena ; and when thereto we add their
careless, confident, insolent manner, we cease to wonder
that the people give them way, and stop, after they have
passed, to look at them again. They are gladiators—
wrestlers, runners, boxers, swordsmen ; professionals unknown in Judea before the coming of the Roman ; fellows
who, what time they are not in training, may be seen
strolling through the king's gardens or sitting with the
guards at the palace gates ; or possibly they are visitors
from Cæsarea, Sebaste, or Jericho ; in which Herod, more
Greek than Jew, and with all a Roman's love of games and
bloody spectacles, has built vast theatres, and now keeps
schools of fighting-men, drawn, as is the custom, from
the Gallic provinces, or the Slavic tribes on the Danube.

" By Bacchus ! " says one of them, drawing his clenched
hand to his shoulder, " their skulls are not thicker than
eggshells."

The brutal look which goes with the gesture disgusts
us, and we turn happily to something more pleasant.

A person follows him challenging all our wonder. He
comes up the road slowly, his face towards the ground ;
at intervals he stops, crosses his hands upon his breast,
lengthens his countenance, and turns his eyes towards
heaven, as if about to break into prayer. Nowhere, except
in Jerusalem, can such a character be found. On his
forehead, attached to the band which keeps the mantle

in place, projects a leathern case, square in form ; another similar case is tied by a thong to the left arm ; the borders of his robe are decorated with deep fringe ; and by such signs—the phylacteries, the enlarged borders of the garment, and the savour of intense holiness pervading the whole man—we know him to be a Pharisee, one of an organization (in religion a sect, in politics a party) whose bigotry and power will shortly bring the world to grief.

And so, till towards noon, sometimes later, the steady currents of business habitually flow in and out of the Joppa Gate, carrying with them every variety of character ; including representatives of all the tribes of Israel, all the sects among whom the ancient faith has been parcelled and refined away, all the religious and social divisions, all the adventurous rabble who, as children of art and ministers of pleasure, riot in the prodigalities of Herod, and all the peoples of note at any time compassed by the Cæsars and their predecessors, especially those dwelling within the circuit of the Mediterranean.

In other words, Jerusalem rich in sacred history, richer in connexion with sacred prophecies—the Jerusalem of Solomon, in which silver was as stones, and cedars as the sycamores of the vale—had come to be but a copy of Rome, a centre of unholy practices, a seat of pagan power. A Jewish king one day put on priestly garments, and went into the Holy of Holies of the first temple to offer incense, and he came out a leper ; but in the time of which we are reading, Pompey entered Herod's temple and the same Holy of Holies, and came out without harm, finding but an empty chamber, and of God not a sign.

CHAPTER V

THE reader, who in thought has been standing beside the Joppa Gate, is now besought to pass through the arched entrance into a narrow lane and court, which passing by the walls of the great tower conduct on into the city. This court is part of the market. It was the third hour of the day, and many of the people had gone away ; yet the

B

press continued without apparent abatement. Of the new-comers, there was a group over by the south wall, con-sisting of a man, a woman and a donkey, which requires extended notice.

The man stood by the animal's head, holding a leading-strap, and leaning upon a stick which seemed to have been chosen for the double purpose of goad and staff. His dress was like that of the ordinary Jews around him, except that it had an appearance of newness. His features were exposed, and they told of fifty years of life, a surmise confirmed by the grey that streaked his otherwise black beard. He looked around him with the half-curious, half-vacant stare of a stranger and provincial.

The donkey ate leisurely from an armful of green grass, unmindful of the woman sitting upon its back in a cushioned pillion. An outer robe of dull woollen stuff completely covered her person, while a white wimple veiled her head and neck.

At length the man was accosted.

" Are you not Joseph of Nazareth ? "

The speaker was standing close by.

" I am so called," answered Joseph, turning gravely around. " And you—ah, peace be unto you, my friend, Rabbi Samuel ! "

" The same give I back to you." The Rabbi paused, looking at the woman, then added, " To you, and unto your house and all your helpers, be peace. What are the Zealots doing down in Galilee ? "

" I am a carpenter, and Nazareth is a village," said Joseph cautiously. " The street on which my bench stands is not a road leading to any city. Hewing wood and sawing plank leave me no time to take part in the disputes of parties."

" But you are a Jew," said the Rabbi earnestly. " You are a Jew, and of the line of David. It is not possible you can find pleasure in the payment of any tax except the shekel given by ancient custom to Jehovah."

Joseph held his peace.

" I do not complain," his friend continued, " of the amount of the tax—a denarius is a trifle. Oh no ! The imposition of the tax is the offence. And, besides, what is paying it but submission to tyranny? Tell me, is it true that Judas claims to be the Messiah? You live in the midst of his followers."

"I have heard his followers say he was the Messiah," Joseph replied.

At this point the wimple was drawn aside, and for an instant the whole face of the woman was exposed. The eyes of the Rabbi wandered that way, and he had time to see a countenance of rare beauty, kindled by a look of intense interest; then a blush overspread her cheeks and brow, and the veil was returned to its place.

The politician forgot his subject.

"Your daughter is comely," he said, speaking lower.

"She is not my daughter," Joseph repeated.

The curiosity of the Rabbi was aroused; seeing which, the Nazarene hastened to say further, "She is the child of Joachim and Anna of Bethlehem, of whom you have at least heard; for they were of great repute——"

"Yes," remarked the Rabbi, deferentially, "I know them. They were lineally descended from David. I knew them well."

"Well, they are dead now," the Nazarene proceeded. "They died in Nazareth. Joachim was not rich, yet he left a house and garden to be divided between his daughters Marian and Mary. This is one of them; and to save her portion of the property, the law required her to marry her next of kin. She is now my wife."

"And you were——"

"Her uncle."

"Yes, yes! And as you were both born in Bethlehem, the Roman compels you to take her there with you to be also counted."

The Rabbi clasped his hands, and looked indignantly to heaven, exclaiming, "The God of Israel still lives! The vengeance is His!"

With that he turned and abruptly departed. A stranger near by, observing Joseph's amazement, said quietly, "Rabbi Samuel is a zealot. Judas himself is not more fierce."

Joseph, not wishing to talk with the man, appeared not to hear, and busied himself gathering in a little heap the grass which the donkey had tossed abroad ; after which he leaned upon his staff again, and waited.

In another hour the party passed out the gate, and, turning to the left, took the road to Bethlehem. The descent into the valley of Hinnom was quite broken, garnished here and there with straggling wild olive-trees. Carefully, tenderly, the Nazarene walked by the woman's side, leading-strap in hand.

She was not more than fifteen. Her form, voice and manner belonged to the period of transition from girlhood. Her face was perfectly oval, her complexion more pale than fair. The nose was faultless ; the lips, slightly parted, were full and ripe, giving to the lines of the mouth warmth, tenderness and trust ; the eyes were blue and large, and shaded by drooping lids and long lashes ; and, in harmony with all, a flood of golden hair, in the style permitted to Jewish brides, fell unconfined down her back to the pillion on which she sat. The throat and neck had the downy softness sometimes seen which leaves the artist in doubt whether it is an effect of contour or colour. To these charms of feature and person were added others more indefinable—an air of purity which only the soul can impart, and of abstraction natural to such as think much of things impalpable. Often, with trembling lips, she raised her eyes to heaven, itself not more deeply blue ; often she crossed her hands upon her breast, as in adoration and prayer ; often she raised her head like one listening eagerly for a calling voice. Now and then, amidst his slow utterances, Joseph turned to look at her, and, catching the expression kindling her face as with light, with bowed head, wondering, plodded on.

So they skirted the great plain of Rephaim, and at length reached the elevation Mar Elias ; from which, across a valley, they beheld Bethlehem, the old, old House of Bread, its white walls crowning a ridge, and shining above the brown scumbling of leafless orchards. They then went down into the valley to the well which was the scene of one of the marvellous exploits of David's strong men.

The narrow space was crowded with people and animals. A fear came upon Joseph—a fear lest, if the town were so thronged, there might not be house-room for the gentle Mary. Without delay, he hurried on, until he stopped before the portal of the khan that then stood outside the village gates, near a junction of roads.

CHAPTER VI

To understand thoroughly what happened to the Nazarene at the khan, the reader must be reminded that Eastern inns were different from the inns of the Western world. They were called khans, from the Persian, and in simplest form were fenced enclosures, without house or shed, often without a gate or entrance. Their sites were chosen with reference to shade, defence or water. In ordinary, they were no more than the house or possession of a sheik, in which, as in head-quarters, he swayed his tribe. Lodging the traveller was the least of their uses ; they were markets, factories, forts ; places of assemblage and residence for merchants and artisans quite as much as places of shelter for belated and wandering wayfarers. Within their walls, all the year round, occurred the multiplied daily transactions of a town.

The singular management of these hostelries was the feature likely to strike a Western mind with most force. There was no host or hostess ; no clerk, cook, or kitchen; a steward at the gate was all the assertion of government or proprietorship anywhere visible. Strangers arriving stayed at will without rendering account. Water, rest, shelter and protection were all he looked for from the proprietor, and they were gratuities. The peace of synagogues was sometimes broken by brawling disputants, but that of the khans never. The houses and all their appurtenances were sacred ; a well was not more so.

The khan at Bethlehem, before which Joseph and his wife stopped, was a good specimen of its class, being neither very primitive nor very princely. The building was purely Oriental ; that is to say, a quadrangular block of

rough stones, one story high, flat-roofed, externally unbroken by a window, and with but one principal entrance
—a doorway, which was also a gateway, on the eastern side,
or front. The road ran by the door so near that the chalk
dust half covered the lintel. A fence of flat rocks, beginning at the north-eastern corner of the pile, extended many
yards down the slope to a point from whence it swept
westwardly to a lime-stone bluff ; making what was in the
highest degree essential to a respectable khan—a safe
enclosure for animals.

Before Joseph drew nigh the great house, while he was
yet climbing the slope, in the steep places toiling to hasten
the donkey, the fear that he might not find accommodations
in the khan became a painful anxiety ; for he found the
road thronged with men and boys who, with great ado, were
taking their cattle, horses and camels to and from the
valley, some to water, some to the neighbouring caves.
And when he was come close by, his alarm was not allayed
by the discovery of a crowd investing the door of the establishment, while the enclosure adjoining, broad as it was,
seemed already full.

" We cannot reach the door," Joseph said, in his slow
way. " Let us stop here, and learn, if we can, what has
happened."

The wife, without answering, quietly drew the wimple
aside. The look of fatigue at first upon her face changed
to one of interest. She found herself at the edge of an
assemblage that could not be other than a matter of
curiosity to her, although it was common enough at the
khans on any of the highways which the great caravans
were accustomed to traverse. There were men on foot,
running hither and thither, talking shrilly and in all the
tongues of Syria ; men on horseback screaming to men on
camels ; men struggling doubtfully with fractious cows
and frightened sheep ; men peddling bread and wine ; and
among the mass a herd of boys apparently in chase of a
herd of dogs. Everybody and everything seemed to be in
motion at the same time. Possibly the fair spectator was
too weary to be long attracted by the scene ; in a little
while she sighed, and settled down on the pillion, and, as

if in search of peace and rest, or in expectation of some one, looked off to the south, and up to the tall cliffs of the Mount of Paradise, then faintly reddening under the setting sun.

Joseph's will was slow, like his mind ; he hesitated, but at length replied, " Let me speak to the gate-keeper myself. I will return quickly."

The keeper sat on a great cedar block outside the gate. Against the wall behind him leaned a javelin. A dog squatted on the block by his side.

" The peace of Jehovah be with you," said Joseph, at last confronting the keeper.

" What you give, may you find again ; and, when found, be it many times multiplied to you and yours," returned the watchman, gravely though without moving.

" I am a Bethlehemite," said Joseph, in his most deliberate way. " Is there not room for——? "

" There is not."

" You may have heard of me—Joseph of Nazareth. This is the house of my fathers. I am of the line of David."

These words held the Nazarene's hope. If they failed him, further appeal was idle, even that of the offer of many shekels. To be a son of Judah was one thing—in the tribal opinion a great thing ; to be of the house of David was yet another ; on the tongue of a Hebrew there could be no higher boast.

The appeal was not without effect. The keeper of the gate slid down from the cedar block, and, laying his hand upon his beard, said respectfully, " Rabbi, I cannot tell you when this door first opened in welcome to the traveller, but it was more than a thousand years ago ; and in all that time there is no known instance of a good man turned away, save when there was no room to rest him in. If it has been so with the stranger, just cause must the steward have who says no to one of the line of David. Wherefore, I salute you again ; and, if you care to go with me, I will show you that there is not a lodging-place left in the house ; neither in the chambers, nor in the lewens, nor in the court —not even on the roof."

Still Joseph persisted.

" The court is large," he said.

" Yes, but it is heaped with cargoes—with bales of silk, and pockets of spices, and goods of every kind."

Then for a moment the face of the applicant lost its stolidity ; the lustreless, staring eyes dropped. With some warmth he next said, " I do not care for myself, but I have with me my wife, and the night is cold—colder on these heights than in Nazareth. She cannot live in the open air. Is there not room in the town ? "

" These people "—the keeper waved his hand to the throng before the door—" have all besought the town, and they report its accommodations all engaged."

Again Joseph studied the ground, saying, half to himself, " She is so young ! if I make her bed on the hill, the frosts will kill her."

Then he spoke to the keeper again.

" It may be you knew her parents, Joachim and Anna, once of Bethlehem, and, like myself, of the line of David."

" Yes, I knew them. They were good people. That was in my youth."

This time the keeper's eyes sought the ground in thought. Suddenly he raised his head.

" If I cannot make room for you," he said, " I cannot turn you away. Rabbi, I will do the best I can for you. You shall not lie out on the ridge. Bring your wife, and hasten ; for, when the sun goes down behind the mountain, you know the night comes quickly, and it is nearly there now."

" I give you the blessing of the houseless traveller ; that of the sojourner will follow."

So saying, the Nazarene went back joyfully and brought Mary on the donkey.

The guide lingered till Mary came to his side.

" The cave to which we are going," he said to her, " must have been a resort of your ancestor David. From the field below us, and from the well down in the valley, he used to drive his flocks to it for safety ; and afterwards, when he was king, he came back to the old house here for rest and health, bringing great trains of animals. The mangers yet remain as they were in his day. Better a bed upon the floor where he has slept than one in the court-yard or out by the roadside. Ah, here is the house before the cave!"

The building was low and narrow, projecting but a little from the rock to which it was joined at the rear, and wholly without a window. In its blank front there was a door, swung on enormous hinges, and thickly daubed with ochreous clay. While the wooden bolt of the lock was being pushed back, Mary was assisted from her pillion. Upon the opening of the door, the keeper called out:

"Come in!"

The guests entered, and stared about them. It became apparent immediately that the house was but a mask or covering for the mouth of a natural cave or grotto, probably forty feet long, nine or ten high, and twelve or fifteen in width. The light streamed through the doorway, over an uneven floor, falling upon piles of grain and fodder, and earthenware and household property, occupying the centre of the chamber. Along the sides were mangers, low enough for sheep, and built of stones laid in cement. There were no stalls or partitions of any kind. Dust and chaff yellowed the floor, filled all the crevices and hollows, and thickened the spiderwebs, which dropped from the ceiling like bits of dirty linen; otherwise the place was cleanly, and to appearance, as comfortable as any of the arched lewens of the khan proper. In fact, a cave was the model and first suggestion of the lewen.

"Come in!" said the guide. "These piles upon the floor are for travellers like yourselves. Take what of them you need."

Then he spoke to Mary.

"Can you rest here?"

"The place is sanctified," she answered.

"I leave you then. Peace be with you all!"

When he was gone, they busied themselves making the cave habitable.

CHAPTER VII

A MILE and a half, it may be two miles, south-east of Bethlehem, there is a plain separated from the town by an intervening swell of the mountain. Besides being well sheltered from the north winds, the vale was covered with a growth of sycamore, dwarf-oak and pine-trees, while in the glens and ravines adjoining there were thickets of olive and mulberry; all at this season of the year invaluable for the support of sheep, goats and cattle, of which the wandering flocks consisted.

At the side farthest from the town, close under a bluff, there was an extensive *mârâh*, or sheepcot, ages old. In some long-forgotten foray, the building had been unroofed and almost demolished. The enclosure attached to it remained intact, however, and that was of more importance to the shepherds who drove their charges thither than the house itself. The stone wall around the lot was high as a man's head, yet not so high but that sometimes a panther or a lion, hungering from the wilderness, leaped boldly in. On the inner side of the wall, and as an additional security against the constant danger, a hedge of the rhamnus had been planted, an invention so successful that now a sparrow could hardly penetrate the overtopping branches, armed as they were with great clusters of thorns hard as spikes.

The day of the occurrences which occupy the preceding chapters, a number of shepherds, seeking fresh walks for their flocks, led them up to this plain; and from early morning the groves had been made ring with calls, and the blows of axes, the bleating of sheep and goats, the tinkling of bells, the lowing of cattle, and the barking of dogs. When the sun went down, they led the way to the *mârâh*, and by nightfall had everything safe in the field: then they kindled a fire down by the gate, partook of their humble supper, and sat down to rest and talk, leaving one on watch.

There were six of these men, omitting the watchman; and after a while they assembled in a group near the fire, some sitting, some lying prone. As they went bareheaded habitually their hair stood out in thick, coarse, sunburnt shocks; their beard covered their throats, and fell in mats down the breast; mantles of the skin of kids and lambs, with the fleece on, wrapped them from neck to knee, leaving the arms exposed; broad belts girthed the rude garments to their waists; their sandals were of the coarsest quality; from their right shoulders hung scrips containing food and selected stones for slings, with which they were armed; on the ground near each one lay his crook, a symbol of his calling and a weapon of offence.

Such were the shepherds of Judea! In appearance, rough and savage as the gaunt dogs sitting with them around the blaze; in fact, simple-minded, tender-hearted; effects due, in part, to the primitive life they led, but chiefly to their constant care of things lovable and helpless.

While they talked, and before the first watch was over, one by one the shepherds went to sleep, each lying where he had sat.

The night, like most nights of the winter season in the hill country, was clear, crisp and sparkling with stars. There was no wind. The atmosphere seemed never so pure, and the stillness was more than silence; it was a holy hush, a warning that heaven was stooping low to whisper some good thing to the listening earth.

By the gate, hugging his mantle close, the watchman walked; at times he stopped, attracted by a stir among the sleeping herds, or by a jackal's cry off on the mountain side. The midnight was slow coming to him; but at last it came. His task was done; now for the dreamless sleep with which labour blesses its wearied children! He moved toward the fire, but paused; a light was breaking around him, soft and white, like the moon's. He waited breathlessly. The light deepened; things before invisible came to view; he saw the whole field, and all it sheltered. A chill sharper than that of the frosty air—a chill of fear —smote him. He looked up; the stars were gone; the light was dropping as from a window in the sky; as he looked, it became a splendour; then, in terror, he cried:

" Awake, awake ! "

Up sprang the dogs, and howling, ran away.

The herds rushed together bewildered.

The men clambered to their feet, weapons in hand.

"What is it?" they asked in one voice.

"See!" cried the watchman, "the sky is on fire!"

Suddenly the light became intolerably bright, and they covered their eyes, and dropped upon their knees; then, as their souls shrank with fear, they fell upon their faces blind and fainting, and would have died had not a voice said to them:

"Fear not!"

And they listened.

"Fear not: for behold, I bring you good tidings of great joy, which shall be to all people."

The voice, in sweetness and soothing more than human, and low and clear, penetrated all their being, and filled them with assurance. They rose upon their knees, and, looking worshipfully, beheld in the centre of a great glory the appearance of a man, clad in a robe intensely white; above its shoulders towered the tops of wings shining and folded; a star over its forehead glowed with steady lustre, brilliant as Hesperus; its hands were stretched towards them in blessing; its face was serene and divinely beautiful.

They had often heard, and, in their simple way, talked, of angels; and they doubted not now, but said, in their hearts, The glory of God is about us, and this is he who of old came to the prophet by the river of Ulai.

Directly the angel continued:

"For unto you is born this day, in the city of David, a Saviour, which is Christ the Lord!"

Again there was a rest, while the words sank into their minds.

"And this shall be a sign unto you," the annunciator said next. "Ye shall find the babe, wrapped in swaddling-clothes, lying in a manger."

The herald spoke not again; his good tidings were told; yet he stayed awhile. Suddenly the light, of which he seemed the centre, turned roseate and began to tremble; then up, far as the men could see, there was flashing of white wings, and coming and going of radiant forms, and voices as of a multitude chanting in unison:

" Glory to God in the highest, and on earth peace. good-will towards men ! "

Not once the praise, but many times.

Then the herald raised his eyes as seeking approval of one far off ; his wings stirred, and spread slowly and majestically, on their upper side white as snow, in the shadow vari-tinted, like mother-of-pearl ; when they were expanded many cubits beyond his stature, he arose lightly, and without effort, floated out of view, taking the light up with him. Long after he was gone, down from the sky fell the refrain in measure mellowed by distance, " Glory to God in the highest, and on earth peace, goodwill towards men."

When the shepherds came fully to their senses, they stared at each other stupidly, until one of them said, " It was Gabriel, the Lord's messenger unto men."

None answered.

" Christ the Lord is born ; said he not so ? "

Then another recovered his voice, and replied, " That is what he said."

" And did he not also say, in the city of David, which is our Bethlehem yonder ? And that we should find Him a babe in swaddling-clothes ? "

" And lying in a manger ! "

The first speaker gazed into the fire thoughtfully, but at length said, like one possessed of a sudden resolve, " There is but one place in Bethlehem where there are mangers ; but one, and that is in the cave near the old khan. Brethren, let us go see this thing which has come to pass. The priests and doctors have been a long time looking for the Christ. Now He is born, and the Lord has given us a sign by which to know Him. Let us go and worship Him."

" But the flocks ! "

" The Lord will take care of them. Let us make haste."

Then they all arose and left the *mârâh.*

* * * * *

Around the mountain and through the town they passed. They went through the court-yard without notice, although there were some up even then talking about the wonderful light. The door of the cavern was open. A lantern was burning within, and they entered unceremoniously.

"I give you peace," they said to Joseph. "Here are people looking for a child born this night whom they are to know by finding him in swaddling-clothes and lying in a manger."

For a moment the face of the stolid Nazarene was moved: turning away, he said, "The child is here."

They were led to one of the mangers, and there the child was. The lantern was brought and the shepherds stood by mute. The little one made no sign; it was as others just born.

"Where is the mother?" they asked.

One of the women took the baby, and went to Mary, lying near, and put it in her arms. Then the bystanders collected about the two.

"It is the Christ!" said a shepherd, at last.

"The Christ!" they all repeated, falling upon their knees in worship. One of them repeated several times over:

"It is the Lord, and His glory is above the earth and heaven."

And the simple men, never doubting, kissed the hem of the mother's robe, and with joyful faces departed. In the khan, to all the people aroused and pressing about them, they told their story; and through the town, and all the way back to the *mârâh*, they chanted the refrain of the angels, "Glory to God in the highest, and on earth peace, goodwill towards men!"

The story went abroad, confirmed by the light so generally seen; and the next day, and for days thereafter, the cave was visited by curious crowds, of whom some believed, though the greater part laughed and mocked.

CHAPTER VIII

THE eleventh day after the birth of the Child in the cave, about mid-afternoon, the three wise men approached

Jerusalem by the road from Shechem. After crossing Brook Cedron, they met many people, of whom none failed to stop and look after them curiously.

Judea was of necessity an international thoroughfare; a narrow ridge, raised, apparently, by the pressure of the desert on the east, and the sea on the west, was all she could claim to be; over the ridge, however, Nature had stretched the line of trade between the east and the south; and that was her wealth. In other words, the riches of Jerusalem were the tolls she levied on passing commerce. Nowhere else, consequently, unless in Rome, was there such constant assemblage of so many people of so many different nations; in no other city was a stranger less strange to the residents than within her walls and purlieus. And yet these three men excited the wonder of all whom they met on the way to the gates by the question put by the man who rode foremost of the three.

"Where is He that is born King of the Jews?"

A large company whom they met going to the Grotto of Jeremiah were so astonished by the inquiry and the appearance of the travellers that they turned about and followed them into the city.

They came, at length, to a tower of great height and strength, overlooking the gate which, at that time, answered to the present Damascus Gate, and marked the meeting-place of the three roads from Shechem, Jericho and Gibeon. A Roman guard kept the passage-way. By this time the people following the camels formed a train sufficient to draw the idlers hanging about the portal; so that when Balthasar stopped to speak to the sentinel, the three became instantly the centre of a close circle eager to hear all that passed.

"I give you peace," the Egyptian said in a clear voice.

The sentinel made no reply.

"We have come great distances in search of one who is born King of the Jews. Can you tell us where He is?"

The soldier raised the visor of his helmet, and called loudly. From an apartment at the right of the passage an officer appeared.

"Give way," he cried to the crowd which now pressed

closer in, and as they seemed slow to obey, he advanced, twirling his javelin vigorously, now right, now left ; and so he gained room.

"What would you ? " he asked of Balthasar, speaking in the idiom of the city.

And Balthasar answered in the same

" Where is He that is born King of the Jews ? "

" Herod ? " asked the officer, confounded.

" Herod's kingship is from Cæsar ; not Herod."

" There is no other King of the Jews."

" But we have seen the star of Him we seek, and come to worship Him."

The Roman was perplexed.

" Go farther," he said at last.   " Go farther.   I am not a Jew.   Carry the question to the doctors in the Temple, or to Hannas the priest, or, better still, to Herod himself. If there be another King of the Jews, he will find him."

Thereupon he made way for the strangers, and they passed the gate.   But, before entering the narrow street, Balthasar lingered to say to his friends, " We are sufficiently proclaimed.   By midnight the whole city will have heard of us and of our mission.   Let us to the khan now."

CHAPTER IX

LATE in the evening the wise men were lying in a lewen of the khan awake.   The stones which served them as pillows raised their heads so they could look out of the open arch into the depths of the sky ; and as they watched the twinkling of the stars, they thought of the next mani- festation.   How would it come ?   What would it be ? They were in Jerusalem at last ; they had asked at the gate for Him they sought ; they had borne witness of His birth ; it remained only to find Him ; and as to that, they placed all trust in the Spirit.   Men listening for the voice of God, or waiting a sign from Heaven, cannot sleep.

While they were in this condition, a man stepped in under the arch, darkening the lewen.

" Awake ! " he said to them ; " I salute you, and give

you peace, and pray your pardon; but my master, the king, has sent me to invite you to the palace, where he would have speech with you privately."

Thus the messenger discharged his duty.

"The king's will is our will," said Balthasar to the messenger. "We will follow you."

The streets of the Holy City were narrow then as now, but not so rough and foul; for the great builder, not content with beauty, enforced cleanliness and convenience also. Following their guide, the brethren proceeded without a word. Through the dim starlight, made dimmer by the walls on both sides, sometimes almost lost under bridges connecting the house-tops, out of a low ground they ascended a hill. At last they came to a portal reared across the way. In the light of fires blazing before it in two great braziers, they caught a glimpse of the structure, and also of some guards leaning motionlessly upon their arms. They passed into a building unchallenged. Then by passages and arched halls; through courts, and under colonnades not always lighted; up long flights of stairs, past innumerable cloisters and chambers, they were conducted into a tower of great height. Suddenly the guide halted, and, pointing through an open door, said to them:

"Enter. The king is there."

The air of the chamber was heavy with the perfume of sandal-wood, and all the appointments within were effeminately rich. Upon the floor, covering the central space, a tufted rug was spread, and upon that a throne was set. The visitors had but time, however, to catch a confused idea of the place—of carved and gilt ottomans and couches; of fans and jars and musical instruments; of golden candlesticks glittering in their own lights; of walls painted in the style of the voluptuous Grecian school, one look at which had made a Pharisee hide his head with holy horror. Herod, sitting upon the throne to receive them, claimed all their minds.

At the edge of the rug, to which they advanced uninvited, they prostrated themselves. The king touched a bell. An attendant came in, and placed three stools before the throne.

C

"Seat yourselves," said the monarch graciously.

"From the North Gate," he continued, when they were at rest, "I had this afternoon report of the arrival of three strangers, curiously mounted, and appearing as if from far countries. Are you the men?"

The Egyptian took the sign from the Greek and the Hindu, and answered, with the profoundest salaam, "Were we other than we are, the mighty Herod, whose fame is as incense to the whole world, would not have sent for us. We may not doubt that we are the strangers."

Herod acknowledged the speech with a wave of the hand.

"Who are you? Whence do you come?" he asked, adding, significantly, "Let each speak for himself."

In turn they gave him account, referring simply to the cities and lands of their birth, and the routes by which they came to Jerusalem. Somewhat disappointed, Herod plied them more directly.

"What was the question you put to the officer at the gate?"

"We asked him, Where is He that is born King of the Jews?"

"I see now why the people were so curious. You excite me no less. Is there another King of the Jews?"

The Egyptian did not blanch.

"There is one newly born."

An expression of pain knit the dark face of the monarch, as if his mind were swept by a harrowing recollection.

"Not to me, not to me!" he exclaimed.

Possibly the accusing images of his murdered children flitted before him; recovering from the emotion, whatever it was, he asked steadily, "Where is the new king?"

"That, O king, is what we would ask."

"You bring me a wonder—a riddle surpassing any of Solomon's," the inquisitor said next. "As you see, I am in the time of life when curiosity is as ungovernable as it was in childhood, when to trifle with it is cruelty. Tell me further, and I will honour you as kings honour each other. Give me all you know about the newly born, and I will join you in the search for him; and when we have

found him, I will do what you wish ; I will bring him to
Jerusalem, and train him in kingcraft ; I will use my grace
with Cæsar for his promotion and glory. Jealousy shall
not come between us, so I swear. But tell me first how,
so widely separated by seas and deserts, you all came to
hear of him."

"I will tell you truly, O king."

"Speak on," said Herod.

Balthasar raised himself erect, and said solemnly :

"There is an Almighty God."

Herod was visibly startled.

"He bade us come hither, promising that we should
find the Redeemer of the World ; that we should see and
worship Him, and bear witness that He was come ; and,
as a sign, we were each given to see a star. His Spirit
stayed with us. O king, His Spirit is with us now ! "

An overpowering feeling seized the three. The Greek
with difficulty restrained an outcry. Herod's gaze darted
quickly from one to the other ; he was more suspicious and
dissatisfied than before.

"You are mocking me," he said. "If not, tell me
more. What is to follow the coming of the new king ? "

"The salvation of men."

"From what ? "

"Their wickedness."

"How ? "

"By the Divine agencies—Faith, Love and Good
Works."

"Then"—Herod paused, and from his look no man
could have said with what feeling he continued—" you are
the heralds of the Christ. Is that all ? "

Balthasar bowed low.

"We are your servants, O king."

The monarch touched a bell, and the attendant appeared.

"Bring the gifts," the master said.

The attendant went out, but in a little while returned,
and, kneeling before the guests, gave to each one an outer
robe or mantle of scarlet and blue, and a girdle of gold.
They acknowledged the honours with Eastern prostra-
tions.

"A word further," said Herod, when the ceremony was ended. "To the officer of the gate, and but now to me, you spoke of seeing a star in the east."

"Yes," said Balthasar, "His star, the star of the newly born."

"What time did it appear?"

"When we were bidden come hither."

Herod arose, signifying the audience was over. Stepping from the throne towards them, he said, with all graciousness:

"If, as I believe, O illustrious men, you are indeed the heralds of the Christ just born, know that I have this night consulted those wisest in things Jewish, and they say with one voice He should be born in Bethlehem of Judea. I say to you, go thither; go and search diligently for the young child; and when you have found Him bring me word again, that I may come and worship Him. To your going there shall be no let or hindrance. Peace be with you!"

And, folding his robe about him, he left the chamber.

Directly the guide came, and led them back to the street, and thence to the khan, at the portal of which the Greek said, impulsively, "Let us to Bethlehem, O brethren, as the king has advised."

"Yes," cried the Hindu. "The Spirit burns within me."

"Be it so," said Balthasar, with equal warmth. "The camels are ready."

They gave gifts to the steward, mounted into their saddles, received directions to the Joppa Gate, and departed. At their approach the great valves were unbarred, and they passed out into the open country, taking the road so lately travelled by Joseph and Mary. As they came up out of Hinnom, on the plain of Rephaim, a light appeared, at first widespread and faint. Their pulses fluttered fast. The light intensified rapidly; they closed their eyes against its burning brilliance: when they dared look again, lo! the star, perfect as any in the heavens, but low down and moving slowly before them. And they folded their hands, and shouted, and rejoiced with exceeding great joy.

"God is with us! God is with us!" they repeated, in

frequent cheer, all the way, until the star, rising out of the valley beyond Mar Elias, stood still over a house upon the slope of the hill near the town.

CHAPTER X

IT was now the beginning of the third watch, and at Bethlehem the morning was breaking over the mountains in the east, but so feebly that it was yet night in the valley. The watchman on the roof of the old khan, shivering in the chilly air, was listening for the first distinguishable sounds with which life, awakening, greets the dawn, when a light came moving up the hill towards the house. He thought it a torch in some one's hand; next moment, he thought it a meteor; the brilliance grew, however, until it became a star. Sore afraid, he cried out, and brought everybody within the walls to the roof. The phenomenon, in eccentric motion, continued to approach; the rocks, trees and roadway under it shone as in a glare of lightning; directly its brightness became blinding. The more timid of the beholders fell upon their knees, and prayed, with their faces hidden; the boldest, covering their eyes, crouched, and now and then snatched glances fearfully. After a while the khan and everything thereabout lay under the intolerable radiance. Such as dared look beheld the star standing still directly over the house in front of the cave where the Child had been born.

In the height of this scene the wise men came up, and at the gate dismounted from their camels, and shouted for admission. When the steward so far mastered his terror as to give them heed, he drew the bars and opened to them. The camels looked spectral in the unnatural light, and, besides their outlandishness, there were in the faces and manner of the three visitors an eagerness and exaltation which still further excited the keeper's fears and fancy; he fell back and for a time could not answer the question they put to him.

"Is not this Bethlehem of Judea?"

But others came, and by their presence gave him assurance.

"No, this is but the khan; the town lies farther on."

"Is there not here a child newly born?"

The bystanders turned to each other marvelling, though some of them answered, "Yes, yes."

"Show us to Him!" said the Greek impatiently.

"Show us to Him!" cried Balthasar, breaking through his gravity; "for we have seen His star, even that which ye behold over the house, and are come to worship Him."

The Hindu clasped his hands, exclaiming, "God indeed lives. Make haste, make haste! The Saviour is found. Blessed, blessed are we above men!"

The people from the roof came down and followed the strangers as they were taken through the court and out into the enclosure; at sight of the star yet above the cave, though less candescent than before, some turned back afraid; the greater part went on. As the strangers neared the house, the orb arose; when they were at the door, it was high up overhead vanishing; when they entered it went out lost to sight. And to the witnesses of what then took place came a conviction that there was a Divine relation between the star and the strangers, which extended also to at least some of the occupants of the cave. When the door was opened, they crowded in.

The apartment was lighted by a lantern enough to enable the strangers to find the mother, and the Child awake in her lap.

"Is the Child thine?" asked Balthasar of Mary.

And she, who had kept all the things in the least affecting the little one, and pondered in her heart, held it up in the light, saying:

"He is my son!"

And they fell down and worshipped Him.

They saw the Child was as other children: about its head was neither nimbus nor material crown; its lips opened not in speech; if it heard their expressions of joy, their invocations, their prayers, it made no sign whatever, but, baby-like, looked longer at the flame in the lantern than at them.

In a little while they arose, and, returning to the camels, brought gifts of gold, frankincense and myrrh, and laid them before the Child, abating nothing of their worshipful speeches; of which no part is given, for the thoughtful know that the pure worship of the pure heart was then what it is now, and has always been, an inspired song.

And this was the Saviour they had come so far to find! Yet they worshipped without a doubt.

BOOK SECOND

CHAPTER I

IT is necessary now to carry the reader forward twenty-one years, to the beginning of the administration of Valerius Gratus, the fourth imperial governor of Judea—a period which will be remembered as rent by political agitations in Jerusalem, if, indeed, it be not the precise time of the opening of the final quarrel between the Jew and the Roman.

In the interval Judea had been subjected to changes affecting her in many ways, but in nothing so much as her political status. Herod the Great died within one year after the birth of the Child—died so miserably that the Christian world had reason to believe him overtaken by the Divine wrath. Like all great rulers who spend their lives in perfecting the power they create, he dreamed of transmitting his throne and crown—of being the founder of a dynasty. With that intent, he left a will dividing his territories between his three sons, Antipas, Philip and Archelaus, of whom the last was appointed to succeed to the title. The testament was necessarily referred to Augustus, the emperor, who ratified all its provisions with one exception : he withheld from Archelaus the title of king until he proved his capacity and loyalty ; in lieu thereof, he created him ethnarch, and as such permitted him to govern nine years, when, for misconduct, and inability to stay the turbulent elements that grew and strengthened around him, he was sent into Gaul as an exile.

Cæsar was not content with deposing Archelaus ; he struck the people of Jerusalem in a manner that touched their pride, and keenly wounded the sensibilities of the haughty habitués of the Temple. He reduced Judea to a Roman province, and annexed it to the prefecture of Syria. So, instead of a king ruling royally from the palace left by Herod on Mount Zion, the city fell into the hands of an officer of the second grade, an appointee called procurator, who communicated with the court in Rome through the Legate of Syria, residing in Antioch. To make the hurt more painful, the procurator was not permitted to establish himself in Jerusalem ; Cæsarea was his seat of government. Most humiliating, however, most exasperating, most studied, Samaria, of all the world the most despised— Samaria was joined to Judea as a part of the same province ! What ineffable misery the bigoted Separatists or Pharisees endured at finding themselves elbowed and laughed at in the procurator's presence in Cæsarea by the devotees of Gerizim !

Judea had been a Roman province eighty years and more—ample time for the Cæsars to study the idiosyncrasies of the people—time enough, at least, to learn that the Jew, with all his pride, could be quietly governed if his religion were respected. Proceeding upon that policy, the predecessors of Gratus had carefully abstained from interfering with any of the sacred observances of their subjects. But he chose a different course ; almost his first official act was to expel Hannas from the high priesthood, and give the place to Ishmael, son of Fabus.

The reader shall be spared a chapter on Jewish politics ; a few words upon the subject, however, are essential to such as may follow the succeeding narration critically. At this time, leaving origin out of view, there were in Judea the party of the nobles and the Separatist or popular party. Upon Herod's death, the two united against Archelaus ; from Temple to palace, from Jerusalem to Rome, they fought him ; sometimes with intrigue, sometimes with the actual weapons of war. More than once the holy cloisters on Moriah resounded with the cries of fighting-men. Finally, they drove him into exile. Meantime throughout this struggle the allies had their diverse objects in view. The nobles hated Joazar, the high-priest ; the Separatists, on the other hand, were his zealous adherents. When Herod's settlement went down with Archelaus, Joazar shared the fall. Hannas, the son of Seth, was selected by the nobles to fill the great office; thereupon the allies divided. The induction of the Sethian brought them face to face in fierce hostility.

In the course of the struggle with the unfortunate ethnarch, the nobles had found it expedient to attach themselves to Rome. Discerning that when the existing settlement was broken up some form of government must needs follow, they suggested the conversion of Judea into a province. The fact furnished the Separatists an additional cause for attack; and, when Samaria was made part of the province, the nobles sank into a minority, with nothing to support them but the imperial court and the prestige of their rank and wealth; yet for fifteen years—down, indeed, to the coming of Valerius Gratus—they managed to maintain themselves in both palace and Temple.

Hannas, the idol of his party, had used his power faithfully in the interest of his imperial patron. A Roman garrison held the Tower of Antonia; a Roman guard kept the gates of the palace; a Roman judge dispensed justice, civil and criminal; a Roman system of taxation, mercilessly executed, crushed both city and country; daily, hourly and in a thousand ways, the people were bruised and galled, and taught the difference between a life of independence and a life of subjection; yet Hannas kept them in comparative quiet. Rome had no truer friend; and he made his loss instantly felt. Delivering his vestments to Ishmael, the new appointee, he walked from the courts of the Temple into the councils of the Separatists, and became the head of a new combination, Bethusian and Sethian.

Gratus, the procurator, left thus without a party, saw the fires, which in the fifteen years had sunk into sodden smoke, begin to glow with returning life. A month after Ishmael took the office, the Roman found it necessary to visit him in Jerusalem. When from the walls, hooting and hissing him, the Jews beheld his guard enter the north gate of the city and march to the Tower of Antonia, they understood the real purpose of the visit—a full cohort of legionaries was added to the former garrison, and the keys of their yoke could now be tightened with impunity. If the procurator deemed it important to make an example, alas for the first offender !

CHAPTER II

WITH the foregoing explanation in mind, the reader is invited to look into one of the gardens of the palace on Mount Zion. The time was noonday in the middle of July, when the heat of summer was at its highest.

In all directions the grade sloped gently from the centre, where there was a reservoir, or deep marble basin, broken at intervals by little gates which, when raised, emptied the water into sluices bordering the walks—a cunning device for the rescue of the place from the aridity too prevalent elsewhere in the region.

Not far from the fountain, there was a small pool of clear water nourishing a clump of cane and oleander, such as grow on the Jordan and down by the Dead Sea. Between the clump and the pool, unmindful of the sun shining full upon them in the breathless air, two boys, one about nineteen, the other seventeen, sat engaged in earnest conversation.

They were both handsome, and, at first glance, would have been pronounced brothers. Both had hair and eyes black ; their faces were deeply browned ; and, sitting, they seemed of a size proper for the difference in their ages.

The elder was bareheaded. A loose tunic, dropping to the knees, was his attire complete, except sandals and a light-blue mantle spread under him on the seat. The costume left his arms and legs exposed, and they were brown as the face : nevertheless, a certain grace of manner, refinement of features, and culture of voice decided his rank. The tunic, of softest woollen, grey-tinted, at the neck, sleeves and edge of the skirt bordered with red, and bound to the waist by a tasselled silken cord, certified him the Roman he was. And if in speech he now and then gazed haughtily at his companion and addressed him as an inferior, he might almost be excused, for he was of a family noble even in Rome—a circumstance which in that age justified any assumption. In the terrible wars between the first Cæsar and his great enemies, a Messala had been the friend of Brutus. After Philippi, without sacrifice of his honour, he and the conqueror became reconciled. Yet later, when Octavius disputed for the empire, Messala supported him. Octavius, as the Emperor Augustus, remembered the service, and showered the family with honours. Among other things, Judea being reduced to a province, he sent the son of his old client or retainer to Jerusalem, charged with the receipt and management of the taxes levied in that region ; and in that service the son had since remained, sharing the palace with the high-priest. The youth just described was his son, whose habit it was to carry about with him all too faithfully a remembrance of the relation between his grandfather and the great Romans of his day.

The associate of the Messala was slighter in form, and his garments were of fine white linen and of the prevalent style in Jerusalem ; a cloth covered his head, held by a yellow cord, and arranged so as to fall away from the forehead down low over the back of the neck. An observer skilled in the distinctions of race, and studying his features more than his costume, would have soon discovered him to be of Jewish descent. The comeliness of the Roman was severe and chaste, that of the Jew rich and voluptuous.

"Did you not say the new procurator is to arrive to-morrow ? "

The question proceeded from the younger of the friends, and was couched in Greek, at the time, singularly enough, the language everywhere prevalent in the politer circles of Judea ; having passed from the palace into the camp and college ; thence, nobody knew exactly when or how, into the Temple itself, and, for that matter, into precincts of the Temple far beyond the gates and cloisters—precincts of a sanctity intolerable for a Gentile.

"Yes, to-morrow," Messala answered.

"Who told you ? "

"I heard Ishmael, the new governor in the palace—you call him high-priest—tell my father so last night. The news had been more credible, I grant you, coming from an Egyptian, who is of a race that has forgotten what truth is, or even from an Idumæan, whose people never knew what truth was ; but, to make quite certain, I saw a centurion from the Tower this morning, and he told me preparations were going on for the reception ; that the armourers were furbishing the helmets and shields, and re-gilding the eagles and globes ; and that apartments long unused were being cleansed and aired as if for an addition to the garrison—the body-guard, probably, of the great man."

The Jewish lad remained silent, looking absently into the depths of the pool.

"Our farewell took place in this garden. 'The peace of the Lord go with you ! '—your last words. 'The gods keep you ! ' I said. Do you remember. How many years, Judah, have passed since then ? "

Judah bent his large eyes upon the questioner ; the gaze was grave and thoughtful, and caught the Roman's, and held it while he replied, " Five years. I remember the parting ; you went to Rome ; I saw you start, and cried, for I loved you. The years are gone, and you have come back to me accomplished and princely—I do not jest ; and yet—yet—I wish you were the Messala you went away."

The Roman smiled.

" O my solemn Judah, wherein have I hurt you ? "

The other drew a long breath, and said, pulling at the cord about his waist, " In the five years I, too, have learned somewhat. Attendance at the Great College, and study of what I heard there, have taught me that Judea is not as she used to be. I know the space that lies between an independent kingdom and the petty province Judea is. I were meaner, viler, than a Samaritan not to resent the degradation of my country. Ishmael is not lawfully high-priest, and he cannot be while the noble Hannas lives ; yet he is a Levite ; one of the devoted who for thousands of years have acceptably served the Lord God of our faith and worship. His——"

Messala broke in upon him with a biting laugh.

" Oh, I understand you now. Ishmael, you say, is a usurper, yet to believe an Idumæan sooner than Ishmael is to sting like an adder. By the drunken son of Semele, what it is to be a Jew ! All men and things, even heaven and earth, change ; but a Jew never. To him there is no backward, no forward ; he is what his ancestor was in the beginning. In this sand I draw you a circle—there ! Now tell me what more a Jew's life is. Round and round, Abraham here, Isaac and Jacob yonder, God in the middle. And the circle—by the master of all thunders, the circle is too large ! I draw it again." He stopped, put his thumb upon the ground, and swept the fingers about it. "See, the thumb spot is the Temple, the finger-lines Judea. Outside the little space is there nothing of value ? The arts ! Herod was a builder ; therefore he is accursed. Painting, sculpture ! to look upon them is sin. Poetry you make fast to your altars. Except in the synagogue, who of you attempts eloquence ? In war all you conquer in the six days you lose on the seventh. Such your life and limit ; who shall say no if I laugh at you ? O my Judah, I pity you : what can you be ? "

The Jew moved nearer the pool ; Messala's drawl deepened.

"Yes, I pity you, my fine Judah. From the college to the synagogue ; then to the Temple ; then—oh, a crowning glory !—the seat in the Sanhedrin. A life without opportunities ; the gods help you ! But I——"

Judah answered, coldly :

"We had better part. I wish I had not come. I sought a friend and find a——"

"Roman," said Messala quickly.

The hands of the Jew clenched, but controlling himself again, he started off. Messala arose, and, taking the mantle from the bench, flung it over his shoulder, and followed after ; when he gained his side, he put his hand upon his shoulder and walked with him.

"This is the way—my hand thus—we used to walk when we were children. Let us keep it as far as the gate."

Apparently Messala was trying to be serious and kind, though he could not rid his countenance of the habitual satirical expression. Judah permitted the familiarity.

"You are a boy ; I am a man ; let me talk like one."

The complacency of the Roman was superb. Mentor lecturing the young Telemachus could not have been more at ease.

When they had gone a few yards, the Roman spoke again.

"I think you can hear me now, especially as what I have to say concerns yourself. I would serve you, O handsome as Ganymede; I would serve you with real good-will. I love you—all I can. I told you I meant to be a soldier. Why not you also? Why not you step out of the narrow circle which, as I have shown, is all of noble life your laws and customs allow?"

Judah made no reply.

"Be wise," continued Messala. "Give up the follies of Moses and the traditions; see the situation as it is. Dare look the Parcæ in the face, and they will tell you, Rome is the world. Ask them of Judea, and they will answer, She is what Rome wills."

They were now at the gate. Judah stopped, and took the hand gently from his shoulder, and confronted Messala, tears trembling in his eyes.

"I understand you, because you are a Roman; you cannot understand me—I am an Israelite. You have given me suffering to-day by convincing me that we can never be the friends we have been—never! Here we part. The peace of the God of my fathers abide with you!"

Messala offered him his hand; the Jew walked on through the gateway. When he was gone, the Roman was silent awhile; then he, too, passed through, saying to himself, with a toss of the head:

"Be it so. Eros is dead, Mars reigns!"

CHAPTER III

Not long after the young Jew parted from the Roman at the palace up on the Market-place, he stopped before the western gate of a house fortelesque in style, except for the windows with which it was unusually garnished and the ornate finish of the doorways or gates. The wicket (a door hung in one of the valves of the gate) was opened to admit him. He stepped in hastily, and failed to acknowledge the low salaam of the porter.

Twelve or fifteen steps along a passage carried him into a court-yard, oblong north and south, and in every quarter, except the east, bounded by what seemed the fronts of two-story houses; of which the lower floor was divided into lewens, while the upper was terraced and defended by strong balustrading. The servants coming and going along the terraces; the noise of millstones grinding; the garments fluttering from ropes stretched from point to point; the chickens and pigeons in full enjoyment of the place; the goats, cows, donkeys and horses stabled in the lewens; a massive trough of water, apparently for the common use, declared this court appurtenant to the domestic management of the owner. Eastwardly there was a division wall broken by another passage-way in all respects like the first one.

Clearing the second passage, the young man entered a second court, spacious, square and set with shrubbery and vines, kept fresh and beautiful by water from a basin erected near a porch on the north side.

A few steps within the second court, the lad turned to the right, and, choosing a walk through the shrubbery, part of which was in flower, passed to the stairway, and ascended to the terrace—a broad pavement of white and brown flags closely laid, and much worn. Making way under the awning to a doorway on the north side, he entered an apartment which the dropping of the screen behind him returned to darkness. Nevertheless, he proceeded, moving over a tiled floor to a divan, upon which he flung himself face downwards, and lay at rest, his forehead upon his crossed arms.

About nightfall a woman came to the door and called; he answered, and she went in.

" Supper is over, and it is night. Is not my son hungry ? " she asked.

" No," he replied.

" Are you sick ? "

" I am sleepy."

" Your mother has asked for you."

" Where is she ? "

" In the summer-house on the roof."

He stirred himself, and sat up.

"Very well. Bring me something to eat."

After a while she returned, bearing on a wooden platter a bowl of milk, some thin cakes of white bread broken, a delicate paste of brayed wheat, a bird broiled, and honey and salt. On one end of the platter was a silver goblet full of wine, on the other a brazen hand-lamp, lighted.

The light also gave the woman to view. Her face was that of a woman of fifty, dark-skinned, dark-eyed, and at the moment softened by a look of tenderness almost maternal. A white turban covered her head, leaving the lobes of the ear exposed, and in them the sign that settled her condition—an orifice bored by a thick awl. She was a slave of Egyptian origin, to whom not even the sacred fiftieth year could have brought freedom : nor would she have accepted it, for the boy she was attending was her life. She had nursed him through babyhood, tended him as a child, and could not break the service. To her love he could never be a man.

He spoke but once during the meal.

"You remember, O my Amrah," he said, "the Messala who used to visit me here days at a time."

"I remember him."

"He went to Rome some years ago, and is now back. I called upon him to-day."

A shudder of disgust seized the lad.

"I knew something had happened," she said, deeply interested. "I never liked the Messala. Tell me all."

But he fell into musing, and to her repeated inquiries only said, "He is much changed, and I shall have nothing more to do with him."

When Amrah took the platter away, he also went out, and up from the terrace to the roof.

The lad whom we are following walked slowly across the house-top to a tower built over the north-west corner of the palace. Had he been a stranger, he might have bestowed a glance upon the structure as he drew nigh it, and seen all the dimness permitted—a darkened mass, low, latticed, pillared and domed. He entered, passing under a half-raised curtain. The interior was all darkness, except that on four sides there were arched openings like doorways,

D

through which the sky, lighted with stars, was visible. In one of the openings, reclining against a cushion from a divan, he saw the figure of a woman, indistinct even in white floating drapery. At the sound of his steps upon the floor, the fan in her hand stopped, glistening where the starlight struck the jewels with which it was sprinkled, and she sat up, and called his name.

" Judah, my son ! "

" It is I, mother," he answered, quickening his approach.

Going to her, he knelt, and she put her arms around him, and with kisses pressed him to her bosom.

CHAPTER IV

THE mother resumed her easy position against the cushion, while the son took place on the divan, his head in her lap.

" Amrah tells me something has happened to you," she said, caressing his cheek. " When my Judah was a child I allowed small things to trouble him, but he is now a man. He must not forget "—her voice became very soft—" that one day he is to be my hero."

He kissed the hand over and over again.

" I will be your hero, but you must put me in the way. You know the law—every son of Israel must have some occupation. I am not exempt, and ask now, shall I tend the herds ? or till the soil ? or drive the saw ? or be a clerk or lawyer ? What shall I be ? Dear, good mother, help me to an answer."

" Gamaliel has been lecturing to-day," she said thoughtfully.

" If so, I did not hear him. I have been up on the Market-place, not to the Temple. I visited the young Messala. What Messala said, my mother, was sharp enough in itself ; but, taken with the manner, some of the sayings were intolerable. Tell me, O my mother—and this is the sum of my trouble—why may not a son of Israel do all a Roman may ? "

She swept the heavens with a rapid glance, trying to compass all the meaning of his questions.

"If Messala is the enemy, do not leave me to fight him in the dark. Tell me all he said."

The young Israelite proceeded then, and rehearsed his conversation with Messala, dwelling with particularity upon the latter's speeches in contempt of the Jews, their customs, and much-pent round of life.

Afraid to speak the while, the mother listened, discerning the matter plainly.

"There never has been a people," she began, "who did not think themselves at least equal to any other ; never a great nation, my son, that did not believe itself the very superior. When the Roman looks down upon Israel and laughs, he merely repeats the folly of the Egyptian, the Assyrian, and the Macedonian ; and as the laugh is against God, the result will be the same."

Her voice became firmer.

"Your friend—or your former friend—charged, if I understood you rightly, that we have had no poets, artists, or warriors ; by which he meant, I suppose, to deny that we have had great men.

"There is an idea that war is the most noble occupation of men, and that the most exalted greatness is the growth of battlefields. Because the world has adopted the idea, be not you deceived. The Greeks have their great glory because they were the first to set Mind above Strength. But was the Hellene the first to do this ? No. My son, that glory is ours. So it happens, O my son, that of the whole world our Israel alone can dispute the superiority of the Greek, and with him contest the palm of original genius."

For a time the rustling of the fan was all the sound heard in the chamber.

"In the sense which limits art to sculpture and painting, it is true," she next said, "Israel has had no artists."

The admission was made regretfully, for it must be remembered she was a Sadducee, whose faith, unlike that of the Pharisees, permitted a love of the beautiful in every form, and without reference to its origin.

"Still he who would do justice," she proceeded, "will not forget that the cunning of our hands was bound by the prohibition, ' Thou shalt not make unto thee any graven image, or any likeness of anything'; which the Sopherim wickedly extended beyond its purpose and time."

"Oh, I see now why the Greek outstripped us," said Judah, intensely interested.

"In such light as I can, my Judah, I will set our great men before you—patriarchs, legislators, warriors, singers, prophets. Turn we to the best of Rome. Against Moses place Cæsar, and Tarquin against David; Sylla against either of the Maccabees; the best of the consuls against the judges; Augustus against Solomon, and you are done: comparison ends there. But think then of the prophets—greatest of the great."

She laughed scornfully.

"Pardon me. I was thinking of the soothsayer who warned Caius Julius against the ides of March, and fancied him looking for the omens of evil, which his master despised, in the entrails of a chicken. From that picture turn to Elijah sitting on the hill-top on the way to Samaria, amid the smoking bodies of the captains and their fifties, warning the son of Ahab of the wrath of our God. Finally, O my Judah—if such speech be reverent—how shall we judge Jehovah and Jupiter unless it be by what their servants have done in their names? And as for what you shall do——"

She spoke the latter words slowly, and with a tremulous utterance.

"As for what you shall do, my boy—serve the Lord, the Lord God of Israel, not Rome. For a child of Abraham there is no glory except in the Lord's ways, and in them there is much glory."

"I may be a soldier then?" Judah asked.

"Why not? Did not Moses call God a man of war?"

There was then a long silence in the summer chamber.

"You have my permission," she said finally; "if only you serve the Lord instead of Cæsar."

He was content with the condition, and by and by fell asleep. She arose then, and put the cushion under his head, and, throwing a shawl over him and kissing him tenderly, went away.

CHAPTER V

THE favours of Herod had left surviving him many persons of vast estate. Where this fortune was joined to undoubted lineal descent from some famous son of one of the tribes, especially Judah, the happy individual was accounted a Prince of Jerusalem. Of this class none had won in private or public life a higher regard than the father of the lad whom we have been following. With a remembrance of his nationality which never failed him, he had yet been true to the king, and served him faithfully at home and abroad. Some offices had taken him to Rome, where his conduct attracted the notice of Augustus, who strove without reserve to engage his friendship. Such a man could not fail to be rich ; yet his wealth was not altogether the largess of royal patrons. He had welcomed the law that bound him to some pursuit ; and, instead of one, he entered into many. Of the herdsmen watching flocks on the plains and hill-sides, far as old Lebanon, numbers reported to him as their employer ; in the cities by the sea, and in those inland, he found houses of traffic ; his ships brought him silver from Spain, whose mines were then the richest known ; while his caravans came twice a year from the East, laden with silks and spices. He perished at sea some ten years before this second period of our story, in the prime of life, and was lamented everywhere in Judea. We are already acquainted with two members of his family—his widow and son ; the only other was a daughter. The morning after the discussion reported in the last chapter, Judah was awakened by his sister's singing.

Tirzah was her name, and as the two looked at each other, their resemblance was plain. Her features had the regularity of his, and were of the same Jewish type : they had also the charm of childish innocency of expression. The edges of her eyelids were painted, and the tips of her fingers stained. Her hair fell in two long plaits down her back. A curled lock rested upon each cheek in front of the ear. Altogether it would have been impossible to deny her grace, refinement and beauty.

"Very pretty, my Tirzah, very pretty!" he said with animation.

"The song?" she asked.

"Yes—and the singer, too. I am proud of my little sister. Have you another song as good?"

"Very many. But let them go now. Amrah sent me to tell you she will bring you your breakfast, and that you need not come down."

At that moment Amrah entered the summer chamber, bearing a platter, with wash-bowl, water and napkins.

Not being a Pharisee, the ablution was short and simple with Judah. The servant then went out, leaving Tirzah to dress his hair. When a lock was disposed to her satisfaction, she would unloose the small metallic mirror which, as was the fashion among her fair country-women, she wore at her girdle, and give it to him, that he might see the triumph, and how handsome it made him. Meanwhile they kept up their conversation.

"What do you think, Tirzah?—I am going away."

She dropped her hands with amazement.

"Going away? When? For what?"

He laughed.

"Three questions, all in a breath! What a body you are!" Next instant he became serious. "You know the law requires me to follow some occupation. Our good father set me an example. Even you would despise me if I spent in idleness the results of his industry and knowledge. I am going to Rome."

"But must you go? Here in Jerusalem you can learn all that is needed to be a merchant—if that is what you are thinking of."

"But that is not what I am thinking of. The law does not require the son to be what the father was."

"What else can you be?"

"A soldier," he replied, with a certain pride of voice. Tears came into her eyes.

"You will be killed."

"If God's will, be it so. But, Tirzah, the soldiers are not all killed."

She answered with sobs.

" War is a trade," he continued, more soberly. " To learn it thoroughly, one must go to school, and there is no school like a Roman camp."

" You would not fight for Rome ? " she asked, holding her breath.

" And you—even you hate her. The whole world hates her. In that, O Tirzah, find the reason of the answer I give you—Yes, I will fight for her, if, in return, she will teach me how one day to fight against her."

" When will you go ? "

Amrah's steps were then heard returning.

" Hist ! " he said. " Do not let her know of what I am thinking."

The faithful slave came in with breakfast, and placed the waiter holding it upon a stool before them ; then, with white napkins upon her arm, she remained to serve them. They dipped their fingers in a bowl of water, and were rinsing them, when a noise arrested their attention. They listened, and distinguished martial music in the street on the north side of the house.

" Soldiers from the Prætorium ! I must see them," he cried, springing from the divan and running out.

In a moment more he was leaning over the parapet of tiles which guarded the roof at the extreme north-east corner, so absorbed that he did not notice Tirzah by his side, resting one hand upon his shoulder.

The array after a while came into view of the two upon the house of the Hurs. First, a vanguard of the light-armed—mostly slingers and bowmen—marching with wide intervals between their ranks and files ; next a body of heavy-armed infantry, bearing large shields, and *hastæ longæ*, or spears identical with those used in the duels before Ilium ; then the musicians ; and then an officer riding alone, but followed closely by a guard of cavalry ; after them again, a column of infantry also heavy-armed, which, moving in close order, crowded the street from wall to wall, and appeared to be without end.

The officer was riding alone in the midst of the column. His head was bare ; otherwise he was in full armour.

While the man was yet in the distance, Judah observed

that his presence was sufficient to throw the people looking at him into angry excitement. They would lean over the parapets or stand boldly out, and shake their fists at him ; they followed him with loud cries, and spat at him as he passed under the bridges ; the women even flung their sandals, sometimes with such good effect as to hit him. When he was nearer, the yells became distinguishable—" Robber, tyrant, dog of a Roman ! Away with Ishmael ! Give us back our Hannas ! "

Now the lad had heard of the custom, borrowed from a habit of the first Cæsar, by which chief commanders, to indicate their rank, appeared in public with only a laurel vine upon their heads. By that sign he knew this officer—VALERIUS GRATUS, THE NEW PROCURATOR OF JUDEA !

To say truth, now, the Roman under the unprovoked storm had the young Jew's sympathy ; so that when he reached the corner of the house, the latter leaned yet farther over the parapet to see him go by, and in the act rested a hand upon a tile which had been a long time cracked and allowed to go unnoticed. The pressure was strong enough to displace the outer piece, which started to fall. A thrill of horror shot through the youth. He reached out to catch the missile. In appearance the motion was exactly that of one pitching something from him. The effort failed—nay, it served to push the descending fragment farther out over the wall. He shouted with all his might. The soldiers of the guard looked up ; so did the great man, and that moment the missile struck him, and he fell from his seat as dead.

The cohort halted ; the guards leaped from their horses, and hastened to cover the chief with their shields. On the other hand, the people who witnessed the affair, never doubting that the blow had been purposely dealt, cheered the lad as he yet stooped in full view over the parapet, transfixed by what he beheld, and by anticipation of the consequences flashed all too plainly upon him.

A mischievous spirit flew with incredible speed from roof to roof along the line of march, seizing the people, and urging them all alike. They laid hands upon the parapets and tore up the tiling and the sunburnt mud of which the house-tops were for the most part made, and with blind fury began to fling them upon the legionaries halted below. A battle then ensued. Discipline, of course, prevailed. The struggle, the slaughter, the skill of one side, the desperation of the other, are alike unnecessary to our story. Let us look rather to the wretched author of it all.

He arose from the parapet, his face very pale.

" O Tirzah, Tirzah ! What will become of us ? "

She had not seen the occurrence below, but was listening to the shouting, and watching the mad activity of the people in view on the houses. Something terrible was going on, she knew ; but what it was, or the cause, or that she or any of those dear to her were in danger, she did not know.

" What has happened ? What does it all mean ? " she asked, in sudden alarm.

" I have killed the Roman governor. The tile fell upon him."

" What will they do ? " she asked.

He was leading her to the summer-house, when the roof jarred under their feet, and a crash of strong timbers being burst away, followed by a cry of surprise and agony, arose apparently from the court-yard below. He stopped and listened. The cry was repeated ; then came a rush of many feet, and voices lifted in rage blent with voices in prayer ; and then the screams of women in mortal terror. The soldiers had beaten in the north gate, and were in possession of the house. The terrible sense of being hunted smote him. His first impulse was to fly ; but where ? Nothing but wings would serve. Tirzah, her eyes wild with fear, caught his arm.

" O Judah, what does it mean ? "

The servants were being butchered—and his mother ! Was not one of the voices he heard hers ? With all the will left him, he said, " Stay here, and wait for me, Tirzah. I will go down and see what is the matter, and come back to you."

His voice was not steady as he wished. She clung closer to him.

Clearer, shriller, no longer a fancy, his mother's cry arose. He hesitated no longer.

"Come, then, let us go."

The terrace or gallery at the foot of the steps was crowded with soldiers. Other soldiers with drawn swords ran in and out of the chambers. At one place a number of women on their knees clung to each other or prayed for mercy. Apart from them, one with torn garments, and long hair streaming over her face, struggled to tear loose from a man all whose strength was tasked to keep his hold. Her cries were shrillest of all; cutting through the clamour, they had risen distinguishably to the roof. To her Judah sprang—his steps were long and swift, almost a winged flight—" Mother, mother l " he shouted. She stretched her hands towards him ; but when almost touching them he was seized and forced aside. Then he heard some one say, speaking loudly :

"That is he ! "

Judah looked, and saw—Messala.

"What, the assassin—that ? " said a tall man, in legionary armour of beautiful finish. "Why, he is but a boy."

"Gods ! " replied Messala, not forgetting his drawl. "A new philosophy ! What would Seneca say to the proposition that a man must be old before he can hate enough to kill ? You have him ; and that is his mother ; yonder is his sister. You have the whole family."

For love of them, Judah forgot his quarrel.

"Help them, O my Messala ! Remember our childhood and help them. I—Judah—pray you."

Messala affected not to hear.

"I cannot be of further use to you," he said to the officer. "There is richer entertainment in the street. Down Eros, up Mars ! "

With the last words he disappeared. Judah understood him, and, in the bitterness of his soul, prayed to heaven.

"In the hour of Thy vengeance, O Lord," he said, "be mine the hand to put it upon him ! "

By great exertion, he drew nearer the officer.

"O sir, the woman you hear is my mother. Spare her, spare my sister yonder. God is just, He will give you mercy for mercy."

The man appeared to be moved.

" To the Tower with the women ! " he shouted, " but do them no harm. I will demand them of you." Then to those holding Judah, he said, " Get cords, and bind his hands, and take him to the street. His punishment is reserved."

The mother was carried away. The little Tirzah, in her home attire, stupefied with fear, went passively with her keepers. Judah gave each of them a last look, and covered his face with his hands, as if to possess himself of the scene fadelessly. He may have shed tears, though no one saw them. When he raised his head, and held his arms out to be bound, the bend of the Cupid's bow had vanished from his lips. In that instant he had put off childhood and become a man.

A trumpet sounded in the courtyard. With the cessation of the call, the gallery was cleared of the soldiery ; many of whom, as they dared not appear in the ranks with visible plunder in their hands, flung what they had upon the floor, until it was strewn with articles of richest *vertu*. When Judah descended, the formation was complete, and the officer waiting to see his last order executed.

The mother, daughter and entire household were led out of the north gate, the ruins of which choked the passage-way. The cries of the domestics, some of whom had been born in the house, were most pitiable. When, finally, the horses and all the dumb tenantry of the place were driven past him, Judah began to comprehend the scope of the procurator's vengeance. The very structure was devoted. Far as the order was possible of execution, nothing living was to be left within its walls. If in Judea there were others desperate enough to think of assassinating a Roman governor, the story of what befell the princely family of Hur would be a warning to them, while the ruin of the habitation would keep the story alive.

The officer waited outside while a detail of men temporarily restored the gate.

In the street the fighting had almost ceased. Upon the houses here and there clouds of dust told where the struggle was yet prolonged. The cohort was, for the most part, standing at rest, its splendour, like its ranks, in nowise diminished. Borne past the point of care for himself, Judah had heart for nothing in view but the prisoners, among whom he looked in vain for his mother and Tirzah.

Suddenly, from the earth where she had been lying, a woman arose and started swiftly back to the gate. Some of the guards reached out to seize her, and a great shout followed their failure. She ran to Judah, and dropping down, clasped his knees, the coarse black hair powdered with dust veiling her eyes.

" O Amrah, good Amrah," he said to her, " God help you ; I cannot."

She could not speak.

He bent down, and whispered, " Live, Amrah, for Tirzah and my mother. They will come back, and——"

A soldier drew her away ; whereupon she sprang up and rushed through the gateway and passage into the vacant court-yard.

" Let her go," the officer shouted. " We will seal the house, and she will starve."

The men resumed their work, and, when it was finished there, passed round to the west side. That gate was also secured, after which the palace of the Hurs was lost to use.

The cohort at length marched back to the Tower, where the procurator stayed to recover from his hurts and dispose of his prisoners. On the tenth day following, he visited the Market-place.

CHAPTER VI

NEXT day a detachment of legionaries went to the desolated palace, and closing the gates permanently, plastered the corners with wax, and at the sides nailed a notice in Latin:

" THIS IS THE PROPERTY OF
THE EMPEROR."

In the haughty Roman idea, the sententious announcement was thought sufficient for the purpose—and it was. The day after that again, about noon, a decurion with his command of ten horsemen approached Nazareth from the south—that is, from the direction of Jerusalem.

A trumpet, sounded when the cavalcade drew near the village, had a magical effect upon the inhabitants. The gates and front doors cast forth groups eager to be the first to catch the meaning of a visitation so unusual.

A prisoner whom the horsemen were guarding was the object of curiosity. He was afoot, bareheaded, half naked, his hands bound behind him. A thong fixed to his wrists was looped over the neck of a horse. The dust went with the party when in movement, wrapping him in yellow fog, sometimes in a dense cloud. He drooped forward, foot-sore and faint. The villagers could see he was young.

At the well the decurion halted, and, with most of the men, dismounted. The prisoner sank down in the dust of the road, stupefied, and asked nothing : apparently he was in the last stage of exhaustion. Seeing, when they came near, that he was but a boy, the villagers would have helped him had they dared.

In the midst of their perplexity, and while the pitchers were passing among the soldiers, a man was descried coming down the road from Sepphoris. At sight of him a woman cried out, " Look ! Yonder comes Joseph the carpenter."

The person spoken of was quite venerable in appearance. Thin white locks fell below the edge of his full turban, and a mass of still whiter beard flowed down the front of his coarse grey gown. He came slowly, for, in addition to his age, he carried some tools—an axe, a saw and a drawing-knife, all very rude and heavy—and had evidently travelled some distance without rest.

He stepped close by to survey the assemblage.

" The Lord help him ! " said Joseph, for once moved out of his stolidity.

Thereupon a youth who came up with Joseph, but had stood behind him unobserved, laid down an axe he had been carrying, and, going to the great stone standing by the well, took from it a pitcher of water. The action was so quiet that before the guard could interfere, had they been disposed to do so, he was stooping over the prisoner, and offering him drink.

The hand laid kindly upon his shoulder awoke the unfortunate Judah, and, looking up, he saw a face he never forgot—the face of a boy about his own age, shaded by locks of yellowish bright chestnut hair ; a face lighted by dark-blue eyes, at the time so soft, so appealing, so full of love and holy purpose, that they had all the power of command and will. The spirit of the Jew, hardened though it was by days and nights of suffering, and so embittered by wrong that its dreams of revenge took in all the world, melted under the stranger's look, and became as a child's. He put his lips to the pitcher, and drank long and deep. Not a word was said to him, nor did he say a word.

When the draught was finished, the hand that had been resting upon the sufferer's shoulder was placed upon his head, and stayed there in the dusty locks time enough to say a blessing ; the stranger then returned the pitcher to its place on the stone, and, taking his axe again, went back to Rabbi Joseph. All eyes went with him, the decurion's as well as those of the villagers.

This was the end of the scene at the well. When the men had drunk, and the horses, the march was resumed. But the temper of the decurion was not as it had been; he himself raised the prisoner from the dust, and helped him on a horse behind a soldier. The Nazarenes went to their houses—among them Rabbi Joseph and his apprentice.

And so, for the first time, Judah and the Son of Mary met and parted.

BOOK THIRD

CHAPTER I

THE city of Misenum gave name to the promontory which it crowned, a few miles south-west of Naples. An account of ruins is all that remains of it now ; yet in the year of our Lord twenty-four—to which it is desirable to advance the reader—the place was one of the most important on the western coast of Italy.[1]

In the old time there was a gateway in the wall at a certain point fronting the sea—an empty gateway forming the outlet of a street which, after the exit, stretched itself, in the form of a broad mole, out many stadia into the waves.

The watchman on the wall above the gateway was disturbed, one cool September morning, by a party coming down the street in noisy conversation. He gave one look, then settled into his drowse again.

There were twenty or thirty persons in the party, of whom the greater number were slaves with torches which flamed little and smoked much, leaving on the air the perfume of the Indian nard. The masters walked in advance arm-in-arm. One of them, apparently fifty years old, slightly bald, and wearing over his scant locks a crown of laurel, seemed, from the attentions paid him, the central object of some affectionate ceremony. They all sported ample togas of white wool broadly bordered with

[1] The Roman government, it will be remembered, had two harbours in which great fleets were constantly kept—Ravenna and Misenum.

purple. A glance had sufficed the watchman. He knew, without question, they were of high rank, and escorted a friend to ship after a night of festivity. Further explanation will be found in the conversation they carried on.

"No, my Quintus," said one, speaking to him with the crown, "it is ill of Fortune to take thee from us so soon. Only yesterday thou didst return from the seas beyond the Pillars. Why, thou hast not even got back thy land legs."

"The Greeks are taking him away," another broke in. "Let us abuse them, not the gods. In learning to trade, they forgot how to fight."

With these words, the party passed the gateway, and came upon the mole, with the bay before them beautiful in the morning light. To the veteran sailor the plash of the waves was like a greeting. He drew a long breath, as if the perfume of the water were sweeter than that of the nard, and held his hand aloft.

"She comes—yonder!" he said, pointing to a galley outside the mole.

"What grace, what freedom! A bird hath not less care for the fretting of the waves. I am going to the Ægean; and as my departure is so near, I will tell the occasion—only keep it under the rose. The trade between Greece and Alexandria, as ye may have heard, is hardly inferior to that between Alexandria and Rome, and is so grown that it will not brook interruption a day. Ye may also have heard of the Chersonesan pirates, nested up in the Euxine; none bolder, by the Bacchæ! Yesterday word came to Rome that, with a fleet, they had rowed down the Bosphorus, sunk the galleys off Byzantium and Chalcedon, swept the Propontis, and, still unsated, burst through into the Ægean. The corn-merchants who have ships in the East Mediterranean are frightened. They had audience with the Emperor himself, and from Ravenna there go to-day a hundred galleys, and from Misenum"—he paused as if to pique the curiosity of his friends, and ended with an emphatic—"one."

"Happy Quintus! We congratulate thee!"

"The preferment forerunneth promotion. We salute thee duumvir; nothing less."

" Quintus Arrius, the duumvir, hath a better sound than Quintus Arrius, the tribune."

In such manner they showered him with congratulations.

Arrius gave little heed to them.   As the ship drew more plainly out of the perspective, she became more and more an attraction to him.   The look with which he watched her was that of an enthusiast.   At length he tossed the loosened folds of his toga in the air ; in reply to the signal, over the *aplustre*, or fan-like fixture at the stern of the vessel, a scarlet flag was displayed ; while several sailors appeared upon the bulwarks, and swung themselves hand over hand up the ropes to the *antenna*, or yard, and furled the sail.   The bow was put round, and the time of the oars increased one half ; so that at racing speed she bore down directly towards him and his friends.   He observed the manœuvring with a perceptible brightening of the eyes.   Her instant answer to the rudder, and the steadiness with which she kept her course, were especially noticeable as virtues to be relied upon in action.

The vessel was of the class called *naves liburnicæ*—long, narrow, low in the water, and modelled for speed and quick manœuvre.   The bow was beautiful.   Below it, fixed to the keel, and projecting forward under the water-line, was the *rostrum*, or beak, a device of solid wood, reinforced and armed with iron, in action used as a ram.   A stout moulding extended from the bow the full length of the ship's sides, defining the bulwarks, which were tastefully crenelated ; below the moulding in three rows, each covered with a cap or shield of bull-hide, were the holes in which the oars were worked—sixty on the right, sixty on the left.   In further ornamentation, *caducei* leaned against the lofty prow.   Two immense ropes passing across the bow marked the number of anchors stowed on the fore-deck.

The simplicity of the upper works declared the oars the chief dependence of the crew.   A mast, set a little forward of midship, was held by fore and back stays and shrouds fixed to rings on the inner side of the bulwarks.   The tackle was that required for the management of one great square sail and the yard to which it was hung.   Above the bulwark the deck was visible.

E

Save the sailors who had reefed the sail, and yet lingered on the yard, but one man was to be seen by the party on the mole, and he stood by the prow helmeted and with a shield.

The hundred and twenty oaken blades, kept white and shining by pumice and the constant wash of the waves, rose and fell as if operated by the same hand, and drove the galley forward with a speed rivalling that of a modern steamer.

So rapidly, and apparently so rashly, did she come, that the landsmen of the tribune's party were alarmed. Suddenly the man by the prow raised his hand with a peculiar gesture ; whereupon all the oars flew up, poised a moment in air, then fell straight down. The water boiled and bubbled about them ; the galley shook in every timber, and stopped as if scared. Another gesture of the hand, and again the oars arose, feathered and fell ; but this time those on the right, dropping towards the stern, pushed forward ; while those on the left, dropping towards the bow, pulled backward. Three times the oars thus pushed and pulled against each other. Round to the right the ship swung as upon a pivot ; then, caught by the wind, she settled gently broadside to the mole.

In the midst of the rounding-to, a trumpet was blown brief and shrill, and from the hatchways out poured the marines, all in superb equipment, brazen helms, burnished shields and javelins. While the fighting-men thus went to quarters as for action, the sailors proper climbed the shrouds and perched themselves along the yard. The officers and musicians took their posts. There was no shouting or needless noise. When the oars touched the mole, a bridge was sent out from the helmsman's deck. Then the tribune turned to his party and said, with a gravity he had not before shown :

" Duty now, O my friends."

He took the chaplet from his head.

To the company he opened his arms, and they came one by one and received his parting embrace.

" The gods go with thee, O Quintus ! " they said.

" Farewell," he replied.

To the slaves waving their torches he waved his hand; then he turned to the waiting ship, beautiful with ordered ranks and crested helms, and shields and javelins. As he stepped upon the bridge the trumpets sounded, and over the aplustre rose the *vexillum purpureum*, or pennant of a commander of a fleet.

CHAPTER II

At noon that day the galley was skimming the sea off Pæstum. The wind was yet from the west, filling the sail to the master's content. The better to study his men, he was seated in the great cabin, a very martial figure.

The cabin, it should be stated, was the central compartment of the galley, in extent quite sixty-five by thirty feet, and lighted by three broad hatchways. A row of stanchions ran from end to end, supporting the roof, and near the centre the mast was visible, all bristling with axes and spears and javelins. To each hatchway there were double stairs descending right and left, with a pivotal arrangement at the top to allow the lower ends to be hitched to the ceiling ; and, as these were now raised, the compartment had the appearance of a skylighted hall.

The reader will understand readily that this was the heart of the ship, the home of all aboard—eating-room, sleeping-chamber, field of exercise, lounging-place off duty —uses made possible by the laws which reduced life there to minute details and a routine relentless as death.

At the after-end of the cabin there was a platform, reached by several steps. Upon it the chief of the rowers sat ; in front of him a sounding-table, upon which, with a gavel, he beat time for the oarsmen ; at his right a clepsydra, or water-clock, to measure the reliefs and watches. Above him on a higher platform, well guarded by gilded railing, the tribune had his quarters, overlooking everything, and furnished with a couch, a table, and a *cathedra*, or chair, cushioned, and with arms and high back—articles which the imperial dispensation permitted of the utmost elegance.

Thus at ease, lounging in the great chair, swaying with

the motion of the vessel, the military cloak half draping his tunic, sword in belt, Arrius kept watchful eye over his command, and was as closely watched by them. He saw critically everything in view, but dwelt longest upon the rowers. The reader would doubtless have done the same : only he would have looked with much sympathy, while, as is the habit with masters, the tribune's mind ran forward of what he saw, inquiring for results.

The spectacle was simple enough of itself. Along the sides of the cabin, fixed to the ship's timbers, were what at first appeared to be three rows of benches ; a closer view, however, showed them a succession of rising banks, in each of which the second bench was behind and above the first one, and the third above and behind the second. To accommodate the sixty rowers on a side, the space devoted to them permitted nineteen banks separated by intervals of one yard, with a twentieth bank divided so that what would have been its upper seat or bench was directly above the lower seat of the first bank. The arrangement gave each rower when at work ample room, if he timed his movements with those of his associates, the principle being that of soldiers marching with cadenced step in close order. The arrangement also allowed a multiplication of banks, limited only by the length of the galley.

As to the rowers, those upon the first and second benches sat, while those upon the third, having longer oars to work, were suffered to stand. The oars were loaded with lead in the handles, and near the point of balance hung to pliable thongs, making possible the delicate touch called feathering, but, at the same time, increasing the need of skill, since an eccentric wave might at any moment catch a heedless fellow and hurl him from his seat. Each oar-hole was a vent through which the labourer opposite it had his plenty of sweet air. Light streamed down upon him from the grating which formed the floor of the passage between the deck and the bulwark over his head. In some respects, therefore, the condition of the men might have been much worse. Still, it must not be imagined that there was any pleasantness in their lives. Communication between them was not allowed. Day after day they filled their places without speech ; in hours of labour they could not see each other's faces ; their short respites were given to sleep and the snatching of food. They never laughed ; no one ever heard one of them sing.

When Druilius won the first sea-fight for his country, Romans plied the oars, and the glory was to the rower not less than the marine. These benches which now we are trying to see as they were testified to the change come with conquest, and illustrated both the policy and the prowess of Rome. Nearly all the nations had sons there, mostly prisoners of war, chosen for their brawn and endurance. In one place a Briton ; before him a Libyan ; behind him a Crimean. Elsewhere a Scythian, a Gaul, and a Thebasite. Roman convicts cast down to consort with Goths and Longobardi, Jews, Ethiopians, and barbarians from the shores of Mæotis. Here an Athenian, there a redhaired savage from Hibernia, yonder blue-eyed giants of the Cimbri.

There was no need of keeping the proper names of the slaves brought to the galleys as to their graves ; so, for convenience, they were usually identified by the numerals painted upon the benches to which they were assigned. As the sharp eyes of the great man moved from seat to seat on either hand, they came at last to number sixty, which, as has been said, belonged properly to the last bank on the left-hand side, but, wanting room aft, had been fixed above the first bench of the first bank. There they rested.

The bench of number sixty was slightly above the level of the platform, and but a few feet away. The light glinting through the grating over his head gave the rower fairly to the tribune's view—erect, and, like all his fellows, naked except a cincture about the loins. There were, however, some points in his favour. He was very young, not more than twenty.

In course of the study, Arrius observed the subject's youth ; wholly unconscious of tenderness on that account, he also observed that he seemed of good height, and that his limbs, upper and nether, were singularly perfect. The arms, perhaps, were too long, but the objection was well hidden under a mass of muscle which, in some movements, swelled and knotted like kinking cords. Every rib in the round body was discernible ; yet the leanness was the healthful reduction so strained after in the palæstræ. And altogether there was in the rower's action a certain harmony which, besides addressing itself to the tribune's theory, stimulated both his curiosity and general interest.

Very soon he found himself waiting to catch a view of the man's face in full. The head was shapely, and balanced upon a neck broad at the base, but of exceeding pliancy and grace. The features in profile were of Oriental outline, and of that delicacy of expression which has always been thought a sign of blood and sensitive spirit. With these observations, the tribune's interest in the subject deepened.

" By the gods," he said to himself, " the fellow impresses me ! He promises well. I will know more of him."

Directly the tribune caught the view he wished—the rower turned and looked at him.

" A Jew ! and a boy ! "

Under the gaze then fixed steadily upon him, the large eyes of the slave grew larger—the blood surged to his very brow—the blade lingered in his hands. But instantly, with an angry crash, down fell the gavel of the hortator. The rower started, withdrew his face from the inquisitor, and, as if personally chidden, dropped the oar half-feathered. When he glanced again at the tribune, he was vastly more astonished—he was met with a kindly smile.

Meantime the galley entered the Straits of Messina, and, skimming past the city of that name, was after a while turned eastward, leaving the cloud over Etna in the sky astern.

Often as Arrius returned to his platform in the cabin, he returned to study the rower, and he kept saying to himself, " The fellow hath a spirit. A Jew is not a barbarian. I will know more of him."

CHAPTER III

THE fourth day out, and the *Astræa*—so the galley was named—was speeding through the Ionian Sea. The sky was clear, and the wind blew as if bearing the goodwill of all the gods.

Arrius stood under the aplustre of the galley. Lifting his eyes from the solarium set under the aplustre for reference in keeping the course, Arrius beheld the rower from number sixty approaching.

" The chief called thee the noble Arrius, and said it was thy will that I should seek thee here. I am come."

" The hortator tells me thou art his best rower."

" The hortator is very kind," the rower answered.

" Hast thou seen much service ? "

" About three years."

" At the oars ? "

" I cannot recall a day of rest from them."

" From thy speech, thou art a Jew."

" My father was a prince of Jerusalem, and, as a merchant, he sailed the seas. He was known and honoured in the guest-chamber of the great Augustus."

" His name ? "

" Ithamar, of the House of Hur."

The tribune raised his hand in astonishment.

" A son of Hur—thou ? "

After a silence, he asked :

" What brought thee here ? "

Judah lowered his head, and his breast laboured hard. When his feelings were sufficiently mastered, he looked the tribune in the face, and answered :

" I was accused of attempting to assassinate Valerius Gratus, the procurator."

" Dost thou admit thy guilt ? " asked Arrius sternly.

" Thou hast heard of the God of my fathers," he said ; " of the infinite Jehovah. By His truth and almightiness, and by the love with which He hath followed Israel from the beginning, I swear I am innocent ! "

The tribune was much moved.

" Didst thou not have a trial ? " he asked.

" No ! "

The Roman raised his head, surprised.

" No trial—no witnesses ! Who passed judgment upon thee ? "

Romans, it should be remembered, were at no time such lovers of the law and its forms as in the ages of their decay.

"They bound me with cords, and dragged me to a vault in the Tower. I saw no one. No one spoke to me. Next day soldiers took me to the seaside. I have been a galley-slave ever since."

"What couldst thou have proven?"

Judah told him of the accident of the loose tile.

Arrius listened intently. He brought all his experience with slaves to his aid. If the feeling shown in this instance were assumed, the acting was perfect; on the other hand, if it were real, the Jew's innocence might not be doubted; and if he were innocent, with what blind fury the power had been exercised! A whole family blotted out to atone an accident! The thought shocked him.

For once the tribune was at loss, and hesitated. His power was ample. He was monarch of the ship. His prepossessions all moved him to mercy. His faith was won. Yet, he said to himself, there was no haste—or, rather, there was haste to Cythera; the best rower could not then be spared; he would wait; he would learn more; he would at least be sure this was the prince Ben-Hur, and that he was of a right disposition. Ordinarily slaves were liars.

"Go now," Arrius said, "and do not build upon what has passed between us. Go!"

A short while after Ben-Hur was upon his bench again.

A man's task is always light if his heart is light. Handling the oar did not seem so toilsome to Judah. A hope had come to him, like a singing bird. He could hardly see the visitor or hear its song; that it was there, though, he knew; his feelings told him so. That he had been called by the great man and asked his story was the bread upon which he fed his hungry spirit. Surely something good would come of it. The light about his bench was clear and bright with promises, and he prayed.

"O God! I am a true son of the Israel Thou hast so loved! Help me, I pray Thee!"

CHAPTER IV

IN the Bay of Antemona, east of Cythera the island, the hundred galleys assembled. There the tribune gave one day to inspection. He sailed then to Naxos, the largest of the Cyclades, midway the coasts of Greece and Asia, like a great stone planted in the centre of a highway, from which he could challenge everything that passed; at the same time, he would be in position to go after the pirates instantly, whether they were in the Ægean or out on the Mediterranean.

As the fleet, in order, rowed in towards the mountain shores of the island, a galley was descried coming from the north. Arrius went to meet it. She proved to be a transport just from Byzantium, and from her commander he learned the particulars of which he stood in most need.

The pirates were from all the farther shores of the Euxine. There were quite sixty galleys in the squadron, all well manned and supplied. A few were biremes, the rest stout triremes. A Greek was in command, and the pilots, said to be familiar with all the Eastern seas, were Greek. The plunder had been incalculable. The panic, consequently, was not on the sea alone; cities, with closed gates, sent their people nightly to the walls. Traffic had almost ceased.

Where were the pirates now?

To this question, of most interest to Arrius, he received answer.

After sacking Hephæstia, on the island of Lemnos, the enemy had coursed across to the Thessalian group, and, by last account, disappeared in the gulfs between Eubœa and Hellas.

Such were the tidings.

If the reader will take a map of Greece and the Ægean, he will notice the island of Eubœa lying along the classic coast like a rampart against Asia, leaving a channel between it and the continent quite a hundred and twenty miles in length, and scarcely an average of eight in width. The inlet on the north had admitted the fleet of Xerxes, and now it received the bold raiders from the Euxine. The

towns along the Pelasgic and Meliac gulfs were rich and
their plunder seductive. All things considered, therefore,
Arrius judged that the robbers might be found somewhere
below Thermopylæ. Welcoming the chance, he resolved
to enclose them north and south, to do which not an hour
could be lost ; even the fruits and wines and women of
Naxos must be left behind. So he sailed away without
stop or tack, until, a little before nightfall, Mount Ocha
was seen upreared against the sky, and the pilot reported
the Eubœan coast.

At a signal the fleet rested upon its oars. When the
movement was resumed, Arrius led a division of fifty of
the galleys, intending to take them up the channel, while
another division, equally strong, turned their prows to
the outer or seaward side of the island, with orders to
make all haste to the upper inlet, and descend sweeping
the waters.

Meantime Ben-Hur kept his bench, relieved every six
hours. The rest in the Bay of Antemona had freshened
him, so that the oar was not troublesome, and the chief on
the platform found no fault.

In his long service, by watching the shifting of the
meagre sunbeams upon the cabin floor when the ship was
under way, he had come to know, generally, the quarter
into which she was sailing. In common with his fellow-
slaves, he knew nothing of the situation, and had no interest
in the voyage. His place was at the oar, and he was held
there inexorably, whether at anchor or under sail. Once
only in three years had he been permitted an outlook from
the deck. The occasion we have seen. He had no idea
that, following the vessel he was helping to drive, there was
a great squadron close at hand and in beautiful order ; no
more did he know the object of which it was in pursuit.

When the sun, going down, withdrew his last ray from
the cabin, the galley still held northward. Night fell,
yet Ben-Hur could discern no change. About that time
the smell of incense floated down the gangways from the
deck.

"The tribune is at the altar," he thought. "Can it
be we are going into battle ? "

He became observant.

Now he had been in many battles without having seen one. From his bench he had heard them above and about him, until he was familiar with all their notes, almost as a singer with a song. So, too, he had become acquainted with many of the preliminaries of an engagement, of which, with a Roman as well as a Greek, the most invariable was the sacrifice to the gods. The rites were the same as those performed at the beginning of a voyage, and to him, when noticed, they were always an admonition.

In good time the lanterns were lighted and hung by the stairs, and the tribune came down from the deck. At his word the marines put on their armour. At his word again, the machines were looked to, and spears, javelins and arrows, in great sheaves, brought and laid upon the floor, together with jars of inflammable oil, and baskets of cotton balls wound loose like the wicking of candles. And when, finally, Ben-Hur saw the tribune mount his platform and don his armour, and get his helmet and shield out, the meaning of the preparations might not be any longer doubted, and he made ready for the last ignominy of his service.

To every bench, as a fixture, there was a chain with heavy anklets. These the hortator proceeded to lock upon the oarsmen, going from number to number, leaving no choice but to obey, and, in event of disaster, no possibility of escape.

The hortator approached. Now he was at number one—the rattle of the iron links sounded horribly. At last number sixty ! Calm from despair, Ben-Hur held his oar at poise, and gave his foot to the officer. Then the tribune stirred—sat up—beckoned to the chief.

A strong revulsion seized the Jew. From the hortator, the great man glanced at him ; and when he dropped his oar all the section of the ship on his side seemed aglow. He heard nothing of what was said ; enough that the chain hung idly from its staple in the bench, and that the chief, going to his seat, began to beat the sounding-board. The notes of the gavel were never so like music. With his breast against the leaded handle, he pushed with all his might—pushed until the shaft bent as if about to break.

The chief went to the tribune, and, smiling, pointed to number sixty.

"What strength!" he said.

"And what spirit!" the tribune answered. "*Perpol!* He is better without the irons. Put them on him no more."

So saying, he stretched himself upon the couch again. The ship sailed on hour after hour under the oars in water scarcely rippled by the wind. And the people not on duty slept, Arrius in his place, the marines on the floor.

The deeper darkness before the dawn was upon the waters, and all things going well with the *Astræa*, when a man, descending from the deck, walked swiftly to the platform where the tribune slept, and awoke him. Arrius arose, put on his helmet, sword and shield, and went to the commander of the marines.

"The pirates are close by. Up and ready!" he said, and passed to the stairs, calm, confident, insomuch that one might have thought, "Happy fellow! Apicius has set a feast for him."

CHAPTER V

EVERY soul aboard, even the ship, awoke. Officers went to their quarters. The marines took arms, and were led out, looking in all respects like legionaries. Sheaves of arrows and armfuls of javelins were carried on deck. By the central stairs the oil-tanks and fire-balls were set ready for use. Additional lanterns were lighted. Buckets were filled with water. The rowers in relief assembled under guard in front of the chief. As Providence would have it, Ben-Hur was one of the latter. Overhead he heard the muffled noises of the final preparations—of the sailors furling sail, spreading the nettings, unslinging the machines, and hanging the armour of bull-hide over the sides. Presently quiet settled about the galley again; quiet full of vague dread and expectation, which, interpreted, means *ready*.

At a signal passed down from the deck, and communicated to the hortator by a petty officer stationed on the
stairs, all at once the oars stopped.

What did it mean ?

A sound like the rowing of galleys astern attracted
Ben-Hur, and the *Astræa* rocked as if in the midst of coun-
tering waves. The idea of a fleet at hand broke upon him
—a fleet in manœuvre—forming probably for attack. His
blood started with the fancy.

Another signal came down from the deck. The oars
dipped, and the galley started imperceptibly. No sound
from without, none from within, yet each man in the cabin
instinctively poised himself for a shock ; the very ship
seemed to catch the sense, and hold its breath, and go
crouched tiger-like.

In such a situation time is inappreciable ; so that Ben-
Hur could form no judgment of distance gone. At last
there was a sound of trumpets on deck, full, clear, long
blown. The chief beat the sounding-board until it rang ;
the rowers reached forward full length, and deepening the
dip of their oars, pulled suddenly with all their united force.
The galley, quivering in every timber, answered with a
leap. Other trumpets joined in the clamour—all from the
rear, none forward—from the latter quarter only a rising
sound of voices in tumult heard briefly. There was a
mighty blow ; the rowers in front of the chief's platform
reeled, some of them fell ; the ship bounded back, recovered,
and rushed on more irresistibly than before. Shrill and
high arose the shrieks of men in terror ; over the blare of
trumpets, and the grind and crash of the collision, they
arose ; then under his feet, under the keel, pounding,
rumbling, breaking to pieces, drowning, Ben-Hur felt
something overridden. The men about him looked at
each other afraid. A shout of triumph from the deck—
the beak of the Roman had won ! But who were they whom
the sea had drunk ? Of what tongue, from what land were
they ?

No pause, no stay ! Forward rushed the *Astræa* ; and,
as it went, some sailors ran down, and plunging the cotton
balls into the oil-tanks, tossed them dripping to comrades

at the head of the stairs ; fire was to be added to other horrors of the combat.

Directly the galley heeled over so far that the oarsmen on the uppermost side with difficulty kept their benches. Again the hearty Roman cheer, and with it despairing shrieks. An opposing vessel, caught by the grappling-hooks of the great crane swinging from the prow, was being lifted into the air that it might be dropped and sunk.

The shouting increased on the right hand and on the left ; before, behind, swelled an indescribable clamour. Occasionally there was a crash, followed by sudden peals of fright, telling of other ships ridden down, and their crews drowned in the vortexes.

Nor was the fight all on one side. Now and then a Roman in armour was borne down the hatchway, and laid bleeding, sometimes dying, on the floor.

Sometimes, also, puffs of smoke, blended with steam, and foul with the scent of roasting human flesh, poured into the cabin, turning the dimming light into yellow murk. Gasping for breath the while, Ben-Hur knew they were passing through the cloud of a ship on fire, and burning up with the rowers chained to the benches.

The *Astræa* all this time was in motion. Suddenly she stopped. The oars forward were dashed from the hands of the rowers, and the rowers from their benches. On deck, then, a furious trampling, and on the sides a grinding of ships afoul of each other. For the first time the beating of the gavel was lost in the uproar. Men sank on the floor in fear or looked about seeking a hiding-place. In the midst of the panic a body plunged or was pitched headlong down the hatchway, falling near Ben-Hur. He beheld the half-naked carcass, a mass of hair blackening the face, and under it a shield of bull-hide and wicker-work—a barbarian from the white-skinned nations of the North whom death had robbed of plunder and revenge. How came he there ? An iron hand had snatched him from the opposing deck—no, the *Astræa* had been boarded ! The Romans were fighting on their own deck ! A chill smote the young Jew ; Arrius was hard pressed—he might be defending his own life. If he should be slain ! God of

Abraham forefend ! The hopes and dreams so lately come, were they only hopes and dreams ? Mother and sister—house—home—Holy Land—was he not to see them, after all ?

It should not be—Arrius should not die. At least, better perish with him than survive a galley-slave.

Once more Ben-Hur looked around. Upon the roof of the cabin the battle yet beat ; against the sides the hostile vessels yet crushed and grided. On the benches, the slaves struggled to tear loose from their chains, and, finding their efforts vain, howled like madmen ; the guards had gone upstairs ; discipline was out, panic in. No, the chief kept his chair, unchanged, calm as ever—except the gavel, weaponless. Vainly with his clangour he filled the lulls in the din. Ben-Hur gave him a last look, then broke away—not in flight, but to seek the tribune.

A very short space lay between him and the stairs of the hatchway aft. He took it with a leap, and was half-way up the steps—up far enough to catch a glimpse of the sky blood-red with fire, of the ships alongside, of the sea covered with ships and wrecks, of the fight closed in about the pilot's quarter, the assailants many, the defenders few —when suddenly his foothold was knocked away, and he pitched backward. The floor, when he reached it, seemed to be lifting itself and breaking to pieces ; then, in a twinkling, the whole afterpart of the hull broke asunder, and, as it had all the time been lying in wait, the sea, hissing and foaming, leaped in, and all became darkness and surging water to Ben-Hur.

It cannot be said that the young Jew helped himself in this stress. Besides his usual strength, he had the indefinite extra force which nature keeps in reserve for just such perils to life ; yet the darkness, and the whirl and roar of water stupefied him. Even the holding his breath was involuntary.

The influx of the flood tossed him like a log forward into the cabin, where he would have drowned but for the reflu-ence of the sinking motion. As it was, fathoms under the surface the hollow mass vomited him forth, and he arose along with the loosed débris. In the act of rising, he

clutched something, and held to it.   The time he was under
seemed an age longer than it really was ; at last he gained
the top ; with a great gasp he filled his lungs afresh, and,
tossing the water from his hair and eyes, climbed higher
upon the plank he held, and looked about him.

Smoke lay upon the sea like a semi-transparent fog,
through which here and there shone cores of intense brilliance.   A quick intelligence told him that they were ships
on fire.   The battle was yet on ; nor could he say who was
victor.   Within the radius of his vision now and then ships
passed, shooting shadows athwart lights.   Out of the dun
clouds farther on he caught the crash of other ships colliding.
The danger, however, was closer at hand.   When the *Astræa*
went down, her deck, it will be recollected, held her own
crew, and the crews of the two galleys which had attacked
her at the same time, all of whom were engulfed.   Many
of them came to the surface together, and on the same
plank or support of whatever kind continued the combat,
begun possibly in the vortex fathoms down.   Writhing
and twisting in deadly embrace, sometimes striking with
sword or javelin, they kept the sea around them in agitation,
at one place inky-black, at another aflame with fiery re-
flections.   With their struggles he had nothing to do ; they
were all his enemies : not one of them but would kill him
for the plank upon which he floated.   He made haste to
get away.

About that time he heard oars in quickest movement,
and beheld a galley coming down upon him.   The tall
prow seemed doubly tall, and the red light playing upon
its gilt and carving gave it an appearance of snaky life.
Under its foot the water churned to flying foam.

He struck out, pushing the plank, which was very broad
and unmanageable.   Seconds were precious—half a second
might save or lose him.   In the crisis of the effort, up from
the sea, within arm's reach, a helmet shot like a gleam of
gold.   Next came two hands with fingers extended—large
hands were they, and strong—their hold once fixed might
not be loosed.   Ben-Hur swerved from them appalled.
Up rose the helmet and the head it encased—then two
arms, which began to beat the water wildly—the head

turned back, and gave the face to the light. The mouth gaping wide; the eyes open, but sightless, and the bloodless pallor of a drowning man—never anything more ghastly ! Yet he gave a cry of joy at the sight, and as the face was going under again, he caught the sufferer by the chain which passed from the helmet beneath the chin and drew him to the plank.

The man was Arrius, the tribune.

For a while the water foamed and eddied violently about Ben-Hur, taxing all his strength to hold to the support and at the same time keep the Roman's head above the surface. The galley had passed, leaving the two barely outside the stroke of its oars. Right through the floating men, over heads helmeted as well as heads bare, she drove, in her wake nothing but the sea sparkling with fire. A muffled crash, succeeded by a great outcry, made the rescuer look again from his charge. A certain savage pleasure touched his heart—the *Astræa* was avenged.

After that the battle moved on. Resistance turned to flight. But who were the victors ? Ben-Hur was sensible how much his freedom and the life of the tribune depended upon that event. He pushed the plank under the latter until it floated him, after which all his care was to keep him there. The dawn came slowly. He watched its growing hopefully, yet sometimes afraid. Would it bring the Romans or the pirates ? If the pirates, his charge was lost.

At last morning broke in full, the air without a breath. Off to the left he saw the land, too far to think of attempting to make it. Here and there men were adrift like himself. In spots the sea was blackened by charred and sometimes smoking fragments. A galley a long way off was lying to with a torn sail hanging from the tilted yard, and the oars all idle. Still farther away he could discern moving specks, which he thought might be ships in flight or pursuit, or they might be white birds a-wing.

An hour passed thus. His anxiety increased. If relief came not speedily, Arrius would die. Sometimes he seemed already dead, he lay so still. He took the helmet off, and then, with greater difficulty, the cuirass ; the heart he

F

found fluttering. He took hope at the sign, and held on. There was nothing to do but wait, and, after the manner of his people, pray.

CHAPTER VI

THE throes of recovery from drowning are more painful than the drowning. These Arrius passed through, and, at length, to Ben-Hur's delight, reached the point of speech.

Gradually, from incoherent questions as to where he was, and by whom and how he had been saved, he reverted to the battle. The doubt of the victory stimulated his faculties to full return, a result aided not a little by a long rest—such as could be had on their frail support. After a while he became talkative.

" Our rescue, I see, depends upon the result of the fight. I see also what thou hast done for me. To speak fairly, thou hast saved my life at the risk of thy own. I make the acknowledgment broadly ; and, whatever cometh, thou hast my thanks. If I live, I will make thee free, and restore thee to thy home and people ; or thou mayest give thyself to the pursuit that pleaseth thee most. Dost thou hear ? "

" I could not choose but hear. Blessed be the God of my fathers, yonder cometh a ship ! "

" In what direction ? "

" From the north."

" Canst thou tell her nationality by outward signs ? "

" No. My service hath been at the oars."

" Hath she a flag ? "

" I cannot see one."

Arrius remained quiet some time, apparently in deep reflection.

" Does the ship hold this way yet ? " he at length asked.

" Still this way."

" If Roman, she hath a helmet over the mast's top."

" Then be of cheer. I see the helmet."

Still Arrius was not assured.

" She stops and puts a boat over her side. The men

in the small boat are taking in the people afloat. Pirates are not humane."

"They may need rowers," Arrius replied, recurring, possibly, to times when he had made rescues for the purpose.

Ben-Hur was very watchful of the actions of the strangers.

"The ship moves off," he said.

"Whither ? "

"Over on our right there is a galley which I take to be deserted. The new-comer heads towards it. Now she is alongside. Now she is sending men aboard."

Then Arrius opened his eyes and threw off his calm.

"Thank thou thy God," he said to Ben-Hur, after a look at the galleys, "thank thou thy God, as I do my many gods. A pirate would sink, not save, yon ship. By the act and the helmet on the mast I know a Roman. The victory is mine. Fortune hath not deserted me. We are saved. Wave thy hand—call to them—bring them quickly. I shall be duumvir, and thou !—I knew thy father, and loved him. He was a prince indeed. He taught me a Jew was not a barbarian. I will take thee with me. I will make thee my son. Give thy God thanks, and call the sailors. Haste ! The pursuit must be kept. Not a robber shall escape. Hasten them ! "

Judah raised himself upon the plank, and waved his hand, and called with all his might ; at last he drew the attention of the sailors in the small boat, and they were speedily taken up.

Arrius was received on the galley with all the honours due a hero so the favourite of Fortune. Upon a couch on the deck he heard the particulars of the conclusion of the fight. When the survivors afloat upon the water were all saved and the prize secured, he spread his flag of commandant anew, and hurried northward to rejoin the fleet and perfect the victory. In due time the fifty vessels coming down the channel closed in upon the fugitive pirates, and crushed them utterly ; not one escaped. To swell the tribune's glory, twenty galleys of the enemy were captured.

Upon his return from the cruise, Arrius had warm welcome on the mole at Misenum. The young man attending him very early attracted the attention of his friends there; and to their questions as to who he was the tribune proceeded in the most affectionate manner to tell the story of his rescue and introduce the stranger, omitting carefully all that pertained to the latter's previous history. At the end of the narrative, he called Ben-Hur to him, and said, with a hand resting affectionately upon his shoulder:

"Good friends, this is my son and heir, who, as he is to take my property—if it be the will of the gods that I leave any—shall be known to you by my name. I pray you all to love him as you love me."

Speedily as opportunity permitted, the adoption was formally perfected. And in such manner the brave Roman kept his faith with Ben-Hur, giving him happy introduction into the imperial world.

BOOK FOURTH

CHAPTER I

THE month to which we now come is July, the year that of our Lord 29, and the place Antioch, then Queen of the East, and next to Rome the strongest, if not the most populous, city in the world.

A transport galley entered the mouth of the river Orontes from the blue waters of the sea. It was in the forenoon. The heat was great, yet all on board who could avail themselves of the privilege were on deck—Ben-Hur among others.

The five years had brought the young Jew to perfect manhood. Though the robe of white linen in which he was attired somewhat masked his form, his appearance was unusually attractive. For an hour and more he had occupied a seat in the shade of the sail, and in that time several fellow-passengers of his own nationality had tried to engage him in conversation, but without avail.

The galley, in coming, had stopped at one of the ports of Cyprus, and picked up a Hebrew of most respectable appearance, quiet, reserved, paternal. Ben-Hur ventured to ask him some questions ; the replies won his confidence, and resulted finally in an extended conversation.

It chanced also that as the galley from Cyprus entered the receiving bay of the Orontes, two other vessels which had been sighted out in the sea met it and passed into the river at the same time ; and as they did so both the strangers threw out small flags of brightest yellow. There was much conjecture as to the meaning of the signals. At length a passenger addressed himself to the respectable Hebrew for information upon the subject.

"Yes, I know the meaning of the flags," he replied; "they do not signify nationality—they are merely marks of ownership."

"Has the owner many ships?"

"He has."

"You know him?"

"I have dealt with him."

The passengers looked at the speaker as if requesting him to go on. Ben-Hur listened with interest.

"He lives in Antioch," the Hebrew continued in his quiet way. "That he is vastly rich has brought him into notice, and the talk about him is not always kind. There used to be in Jerusalem a prince of very ancient family named Hur."

Judah strove to be composed, yet his heart beat quicker.

"The prince was a merchant, with a genius for business. He set on foot many enterprises, some reaching far East, others West. In the great cities he had branch houses. The one in Antioch was in charge of a man said by some to have been a family servant called Simonides, Greek in name, yet an Israelite. The master was drowned at sea. His business, however, went on, and was scarcely less prosperous. After a while misfortune overtook the family. The prince's only son, nearly grown, tried to kill the procurator Gratus in one of the streets of Jerusalem. He failed by a narrow chance, and has not since been heard of. In fact, the Roman's rage took in the whole House—not one of the name was left alive. Their palace was sealed up, and is now a rookery for pigeons; the estate was confiscated; everything that could be traced to the ownership of the Hurs was confiscated. The procurator cured his hurt with a golden salve."

The passengers laughed.

"You mean he kept the property," said one of them.

"They say so," the Hebrew replied; "I am only telling a story as I received it. And, to go on, Simonides, who had been the prince's agent here in Antioch, opened trade in a short time on his own account, and in a space incredibly brief became the master merchant of the city. In imitation of his master, he sent caravans to India ; and on the sea at present he has galleys enough to make a royal fleet. They say nothing goes amiss with him. His camels do not die, except of old age ; his ships never founder ; if he throw a chip into the river, it will come back to him gold."

" How long has he been going on thus ? "

" Not ten years."

" He must have had a good start."

" Yes, they say the procurator took only the prince's property ready at hand—his horses, cattle, houses, land, vessels, goods. The money could not be found, though there must have been vast sums of it. What became of it has been an unsolved mystery."

" Not to me," said a passenger, with a sneer.

" I understand you," the Hebrew answered. " Others have had your idea. That it furnished old Simonides his start is a common belief. The procurator is of that opinion—or he has been—for twice in five years he has caught the merchant, and put him to torture. The suffering made no impression upon him. All he had was his lawfully, and he was making lawful use of it—that was the most they wrung from him. Now, however, he is past persecution. He has a licence to trade signed by Tiberius himself."

The story ended there.

CHAPTER II

NEXT day early, to the neglect of the city, Ben-Hur sought the house of Simonides. Through an embattled gateway he passed to a continuity of wharves ; thence up the river midst a busy press, to the Seleucian Bridge, under which he paused to take in the scene.

There, directly under the bridge, was the merchant's house, a mass of grey stone, unhewn, referable to no style, looking like a buttress of the wall against which it leaned. Two immense doors in front communicated with the wharf.

Some holes near the top, heavily barred, served as windows. Weeds waved from the crevices, and in places black moss splotched the otherwise bald stones.

The doors were open. Through one of them business went in ; through the other it came out ; and there was hurry, hurry in all its movements.

On the wharf there were piles of goods in every kind of package, and groups of slaves, stripped to the waist, going about in the *abandon* of labour.

Below the bridge lay a fleet of galleys, some loading, others unloading. A yellow flag blew out from each mast-head. From fleet and wharf, and from ship to ship, the bondmen of traffic passed in clamorous counter-currents.

Ben passed boldly into the house.

The interior was that of a vast depôt where, in ordered spaces, and under careful arrangement, goods of every kind were heaped and pent. Though the light was murky and the air stifling, men moved about briskly ; and in places he saw workmen with saws and hammers making packages for shipments. Down a path between the piles he walked slowly, wondering if the man of whose genius there were here such abounding proofs could have been his father's slave ?

At length a man approached and spoke to him.

" What would you have ? "

" I would see Simonides, the merchant."

" Will you come this way ? "

By a number of paths left in the stowage, they finally came to a flight of steps ; ascending which, he found himself on the roof of the depôt, and in front of a structure which cannot be better described than as a lesser stone house built upon another, invisible from the landing below, and out west of the bridge under the open sky. The roof, hemmed in by a low wall, seemed like a terrace, which, to his aston-ishment, was brilliant with flowers ; in the rich surrounding, the house sat squat, a plain square block, unbroken except by a doorway in front. A dustless path led to the door, through a bordering of shrubs of Persian rose in perfect bloom. Breathing a sweet attar-perfume, he followed the guide.

At the end of a darkened passage within, they stopped before a curtain half parted. The man called out:

" A stranger to see the master."

A clear voice replied, " In God's name, let him enter."

A Roman might have called the apartment into which the visitor was ushered his atrium. Above a cornice of gilded balls, the ceiling rose in pavilion style until it broke into a shallow dome set with hundreds of panes of violet mica, permitting a flood of light deliciously reposeful. The floor was carpeted with grey rugs so thick that an invading foot fell half buried and soundless.

In the midlight of the room were two persons—a man resting in a chair high-backed, broad-armed, and lined with pliant cushions ; and at his left, leaning against the back of the chair, a girl well forward into womanhood. At sight of them Ben-Hur felt the blood redden his forehead : bowing, as much to recover himself as in respect, he lost the lifting of the hands, and the shiver and shrink with which the sitter caught sight of him—an emotion as swift to go as it had been to come. When he raised his eyes the two were in the same position, except the girl's hand had fallen and was resting lightly upon the elder's shoulder ; both of them were regarding him fixedly.

" If you are Simonides, the merchant, and a Jew "— Ben-Hur stopped an instant—" then the peace of the God of our father Abraham upon you and—yours."

The last word was addressed to the girl.

" I am the Simonides of whom you speak, by birthright a Jew," the man made answer, in a voice singularly clear. " I am Simonides, and a Jew : and I return you your salutation, with prayer to know who calls upon me."

Ben-Hur looked as he listened, and where the figure of the man should have been in healthful roundness, there was only a formless heap sunk in the depths of the cushions, and covered by a quilted robe of sombre silk. Over the heap shone a head royally proportioned—the ideal head of a statesman and conqueror—a head broad of base and dome-like in front, such as Angelo would have modelled for Cæsar. White hair dropped in thin locks over the white brows, deepening the blackness of the eyes shining through them like sullen lights. The face was bloodless, and much puffed with folds, especially under the chin. To him Ben-Hur stretched his hands, open and palm up, as he would offer peace at the same time he asked it.

"I am Judah, son of Ithamar, late head of the House of Hur, and a prince of Jerusalem."

The merchant's right hand lay outside the robe—a long, thin hand, articulate to deformity with suffering. It closed tightly; otherwise there was not the slightest expression of feeling of any kind on his part; nothing to warrant an inference of surprise or interest; nothing but this calm answer:

"The princes of Jerusalem, of the pure blood, are always welcome in my house; you are welcome. Give the young man a seat, Esther."

The girl took an ottoman near by, and carried it to Ben-Hur. As she arose from placing the seat, their eyes met.

"The peace of our Lord with you," she said modestly. "Be seated and at rest."

Ben-Hur did not take the offered seat, but said, deferentially, "I pray the good master Simonides that he will not hold me an intruder. Coming up the river yesterday, I heard he knew my father."

"I knew the Prince Hur. We were associated in some enterprises lawful to merchants who find profit in lands beyond the sea and the desert. But sit, I pray you—and, Esther, some wine for the young man. Nehemiah speaks of a son of Hur who once ruled the half part of Jerusalem; an old House; very old, by the faith!"

By the time of the conclusion of this speech, Esther was before Ben-Hur with a silver cup filled from a vase upon a table a little removed from the chair. She offered the drink with downcast face. He touched her hand gently to put it away. Again their eyes met, whereat he noticed that she was small, not nearly to his shoulder in height; but very graceful, and fair and sweet of face, with eyes black and inexpressibly soft. When he said aloud:

"No, thy father—if he is thy father?"—he paused.

" I am Esther, the daughter of Simonides," she said, with dignity.

" Then, fair Esther, thy father, when he has heard my further speech, will not think worse of me if yet I am slow to take his wine of famous extract ; nor less I hope not to lose grace in thy sight. Stand thou here with me a moment ! "

Both of them, as in common cause, turned to the merchant. " Simonides ! " he said firmly, " my father, at his death, had a trusted servant of thy name, and it has been told me that thou art the man ! "

There was a sudden start of the wrenched limbs under the robe, and the thin hand clenched.

Simonides returned to his calm, and answered coldly : " Before I make return to thy demand touching my relations to the Prince Hur, and as something which of right should come first, do thou show me proofs of who thou art. Is thy witness in writing ? Or cometh it in person ? "

The demand was plain, and the right of it indisputable. Ben-Hur blushed, clasped his hand, stammered, and turned away at loss. Simonides pressed him.

" The proofs, the proofs, I say ! Set them before me— lay them in my hands ! "

Yet Ben-Hur had no answer. He had not anticipated the requirement ; and, now that it was made, to him as never before came the awful fact that the three years in the galley had carried away all proofs of his identity ; mother and sister gone, he did not live in the knowledge of any human being. Many there were acquainted with him, but that was all. Judah had felt the loneliness before ; to the core of life the sense struck him now. He stood, hands clasped, face averted, in stupefaction. Simonides respected his suffering, and waited in silence.

" Master Simonides," he said, at length, " I can only tell my story ; and I will not that unless you stay judgment so long, and with goodwill deign to hear me."

" Speak," said Simonides, now, indeed, master of the situation—" speak, and I will listen the more willingly that I have not denied you to be the very person you claim yourself."

Ben-Hur proceeded then, and told his life hurriedly, yet with the feeling which is the source of all eloquence; but as we are familiar with it down to his landing at Misenum, in company with Arrius, returned victorious from the Ægean, at that point we will take up the words.

" My benefactor was loved and trusted by the emperor, who heaped him with honourable rewards. The merchants of the East contributed magnificent presents, and he became doubly rich among the rich of Rome. May a Jew forget his religion; or his birthplace, if it were the Holy Land of our fathers? The good man adopted me his son by formal rites of law; and I strove to make him just return: no child was ever more dutiful to father than I to him. I devoted myself to arms, and the acquisition of everything deemed essential to thorough knowledge of the art of war. Master of personal skill in all arms, I seek now the higher knowledge pertaining to the conduct of bodies of men in the field. The consul has admitted me one of his military family.

" O good Simonides ! " Ben-Hur then said, advancing a step, his whole soul seeking expression, " I see thou art not convinced, and that yet I stand in the shadow of thy distrust."

The merchant held his features fixed as marble, and his tongue as still.

Then Judah addressed himself to the merchant again :

" As I have no proof that I am my father's son, I will withdraw that I demanded of thee, O Simonides, and go hence to trouble you no more; only let me say I did not seek thy return to servitude nor account of thy fortune ; in any event, I would have said, as now I say, that all which is product of thy labour and genius is thine ; keep it and welcome. I have no need of any part thereof. When the good Quintus, my second father, sailed on the voyage which was his last, he left me his heir, princely rich. If, therefore, thou dost think of me again, be it with remembrance of this question, which, as I do swear by the prophets and Jehovah, thy God and mine, was the chief purpose of my coming here. What dost thou know— what canst thou tell me—of my mother and Tirzah, my sister—she who should be in beauty and grace even as this one, thy sweetness of life, if not thy very life ? Oh ! what canst thou tell me of them ? "

The tears ran down Esther's cheeks ; but the man was wilful : in a clear voice, he replied :

" I have said I knew the Prince Ben-Hur. I remember hearing of the misfortune which overtook his family. I remember the bitterness with which I heard it. He who wrought such misery to the widow of my friend is the same who, in the same spirit, hath since wrought upon me. I will go further, and say to you, I have made diligent quest concerning the family, but—I have nothing to tell you of them. They are lost."

Ben-Hur uttered a great groan.

" Then—then it is another hope broken ! " he said, struggling with his feelings. " I am used to disappointments. I pray you pardon my intrusion ; and if I have occasioned you annoyance, forgive it because of my sorrow. I have nothing now to live for but vengeance Farewell."

At the curtain he turned, and said simply, " I thank you both."

" Peace go with you," the merchant said.

Esther could not speak for sobbing.

And so he departed.

CHAPTER III

SCARCELY was Ben-Hur gone, when Simonides seemed to wake as from sleep : his countenance flushed ; the sullen light of his eyes changed to brightness ; and he said cheerily :

" Esther, ring—quick ! "

She went to the table, and rang a service-bell.

One of the panels in the wall swung back, exposing a doorway which gave admittance to a man who passed round to the merchant's front, and saluted him with a half salaam.

" Malluch, here—nearer—to the chair," the master said imperiously. " I have a mission which shall not fail though the sun should. Hearken ! A young man is now descend-

ing to the store-room—tall, comely, and in the garb of
Israel; follow him, his shadow not more faithful; and
every night send me report of where he is, what he does,
and the company he keeps; and if, without discovery,
you overhear his conversations, report them word for
word, together with whatever will serve to expose him,
his habits, motives, life. Understand you? Go quickly!
Stay, Malluch: if he leave the city, go after him—and,
mark you, Malluch, be as a friend. If he bespeak you,
tell him what you will to the occasion most suited, except
that you are in my service; of that, not a word. Haste—
make haste."

The man saluted as before, and was gone.

Then Simonides rubbed his wan hands together, and
laughed.

"When the young man was speaking, Esther, I observed
thee, and thought thou wert won by him."

Her eyes fell as she replied:

"Speak you of faith, father, I believed him."

"In thy eyes, then, he is the lost son of the Prince
Hur?"

"If he is not——" She hesitated.

"And if he is not, Esther?"

"I have been thy handmaiden, father, since my mother
answered the call of the Lord God; by thy side I have
heard and seen thee deal in wise ways with all manner of
men seeking profit, holy and unholy; and now I say, if
indeed the young man be not the prince he claims to be,
then before me falsehood never played so well the part
of righteous truth."

"By the glory of Solomon, daughter, thou speakest
earnestly. Dost thou believe thy father his father's
servant?"

"I understood him to ask of that as something he had
but heard."

"Well, thou art a good child, Esther, of genuine Jewish
shrewdness, and of years and strength to hear a sorrowful
tale. . . . I was born in a tomb in the valley of Hinnom,
on the south side of Zion. My father and mother were
Hebrew bondservants, tenders of the fig and olive trees

growing, with many vines, in the King's Garden hard by Siloam ; and in my boyhood I helped them. They were of the class bound to serve for ever. They sold me to the Prince Hur, then, next to Herod the King, the richest man in Jerusalem. From the garden he transferred me to his storehouse in Alexandria of Egypt, where I came of age. I served him six years, and in the seventh, by the law of Moses, I went free."

Esther clapped her hands lightly.

" Oh, then, thou art not his father's servant ! "

" Nay, daughter, hear. Now, in those days there were lawyers in the cloisters of the Temple who disputed vehemently, saying the children of servants bound for ever took the condition of their parents ; but the Prince Hur was a man righteous in all things, and an interpreter of the law after the straitest sect, though not of them. He said I was a Hebrew servant bought, in the true meaning of the great lawgiver, and, by sealed writings, which I yet have, he set me free."

" And my mother ? " Esther asked.

" Thou shalt hear all, Esther ; be patient. Before I am through thou shalt see it were easier for me to forget myself than thy mother. . . . At the end of my service, I came up to Jerusalem to the Passover. My master entertained me. I was in love with him already ; and I prayed to be continued in his service. He consented, and I served him yet another seven years, but as a hired son of Israel. In his behalf I had charge of ventures on the sea by ships, and of ventures on land by caravans eastward to Susa and Persepolis, and the lands of silk beyond them. Perilous passages were they, my daughter ; but the Lord blessed all I undertook. I brought home vast gains for the prince, and richer knowledge for myself, without which I could not have mastered the charges since fallen to me. . . . One day I was a guest in his house in Jerusalem. A servant entered with some sliced bread on a platter. She came to me first. It was then I saw thy mother, and loved her, and took her away in my secret heart. After a while a time came when I sought the prince to make her my wife. He told me she was bondservant for ever ;

but if she wished, he would set her free that I might be
gratified. She gave me love for love, but was happy where
she was, and refused her freedom. I prayed and besought,
going again and again, after long intervals. She would
be my wife, she all the time said, if I would become her
fellow in servitude. Our father Jacob served yet other
seven years for his Rachel. Could I not as much for mine?
But thy mother said I must become as she, to serve for
ever. I came away, but went back. Look, Esther, look
here."

He pulled out the lobe of his left ear.

"See you not the scar of the awl?"

"I see it," she said; "and, oh, I see how thou didst love
my mother!"

"My master was drowned at sea, the first sorrow that
ever fell upon me," the merchant continued. "Now,
Esther, mark you! When the good prince was lost, I had
risen to be his chief steward, with everything of property
belonging to him in my management and control. His
widow continued me in the stewardship. I applied myself
with greater diligence. The business prospered, and grew
year by year. Ten years passed; then came the blow
which you heard the young man tell about—the accident,
as he called it, to the Procurator Gratus. The Roman
gave it out an attempt to assassinate him. Under that
pretext, by leave from Rome, he confiscated to his own
use the immense fortune of the widow and children. Nor
stopped he there. That there might be no reversal of
the judgment, he removed all the parties interested. From
that dreadful day to this the family of Hur have been
lost. The son, whom I had seen as a child, was sentenced
to the galleys. The widow and daughter are supposed to
have been buried in some of the many dungeons of Judea,
which, once closed upon the doomed, are like sepulchres
sealed and locked. They passed from the knowledge of
men as utterly as if the sea had swallowed them unseen.
We could not hear how they died—nay, not even that they
were dead."

Esther's eyes were dewy with tears.

"Thy heart is good, Esther; good as thy mother's was;

and I pray it have not the fate of most good hearts—to
be trampled upon by the unmerciful and blind. But
hearken further. I went up to Jerusalem to give help to
my benefactress, and was seized at the gate of the city
and carried to the sunken cells of the Tower of Antonia ;
why, I knew not, until Gratus himself came and demanded
of me the moneys of the House of Hur, which he knew,
after our Jewish custom of exchange, were subject to my
draft in the different marts of the world. He required
me to sign to his order. I refused. He had the houses,
lands, goods, ships and movable property of those I served ;
he had not their moneys. I saw, if I kept favour in the
sight of the Lord, I could rebuild their broken fortunes.
I refused the tyrant's demands. He put me to torture ;
my will held good, and he set me free, nothing gained.
I came home and began again, in the name of Simonides
of Antioch, instead of the Prince Hur of Jerusalem. Thou
knowest, Esther, how I have prospered ; that the increase
of the millions of the prince in my hands was miraculous ;
thou knowest how, at the end of three years, while going
up to Cæsarea, I was taken and a second time tortured
by Gratus to compel a confession that my goods and
moneys were subject to his order of confiscation ; thou
knowest he failed as before. Broken in body, I came
home and found my Rachel dead of fear and grief for me.
The Lord our God reigned, and I lived. From the emperor
himself I bought immunity and licence to trade throughout
the world. To-day—praised be He who maketh the clouds
His chariot and walketh upon the winds !—to-day, Esther,
that which was in my hands for stewardship is multiplied
into talents sufficient to enrich a Cæsar."

He lifted his head proudly ; their eyes met ; each read
the other's thought. "What shall I with the treasure,
Esther ? " he asked, without lowering his gaze.

"My father," she answered in a low voice, "did not
the rightful owner call for it but now ? "

Still his look did not fail.

"And thou, my child ; shall I leave thee a beggar ? "

"Nay, father, am not I, because I am thy child, his
bond-servant ? And of whom was it written, ' Strength

G

and honour are her clothing, and she shall rejoice in time to come ' ? "

A gleam of ineffable love lighted his face as he said, " The Lord hath been good to me in many ways ; but thou, Esther, art the sovereign excellence of His favour."

He drew her to his breast and kissed her many times.

" Hear now," he said, with clearer voice—" hear now why I laughed this morning. The young man faced me, the apparition of his father in comely youth. My spirit arose to salute him. I felt my trial days were over and my labours ended. Hardly could I keep from crying out. I longed to take him by the hand and show the balance I had earned, and say, ' Lo, 'tis all thine ! and I am thy servant, ready now to be called away.' And so I would have done, Esther, so I would have done, but that moment three thoughts rushed to restrain me. I will be sure he is my master's son—such was the first thought ; if he is my master's son, I will learn somewhat of his nature. Of those born to riches, bethink you, Esther, how many there are in whose hands riches are but breeding curses."

Esther caressed the faded hands, and said, as if her spirit with his were running forward to results, " He is gone. Will he come again ? "

" Ah, Malluch the faithful goes with him, and will bring him back when I am ready."

" And when will that be, father ? "

" Not long, not long. He thinks all his witnesses dead. There is one living who will not fail to know him, if he be indeed my master's son."

" His mother ? "

" Nay, daughter, I will set the witness before him ; till then let us rest the business with the Lord. I am tired. Call Abimelech."

Esther called the servant, and they returned into the house.

CHAPTER IV

WHEN Ben-Hur sallied from the great warehouse it was with the thought that another failure was to be added to the many he had already met in the quest for his people ; and the idea was depressing exactly in proportion as the objects of his quest were dear to him ; it curtained him round about with a sense of utter loneliness on earth, which, more than anything else, serves to take from a soul cast down its remaining interest in life.

He walked rapidly back to the khan.

" The road to Daphne ! " the steward said, surprised at the question Ben-Hur put to him. " You have not been here before ? Well, count this the happiest day of your life. You cannot mistake the road. The next street to the left, going south, leads straight to Mount Sulpius, crowned by the altar of Jupiter and the Amphitheatre ; keep it to the third cross street, known as Herod's Colonnade ; turn to your right there, and hold the way through the whole city of Seleucus to the bronze gates of Epiphanes. There the road to Daphne begins—and may the gods keep you ! "

A few directions respecting his baggage, and Ben-Hur set out.

The Colonnade of Herod was easily found ; thence to the brazen gates, under a continuous marble portico, he passed with a multitude mixed of people from all the trading nations of the earth.

It was about the fourth hour of the day when he passed out the gate, and found himself one of a procession apparently interminable, moving to the famous Grove. The road was divided into separate ways for footmen, for men on horses, and men in chariots ; and those again into separate ways for outgoers and incomers. The lines of division were guarded by low balustrading, broken by massive pedestals, many of which were surmounted with statuary. Right and left of the road extended margins of sward perfectly kept, relieved at intervals by groups of oak and sycamore trees, and vine-clad summer-houses for the accommodation of the weary, of whom, on the return side, there were always multitudes. The ways of the footmen were paved with red stone, and those of the riders strewn with white sand compactly rolled, but not so solid as to give back an echo to hoof or wheel. The number and variety of fountains at play were amazing, all gifts of visiting kings, and called after them.   Out south-west to the gates of the Grove, the magnificent thoroughfare stretched a little over four miles from the city.

In his wretchedness of feeling, Ben-Hur barely observed the royal liberality which marked the construction of the road.   Nor more did he at first notice the crowd going with him. He treated the processional displays with like indifference.   To say truth, besides his self-absorption, he had not a little of the complacency of a Roman visiting the provinces fresh from the ceremonies which daily eddied round and round the golden pillars set up by Augustus as the centre of the world.   It was not possible for the provinces to offer anything new or superior.   At last there was a clapping of hands, and a burst of joyous cries ; following the pointing of many fingers, he looked and saw upon the brow of a hill the templed gate of the consecrated Grove.   The hymns swelled to louder strains ; the music quickened time ; and, borne along by the impulsive current, and sharing the common eagerness, he passed in, and, Romanized in taste as he was, fell to worshipping the place.

Rearward of the structure which graced the entrance-way—a purely Grecian pile—he stood upon a broad esplanade paved with polished stone ; around him a restless exclamatory multitude, in gayest colours, relieved against the iridescent spray flying crystal-white from fountains ; before him, off to the south-west, dustless paths radiated out into a garden, and beyond that into a forest, over which rested a veil of pale-blue vapour.

CHAPTER V

BEN-HUR entered the woods with the processions. He had not interest enough at first to ask where they were going ; yet, to relieve him from absolute indifference, he had a vague impression that they were in movement to the temples, which were the central objects of the Grove, supreme in attractions.

Presently, as singers dreamfully play with a flitting chorus, he began repeating to himself, " Better be a worm, and feed on the mulberries of Daphne, than a king's guest." Then of the much repetition arose questions importunate of answer. Was life in the Grove so very sweet ? Wherein was the charm ? Did it lie in some tangled depth of philosophy ? Or was it something in fact, something on the surface, discernible to every-day wakeful senses ? Every year thousands, forswearing the world, gave themselves to service here. Did they find the charm ? And was it sufficient, when found; to induce forgetfulness profound enough to shut out of mind the infinitely diverse things of life ? those that sweeten and those that embitter ? hopes hovering in the near future as sorrows born of the past ? If the Grove were so good for them, why should it not be good for him ? He was a Jew ; could it be that the excellences were for all the world but children of Abraham ? Forthwith he bent all his faculties to the task of discovery unmindful of the singing of the gift-bringers and the quips of his associates.

A path into the woods began, offering a happy escape from the noisy processions. Ben-Hur availed himself of the offer.

He walked first into a thicket which, from the road, appeared in a state of nature, close, impenetrable, a nesting-place for wild birds.

Out of the thicket, as he proceeded, on his right and left, issued the cry of the pigeon and the cooing of turtle-doves ; blackbirds waited for him, and bided his coming close ; a nightingale kept its place fearless, though he passed in arm's-length ; a quail ran before him at his feet, whistling to the brood she was leading, and as he paused for them to get out of his way, a figure crawled from a bed of honeyed musk brilliant with balls of golden blossoms. Ben-Hur was startled. Had he, indeed, been permitted to see a satyr at home ? The creature looked up at him, and showed in its teeth a hooked pruning-knife ; he smiled at his own scare, and, lo ! the charm was evolved ! Peace without fear—peace a universal condition—that it was !

He sat upon the ground beneath a citron-tree, which

spread its grey roots sprawling to receive a branch of the brook. The nest of a titmouse hung close to the bubbling water, and the tiny creature looked out of the door of the nest into his eyes. "Verily, the bird is interpreting to me," he thought. "It says, ' I am not afraid of you, for the law of this happy place is Love.' "

The charm of the Grove seemed plain to him ; he was glad, and determined to render himself one of the lost in Daphne. In charge of the flowers and shrubs, and watching the growth of all the dumb excellences everywhere to be seen, could not he, like the man with the pruning-knife in his mouth, forego the days of his troubled life—forego them forgetting and forgotten ?

But by and by his Jewish nature began to stir within him.

The charm might be sufficient for some people. Of what kind were they ?

Love is delightful—ah ! how pleasant as a successor to wretchedness like his. But was it all there was of life ? All ?

There was an unlikeness between him and those who buried themselves contentedly here. They had no duties —they could not have had ; but he——

"God of Israel ! " he cried aloud, springing to his feet with burning cheeks—" Mother ! Tirzah ! Cursed be the moment, cursed the place, in which I yield myself happy in your loss ! "

He hurried away through the thicket, and came to a stream flowing with the volume of a river between banks of masonry, broken at intervals by gated sluiceways. A bridge carried the path he was traversing across the stream ; and, standing upon it, he saw other bridges, no two of them alike. Under him the water was lying in a deep pool, clear as a shadow ; down a little way it tumbled with a roar over rocks ; then there was another pool, and another cascade ; and so on, out of view ; and bridges and pools and resounding cascades said, plainly as inarticulate things can tell a story, the river was running by permission of a master, exactly as the master would have it, tractable as became a servant of the gods.

Suddenly a revelation dawned upon him—the Grove was, in fact, a temple—one far-reaching, wall-less temple !

Never anything like it !

The architect had not stopped to pother about columns and porticoes, proportions or interiors, or any limitation upon the epic he sought to materialize ; he had simply made a servant of Nature—art can go no further.   So the cunning son of Jupiter and Callisto built the old Arcadia ; and in this, as in that, the genius was Greek.

From the bridge Ben-Hur went forward into the nearest valley, and came next to a grove luxuriant, in the heart of the vale at the point where it would be most attractive to the observing eye. As it came close to the path he was travelling, there was a seduction in its shade, and through the foliage he caught the shining of what appeared a pretentious statue ; so he turned aside, and entered the cool retreat.

The statue proved to be a Daphne of wondrous beauty. Hardly, however, had he time to more than glance at her face ; at the base of the pedestal a girl and a youth were lying upon a tiger's skin asleep in each other's arms ; close by them the implements of their service—his axe and sickle, her basket—flung carelessly upon a heap of fading roses.

The exposure startled him. Back in the hush of the perfumed thicket he discovered, as he thought, that the charm of the great Grove was peace without fear, and almost yielded to it ; now, in this sleep in the day's broad glare— this sleep at the feet of Daphne—he read a further chapter to which only the vaguest allusion is sufferable.   The law of the place was Love, but Love without Law.

And this was the sweet peace of Daphne !

This the life's end of her ministers !

Ben-Hur walked with a quicker step, holding his head higher ; and, while not less sensitive to the delightfulness of all about him, he made his survey with calmer spirit, though sometimes with curling lip ; that is to say, he could not so soon forget how nearly he himself had been imposed upon.

CHAPTER VI

IN front of Ben-Hur there was a forest of cypress-trees, each a column tall and straight as a mast. Venturing into the shady precinct, he heard a trumpet gaily blown, and an instant after was lying upon the grass close by a countryman whose strong Judean face avouched that he wore the customary Jewish costume of honest right. The man arose, and came to him.

" I give you peace again," he said pleasantly.

" Thank you," Ben-Hur replied, then asked, " Go you my way ? "

" I am for the stadium, if that is your way."

" The stadium ! "

" Yes. The trumpet you heard but now was a call for the competitors."

" Good friend," said Ben-Hur frankly, " I admit my ignorance of the Grove ; and if you will let me be your follower, I will be glad."

" That will delight me. Hark ! I hear the wheels of the chariots. They are taking the track."

Ben-Hur listened a moment, then completed the introduction by laying his hand upon the man's arm and saying, " I am the son of Arrius, the duumvir, and thou ? "

" I am Malluch, a merchant of Antioch."

" Well, good Malluch, the trumpet, and the gride of wheels, and the prospect of diversion excite me   I have some skill in the exercises. In the palæstræ of Rome I am not unknown. Let us to the course."

Malluch lingered to say quickly, " The duumvir was a Roman, yet I see his son in the garments of a Jew."

" The noble Arrius was my father by adoption," Ben-Hur answered.

" Ah ! I see, and beg pardon."

Passing through the belt of forest, they came to a field with a track laid out upon it, in shape and extent exactly like those of the stadia. The course, or track proper, was of soft earth, rolled and sprinkled, and on both sides defined by ropes, stretched loosely upon upright javelins. For the accommodation of spectators, and such as had interests

reaching forward of the mere practice, there were several
stands shaded by substantial awnings, and provided with
seats in rising rows. In one of the stands the two new-
comers found places.

Ben-Hur counted the chariots as they went by—nine in
all.

" I commend the fellows," he said, with goodwill.
" Here in the East, I thought they aspired to nothing better
than the two ; but they are ambitious, and play with royal
fours. Let us study their performance."

Eight of the fours passed the stand, some walking, others
on the trot, and all unexceptionally handled ; then the
ninth one came on the gallop. Ben-Hur burst into exclamation.

" I have been in the stables of the emperor, Malluch, but,
by our father Abraham of blessed memory ! I never saw
the like of these."

The last four was then sweeping past. All at once they
fell into confusion. Some one on the stand uttered a
sharp cry. Ben-Hur turned, and saw an old man half-
risen from an upper seat, his hands clenched and raised, his
eyes fiercely bright, his long white beard fairly quivering.
Some of the spectators nearest him began to laugh.

"They should respect his beard at least. Who is he ? "
asked Ben-Hur.

"A mighty man from the desert, somewhere beyond
Moab, and owner of camels in herds, and horses descended,
they say, from the racers of the first Pharaoh—Sheik
Ilderim by name and title."

Thus Malluch replied.

The driver meanwhile exerted himself to quiet the four,
but without avail. Each ineffectual effort excited the
sheik the more.

" Abaddon seize him ! " yelled the patriarch shrilly.
" Run ! fly ! do you hear, my children ? The question
was to his attendants, apparently of the tribe. " Do you
hear ? They are desert-born, like yourselves. Catch
them—quick ! "

The plunging of the animals increased.

" Accursed Roman ! " and the sheik shook his fist at

the driver. " Did he not swear he could drive them—swear it by all his brood of bastard Latin gods ? Nay, hands off me—off I say ! They should run swift as eagles, and with the temper of hand-bred lambs, he swore. Cursed be he—cursed the mother of liars who calls him son ! See them, the priceless ! Let him touch one of them with a lash, and——" The rest of the sentence was lost in a furious grinding of his teeth. " To their heads, some of you, and speak them—a word, one is enough, from the tent-song your mothers sang you. Oh, fool, fool that I was to put trust in a Roman ! "

Some of the shrewder of the old man's friends planted themselves between him and the horses. An opportune failure of breath on his part helped the stratagem.

Ben-Hur, thinking he comprehended the sheik, sympathized with him.

In this second and closer look at the horses, Ben-Hur read the story of their relation to their master. They had grown up under his eyes, objects of his special care in the day, his visions of pride in the night, with his family at home in the black tent out on the shadeless bosom of the desert, as his children beloved. That they might win him a triumph over the haughty and hated Roman, the old man had brought his loves to the city, never doubting they would win, if only he could find a trusty expert to take them in hand ; not merely one with skill, but of a spirit which their spirits would acknowledge. Unlike the colder people of the West, he could not protest the driver's inability, and dismiss him civilly ; an Arab and a sheik, he had to explode, and rive the air about him with clamour.

Before the patriarch was done with his expletives, a dozen hands were at the bits of the horses, and their quiet assured. About that time, another chariot appeared upon the track ; and, unlike the others, driver, vehicle, and racers were precisely as they would be presented in the Circus the day of final trial. For a reason which will presently be more apparent, it is desirable now to give this turn-out plainly to the reader.

There should be no difficulty in understanding the carriage

known to us all as the chariot of classical renown. One has but to picture to himself a dray with low wheels and broad axle, surmounted by a box open at the tail-end. Such was the primitive pattern. Artistic genius came along in time, and, touching the rude machine, raised it into a thing of beauty—that, for instance, in which Aurora, riding in advance of the dawn, is given to our fancy.

The jockeys of the ancients, quite as shrewd and ambitious as their successors of the present, called their humblest turn-out a *two*, and their best in grade a *four*; in the latter, they contested the Olympics and the other festal shows founded in imitation of them.

The other contestants had been received in silence ; the last comer was more fortunate. While moving towards the stand from which we are viewing the scene, his progress was signalized by loud demonstrations, by clapping of hands and cheers, the effect of which was to centre attention upon him exclusively. His yoke-steeds, the two against the pole, it was observed, were black, while the outside horses, the trace-mates, were snow-white.

In advancing, the stranger at length reached a point where the chariot came into view from the stand, and its appearance would of itself have justified the shouting. The wheels were very marvels of construction. Stout bands of burnished bronze reinforced the hubs, otherwise very light ; the spokes were sections of ivory tusks, set in with the natural curve outward to perfect the dishing, considered important then as now ; bronze tires held the fellies, which were of shining ebony. The axle, in keeping with the wheels, was tipped with heads of snarling tigers done in brass, and the bed was woven of willow wands gilded with gold.

The coming of the beautiful horses and resplendent chariot drew Ben-Hur to look at the driver with increased interest.

Who was he ?

And directly the whole person of the driver was in view. A companion rode with him, in classic description a Myrtilus, permitted men of high estate indulging their passion for the race-course. Ben-Hur could only see the driver, standing erect in the chariot, with the reins passed several times round his body—a handsome figure, scantily covered by a tunic of light-red cloth ; in the right hand a whip ; in the other, the arm raised and lightly extended, the four lines. The pose was exceedingly graceful and animated. The cheers and clapping of hands were received with statuesque indifference. Ben-Hur stood transfixed—his instinct and memory had served him faithfully—*the driver was Messala !*

By the selection of horses, the magnificence of the chariot, the attitude and display of person—above all, by the expression of the cold, sharp, eagle features, imperialized in his countrymen by sway of the world through so many generations, Ben-Hur knew Messala unchanged, as haughty, confident and audacious as ever, the same in ambition, cynicism and mocking *insouciance.*

CHAPTER VII

As Ben-Hur descended the steps of the stand, an Arab arose upon the last one at the foot, and cried out :

" Men of the East and West—hearken ! The good Sheik Ilderim giveth greeting. With four horses, sons of the favourites of Solomon the Wise, he hath come up against the best. Needs he most a mighty man to drive them. Whoso will take them to his satisfaction, to him he promiseth enrichment for ever. Here—there—in the city and in the Circuses, and wherever the strong most do congregate, tell ye this his offer. So saith my master, Sheik Ilderim the Generous."

The proclamation awakened a great buzz among the people under the awning. By night it would be repeated and discussed in all the sporting circles of Antioch. Ben-Hur, hearing it, stopped and looked hesitatingly from the herald to the sheik. Malluch thought he was about to accept the offer, but was relieved when he presently turned to him and asked, " Good Malluch, where to now ? "

" Castalia."

"Oh! that fountain has repute throughout the world. Let us thither."

At the end of an avenue the road, by an easy grade, descended into a lowland, where, on the right hand, there was a precipitous facing of grey rock, and on the left an open meadow of vernal freshness. Then they came in view of the famous Fountain of Castalia.

Edging through a company assembled at the point, Ben-Hur beheld a jet of sweet water pouring from the crest of a stone into a basin of black marble, where, after much boiling and foaming, it disappeared as through a funnel.

By the basin, under a small portico cut in the solid wall, sat a priest, old, bearded, wrinkled, cowled—never being more perfectly eremitish. From the manner of the people present, hardly might one say which was the attraction, the fountain, for ever sparkling, or the priest, for ever there. He heard, saw, was seen, but never spoke. Occasionally a visitor extended a hand to him with a coin in it. With a cunning twinkle of the eyes, he took the money, and gave the party in exchange a leaf of papyrus.

The receiver made haste to plunge the papyrus into the basin ; then, holding the dripping leaf in the sunlight, he would be rewarded with a versified inscription upon its face ; and the fame of the fountain seldom suffered loss by poverty of merit in the poetry. Before Ben-Hur could test the oracle, some other visitors were seen approaching across the meadow, and their appearance piqued the curiosity of the company, his not less than theirs.

He saw first a camel, very tall and very white, in leading of a driver on horseback. A houdah on the animal, besides being unusually large, was of crimson and gold. Two other horsemen followed the camel with tall spears in hand.

But who were the man and woman under the houdah ? Every eye saluted them with the inquiry.

If the former were a prince or a king, the philosophers of the crowd might not deny the impartiality of Time. When they saw the thin shrunken face buried under an immense turban, the skin of the hue of a mummy, making it impossible to form an idea of his nationality, they were pleased to think the limit of life was for the great as well as the small. They saw about his person nothing so enviable as the shawl which draped him.

The woman was seated in the manner of the East, amidst veils and laces of surpassing fineness. Above her elbows she wore armlets fashioned like coiled asps, and linked to bracelets at the wrists by strands of gold; otherwise the arms were bare and of singular natural grace, complemented with hands modelled daintily as a child's. From her elevated seat she looked upon the people calmly, pleasantly, and apparently so intent upon studying them as to be unconscious of the interest she herself was exciting; and, what was unusual—nay, in violent contravention of the custom among women of rank in public—she looked at them with an open face.

It was a fair face to see; quite youthful; in form, oval: complexion not white, like the Greek, nor brunette, like the Roman; nor blond, like the Gaul; but rather the tinting of the sun of the Upper Nile upon a skin of such transparency that the blood shone through it on cheek and brow with nigh the ruddiness of lamplight.

As if satisfied with the survey of people and locality, the fair creature spoke to the driver—an Ethiopian of vast brawn, naked to the waist—who led the camel nearer the fountain, and caused it to kneel; after which he received from her hand a cup, and proceeded to fill it at the basin. That instant the sound of wheels and the trampling of horses in rapid motion broke the silence her beauty had imposed, and, with a great outcry, the bystanders parted in every direction, hurrying to get away.

"The Roman has a mind to ride us down. Look out!" Malluch shouted to Ben-Hur, setting him at the same time an example of hasty flight.

The latter faced to the direction the sounds came from, and beheld Messala in his chariot pushing the four straight at the crowd. This time the view was near and distinct.

The parting of the company uncovered the camel, which might have been more agile than his kind generally; yet the hoofs were almost upon him, and he resting with closed eyes, chewing the endless cud with such sense of security as long favouritism may be supposed to have bred in him. The Ethiopian wrung his hands afraid. In the houdah, the old man moved to escape ; but he was hampered with age, and could not, even in the face of danger, forget the dignity which was plainly his habit. It was too late for the woman to save herself. Ben-Hur stood nearest them, and he called to Messala :

" Hold ! Look where thou goest ! Back, back ! "

The patrician was laughing in hearty good-humour ; and seeing there was but one chance of rescue, Ben-Hur stepped in, and caught the bits of the left yoke-steed and his mate. " Dog of a Roman ! Carest thou so little for life ? " he cried, putting forth all his strength. The two horses reared, and drew the others round ; the tilting of the pole tilted the chariot ; Messala barely escaped a fall, while his complacent Myrtilus rolled back like a clod to the ground. Seeing the peril past, all the bystanders burst into derisive laughter.

The matchless audacity of the Roman then manifested itself. Loosing the lines from his body, he tossed them to one side, dismounted, walked round the camel, looked at Ben-Hur, and spoke partly to the old man and partly to the woman.

" Pardon, I pray you—I pray you both. I am Messala," he said ; " and, by the old Mother of the earth, I swear I did not see you or your camel ! As to these good people— perhaps I trusted too much to my skill. I sought a laugh at them—the laugh is theirs. Good may it do them ! "

The good-natured, careless look and gesture he threw the bystanders accorded well with the speech. To hear what more he had to say, they became quiet. Assured of victory over the body of the offended, he signed his companion to take the chariot to a safer distance, and addressed himself boldly to the woman.

" Thou hast interest in the good man here, whose pardon, if not granted now, I shall seek with the greater diligence hereafter ; his daughter, I should say ? "

She made him no reply.

" O stranger, beautiful as cruel ! " Messala said, waving

his hand to her. " If Apollo get thee not, thou shalt see me again. Not knowing thy country, I cannot name a god to commend thee to ; so, by all the gods, I will commend thee to—myself ! "

Seeing the Myrtilus had the four composed and ready, he returned to the chariot. The woman looked after him as he moved away, and whatever else there was in her look, there was no displeasure.

Immediately the camel was aroused, and on his feet, and about to go, when the old man called :

" Stand thou here."

Ben-Hur went to him respectfully.

" Thou hast served the stranger well to-day. There is but one God. In his holy name I thank thee. I am Balthasar, the Egyptian. In the Great Orchard of Palms, beyond the village of Daphne, in the shade of the palms, Sheik Ilderim the Generous abideth in his tents, and we are his guests. Seek us there. Thou shalt have welcome sweet with the savour of the grateful."

Ben-Hur was left in wonder at the old man's clear voice and reverend manner. As he gazed after the two departing, he caught sight of Messala going as he had come, joyous, indifferent, and with a mocking laugh.

CHAPTER VIII

As a rule, there is no surer way to the dislike of men than to behave well where they have behaved badly. In this instance, happily, Malluch was an exception to the rule. The affair he had just witnessed raised Ben-Hur in his estimation, since he could not deny him courage and address ; could he now get some insight into the young man's history, the results of the day would not be all unprofitable to good master Simonides.

On the latter point, referring to what he had as yet learned, two facts comprehended it all—the subject of his investigation was a Jew, and the adopted son of a famous Roman. Another conclusion which might be of importance was beginning to formulate itself in the shrewd mind of the emissary; between Messala and the son of the duumvir there was a connexion of some kind. But what was it?—and how could it be reduced to assurance? With all his sounding, the ways and means of solution were not at call. In the heat of the perplexity, Ben-Hur himself came to his help, by telling him of the downfall of the house of Hur and of the reasons he had for bitterly hating Messala.

"And, Malluch, he knows and takes with him now the secret I would give my life for; he could tell if she lives, and where she is, and her condition; if she—no, *they*—much sorrow has made the two as one—if they are dead, he could tell where they died, and of what, and where their bones await my finding."

"And will he not?"

"No."

"Why?"

"I am a Jew, and he is a Roman."

"But Romans have tongues, and Jews, though ever so despised, have methods to beguile them."

"For such as he? No; and, besides, the secret is one of state. All my father's property was confiscated and divided."

Malluch nodded his head slowly, much as to admit the argument; then he asked anew, "Did he not recognize you?"

"He could not. I was sent to death in life, and have been long since accounted of the dead."

"I wonder you did not strike him," said Malluch, yielding to a touch of passion.

"That would have been to put him past serving me for ever I would have had to kill him, and against that extreme the possession of the secret is for the present, at least, his safeguard; yet I may punish him, and so you give me help, I will try."

"He is a Roman," said Malluch, without hesitation; "and I am of the tribe of Judah. I will help you. If you choose, put me under oath—under the most solemn oath."

"Give me your hand, that will suffice."

As their hands fell apart, Ben-Hur said, with lightened feeling, "That I would charge you with is not difficult,

H

good friend ; neither is it dreadful to conscience. Let us move on."

They took the road which led to the right across the meadow spoken of in the description of coming to the fountain. Ben-Hur was first to break the silence.

" Do you know Sheik Ilderim the Generous ? "

" Yes."

" Where is his Orchard of Palms ? or, rather, Malluch, how far is it beyond the village of Daphne ? "

" The Orchard of Palms lies beyond the village two hours by horse, and one by a swift camel."

" Thank you ; and to your knowledge once more. Have the games of which you told me been widely published ? and when will they take place ? "

The questions were suggestive ; and if they did not restore Malluch his confidence, they at least stimulated his curiosity.

" Oh yes, they will be of ample splendour. The prefect is rich, and could afford to lose his place ; yet, as is the way with successful men, his love of riches is nowise diminished ; and to gain a friend at court, if nothing more, he must make ado for the Consul Maxentius, who is coming hither to make final preparations for a campaign against the Parthians. The fees offered are royal."

" One thing more now, O Malluch. When will the celebration be ? "

" Ah ! your pardon," the other answered. " To-morrow —and the next day," he said, counting aloud, " then, to speak in the Roman style, if the sea-gods be propitious, the consul arrives. Yes, the sixth day from this we have the games."

" The time is short, Malluch, but it is enough." The last words were spoken decisively. " By the prophets of our old Israel ! I will take to the reins again. Stay ! a condition ; is there assurance that Messala will be a competitor ? "

Malluch saw now the plan, and all its opportunities for the humiliation of the Roman ; and he had not been true descendant of Jacob, if, with all his interest wakened, he had not rushed to a consideration of the chances. His voice actually trembled as he said, "Have you the practice?"

"Fear not, my friend. The winners in the Circus Maximus have held their crowns these three years at my will. Ask them—ask the best of them, and they will tell you so. In the last great games the emperor himself offered me his patronage if I would take his horses in hand and run them against the entries of the world."

"The Messala will drive," Malluch said directly. "He is committed to the race in many ways—by publication in the streets, and in the baths and theatres, the palace and barracks; and, to fix him past retreat, his name is on the tablets of every young spendthrift in Antioch."

"In wager, Malluch?"

"Yes, in wager; and every day he comes ostentatiously to practise, as you saw him."

"Ah! and that is the chariot, and those the horses, with which he will make the race? Thank you, thank you, Malluch! You have served me well already. I am satisfied. Now be my guide to the Orchard of Palms, and give me introduction to Sheik Ilderim the Generous."

"When?"

"To-day. His horses may be engaged to-morrow."

Malluch took a moment for reflection.

"It is best we go straight to the village, which is fortunately near by; if two swift camels are to be had for hire there, we will be on the road but an hour."

"Let us about it, then."

The village was an assemblage of palaces in beautiful gardens, interspersed with khans of princely sort. Dromedaries were happily secured, and upon them the journey to the famous Orchard of Palms was begun.

CHAPTER IX

BEYOND the village the country was undulating and cultivated; in fact, it was the garden-land of Antioch, with not a foot lost to labour. The steep faces of the hills were terraced; even the hedges were brighter of the trailing vines which, besides the lure of shade, offered passers-by sweet promises of wine to come, and grapes in clustered purple ripeness.

In course of their journey the friends came to the river, which they followed with the windings of the road, now over bold bluffs, and then into vales, all alike allotted for country-seats. And down the shore the friends went continuously till they came to a lake fed by back-water from the river, clear, deep and without current. An old palm-tree dominated the angle of the inlet; turning to the left at the foot of the tree, Malluch clapped his hands and shouted:

"Look, look! The Orchard of Palms!"

The scene was nowhere else to be found unless in the favoured oases of Arabia or the Ptolemæan farms along the Nile; and to sustain a sensation new as it was delightful, Ben-Hur was admitted into a tract of land apparently without limit and level as a floor. All underfoot was fresh grass, in Syria the rarest and most beautiful production of the soil; if he looked up, it was to see the sky palely blue through the groinery of countless date-bearers, very patriarchs of their kind, so numerous and old, and of such mighty girth, so tall, so serried, so wide of branch, each branch so perfect with fronds, plumy and wax-like and brilliant, they seemed enchanters enchanted.

The road wound in close parallelism with the shore of the lake; and when it carried the travellers down to the water's edge, there was always on that side a shining expanse limited not far off by the opposite shore, on which, as on this one, no tree but the palm was permitted.

Ben-Hur was moved to say:

"As I saw him at the stand to-day, good Malluch, Sheik Ilderim appeared to be a very common man. The Rabbis in Jerusalem would look down upon him, I fear, as a son of a dog of Edom. How came he in possession of the Orchard? And how has he been able to hold it against the greed of Roman governors?"

"If blood derives excellence from time, son of Arrius, then is old Ilderim a man, though he be an uncircumcised Edomite."

Malluch spoke warmly.

" All his fathers before him were sheiks. One of them—
I shall not say when he lived or did the good deed—once
helped a king who was being hunted with swords. And
the king, it is said, remembered the service, and brought
the son of the desert to this place, and bade him set up his
tent and bring his family and his herds, for the lake and
trees, and all the land from the river to the nearest mountains, were his and his children's for ever. And they have
never been disturbed in the possession. The rulers succeeding have found it policy to keep good terms with the tribe,
to whom the Lord has given increase of men and horses,
and camels and riches, making them masters of many
highways between cities ; so that it is with them any time
they please to say to commerce, ' Go in peace,' or ' Stop,'
and what they say shall be done.

" But Ilderim is not a lover of Rome ; he has a grievance. Three years ago the Parthians rode across the road
from Bozra to Damascus, and fell upon a caravan laden,
among other things, with the incoming tax-returns of a
district over that way. They slew every creature taken,
which the censors in Rome could have forgiven if the imperial treasure had been spared and forwarded. The farmers
of the taxes, being chargeable with the loss, complained to
Cæsar, and Cæsar held Herod to payment, and Herod, on
his part, seized property of Ilderim, whom he charged with
treasonable neglect of duty. The sheik appealed to Cæsar,
and Cæsar has made him such answer as might be looked
for from the unwinking sphinx. The old man's heart has
been aching sore ever since, and he nurses his wrath, and
takes pleasure in its daily growth."

" He can do nothing, Malluch."

" Well," said Malluch, " that involves another explanation, which I will give you, if we can draw nearer. But
see !—the hospitality of the sheik begins early—the children
are speaking to you."

The dromedaries stopped, and Ben-Hur looked down
upon some little girls of the Syrian peasant class, who were
offering him their baskets filled with dates. The fruit was
freshly gathered, and not to be refused ; he stooped and
took it, and as he did so a man in the tree by which

they were halted cried, "Peace to you, and welcome!"

Their thanks said to the children, the friends moved on at such gait as the animals chose.

"You must know," Malluch continued, pausing now and then to dispose of a date, "that the merchant Simonides gives me his confidence, and sometimes flatters me by taking me into council; and as I attend him at his house, I have made acquaintance with many of his friends, who, knowing my footing with the host, talk to him freely in my presence. In that way I became somewhat intimate with Sheik Ilderim. A few weeks ago the old Arab called on Simonides, and found me present. I observed he seemed much moved about something, and, in deference, offered to withdraw, but he himself forbade me. 'As you are an Israelite,' he said, 'stay, for I have a strange story to tell.' The emphasis on the word Israelite excited my curiosity. I remained, and this is in substance his story—I cut it short because we are drawing nigh the tent, and I leave the details to the good man himself. A good many years ago, three men called at Ilderim's tent out in the wilderness. They were all foreigners, a Hindu, a Greek, and an Egyptian; and they had come on camels, the largest he had ever seen, and all white. He welcomed them, and gave them rest. Next morning they arose and prayed a prayer new to the sheik—a prayer addressed to God and His Son—this with much mystery besides. After breaking fast with him, the Egyptian told who they were, and whence they had come. Each had seen a star, out of which a voice had bidden them go to Jerusalem, and ask, 'Where is He that is born King of the Jews?' They obeyed. From Jerusalem they were led by a star to Bethlehem, where, in a cave, they found a child newly born, which they fell down and worshipped; and after worshipping it, and giving it costly presents, and bearing witness of what it was, they took to their camels, and fled without pause to the sheik, because if Herod— meaning him surnamed the Great—could lay hands upon them, he would certainly kill them. And, faithful to his habit, the sheik took care of them, and kept them concealed for a year, when they departed, leaving with him gifts of great value, and each going a separate way."

" Has Ilderim nothing more of the three men ? " asked
Ben-Hur. " What became of them ? "

" Ah, yes, that was the cause of his coming to Simonides
the day of which I was speaking. Only the night before that day, Balthasar the Egyptian reappeared to
him."

" Balthasar, you said ? "

" Yes. Balthasar, the Egyptian."

" That was the name the old man gave us at the fountain
to-day."

Then, at the reminder, Malluch became excited.

" It is true," he said ; " and the camel was the same—
and you saved the man's life."

" But, following the story, did you hear what Simonides
said to him ? "

" If Ilderim is a grave man, Simonides is a wise one,"
Malluch replied. " I listened, and he said—— But hark !
Some one comes overtaking us."

The noise grew louder, until presently they heard the
rumble of wheels mixed with the beating of horse-hoofs—a
moment later Sheik Ilderim himself appeared on horseback,
followed by a train, among which were the four wine-red
Arabs drawing the chariot. The sheik's chin, in its muffling
of long white beard, was drooped upon his breast. Our
friends had out-travelled him ; but at sight of them, he
raised his head, and spoke kindly.

" Peace to you !—Ah, my friend Malluch ! Welcome !
And tell me you are not going, but just come ; that you
have something for me from the good Simonides—may the
Lord of his fathers keep him in life for many years to come !
Ay, take up the straps, both of you, and follow me. I have
bread and leben, or, if you prefer it, arrack, and the flesh
of young kid. Come ! "

They followed after him to the door of the tent, in which,
when they were dismounted, he stood to receive them,
holding a platter with three cups filled with creamy liquor
just drawn from a great smoke-stained skin bottle, pendent
from the central post.

" Drink," he said heartily, " drink, for this is the fear-
naught of the tentmen."

They each took a cup, and drank till but the foam remained.

" Enter now, in God's name."

And when they were gone in, Malluch took the sheik aside, and spoke to him privately ; after which he went to Ben-Hur and excused himself.

" I have told the sheik about you, and he will give you the trial of his horses in the morning. He is your friend. Having done for you all I can, you must do the rest, and let me return to Antioch. There is one there who has my promise to meet him to-night ; I have no choice but to go. I will come back to-morrow prepared, if all goes well in the meantime, to stay with you until the games are over."

With blessings given and received, Malluch set out in return.

CHAPTER X

WHAT time the lower horn of a new moon touched the castellated piles on Mount Sulpius, and two-thirds of the people of Antioch were out on their house-tops comforting themselves with the night breeze when it blew, and with fans when it failed, Simonides sat in the chair which had come to be a part of him, and from the terrace looked down over the river, and his ships a-swing at their moorings.

" Malluch is a laggard to-night," he said, showing where his thoughts were.

" Do you believe he will come ? " Esther asked.

" Unless he has taken to the sea or the desert, and is yet following on, he will come."

Simonides spoke with quiet confidence.

Just then a footstep was heard upon the terrace. " Ha, Esther ! said I not so ? He is here—and we will have tidings. For thy sake, sweet child—my lily just budded— I pray the Lord God, who has not forgotten His wandering sheep of Israel, that they be good and comforting. Now we will know if he will let thee go with all thy beauty, and me with all my faculties."

Malluch came to the chair.

" Peace to you, good master," he said, with a low obeisance—" and to you, Esther, most excellent of daughters."

He stood before them deferentially, and the attitude and the address left it difficult to define his relation to them ; the one was that of a servant, the other indicated the familiar and friend.   On the other side, Simonides, as was his habit in business, after answering the salutation went straight to the subject.

" What of the young man, Malluch ? "

The events of the day were told quietly and in the simplest words, and until he was through there was no interruption ; nor did the listener in the chair so much as move a hand during the narration ; but for his eyes, wide open and bright, and an occasional long-drawn breath, he might have been accounted an effigy.

" Thank you, thank you, Malluch," he said heartily, at the conclusion ;   " you have done well—no one could have done better.   Now what say you of the young man's nationality ? "

" He is an Israelite, good master, and of the tribe of Judah."

" You are positive ? "

" Very positive."

" In what he said or did, Malluch, could you in anywise detect his master-idea ? "

" As to that, Master Simonides, I can answer with much assurance.   He is devoted to finding his mother and sister —that first.   Then he has a grievance against Rome ; and as the Messala of whom I told you had something to do with the wrong, the great present object is to humiliate him. The meeting at the fountain furnished an opportunity, but it was put aside as not sufficiently public."

" The Messala is influential," said Simonides, thoughtfully.

" Yes ; but the next meeting will be in the Circus."

" Well—and then ? "

" The son of Arrius will win."

" How know you ? "

Malluch smiled.

" I am judging by what he says."

" Is that all ? "

" No ; there is a much better sign—his spirit."

" Ay ; but, Malluch, his idea of vengeance—what is its scope ? Does he limit it to the few who did him the wrong, or does he take in the many ? "

" Good, my master," Malluch replied, " one of my reasons for believing the young man a Jew is the intensity of his hate. It was plain to me he had himself under watch, as was natural, seeing how long he has lived in an atmosphere of Roman jealousy ; yet I saw it blaze."

Simonides gazed for a time at the ships and their shadows slowly swinging together in the river ; when he looked up, it was to end the interview.

" Enough, Malluch," he said. " Get you to eat, and make ready to return to the Orchard of Palms ; you must help the young man in his coming trial. Come to me in the morning. I will send a letter to Ilderim." Then in an undertone, as if to himself, he added, " I may attend the Circus myself."

When Malluch after the customary benediction given and received was gone, Simonides took a deep draught of milk, and seemed refreshed and easy of mind.

" Put the meal down, Esther," he said, " it is over."

She obeyed.

" Here now."

She resumed her place upon the arm of the chair close to him.

" God is good to me, very good," he said fervently. " His habit is to move in mystery, yet sometimes He permits us to think we see and understand Him. I am old, dear, and must go ; but now, in this eleventh hour, when my hope was beginning to die, He sends me this one with a promise, and I am lifted up. I see the way to a great part in a circumstance itself so great that it shall be as a new birth to the whole world. And I see a reason for the gift of my great riches, and the end for which they were designed. Verily, my child, I take hold on life anew."

Esther nestled closer to him, as if to bring his thoughts from their far-flying.

" The King has been born," he continued, imagining he

was still speaking to her, " and He must be near the half
of common life. Balthasar says He was a child on His
mother's lap when he saw Him, and gave Him presents
and worship ; and Ilderim holds it was twenty-seven years
ago last December when Balthasar and his companions
came to his tent asking a hiding-place from Herod. Wherefore the coming cannot now be long delayed. To-night—
to-morrow it may be. Holy fathers of Israel, what happiness in the thought ! When the King comes He will need
money and men, for as He was a child born of woman He
will be but a man after all, bound to human ways as you
and I are. And for the money He will have need of getters
and keepers, and for the men leaders. There, there ! See
you not a broad road for my walking, and the running of
the youth our master ?—and at the end of it glory and
revenge for us both ?—and—and "—he paused, struck
with the selfishness of a scheme in which she had no part
or good result ; then added, kissing her, " And happiness
for thy mother's child."

She sat still, saying nothing. Then he remembered the
difference in natures, and the law by which we are not
permitted always to take delight in the same cause or be
equally afraid of the same thing. He remembered she
was but a girl.

" Of what are you thinking, Esther ? " he said in his
common home-like way. " If the thought have the form
of a wish, give it me, little one, while the power remains
mine. For power, you know, is a fretful thing, and hath
its wings always spread for flight."

She answered with a simplicity almost childish.

" Send for him, father. Send for him to-night, and do
not let him go into the Circus."

" Not go into the Circus, Esther ? Why, child ? "

" It is not a place for a son of Israel, father."

" Rabbinical, rabbinical, Esther ! Is that all ? "

The tone of the inquiry was searching, and went to her
heart, which began to beat loudly—so loudly she could not
answer. A confusion new and strangely pleasant fell upon
her.

" The young man is to have the fortune," he said, taking

her hand, and speaking more tenderly; " he is to have the ships and the shekels—all, Esther, all. Yet I did not feel poor, for thou wert left me, and thy love so like the dead Rachel's. Tell me, is he to have that too ? "

She bent over him, and laid her cheek against his head.

" Speak, Esther. I will be the stronger of the knowledge. In warning there is strength."

She sat up then, and spoke as if she were Truth's holy self.

" Comfort thee, father. I will never leave thee ; though he take my love, I will be thy handmaid ever as now."

And stooping she kissed him.

" And more," she said, continuing: " he is comely in my sight, and the pleading of his voice drew me to him, and I shudder to think of him in danger. Yes, father, I would be more than glad to see him again. Still, the love that is unrequited cannot be perfect love, wherefore I will wait a time, remembering I am thy daughter and my mother's."

" A very blessing of the Lord art thou, Esther ! A blessing to keep me rich, though all else be lost. And by His holy name and everlasting life, I swear thou shalt not suffer."

At his request, a little later, the servant came and rolled the chair into the room, where he sat for a time thinking of the coming of the King, while she went off and slept the sleep of the innocent.

CHAPTER XI

THE palace across the river nearly opposite Simonides' place is said to have been completed by the famous Epiphanes, and was all such a habitation can be imagined ; though he was a builder whose taste ran to the immense rather than the classical, now so called—an architectural imitator, in other words, of the Persians instead of the Greeks.

As we have to do with but one apartment in the old pile, the residue of it is left to the reader's fancy ; and as pleases

him, he may go through its gardens, baths, halls and laby-
rinth of rooms to the pavilions on the roof, all furnished as
became a house of fame in a city which was more nearly
Milton's " gorgeous East " than any other in the world.

At this age the apartment alluded to would be termed a
saloon.   It was quite spacious, floored with polished marble
slabs, and lighted in the day by skylights in which coloured
mica served as glass.   Around the room ran a continuous
divan of Indian silks and wool of Cashmere.   The furniture
consisted of tables and stools of Egyptian patterns gro-
tesquely carved.   About the tables, seated or standing, or
moving restlessly from one to another, there are probably
a hundred persons, whom we must study at least for a
moment.

They are all young, some of them little more than boys.
That they are Italians and mostly Romans is past doubt.
They all speak Latin in purity, while each one appears in
the indoor dress of the great capital on the Tiber ; that is,
in tunics short of sleeve and skirt, a style of vesture well
adapted to the climate of Antioch, and especially comfortable in the too close atmosphere of the saloon.   On the
divan also lie sleepers stretched at ease ; whether they were
overcome by the heat and fatigue of the sultry day or by
Bacchus we will not pause to inquire.

The hum of voices is loud and incessant.   Sometimes
there is an explosion of laughter, sometimes a burst of rage
or exultation ; but over all prevails a sharp prolonged
rattle, at first somewhat confusing to the non-familiar.   If
we approach the tables, however, the mystery solves itself.
The company is at the favourite games, draughts and dice,
singly or together, and the rattle is merely of the tesseræ,
or ivory cubes, loudly shaken, and the moving of the *hostes*
on the checkered boards.

Who are the company ?

" Good Flavius," said a player, holding his piece in
suspended movement.   " I would have him tell me the
hour—hour, said I ?—nay, the minute—Maxentius will
arrive to-morrow."

" Good play, good play ! I have you ! And why the
minute ? "

" Hast thou ever stood uncovered in the Syrian sun on
the quay at which he will land ?   The fires of the Vesta
are not so hot ; and, by the Strator of our father Romulus,
I would die, if die I must, in Rome.   Avernus is here ;
there, in the square before the Forum, I could stand, and,
with my hand raised thus, touch the floor of the gods.   Ha,
by Venus, my Flavius, thou didst beguile me ! I have
lost.   My fortune ! "

" Again ? "

" I must have back my sestertium."

" Be it so."

And they played again and again ; and when day, stealing through the skylights, began to dim the lamps, it found
the two in the same places at the same table, still at the
game.   Like most of the company, they were military
attachés of the consul, awaiting his arrival and amusing
themselves meantime.

During this conversation a party entered the room, and,
unnoticed at first, proceeded to the central table.   The
signs were that they had come from a revel just dismissed.
Some of them kept their feet with difficulty.   Around the
leader's brow was a chaplet which marked him master of
the feast, if not the giver.   The wine had made no impression upon him unless to heighten his beauty, which was of
the most manly Roman style ;   he carried his head high
raised ;   the blood flushed his lips and cheeks brightly ;   his
eyes glittered ;   though the manner in which, shrouded in a
toga spotless white and of ample folds, he walked was too
nearly imperial for one sober and not a Cæsar,   In going
to the table, he made room for himself and his followers
with little ceremony and no apologies ; and when at length
he stopped, and looked over it and at the players, they all
turned to him, with a shout like a cheer.

" Messala ! Messala ! " they cried.

Those in distant quarters, hearing the cry, re-echoed it
where they were.   Instantly there were dissolution of
groups, and breaking-up of games, and a general rush
towards the centre.

Messala took the demonstration indifferently, and proceeded presently to show the ground of his popularity.

" A health to thee, Drusus, my friend," he said to the player next at his right; " a health—and thy tablets a moment."

He raised the waxen boards, glanced at the memoranda of wagers, and tossed them down.

" Denarii, only denarii—coin of cartmen and butchers!" he said, with a scornful laugh. " By the drunken Semele, to what is Rome coming, when a Cæsar sits o' nights waiting a turn of fortune to bring him but a beggarly denarius!"

The scion of the Drusi reddened to his brows, but the bystanders broke in upon his reply by surging closer around the table, and shouting, " The Messala! the Messala!"

He turned to Drusus, with a laugh heard throughout the apartment.

" Ha, ha, my friend! Be thou not offended because I levelled the Cæsar in thee down to the denarii. Thou seest I did but use the name to try these fine fledglings of our old Rome. Come, my Drusus, come!" He took up the box again and rattled the dice merrily. " Here, for what sum thou wilt, let us measure fortunes."

The manner was frank, cordial, winsome. Drusus melted in a moment.

" By the Nymphæ, yes!" he said, laughing. " I will throw with thee, Messala—for a denarius. But hold, Messala, hold! I know not if it be ominous to stay the poised dice with a question; but one occurs to me, and I must ask it though Venus slap me with her girdle."

" Nay, my Drusus, Venus with her girdle off is Venus in love. To thy question—I will make the throw and hold it against mischance. Thus."

He turned the box upon the table and held it firmly over the dice.

And Drusus asked, " Did you ever see one Quintus Arrius?"

" The duumvir?"

" No—his son?"

" I knew not he had a son."

" Well, it is nothing," Drusus added indifferently;

" only, my Messala, Pollux was not more like Castor than Arrius is like thee."

The remark had the effect of a signal: twenty voices took it up.

" True, true! His eyes—his face," they cried.

" What! " answered one, disgusted. " Messala is a Roman; Arrius is a Jew."

" Thou sayest right," a third exclaimed. " He is a Jew, or Momus lent his mother the wrong mask."

There was promise of a dispute; seeing which, Messala interposed. " The wine is not come, my Drusus; and, as thou seest, I have the freckled Pythias as they were dogs in leash. As to Arrius, I will accept thy opinion of him, so thou tell me more about him."

" Well, be he Jew or Roman—and by the great god Pan, I say it not in disrespect of thy feelings, my Messala!— this Arrius is handsome and brave and shrewd. The emperor offered him favour and patronage, which he refused. He came up through mystery, and keepeth distance as if he felt himself better or knew himself worse than the rest of us. In the palæstræ he was unmatched; he played with the blue-eyed giants from the Rhine and the hornless bulls of Sarmatia as they were willow wisps. The duumvir left him vastly rich. He has a passion for arms, and thinks of nothing but war. Maxentius admitted him into his family, and he was to have taken ship with us, but we lost him at Ravenna. Nevertheless he arrived safely. We heard of him this morning. *Perpol!* Instead of coming to the palace or going to the citadel, he dropped his baggage at the khan, and hath disappeared again."

At the beginning of the speech Messala listened with polite indifference; as it proceeded, he became more attentive; at the conclusion, he took his hand from the dicebox, and called out, " Ho, my Caius! Dost thou hear? "

A youth at his elbow—his Myrtilus, or comrade, in the day's chariot practice—answered, much pleased with the attention, " Did I not, my Messala, I were not thy friend."

" Dost thou remember the man who gave thee the fall to-day? "

" By the love-locks of Bacchus, have I not a bruised

shoulder to help me keep it in mind ? " and he seconded
the words with a shrug that submerged his ears.

" Well, be thou grateful to the Fates—I have found thy
enemy."

" Thou hast found him, my Messala," Caius answered ;
" or I am not myself."

" Thy pardon, Drusus—and pardon of all—for speaking
in riddles thus," Messala said, in his winsome way. " Thou
didst speak, I think, of mystery in connexion with the
coming of the son of Arrius. Tell me of that."

" 'Tis nothing, Messala, nothing," Drusus replied ; " a
child's story. When Arrius, the father, sailed in pursuit
of the pirates, he was without wife or family ; he returned
with a boy—him of whom we speak—and next day adopted
him."

" Adopted him ? " Messala repeated. " By the gods,
Drusus, thou dost, indeed, interest me ! Where did the
duumvir find the boy ? And who was he ? "

" Who shall answer thee that, Messala ? who but the
young Arrius himself ? *Perpol !* in the fight the duumvir
then but a tribune—lost his galley. A returning vessel
found him and one other—all of the crew who survived—
afloat upon the same plank. I give you now the story of
the rescuers, which hath this excellence at least—it hath
never been contradicted. They say, the duumvir's companion on the plank was a Jew——"

" A Jew ? " echoed Messala.

" And a slave."

" How, Drusus ? A slave ? "

" When the two were lifted to the deck, the duumvir
was in his tribune's armour, and the other in the vesture
of a rower."

Messala arose from leaning against the table.

" A galley—— " He checked the debasing word, and
looked around, for once in his life at loss.

He then stooped and uncovered the dice, saying, with a
laugh, " See, my Drusus, by the ass of Silenus, the denarius
is mine ! "

There was a shout that set the floor to quaking, and the
grim Atlantes to dancing, and the orgies began.

I

CHAPTER XII

SHEIK ILDERIM was a man of too much importance to go about with a small establishment. He took pleasure in a certain state, which, besides magnifying his dignity with strangers, contributed to his personal pride and comfort. Wherefore the reader must not be misled by the frequent reference to his tent in the Orchard of Palms. He had there really a respectable *dowar*; that is to say, he had there three large tents—one for himself, one for visitors, one for his favourite wife and her women; and six or eight lesser ones, occupied by his servants and such tribal retainers as he had chosen to bring with him as a body-guard—strong men of approved courage, and skilful with bow, spear and horses.

To be sure, his property of whatever kind was in no danger at the Orchard; yet as the habits of a man go with him to town not less than the country, and as it is never wise to slip the bands of discipline, the interior of the dowar was devoted to his cows, camels, goats and such property in general as might tempt a lion or a thief.

To do him full justice, Ilderim kept well all the customs of his people, abating none, not even the smallest; in consequence his life at the Orchard was a continuation of his life in the desert; nor that alone, it was a fair reproduction of the old patriarchal modes—the genuine pastoral life of primitive Israel.

Such was the tent at the door of which we left Ben-Hur.

Servants were already waiting the master's direction. One of them took off his sandals; another unlatched Ben-Hur's Roman shoes; then the two exchanged their dusty outer garments for fresh ones of white linen.

" Enter—in God's name, enter and take thy rest," said the host heartily, in the dialect of the Market-place of Jerusalem; forthwith he led the way to the divan.

" I will sit here," he said next, pointing; " and there the stranger."

A woman—in the old time she would have been called a handmaid—answered, and dexterously piled the pillows and bolsters as rests for the back; after which they sat upon the side of the divan, while water was brought fresh from the lake, and their feet bathed and dried with napkins.

Ilderim clapped his hands.

"Seek the stranger in the guest-tent, and say I, Ilderim, have returned with another for breaking of bread; and, if Balthasar the wise careth to share the loaf, three may partake of it, and the portion of the birds be none the less."

The second servant went away.

"Let us take our rest now."

Thereupon Ilderim settled himself upon the divan, as at this day merchants sit on their rugs in the bazaars of Damascus: and when fairly at rest, he stopped combing his beard and said, gravely, "That thou art my guest, and hast drunk my leben, and art about to taste my salt, ought not to forbid a question: Who art thou?"

"Sheik Ilderim," said Ben-Hur, calmly enduring his gaze, "I pray thee not to think me trifling with thy just demand; but was there never a time in thy life when to answer such a question would have been a crime to thyself?"

"By the splendour of Solomon, yes!" Ilderim answered. "Betrayal of self is at times as base as the betrayal of a tribe."

"Thanks, thanks, good sheik!" Ben-Hur exclaimed. "Never answer became thee better. Now I know thou dost not seek assurance to justify the trust I have come to ask, and that such assurance is of more interest to thee than the affairs of my poor life."

The sheik in his turn bowed, and Ben-Hur hastened to pursue his advantage.

"So it please thee then," he said, "first, I am not a Roman, as the name given thee as mine implieth."

Ilderim clasped the beard overflowing his breast, and gazed at the speaker with eyes faintly twinkling through the shade of the heavy close-drawn brows.

"In the next place," Ben-Hur continued, "I am an Israelite of the tribe of Judah."

The sheik raised his brows a little.

" Nor that merely.   Sheik, I am a Jew with a grievance against Rome compared with which thine is not more than a child's trouble.''

The old man combed his beard with nervous haste, and let fall his brows until even the twinkle of the eyes went out.

" Still further : I swear to thee, Sheik Ilderim—I swear by the covenant the Lord made with my fathers—so thou but give me the revenge I seek, the money and the glory of the race shall be thine.''

Ilderim's brows relaxed; his head arose; his face began to beam ; and it was almost possible to see the satisfaction taking possession of him.

" Enough ! '' he said.   " If at the roots of thy tongue there is a lie in coil, Solomon himself had not been safe against thee.   That thou art not a Roman—that as a Jew thou hast a grievance against Rome, and revenge to compass, I believe ; and on that score enough.   But as to thy skill.   What experience hast thou in racing with chariots ? And the horses—canst thou make them creatures of thy will ?—to know thee ? to come at call ? to go, if thou sayest it, to the last extreme of breath and strength ? and then, in the perishing moment, out of the depths of thy life thrill them to one exertion the mightiest of all ?   The gift, my son, is not to every one.   Ho, there ! ''

A servant came forward.

" Let my Arabs come ! ''

The man drew aside part of the division curtain of the tent, exposing to view a group of horses, who lingered a moment where they were as if to make certain of the invitation.

A head of exquisite turn—with large eyes, soft as a deer's, and half hidden by the dense forelock, and small ears, sharp-pointed and sloped well forward—approached then quite to Ben-Hur's breast, the nostrils open, and the upper lip in motion.   " Who are you ? '' it asked, plainly as ever man spoke.   Ben-Hur recognized one of the four racers he had seen on the course, and gave his open hand to the beautiful brute.

The sheik played with the horses, patting their cheeks,

combing their forelocks with his fingers, giving each one a token of remembrance.

"And now, O son of Israel, thou mayest believe my declaration—if I am a lord of the desert, behold my ministers! Take them from me, and I become as a sick man left by the caravan to die. Thanks to them, age hath not diminished the terror of me on the highways between cities; and it will not while I have strength to go with them. Ha, ha, ha! I could tell thee marvels done by their ancestors. In a favouring time I may do so; for the present, enough that they were never overtaken in retreat; nor, by the sword of Solomon, did they ever fail in pursuit! That, mark you, on the sands and under saddle; but now—I do not know—I am afraid, for they are under yoke the first time, and the conditions of success are so many. They have the pride and the speed and the endurance. If I find them a master, they will win. Son of Israel! so thou art the man, I swear it shall be a happy day that brought thee hither. Of thyself now speak."

"I know now," said Ben-Hur, "why it is that in the love of an Arab his horse is next to his children; and I know, also, why the Arab horses are the best in the world; but, good sheik, I would not have you judge me by words alone; for as you know, all promises of men sometimes fail. Give me the trial first on some plain hereabout, and put the four in my hand to-morrow."

Ilderim's face beamed again, and he would have spoken.

"A moment, good sheik, a moment!" said Ben-Hur. "Let me say further. From the masters in Rome I learned many lessons, little thinking they would serve me in a time like this. I tell thee these thy sons of the desert, though they have separately the speed of eagles and the endurance of lions, will fail if they are not trained to run together under the yoke. For bethink thee, sheik, in every four there is one of the slowest and one the swiftest; and while the race is always to the slowest, the trouble is always with the swiftest. It was so to-day; the driver could not reduce the best to harmonious action with the poorest. My trial may have no better result; but if so, I will tell thee of it: that I swear. Wherefore, in the same spirit I say, can I get them to run together, moved by my will, the four as one, thou shalt have the sestertii and the crown, and I my revenge. What sayest thou?"

Ilderim listened, combing his beard the while. At the end he said, with a laugh, "I think better of thee, son of Israel. We have a saying in the desert, 'If you will cook the meal with words, I will promise an ocean of butter.' Thou shalt have the horses in the morning."

At that moment there was a stir at the rear entrance to the tent.

"The supper—it is here! and yonder my friend Balthasar, whom thou shalt know. He hath a story to tell which an Israelite should never tire of hearing."

And to the servants he added:

"Return my jewels to their apartment."

And they did as he ordered.

CHAPTER XIII

BALTHASAR was conducted to the divan, where Ilderim and Ben-Hur received him standing. A loose black gown covered his person; his step was feeble, and his whole movement slow and cautious, apparently dependent upon a long staff and the arm of a servant.

"Peace to you, my friend," said Ilderim respectfully. "Peace and welcome."

The Egyptian raised his head and replied, "And to thee, good sheik—to thee and thine, peace and the blessing of the One God—God, the true and loving."

"This is he, O Balthasar," said the sheik, laying his hand on Ben-Hur's arm, "who will break bread with us this evening."

The Egyptian glanced at the young man, and looked again surprised and doubting; seeing which the sheik continued, "I have promised him my horses for trial tomorrow; and if all goes well, he will drive them in the Circus."

Balthasar continued his gaze.

"He came well recommended," Ilderim pursued, much

puzzled. "You may know him as the son of Arrius, who was a noble Roman sailor, though "—the sheik hesitated, then resumed, with a laugh—" though he declares himself an Israelite of the tribe of Judah ; and, by the splendour of God, I believe that he tells me ! "

Balthasar could no longer withhold explanation.

"To-day, O most generous sheik, my life was in peril, and would have been lost had not a youth, the counterpart of this one—if, indeed, he be not the very same—intervened when all others fled, and saved me." Then he addressed Ben-Hur directly, " Art thou not he ? "

" I cannot answer so far," Ben-Hur replied, with modest deference. " I am he who stopped the horses of the insolent Roman when they were rushing upon thy camel at the Fountain of Castalia."

" What ! " said the sheik to Ben-Hur. " Thou saidst nothing of this to me, when better recommendation thou couldst not have brought ! Am I not an Arab, and sheik of my tribe of tens of thousands ? And is not he my guest ? And is it not in my guest-bond that the good or evil thou dost him is good or evil done to me ? Whither shouldst thou go for reward but here ? And whose the hand to give it but mine ? "

His voice at the end of the speech rose to cutting shrillness.

" Come," he said to them, " the meal is ready."

Ben-Hur gave his arm to Balthasar, and conducted him to the table, where shortly they were all seated on their rugs Eastern fashion. The lavers were brought them, and they washed and dried their hands ; then the sheik made a sign, the servants stopped, and the voice of the Egyptian arose tremulous with holy feeling.

" Father of All—God ! What we have is of Thee ; take our thanks, and bless us, that we may continue to do Thy will."

It was the grace the good man had said simultaneously with his brethren Gaspar the Greek and Melchior the Hindu, the utterance in diverse tongues out of which had come the miracle attesting the Divine Presence at the meal in the desert years before.

With such a company—an Arab, a Jew, and an Egyptian, all believers alike in one God—there could be at that age but one subject of conversation ; and of the three, which should be speaker but he to whom the Deity had been so nearly a personal appearance, who had seen Him in a star, had heard His voice in direction, had been led so far and so miraculously by His Spirit ? And of what should he talk but that of which he had been called to testify ?

CHAPTER XIV

THE Egyptian told his story of the meeting of the three in the desert, and agreed with the sheik that it was in December, twenty-seven years before, when he and his companions fleeing from Herod arrived at the tent praying shelter. The narrative was heard with intense interest ; even the servants lingering when they could catch its details. Ben-Hur received it as became a man listening to a revelation of deep concern to all humanity, and to none of more concern than the people of Israel. In his mind, as we shall presently see, there was crystallizing an idea which was to change his course of life, if not absorb it absolutely.

To Sheik Ilderim the story was not new. He certainly believed the story ; yet, in the nature of things, its mighty central fact could not come home to him with the force and absorbing effect it came to Ben-Hur. He was an Arab, whose interest in the consequences was but general ; on the other hand, Ben-Hur was an Israelite and a Jew, with more than a special interest in—if the solecism can be pardoned—the truth of the fact. He laid hold of the circumstance with a purely Jewish mind.

From his cradle, let it be remembered, he had heard of the Messiah ; at the colleges he had been made familiar with all that was known of that Being at once the hope, the fear, and the peculiar glory of the chosen people ; the prophets from the first to the last of the heroic line foretold Him ; and the coming had been, and yet was, the theme of endless exposition with the Rabbis—in the synagogues, in the schools, in the Temple, of fast-days and feast-days, in public and in private, the national teachers expounded and kept expounding until all the children of Abraham wherever their lots were cast bore the Messiah in expectation, and by it literally, and with iron severity, ruled and moulded their lives.

Doubtless, it will be understood from this that there was much argument among the Jews themselves about the Messiah, and so there was; but the disputation was all limited to one point, and one only—when would He come ?

There was one point connected with the Messiah about which the unanimity among the chosen people was matter of marvellous astonishment : He was to be, when come, the KING OF THE JEWS—their political King, their Cæsar. By their instrumentality He was to make armed conquest of the earth, and then, for their profit and in the name of God, hold it down for ever. On this faith, dear reader, the Pharisees or Separatists—the latter being rather a political term—in the cloisters and around the altars of the Temple, built an edifice of hope far overtopping the dream of the Macedonian.

Upon a youth of Ben-Hur's mind and temperament the influence of five years of affluent life in Rome can be appreciated best by recalling that the great city was then, in fact, the meeting-place of the nations—their meeting-place politically and commercially, as well as for the indulgence of pleasure without restraint.   Round and round the golden mile-stone in front of the Forum—now in gloom of eclipse, now in unapproachable splendour—flowed all the active currents of humanity. As mere assemblages, to be sure, there was nothing to compare with the gatherings at Jerusalem in celebration of the Passover ; yet when he sat under the purple velaria of the Circus Maximus, one of three hundred and fifty thousand spectators, he must have been visited by the thought that possibly there might be some branches of the family of man worthy of Divine consideration—if not mercy, though they were of the uncircumcised—some, by their sorrows, and, yet worse, by their hopelessness in the midst of sorrows, fitted for brotherhood in the promises to his countrymen.

That he should have had such a thought under such circumstances was but natural ; we think so much at least will be admitted : but when the reflection came to him, and he gave himself up to it, he could not have been blind to a certain distinction. The wretchedness of the masses, and their hopeless condition, had no relation whatever to religion ; their murmurs and groans were not against their gods or for want of gods. No, the unhappy condition was not from religion, but misgovernment and usurpations and countless tyrannies. The Avernus men had been tumbled into, and were praying to be relieved from, was terribly but essentially political. The supplication—everywhere alike, in Lodinum, Alexandria, Athens, Jerusalem—was for a king to conquer with, not a god to worship.

Studying the situation after two thousand years, we can see and say that religiously there was no relief from the universal conclusion except some God could prove himself a true God, and a masterful one, and come to the rescue ; but the people of the time, even the discerning and philosophical, discovered no hope except in crushing Rome ; that done, the relief would follow in restorations and reorganizations ; therefore they prayed, conspired, rebelled, fought and died, drenching the soil to-day with blood, to-morrow with tears—and always with the same result.

It remains to be said now that Ben-Hur was in agreement with the mass of men of his time not Romans. The five years' residence in the capital served him with opportunity to see and study the miseries of the subjugated world ; and in full belief that the evils which afflicted it were political, and to be cured only by the sword, he was going forth to fit himself for a part in the day of resort to the heroic remedy. By practice of arms he was a perfect soldier ; but war has its higher fields, and he who would move successfully in them must know more than to defend with shield and thrust with spear. In those fields the general finds his tasks, the greatest of which is the reduction of the many into one, and that one himself ; the consummate captain is a fighting-man armed with an army. This conception entered into the scheme of life to which he was further swayed by the reflection that the vengeance he dreamed of, in connexion with his individual wrongs, would be more surely found in some of the ways of war than in any pursuit of peace.

The feelings with which he listened to Balthasar can be now understood. The story touched two of the most sensitive points of his being, so they rang within him. His heart beat fast—and faster still when, searching himself, he found not a doubt either that the recital was true in every particular, or that the Child so miraculously found was the Messiah. Marvelling much that Israel rested so dead to the revelation, and that he had never heard of it before that day, two questions presented themselves to him as centring all it was at that moment further desirable to know:

Where was the Child then?

And what was His mission?

With apologies for the interruptions, he proceeded to draw out the opinions of Balthasar, who was in nowise loath to speak.

CHAPTER XV

"If I could answer you," Balthasar said in his simple, earnest, devout way—" oh, if I knew where He is, how quickly I would go to Him! The seas should not stay me, nor the mountains."

"You have tried to find Him, then?" asked Ben-Hur.

A smile flitted across the face of the Egyptian.

"The first task I charged myself with after leaving the shelter given me in the desert "—Balthasar cast a grateful look at Ilderim—" was to learn what became of the Child. But a year had passed, and I dared not go up to Judea in person, for Herod still held the throne bloody-minded as ever. In Egypt, upon my return, there were a few friends to believe the wonderful things I told them of what I had seen and heard—a few who rejoiced with me that a Redeemer was born—a few who never tired of the story. Some of them came up for me looking after the Child. They went first to Bethlehem, and found there the khan and the cave; but the steward—he who sat at the gate the night of the

birth, and the night we came following the st ar—was gone
The king had taken him away, and he was no more seen."

"But they found some proofs, surely ? " said Ben-Hur
eagerly.

"Yes, proofs written in blood—a village in mourning ;
mothers yet crying for their little ones. You must know,
when Herod heard of our flight, he sent down and slew
the youngest-born of the children of Bethlehem. Not one
escaped. The faith of my messengers was confirmed ; but
they came to me saying the Child was dead, slain with the
other innocents."

"Dead ! " exclaimed Ben-Hur aghast. "Dead, sayest
thou ? "

"Nay, my son, I did not say so. I said they, my messengers, told me the Child was dead. I did not believe
the report then ; I do not believe it now."

"I see—thou hast some special knowledge."

"I have no special knowledge," Balthasar replied, observing the dejection which had fallen upon Ben-Hur; "but,
my son, I have given the matter much thought, and if you
will listen, I will tell you why I believe the Child is living."

Both Ilderim and Ben-Hur looked assent, and appeared
to summon their faculties that they might understand as
well as hear. The interest reached the servants, who drew
near to the divan, and stood listening. Throughout the
tent there was the profoundest silence.

"We three believe in God."

Balthasar bowed his head as he spoke.

"And He is the Truth," he resumed. "His word is
God. The hills may turn to dust, and the seas be drunk dry
by south winds ; but His word shall stand, because it is
the Truth."

The utterance was in a manner inexpressibly solemn.

"The voice, which was His, speaking to me by the lake,
said, ' Blessed art thou, O son of Mizraim ! The Redemption cometh. With two others from the remotenesses of
the earth, thou shalt see the Saviour.' I have seen the
Saviour—blessed be His name !—but the Redemption,
which was the second part of the promise, is yet to come.
Seest thou now ? If the Child be dead, there is no agent to

bring the Redemption about, and the word is naught, and God—nay, I dare not say it!"

He threw up both hands in horror.

"Wilt thou not taste the wine? It is at thy hand—see," said Ilderim respectfully.

Balthasar drank, and, seeming refreshed, continued:

"The Saviour I saw was born of woman, in nature like us and subject to all our ills—even death. Consider next the work set apart to Him. Was it not a performance for which only a man is fitted?—a man wise, firm, discreet—a man, not a child? To become such He had to grow as we grow. Bethink you now of the dangers His life was subject to in the interval—the long interval between child-hood and maturity. The existing powers were His enemies. See you now. What better way was there to take care of His life in the helpless growing time than by passing Him into obscurity? Wherefore I say to myself, 'He is not dead, but lost; and, His work remaining undone, He will come again.'"

A thrill of awe struck Ben-Hur—a thrill which was but the dying of his half-formed doubt.

"Where thinkest thou He is?" he asked, in a low voice, and hesitating, like one who feels upon his lips the pressure of a sacred silence.

Balthasar looked at him kindly, and replied, his mind not entirely freed from its abstraction:

"In my house on the Nile, so close to the river that the passers-by in boats see it and its reflection in the water at the same time—in my house, a few weeks ago, I sat think-ing. A man thirty years old, I said to myself, should have his fields of life all ploughed, and his planting well done; for after that it is summer-time, with space scarce enough to ripen his sowing. The Child, I said further, is now twenty-seven—His time to plant must be at hand. I asked myself, as you here asked me, my son, and answered by coming hither, as to a good resting-place close by the land thy fathers had from God. Where else should He appear, if not in Judea? In what city should He begin His work, if not in Jerusalem? Who should be first to receive the blessings He is to bring, if not the children of Abraham,

Isaac and Jacob; in love, at least, the children of the Lord? If I were bidden go seek Him, I would search well the hamlets and villages on the slopes of the mountains of Judea and Galilee falling eastwardly into the valley of the Jordan. He is there now. Standing in a door or on a hill-top, only this evening He saw the sun set one day nearer the time when He Himself shall become the light of the world."

Balthasar ceased, with his hand raised and finger pointing as if at Judea. All the listeners, even the dull servants outside the divan, affected by his fervour, were startled as if by a majestic presence suddenly apparent within the tent. Nor did the sensation die away at once: of those at the table, each sat awhile thinking. The spell was finally broken by Ben-Hur.

"I see, good Balthasar," he said, "that thou hast been much and strangely favoured. I see, also, that thou art a wise man indeed. It is not in my power to tell how grateful I am for the things thou hast told me. I am warned of the coming of great events, and borrow somewhat from thy faith. Complete the obligation, I pray thee, by telling further of the mission of Him for whom thou art waiting, and for whom from this night I too shall wait as becomes a believing son of Judah. He is to be a Saviour, thou saidst; is He not to be King of the Jews also?"

"My son," said Balthasar, in his benignant way, "the mission is yet a purpose in the bosom of God. All I think about it is wrung from the words of the Voice in connection with the prayer to which they were in answer. Shall we refer to them again?"

"Thou art the teacher."

"The cause of my disquiet," Balthasar began calmly— "that which made me a preacher in Alexandria and in the villages of the Nile; that which drove me at last into the solitude where the Spirit found me—was the fallen condition of men, occasioned, as I believed, by loss of the knowledge of God I sorrowed for the sorrows of my kind—not of one class, but all of them. So utterly were they fallen it seemed to me there could be no Redemption unless God Himself would make it His work; and I prayed Him to come, and that I might see Him. 'Thy good works have conquered. The Redemption cometh: thou shalt see the Saviour'—thus the Voice spake; and with the answer I went up to Jerusalem rejoicing. Now, to whom is the Redemption? To all the world. The Redemption cannot be for a political purpose—to pull down rulers and powers, and vacate their places merely that others may take and enjoy them. If that were all of it, the wisdom of God would cease to be surpassing. I tell you, though it be but the saying of blind to blind, He that comes is to be a Saviour of souls; and the Redemption means God once more on earth, and righteousness, that His stay here may be tolerable to Himself."

Disappointment showed plainly on Ben-Hur's face—his head drooped; and if he was not convinced, he yet felt himself incapable that moment of disputing the opinion of the Egyptian. Not so Ilderim.

"By the splendour of God!" he cried impulsively, "the judgment does away with all custom. The ways of the world are fixed, and cannot be changed. There must be a leader in every community clothed with power, else there is no reform."

Balthasar received the burst gravely.

"Thy wisdom, good sheik, is of the world; and thou dost forget that it is from the ways of the world we are to be redeemed. Man as a subject is the ambition of a king; the soul of a man for its salvation is the desire of a God."

"When thou dost speak of fact, O father, to hear thee is to believe," said Ben-Hur; "but in the matter of opinion, I cannot understand the kind of king thou wouldst make of the Child—I cannot separate the ruler from his powers and duties."

Balthasar raised his eyes devoutly.

"There is a kingdom on the earth, though it is not of it—a kingdom of wider bounds than the earth—wider than the sea and the earth, though they were rolled together as finest gold and spread by the beating of hammers. Its existence is a fact as our hearts are facts, and we journey through it from birth to death without seeing it; nor shall any man see it until he hath first known his own soul;

ιor the kingdom is not for him, but for his soul. And in its dominion there is glory such as hath not entered imagination —original, imcomparable, impossible of increase."

" What thou sayest, father, is a riddle to me," said Ben-Hur. " I never heard of such a kingdom."

" Nor did I," said Ilderim.

" And I may not tell more of it," Balthasar added, humbly dropping his eyes. " What it is, what it is for, how it may be reached, none can know until the Child comes to take possession of it as His own. He brings the key of the viewless gate, which He will open for His beloved, among whom will be all who love Him, for of such only the redeemed will be."

After that there was a long silence, which Balthasar accepted as the end of the conversation.

" Good sheik," he said, in his placid way, " to-morrow or the next day I will go up to the city for a time. My daughter wishes to see the preparations for the games. I will speak further about the time of our going. And, my son, I will see you again. To you both, peace and good night."

They all arose from the table. The sheik and Ben-Hur remained looking after the Egyptian until he was conducted out of the tent.

" Sheik Ilderim," said Ben-Hur, then, " I have heard strange things to-night. Give me leave, I pray, to walk by the lake that I may think of them."

" Go ; and I will come after you."

They washed their hands again ; after which, at a sign from the master, a servant brought Ben-Hur his shoes, and directly he went out.

CHAPTER XVI

UP a little way from the dowar there was a cluster of palms, which threw its shade half in the water, half on the land. A bulbul sang from the branches a song of invitation. Ben-Hur stopped beneath to listen. At any other time the notes of the bird would have driven thought away ; but the story of the Egyptian was a burden of wonder, and he was a labourer carrying it, and, like other labourers, there was to him no music in the sweetest music until mind and body were happily attuned by rest.

The night was quiet. Not a ripple broke upon the shore. The old stars of the old East were all out, each in its accustomed place ; and there was summer everywhere—on land, on lake, in the sky.

Ben-Hur's imagination was heated, his feelings aroused, his will all unsettled.

His scheme of life had been explained. In all reflection about it heretofore there had been one hiatus which he had not been able to bridge or fill up—one so broad he could see but vaguely to the other side of it. When, finally, he was graduated a captain as well as a soldier, to what object should he address his efforts ?

The hours and days he had given this branch of his scheme were past calculation—all with the same conclusion —a dim, uncertain, general idea of national liberty. Was it sufficient ? He could not say no, for that would have been the death of his hope ; he shrank from saying yes, because his judgment taught him better. He could not assure himself even that Israel was able single-handed to successfully combat Rome. He knew the resources of that great enemy ; he knew her art was superior to her resources. A universal alliance might suffice, but, alas ! that was impossible, except—and upon the exception how long and earnestly he had dwelt !—except a hero would come from one of the suffering nations, and by martial successes accomplish a renown to fill the whole earth. What glory to Judea could she prove the Macedonia of the new Alexander ! Alas, again ! Under the Rabbis valour was possible, but not discipline. And then the taunt of Messala in the garden of Herod—"All you conquer in the six days, you lose on the seventh."

So it happened he never approached the chasm thinking to surmount it, but he was beaten back ; and so incessantly had he failed in the object, that he had about given it over, except as a thing of chance. The hero might be discovered in his day, or he might not. God only knew. Such his

K

BOOK FIFTH

CHAPTER I

THE morning after the bacchanalia in the saloon of the palace, the divan was covered with young patricians.

Not all, however, who participated in the orgy were in the shameful condition. When dawn began to peer through the skylights of the saloon, Messala arose, and took the chaplet from his head, in sign that the revel was at end ; then he gathered his robe about him, gave a last look at the scene, and, without a word, departed for his quarters. Cicero could not have retired with more gravity from a night-long senatorial debate.

Three hours afterwards two courtiers entered his room, and from his own hand received each a dispatch, sealed and in duplicate, and consisting chiefly of a letter to Valerius Gratus, the procurator, still resident in Cæsarea. The importance attached to the speedy and certain delivery of the paper may be inferred. One courier was to proceed overland, the other by sea ; both were to make the utmost haste.

It is of great concern now that the reader should be fully informed of the contents of the letter thus forwarded, and it is accordingly given :

"ANTIOCH, *XII. Kal. Jul.*

"*Messala to Gratus.*

"O my Midas !

"I have to relate to thee an astonishing event, which though as yet somewhat in the field of conjecture, will, I doubt not, justify thy instant consideration.

"Allow me first to revive thy recollection. Remember, a good many years ago, a family of a prince of Jerusalem, incredibly ancient and vastly rich—by name Ben-Hur. If thy memory have a limp

148

or ailment of any kind, there is, if I mistake not, a wound on thy head which may help thee to a revival of the circumstance.

" Next, to arouse thy interest. In punishment of the attempt upon thy life—for dear repose of conscience, may all the gods forbid it should ever prove to have been an accident !—the family were seized and summarily disposed of, and their property confiscated. And inasmuch, O my Midas ! as the action had the approval of our Cæsar, who was as just as he was wise—be there flowers upon his altars for ever !—there should be no shame in referring to the sums which were realized to us respectively from that source, for which it is not possible I can ever cease to be grateful to thee, certainly not while I continue, as at present, in the uninterrupted enjoyment of the part which fell to me.

" In vindication of thy wisdom I recall further that thou didst make disposition of the family of Hur, both of us at the time supposing the plan hit upon to be the most effective possible for the purposes in view, which were silence and delivery over to inevitable but natural death. Thou wilt remember what thou didst with the mother and sister of the malefactor ; yet, if now I yield to a desire to learn whether they be living or dead, I know, from knowing the amiability of thy nature, O my Gratus, that thou wilt pardon me as one scarcely less amiable than thyself.

" As more immediately essential to the present business, however, I take the liberty of inviting to thy remembrance that the actual criminal was sent to the galleys a slave for life.

" Referring to the limit of life at the oar, the outlaw thus justly disposed of should be dead, or, better speaking, some one of the three thousand Oceanides should have taken him to husband at least five years ago. And if thou wilt excuse a momentary weakness, O most virtuous and tender of men ! inasmuch as I loved him in childhood, and also because he was very handsome—I used in much admiration to call him my Ganymede—he ought in right to have fallen into the arms of the most beautiful daughter of the family. Of opinion, however, that he was certainly dead, I have lived quite five years in calm and innocent enjoyment of the fortune for which I am in a degree indebted to him. I make the admission of indebtedness without intending it to diminish my obligation to thee.

" Now I am at the very point of interest.

" Last night, while acting as master of the feast for a party just from Rome—their extreme youth and inexperience appealed to my compassion—I heard a singular story. Maxentius, the consul, as you know, comes to-day to conduct a campaign against the Parthians. Of the ambitious who are to accompany him there is one, a son of the late duumvir Quintus Arrius. I had occasion to inquire about him particularly. When Arrius set out in pursuit of the pirates, whose defeat gained him his final honours, he had no family ; when he returned from the expedition, he brought back with him an heir. Now be thou composed as becomes the owner of so many talents in ready sestertia ! The son and heir of whom I speak is he whom thou didst send to the galleys—the very Ben

Hur who should have died at his oar five years ago—returned now with fortune and rank, and possibly as a Roman citizen, to—— Well, thou art too firmly seated to be alarmed, but I, O my Midas! I am in danger—no need to tell thee of what. Who should know, if thou dost not?

"When Arrius, the father, by adoption, joined battle with the pirates, his vessel was sunk, and but two of all her crew escaped drowning—Arrius himself and this one, his heir.

" The officers who took them from the plank on which they were floating say the associate of the fortunate tribune was a young man who, when lifted to the deck, was in the dress of a galley slave.

" This should be convincing, to say least; but lest thou say tut-tut, I tell thee, O my Midas! that yesterday, by good chance, I met the mysterious son of Arrius face to face; and I declare now that, though I did not then recognize him, he is the very Ben-Hur who was for years my playmate; the very Ben-Hur who, if he be a man, though of the commonest grade, must this very moment of my writing be thinking of vengeance—for so would I were I he —vengeance not to be satisfied short of life; vengeance for country, mother, sister, self, and—I say it last, though thou mayst think it should be first—for fortune lost.

" The sun is now fairly risen. An hour hence two messengers will depart from my door, each with a sealed copy hereof; one of them will go by land, the other by sea, so important do I regard it that thou shouldst be early and particularly informed of the appearance of our enemy in this part of our Roman world.

" I will await thy answer here.

" Ben-Hur's going and coming will of course be regulated by his master, the consul, who, though he exert himself without rest day and night, cannot get away under a month. Thou knowest what work it is to assemble and provide for an army destined to operate in a desolate, townless country.

" I saw the Jew yesterday in the Grove of Daphne; and if he be not there now, he is certainly in the neighbourhood, making it easy for me to keep him in eye. Indeed, wert thou to ask me where he is now, I should say, with the most positive assurance, he is to be found at the old Orchard of Palms, under the tent of the traitor Sheik Ilderim, who cannot long escape our strong hand. Be not surprised if Maxentius, as his first measure, places the Arab on ship for forwarding to Rome.

" I am so particular about the whereabouts of the Jew because it will be important to thee, O illustrious! when thou comest to consider what is to be done; for already I know, and by the knowledge I flatter myself I am growing in wisdom, that in every scheme involving human action there are three elements always to be taken into account—time, place, and agency.

" If thou sayest this is the place, have thou then no hesitancy in trusting the business to thy most loving friend, who would be thy aptest scholar as well.

" MESSALA."

CHAPTER II

ABOUT the time the couriers departed from Messala's door
with the dispatches (it being yet the early morning hour),
Ben-Hur entered Ilderim's tent. He had taken a plunge
into the lake, and breakfasted, and appeared now in an
under-tunic, sleeveless, and with skirt scarcely reaching to
the knee.

The sheik saluted him from the divan.

" I give thee peace, son of Arrius," he said, with admiration, for, in truth, he had never seen a more perfect illustration of glowing, powerful, confident manhood. " I give
thee peace and goodwill. The horses are ready, I am
ready. And thou ? "

" The peace thou givest me, good sheik, I give thee in
return. I thank thee for so much goodwill. I am ready."

Ilderim clapped his hands.

" I will have the horses brought. Be seated."

" Are they yoked ? "

" No."

" Then suffer me to serve myself," said Ben-Hur. " It
is needful that I make the acquaintance of thy Arabs.
I must know them by name, O sheik, that I may speak to
them singly ; nor less must I know their temper, for they
are like men ; if bold, the better of scolding ; if timid, the
better of praise and flattery. Let the servants bring me
the harness."

" And the chariot ? " asked the sheik.

" I will let the chariot alone to-day. In its place, let
them bring me a fifth horse, if thou hast it ; he should be
barebacked, and fleet as the others."

Ilderim's wonder was aroused, and he summoned a servant immediately.

" Bid them bring the harness for the four," he said ;
" the harness for the four, and the bridle for Sirius."

The harness was brought. With his own hands Ben-Hur
equipped the horses ; with his own hands he led them out
of the tent, and there attached the reins.

" Bring me Sirius," he said.

An Arab could not have better sprung to seat on the courser's back.

" And now the reins."

They were given him, and carefully separated.

" Good sheik," he said, " I am ready. Let a guide go before me to the field, and send some of thy men with water."

There was no trouble at starting. The horses were not afraid. Already there seemed a tacit understanding between them and the new driver, who had performed his part calmly, and with the confidence which always begets confidence. The order of going was precisely that of driving, except that Ben-Hur sat upon Sirius instead of standing in the chariot. Ilderim's spirit arose. He combed his beard, and smiled with satisfaction as he muttered, " He is not a Roman, no, by the splendour of God ! " He followed on foot, the entire tenantry of the dowar—men, women, and children—pouring after him, participants all in his solicitude if not in his confidence.

The field, when reached, proved ample and well fitted for the training, which Ben-Hur began immediately by driving the four at first slowly, and in perpendicular lines, and then in wide circles. Advancing a step in the course, he put them next into a trot ; again progressing, he pushed into a gallop ; at length he contracted the circles, and yet later drove eccentrically here and there, right, left, forward, and without a break. An hour was thus occupied. Slowing the gait to a walk, he drove up to Ilderim.

" The work is done, nothing now but practice," he said. " I give you joy, Sheik Ilderim, that you have such servants as these. See," he continued, dismounting and going to the horses, " see, the gloss of their red coats is without spot ; they breathe lightly as when I began. I give thee great joy, and it will go hard if "—he turned his flashing eyes upon the old man's face—" if we have not the victory and our——"

He stopped, coloured, bowed. At the sheik's side he observed, for the first time, Balthasar, leaning upon his staff, and two women closely veiled. At one of the latter he looked a second time, saying to himself, with a flutter about his heart, " 'Tis she—'tis the Egyptian!" Ilderim picked up his broken sentence—

" The victory, and our revenge!" Then he said aloud, " I am not afraid; I am glad. Son of Arrius, thou art the man. Be the end like the beginning, and thou shalt see of what stuff is the lining of the hand of an Arab who is able to give."

" I thank thee, good sheik," Ben-Hur returned modestly. " Let the servants bring drink for the horses."

With his own hands he gave the water.

Remounting Sirius, he renewed the training, going as before from walk to trot, from trot to gallop; finally, he pushed the steady racers into the run, gradually quickening it to full speed. The performance then became exciting; and there were applause for the dainty handling of the reins, and admiration for the four, which were the same, whether they flew forward or wheeled in varying curvature. In their action there were unity, power, grace, pleasure, all without effort or sign of labour. The admiration was unmixed with pity or reproach, which would have been as well bestowed upon swallows in their evening flight.

In the midst of the exercises, and the attention they received from all the bystanders, Malluch came upon the ground, seeking the sheik.

" I have a message for you, O sheik," he said, availing himself of a moment he supposed favourable for the speech —" a message from Simonides, the merchant."

" Simonides!" ejaculated the Arab. " Ah! 'tis well, May Abaddon take all his enemies!"

" He bade me give thee first the holy peace of God," Malluch continued; " and then this dispatch, with prayer that thou read it the instant of receipt."

Ilderim, standing in his place, broke the sealing of the package delivered to him, and from a wrapping of fine linen took two letters, which he proceeded to read.

[No. 1.]
" *Simonides to Sheik Ilderim.*

" O friend!
" Assure thyself first of a place in my inner heart.
" Then—

"There is in thy dowar a youth of fair presence, calling himself the son of Arrius; and such he is by adoption.

"He is very dear to me.

"He hath a wonderful history, which I will tell thee; come thou to-day or to-morrow, that I may tell thee the history, and have thy counsel.

"Meantime, favour all his requests, so they be not against honour. Should there be need of reparation, I am bound to thee for it.

"That I have interest in this youth, keep thou private.

"Remember me to thy other guest. He, his daughter, thyself, and all whom thou mayst choose to be of thy company, must depend upon me at the Circus the day of the games. I have seats already engaged.

"To thee and all thine, peace.

"What should I be, O my friend, but thy friend?

"SIMONIDES."

[No. 2.]

"Simonides to Sheik Ilderim.

"O friend!

"Out of the abundance of my experience, I send you a word.

"There is a sign which all persons not Romans, and who have moneys or goods subject to despoilment, accept as warning—that is, the arrival at a seat of power of some high Roman official charged with authority.

"To-day comes the Consul Maxentius.

"Be thou warned!

"Another word of advice.

"A conspiracy, to be of effect against thee, O friend, must include the Herods as parties; thou hast great properties in their dominions.

"Wherefore keep thou watch.

"Send this morning to thy trusty keepers of the roads leading south from Antioch, and bid them search every courier going and coming; if they should find private dispatches relating to thee or thy affairs, *thou shouldst see them.*

"You should have received this yesterday, though it is not too late, if you act promptly.

"If couriers left Antioch this morning, your messengers know the byways, and can get before them with your orders.

"Do not hesitate.

"Burn this after reading.

"O my friend! thy friend.

"SIMONIDES."

Ilderim read the letters a second time, and refolded them in the linen wrap, and put the package under his girdle.

The exercises in the field continued but a little longer—in all about two hours. At their conclusion, Ben-Hur brought the four to a walk, and drove to Ilderim.

" With leave, O sheik," he said, " I will return thy Arabs to the tent, and bring them out again this afternoon."

Ilderim walked to him as he sat on Sirius, and said, " I give them to you, son of Arrius, to do with as you will until after the games. You have done with them in two hours what the Roman—may jackals gnaw his bones fleshless !—could not in as many weeks. We will win— by the splendour of God, we will win ! "

At the tent Ben-Hur remained with the horses while they were being cared for ; then, after a plunge in the lake and a cup of arrack with the sheik, whose flow of spirits was royally exuberant, he dressed himself in his Jewish garb again, and walked with Malluch on into the Orchard.

There was much conversation between the two, not all of it important. One part, however, must not be over-looked. Ben-Hur was speaking.

" To save all forfeit or hindrance in connexion with the race, you would put me perfectly at rest by going to the office of the Circus, and seeing that he has complied with every preliminary rule ; and if you can get a copy of the rules, the services may be of great avail to me. I would like to know the colours I am to wear, and particularly the number of the crypt I am to occupy at the starting ; if it be next Messala's on the right or left, it is well ; if not, and you can have it changed so as to bring me next the Roman, do so. Have you good memory, Malluch ? "

" It has failed me, but never, son of Arrius, where the heart helped it as now."

" I will venture, then, to charge you with one further service. I saw yesterday that Messala was proud of his chariot, as he might be, for the best of Cæsar's scarcely surpass it. Can you not make its display an excuse which will enable you to find if it be light or heavy ? I would like to have its exact weight and measurements—and, Malluch, though you fail in all else, bring me exactly the height his axle stands above the ground. You understand, Malluch ? I do not wish him to have any actual advantage of me. I do not care for his splendour ; if I beat him, it will make his fall the harder, and my triumph the more

156 BEN-HUR: A TALE OF THE CHRIST

complete. If there are advantages really important, I want them."

"I see, I see!" said Malluch. "A line dropped from the centre of the axle is what you want."

"Thou hast it; and be glad, Malluch—it is the last of my commissions. Let us return to the dowar."

At the door of the tent they found a servant replenishing the smoke-stained bottles of leben freshly made, and stopped to refresh themselves. Shortly afterwards Malluch returned to the city.

During their absence, a messenger well mounted had been dispatched with orders as suggested by Simonides. He was an Arab, and carried nothing written.

CHAPTER III

"IRAS, the daughter of Balthasar, sends me with salutation and a message," said a servant to Ben-Hur, who was taking his ease in the tent.

"Give me the message."

"Would it please you to accompany her upon the lake?"

"I will carry the answer myself. Tell her so."

His shoes were brought him, and in a few minutes Ben-Hur sallied out to find the fair Egyptian. The shadow of the mountains was creeping over the Orchard of Palms in advance of night. Afar through the trees came the tinkling of sheep-bells, the lowing of cattle, and the voices of the herdsmen bringing their charges home. Life at the Orchard, it should be remembered, was in all respects as pastoral as life on the scantier meadows of the desert.

Sheik Ilderim had witnessed the exercises of the afternoon, being a repetition of those of the morning; after which he had gone to the city in answer to the invitation of Simonides; he might return in the night; but, considering the immensity of the field to be talked over with his friend, it was hardly possible. Ben-Hur, thus left alone, had seen his horses cared for; cooled and purified himself in the lake; exchanged the field garb for his customary vestments, all white, as became a Sadducean of the pure blood ; supped early ; and, thanks to the strength of youth, was well recovered from the violent exertion he had undergone.

It is neither wise nor honest to detract from beauty as a quality. There cannot be a refined soul insensible to its influence. The story of Pygmalion and his statue is as natural as it is poetical. Beauty is of itself a power ; and it was now drawing Ben-Hur.

The Egyptian was to him a wonderfully beautiful woman —beautiful of face, beautiful of form. It was not love that was taking him, but admiration and curiosity which might be the heralds of love.

The landing was a simple affair, consisting of a short stairway, and a platform garnished by some lamp-posts ! yet at the top of the steps he paused, arrested by what he beheld.

There was a shallop resting upon the clear water lightly as an egg-shell. An Ethiop—the camel-driver at the Castalian fount—occupied the rower's place, his blackness intensified by a livery of shining white. All the boat aft was cushioned and carpeted with stuffs brilliant with Tyrian red. On the rudder-seat sat the Egyptian herself, sunk in Indian shawls and a very vapour of most delicate veils and scarfs. Her arms were bare to the shoulders ; and, not merely faultless in shape, they had the effect of compelling attention to them—their pose, their action, their expression ; the hands, the fingers even, seemed endowed with graces and meaning ; each was an object of beauty. The shoulders and neck were protected from the evening air by an ample scarf, which yet did not hide them.

" Come," she said, observing him stop, " come, or I shall think you a poor sailor."

The red of his cheek deepened. Did she know anything of his life upon the sea ? He descended to the platform at once.

" I was afraid," he said, as he took the vacant seat before her.

" Of what ? "

" Of sinking the boat," he replied, smiling.

" Wait until we are in deeper water," she said, giving a

That instant the lamps burning before the door of the tent came into view.

" The dowar ! " she cried.

" Ah, then, we have not been to Egypt.   I have not seen Karnak or Philæ or Abydos.   This is not the Nile.   I have but been boating in a dream."

" Philæ—Karnak.   Mourn rather that you have not seen the Rameses at Aboo Simbel, looking at which makes it so easy to think of God, the Maker of the heavens and earth.   Or why should you mourn at all ?   Let us go on to the river ;   and I can tell you stories of Egypt.

" Go on !   Ay, till morning comes, and the evening, and the next morning ! " he said vehemently."

At the conclusion of the outing, Ben-Hur was sitting at the Egyptian's feet, and her hand upon the tiller was covered by his hand.

" You are a good companion, O son of Arrius."

As they stepped ashore, she said :

" To-morrow we go to the city."

" But you will be at the games ? " he asked.

" Oh yes."

" I will send you my colours."

With that they separated.

CHAPTER IV

THE sheik waited, well satisfied, until Ben-Hur drew his horses off the field for the forenoon—well satisfied, for he had seen them, after being put through all the other paces, run full speed in such manner that it did not seem there were one the slowest and another the fastest—run, in other words, as the four were one.

At the door of the tent they dismounted.

Ilderim drew forth a package, and opened it slowly, while they walked to the divan and seated themselves— " son of Arrius, see thou here, and help me with thy Latin."

He passed the dispatch to Ben-Hur.

" There; read—and read aloud, rendering what thou findest into the tongue of thy fathers.   Latin is an abomination."

Ben-Hur was in good spirits, and began the reading carelessly.   "'*Messala to Gratus!*'" He paused.   A premonition drove the blood to his heart.   Ilderim observed his agitation.

" Well; I am waiting."

Ben-Hur prayed pardon, and recommenced the paper, which, it is sufficient to say, was one of the duplicates of the letter dispatched so carefully to Gratus by Messala the morning after the revel in the palace.

The paragraphs in the beginning were remarkable only as proof that the writer had not outgrown his habit of mockery ; when they were passed, and the reader came to the parts intended to refresh the memory of Gratus, his voice trembled, and twice he stopped to regain his self-control.

The sheik had been a silent, but not unsympathetic, witness of the young man's suffering ; now he arose and said, " Son of Arrius, it is for me to beg thy pardon.   Read the paper by thyself.   When thou art strong enough to give the rest of it to me, send word, and I will return."

He went out of the tent, and nothing in all his life became him better.

Ben-Hur resumed the reading.   " Thou wilt remember," the missive ran, " what thou didst with the mother and sister of the malefactor ; yet, if now I yield to a desire to learn if they be living or dead "—Ben-Hur started, and read again, and then again, and at last broke into exclamation.

" They are not dead," he said, after reflection ; " they are not dead, or he would have heard of it."

A second reading, more careful than the first, confirmed him in the opinion.   Then he sent for the sheik.

" In coming to your hospitable tent, O sheik," he said calmly, when the Arab was seated, and they were alone, " it was not in my mind to speak of myself further than to assure you I had sufficient training to be entrusted with your horses.   I declined to tell you my history.   But the chances which have sent this paper to my hand and given

L

it to me to be read are so strange that I feel bidden to trust you with everything. And I am the more inclined to do so by knowledge here conveyed that we are both of us threatened by the same enemy, against whom it is needful that we make common cause. I will read the letter and give you explanation ; after which you will not wonder I was so moved. If you thought me weak or childish, you will then excuse me."

The sheik held his peace, listening closely until Ben-Hur came to the paragraph in which he was particularly mentioned : " Be not surprised if Maxentius, as his first measure, places the Arab on ship for forwarding to Rome."

" To Rome ! Me—Ilderim—sheik of ten thousand horsemen with spears—me to Rome ! "

He leaped rather than rose to his feet, his arms outstretched, his fingers spread and curved like claws, his eyes glittering like a serpent's.

" O God ;—nay, by all the gods except of Rome !—when shall this insolence end ? A freeman am I ; free are my people. Must we die slaves ? Or, worse, must I live a dog, crawling to a master's feet ? Must I lick his hand lest he lash me ? What is mine is not mine ; I am not my own ; for breath of body I must be beholden to a Roman. Oh, if I were young again ! Oh, could I shake off twenty years—or ten—or five ! "

He ground his teeth and shook his hands overhead ; then, under the impulse of another idea, he walked away and back again to Ben-Hur swiftly, and caught his shoulder with a strong grasp.

" If I were as thou, son of Arrius—as young, as strong, as practised in arms ; if I had a motive hissing me to revenge—a motive, like thine, great enough to make hate holy—— Away with disguise on thy part and on mine ! Son of Hur, son of Hur, I say——"

At that name all the currents of Ben-Hur's blood stopped ; surprised, bewildered, he gazed into the Arab's eyes, now close to his, and fiercely bright.

" Son of Hur, I say, were I as thou, with half thy wrongs, bearing about with me memories like thine, I would not, I could not rest." Never pausing, his words following each other torrent-like, the old man swept on. "To all my grievances, I would add those of the world, and devote myself to vengeance. From land to land I would go firing all mankind. No war for freedom but should find me engaged; no battle against Rome in which I would not bear a part. To the flames everything Roman; to the sword every Roman born. Oh, I could not sleep. I—I——"

The sheik stopped for want of breath, panting, wringing his hands.

For the first time in years, the desolate youth heard himself addressed by his proper name. One man at least knew him, and acknowledged it without demand of identity; and he an Arab fresh from the desert.

"Good sheik, tell me how you came by this letter."

"My people keep the roads between cities," Ilderim answered bluntly. "They took it from a courier."

"Are they known to be thy people?"

"No. To the world they are robbers, whom it is mine to catch and slay."

"What sayest thou?" he asked, while waiting for his horse and retinue. "I told what I would do were I thou, and thou hast made no answer."

"I intended to answer, sheik, and I will." Ben-Hur's countenance and voice changed with the feeling invoked. "All thou hast said, I will do—all at least in the power of a man. I devoted myself to vengeance long ago. Every hour of the five years passed, I have lived with no other thought. The blandishments of Rome were not for me. I wanted her to educate me for revenge. I resorted to her most famous masters and professors—not those of rhetoric or philosophy: alas! I had no time for them. The arts essential to a fighting-man were my desire. I associated with gladiators, and with winners of prizes in the circus; and they were my teachers. The drill-masters in the great camp accepted me as a scholar, and were proud of my attainments in their line. O sheik, I am a soldier; but the things of which I dream require me to be a captain. With that thought, I have taken part in the campaign against the Parthians; when it is

over, then, if the Lord spare my life and strength—then "
—he raised his clenched hands, and spoke vehemently—
" then I will be an enemy Roman-taught in all things;
then Rome shall account to me in Roman lives for her
ills. You have my answer, sheik."

Ilderim put an arm over his shoulder, and kissed him,
saying passionately, " If thy God favour thee not, son of
Hur, it is because He is dead. Take thou this from me—
sworn to, if so thy preference run; thou shalt have my
hands, and their fullness—men, horses, camels, and the
desert for preparation. I swear it! For the present,
enough. Thou shalt see or hear from me before night."

Turning abruptly off, the sheik was speedily on the road
to the city.

CHAPTER V

THE intercepted letter was conclusive upon a number of
points of great interest to Ben-Hur. It had all the effect
of a confession.

And, now that the letter had reached the hand of him
really its subject, it was notice of danger to come, as well
as a confession of guilt. So when Ilderim left the tent,
Ben-Hur had much to think about, requiring immediate
action. His enemies were as adroit and powerful as any
in the East. If they were afraid of him, he had greater
reason to be afraid of them. He strove earnestly to reflect upon the situation, but could not ; his feelings constantly overwhelmed him. There was a certain qualified
pleasure in the assurance that his mother and sister were
alive ; and it mattered little that the foundation of the
assurance was a mere inference.

And patient he would have been if only he could have
believed Tirzah and his mother were waiting for him
under circumstances permitting hope on their part strong
as his ; if, in other words, conscience had not stung him
with accusations respecting them.

The midday meal disposed of, still further to occupy
himself, Ben-Hur had the chariot rolled out into the sun-

light for inspection. The word but poorly conveys the careful study the vehicle underwent. No point or part of it escaped him. With a pleasure which will be better understood hereafter, he saw the pattern was Greek, in his judgment preferable to the Roman in many respects; it was wider between the wheels, and lower and stronger, and the disadvantage of greater weight would be more than compensated by the greater endurance of his Arabs. Speaking generally, the carriage-makers of Rome built for the games almost solely, sacrificing safety to beauty, and durability to grace; while the chariots of Achilles and "the king of men," designed for war and all its extreme tests, still ruled the tastes of those who met and struggled for the crowns Isthmian and Olympic.

After nightfall, Ben-Hur sat by the door of the tent waiting for Ilderim, not yet returned from the city. He was not impatient, or vexed, or doubtful. The sheik would be heard from, at least. Indeed, whether it was from satisfaction with the performance of the four, or the refreshment there is in cold water succeeding bodily exercise, or supper partaken with royal appetite, or the reaction which, as a kindly provision of nature, always follows depression, the young man was in good humour verging upon elation. He felt himself in the hands of Providence no longer his enemy. At last there was a sound of horses' feet coming rapidly and Malluch rode up.

"Son of Arrius," he said cheerily, after salutation, "I salute you for Sheik Ilderim, who requests you to mount and go to the city. He is waiting for you."

Ben-Hur asked no questions. Very shortly the two were on the road, going swiftly and in silence.

Some distance below the Seleucian Bridge, they crossed the river by a ferry, and, riding far round on the right bank, and recrossing by another ferry, entered the city from the west. The detour was long, but Ben-Hur accepted it as a precaution for which there was good reason.

Down to Simonides' landing they rode, and in front of the great warehouse under the bridge, Malluch drew rein.

"We are come," he said. "Dismount."

Ben-Hur recognized the place.

"Where is the sheik?" he asked.

"Come with me. I will show you."

A watchman took the horses, and almost before he realized it Ben-Hur stood once more at the door of the house up on the greater one, listening to the response from within—"In God's name, enter."

CHAPTER VI

MALLUCH stopped at the door; Ben-Hur entered alone.

The room was the same in which he had formerly interviewed Simonides.

Within, a few steps, Ben-Hur stopped.

Three persons were present, looking at him—Simonides, Ilderim and Esther.

He glanced hurriedly from one to another, as if to find answer to the question half formed in his mind, What business can these have with me? He became calm, with every sense on the alert, for the question was succeeded by another, Are they friends or enemies?

At length his eyes rested upon Esther.

The men returned his look kindly; in her face there was something more than kindness—something too *spirituel* for definition, which yet went to his inner consciousness without definition.

"Son of Hur——"

The guest turned to the speaker.

"Son of Hur," said Simonides, repeating the address slowly, and with distinct emphasis, as if to impress all its meaning upon him most interested in understanding it, "take thou the peace of the Lord God of our fathers —take it from me." He paused, then added, "From me and mine."

"Simonides," Ben-Hur answered, much moved, "the holy peace you tender is accepted. As son to father, I return it to you. Only let there be perfect understanding between us."

Simonides let fall his hands, and turning to Esther, said, "A seat for the master, daughter."

She hastened, and brought a stool, and stood with suffused face, looking from one to the other—from Ben-Hur to Simonides, from Simonides to Ben-Hur ; and they waited, each declining the superiority direction would imply. When at length the pause began to be embarrassing, Ben-Hur advanced, and gently took the stool from her, and, going to the chair, placed it at the merchant's feet.

" I will sit here," he said.

His eyes met hers—an instant only ; but both were better for the look. He recognized her gratitude, she his generosity and forbearance.

Simonides bowed his acknowledgment.

" Esther, child, bring me the paper," he said, with a breath of relief.

She went to a panel in the wall, opened it, took out a roll of papyri, and brought and gave it to him.

" This," said Simonides, drawing out the first leaf, " shows the money I had of thy father's, being the amount saved from the Romans ; there was no property saved, only money, and that the robbers would have secured but for our Jewish custom of bills of exchange. The amount saved, being sums I drew from Rome, Alexandria, Damascus, Carthage, Valentia, and elsewhere within the circle of trade, was one hundred and twenty talents Jewish money."

He gave the sheet to Esther, and took the next one.

" With that amount—one hundred and twenty talents —I charged myself. Hear now my credits. I use the word, as thou wilt see, with reference rather to the proceeds gained from the use of the money."

From separate sheets he then read footings, which, fractions omitted, were as follows :

CR.		
By ships	60	talents.
„ goods in store	110	„
„ cargoes in transit	75	„
„ camels, horses, etc. . . .	20	„
„ warehouses	10	„
„ bills due	54	„
„ money on hand and subject to draft	224	„
Total	553	„

"To these now, to the five hundred and fifty-three talents gained, add the original capital I had from thy father, and thou hast SIX HUNDRED AND SEVENTY-THREE TALENTS!—and all thine—making thee, O son of Hur, the richest subject in the world.

"And there is nothing," he added, dropping his voice, but not his eyes—"there is nothing now thou mayest not do."

Taking the roll, Ben-Hur arose, struggling with emotion. "I give first thanks to the Lord, who has not abandoned me, and my next to thee, O Simonides. Thy faithfulness outweighs the cruelty of others, and redeems our human nature. 'There is nothing I cannot do': be it so. Shall any man in this my hour of such mighty privilege be more generous than I? Serve me as a witness now, Sheik Ilderim. Hear thou my words as I shall speak them—hear and remember. And thou, Esther, good angel of this good man! hear thou also."

He stretched his hand with the roll to Simonides.

"The things these papers take into account—all of them : ships, houses, goods, camels, horses, money—the least as well as the greatest—give I back to thee, O Simonides, making them all thine, and sealing them to thee and thine for ever."

Esther smiled through her tears ; Ilderim pulled his beard with rapid motion, his eyes glistening like beads of jet. Simonides alone was calm.

"Sealing them to thee and thine for ever," Ben-Hur continued, with better control of himself, "with one exception, and upon one condition."

The breath of the listeners waited upon his words.

"The hundred and twenty talents which were my father's thou shalt return to me."

Ilderim's countenance brightened.

"And thou shalt join me in search of my mother and sister, holding all thine subject to the expense of discovery, even as I will hold mine."

Simonides was much affected. Stretching out his hand, he said, "I see thy spirit, son of Hur, and I am grateful to the Lord that He hath sent thee to me such as thou art.

If I served well thy father in life, and his memory after-wards, be not afraid of default to thee ; yet must I say the exception cannot stand."

Exhibiting, then, the reserved sheet, he continued :

" Thou hast not all the account. Take this and read —read aloud."

Ben-Hur took the supplement, and read it.

" Statement of the servants of Hur, rendered by Simonides, steward of the estate.

1. Amrah, Egyptian, keeping the palace in Jerusalem.
2. Simonides, the steward, in Antioch.
3. Esther, daughter of Simonides."

Now, in all his thoughts of Simonides, not once had it entered Ben-Hur's mind that, by the law, a daughter fol-lowed the parent's condition. In all his visions of her, the sweet-faced Esther had figured as the rival of the Egyptian, and an object of possible love. He shrank from the revelation so suddenly brought him, and looked at her blushing ; and, blushing, she dropped her eyes before him. Then he said, while the papyrus rolled itself to-gether :

" A man with six hundred talents is indeed rich, and may do what he pleases ; but, rarer than the money, more priceless than the property, is the mind which amassed the wealth, and the heart it could not corrupt when amassed. O Simonides—and thou, fair Esther—fear not. Sheik Ilderim here shall be witness that in the same moment ye were declared my servants, that moment I declared ye free ; and what I declare, that will I put in writing. Is it not enough ? Can I do more ? "

" Son of Hur," said Simonides, " verily thou dost make servitude lightsome. I was wrong ; there are some things thou canst not do : thou canst not make us free in law. I am thy servant for ever, because I went to the door with thy father one day, and in my ear the awl-marks yet abide."

" Did my father that ? "

" Judge him not," cried Simonides quickly. " He accepted me a servant of that class because I prayed him to do so. I never repented the step. It was the price I paid for Rachel, the mother of my child here ; for Rachel, who would not be my wife unless I became what she was."

"Was she a servant for ever ? "

"Even so."

Ben-Hur walked the floor in pain of impotent wish.

"I was rich before," he said, stopping suddenly. "I was rich with the gifts of the generous Arrius ; now comes this greater fortune, and the mind which achieved it. Is there not a purpose of God in it all ? Counsel me, O Simonides ! Help me to see the right and do it. Help me to be worthy my name, and what thou art in law to me, that will I be to thee in fact and deed. I will be thy servant for ever."

Simonides' face actually glowed.

"O son of my dead master ! I will do better than help ; I will serve thee with all my might of mind and heart. Body I have not ; it perished in thy cause ; but with mind and heart I serve thee. I swear it, by the altar of our God, and the gifts upon the altar ! Only make me formally what I have assumed to be."

"Name it," said Ben-Hur eagerly.

"As steward the care of the property will be mine."

"Count thyself steward now ; or wilt thou have it in writing ? "

"Thy word simply is enough ; it was so with the father, and I will not more from the son. And now, if the understanding be perfect——" Simonides paused.

"It is with me," said Ben-Hur.

"And thou, daughter of Rachel, speak ! " said Simonides, lifting her arm from his shoulder.

Esther, left thus alone, stood a moment abashed, her colour coming and going ; then she went to Ben-Hur, and said, with a womanliness singularly sweet, " I am not better than my mother was ; and, as she is gone, I pray you, O my master, let me care for my father."

Ben-Hur took her hand, and led her back to the chair, saying, " Thou art a good child. Have thy will."

Simonides replaced her arm upon his neck, and there was silence for a time in the room.

CHAPTER VII

SIMONIDES looked up, none the less a master.

"Esther," he said quietly, "the night is going fast ; and, lest we become too weary for that which is before us, let the refreshments be brought."

She rang a bell. A servant answered with wine and bread, which she bore round.

"The understanding, good my master," continued Simonides, when all were served, "is not perfect in my sight. Henceforth our lives will run on together like rivers which have met and joined their waters. I think their flowing will be better if every cloud is blown from the sky above them. You left my door the other day with what seemed a denial of the claims which I have just allowed in the broadest terms ; but it was not so, indeed it was not. Esther is witness that I recognized you ; and that I did not abandon you, let Malluch say."

"Malluch ! " exclaimed Ben-Hur.

"One bound to a chair, like me, must have many hands far-reaching, if he would move the world from which he is so cruelly barred. I have many such, and Malluch is one of the best of them. And, sometimes "—he cast a grateful glance at the sheik—" sometimes I borrow from others good of heart, like Ilderim the Generous—good and brave. Let him say if I either denied or forgot you."

Ben-Hur looked at the Arab.

"This is he, good Ilderim, this is he who told you of me ? "

Ilderim's eyes twinkled as he nodded his answer.

"How, O my master," said Simonides, "may we without trial tell what a man is ? I knew you ; I saw your father in you ; but the kind of man you were I did not know. There are people to whom fortune is a curse in disguise. Were you of them ? I sent Malluch to find out for me, and in the service he was my eyes and ears. Do not blame him. He brought me report of you which was all good."

" I do not," said Ben-Hur heartily. " There was wisdom in your goodness."

" The words are very pleasant to me," said the merchant, with feeling, " very pleasant. My fear of misunderstanding is laid. Let the rivers run on now as God may give them direction."

After an interval he continued :

" I am compelled now by truth. You have seen Balthasar ? "

" And heard him tell his story," said Ben-Hur.

" A miracle !—a very miracle ! " cried Simonides. " As he told it to me, good my master, I seemed to hear the answer I had so long waited ; God's purpose burst upon me. Poor will the King be when He comes—poor and friendless ; without following, without armies, without cities or castles ! a kingdom to be set up, and Rome reduced and blotted out. See, see, O my master ! thou flushed with strength, thou trained to arms, thou burdened with riches ; behold the opportunity the Lord hath sent thee ! Shall not His purpose be thine ? Could a man be born to a more perfect glory ? "

Simonides put his whole force in the appeal.

" But the kingdom, the kingdom ! " Ben-Hur answered eagerly. " Balthasar says it is to be of souls."

The pride of the Jew was strong in Simonides, and therefore the slightly contemptuous curl of the lip with which he began his reply :

" Balthasar has been a witness of wonderful things— of miracles, my master ; and when he speaks of them, I bow with belief, for they are of sight and sound personal to him. But he is a son of Mizraim, and not even a proselyte. Hardly may he be supposed to have special knowledge by virtue of which we must bow to him in a matter of God's dealing with our Israel. The prophets had their light from Heaven directly, even as he had his—many to one, and Jehovah the same for ever. I must believe the prophets. May the testimony of a whole people be slighted, my master ? Though you travel from Tyre, which is by the sea in the north, to the capital of Edom, which is in the desert south, you will not find a lisper of the Shema, an alms-giver in the Temple, or any one who has ever eaten of the lamb of the Passover, to tell you the kingdom the King is coming to build for us, the children of the covenant, is other than of this world, like our father David's. Now where got they the faith, ask you ? "

Ben-Hur looked away.

" What see you, O my master ? "

" Rome ! " he answered gloomily—" Rome, and her legions. I have dwelt with them in their camps. I know them."

" Ah ! " said Simonides. " Thou shalt be a master of legions for the King, with millions to choose from."

" Millions ! " cried Ben-Hur.

Simonides sat a moment thinking.

" The question of power should not trouble you," he next said.

Ben-Hur looked at him inquiringly.

" You were seeing the lowly King in the act of coming to His own," Simonides answered—" seeing Him on the right hand, as it were, and on the left the brassy legions of Cæsar, and you were asking, What can He do ? "

" It was my very thought."

" O my master ! " Simonides continued. " You do not know how strong our Israel is. You think of him as a sorrowful old man weeping by the rivers of Babylon. But go up to Jerusalem next Passover, and stand on the Xystus or in the street of Barter, and see him as he is. The promise of the Lord to father Jacob coming out of Padan-aram was a law under which our people have not ceased multiplying—not even in captivity ; they grew under foot of the Egyptian ; the clench of the Roman has been but wholesome nurture to them ; now they are indeed ' a nation, and a company of nations.' Nor that only, my master ; in fact, to measure the strength of Israel—which is, in fact, measuring what the King can do—you shall not abide solely by the rule of natural increase, but add thereto the other—I mean the spread of the faith, which will carry you to the far and near of the whole known earth. Further, the habit is, I know, to think and speak of Jerusalem as Israel, which may be likened to our finding an embroidered shred, and holding it up as a magisterial robe of Cæsar's. Jerusalem is but a stone of the Temple, or the heart in the body. Turn from beholding the legions, strong though they be, and count the hosts of the faithful waiting the old alarm, ' To your tents, O Israel! '—count the many in Persia, children of those who chose not to return with the returning ; count the brethren who swarm the marts of Egypt and farther Africa ; count the Hebrew colonists eking profit in the West—in Lodinum and the trade-courts of Spain ; count the pure of blood and the proselytes in Greece and in the isles of the sea, and over in Pontus, and here in Antioch, and, for that matter, those of that city lying accursed in the shadow of the unclean walls of Rome herself ; count the worshippers of the Lord dwelling in tents along the deserts next us, as well as in the deserts beyond the Nile ; and in the regions across the Caspian, and up in the old lands of Gog and Magog even, separate those who annually send gifts to the Holy Temple in acknowledgment of God—separate them, that they may be counted also. And when you have done counting, lo ! my master, a census of the sword hands that await you ; lo ! a kingdom ready fashioned for Him who is to do ' judgment and justice in the whole earth '—in Rome not less than in Zion. Have then the answer, What Israel can do, that can the King."

The picture was fervently given.

Upon Ilderim it operated like the blowing of a trumpet. "Oh, that I had back my youth ! " he cried, starting to his feet.

" Let us concede all you say, O Simonides," said Ben-Hur—" that the King will come, and His kingdom be as Solomon's ; say also I am ready to give myself and all I have to Him and His cause ; yet more, say that I should do as was God's purpose in the ordering of my life and in your quick amassment of astonishing fortune ; then what ? Shall we proceed like blind men building ? Shall we wait till the King comes ? Or until He sends for me ? You have age and experience on your side. Answer."

Simonides answered at once.

" There is a work, a work for the King, which should be

done in advance of His coming. We may not doubt that
Israel is to be His right hand; but, alas! it is a hand of
peace, without cunning in war. Of the millions, there
is not one trained band, not a captain. The mercenaries
of the Herods I do not count, for they are kept to crush
us. The condition is as the Roman would have it; his
policy has fruited well for his tyranny; but the time of
change is at hand, when the shepherd shall put on armour,
and take to spear and sword, and the feeding flocks be
turned to fighting lions. Some one, my son, must have
place next the King at His right hand. Who shall it be
if not he who does this work well?"

Ben-Hur's face flushed at the prospect, though he
said, "I see; but speak plainly. A deed to be done is
one thing; how to do it is another."

Simonides sipped the wine Esther brought him, and
replied:

"The sheik, and thou, my master, shall be principals,
each with a part. I will remain here, carrying on as now,
and watchful that the spring go not dry. Thou shalt
betake thee to Jerusalem, and thence to the wilderness,
and begin numbering the fighting-men of Israel, and
telling them into tens and hundreds, and choosing captains
and training them, and in secret places hoarding arms, for
which I shall keep thee supplied. Commencing over in
Perea, thou shalt go then to Galilee, whence it is but a
step to Jerusalem. In Perea, the desert will be at thy
back, and Ilderim in reach of thy hand. He will keep
the roads, so that nothing shall pass without thy knowledge. He will help thee in many ways. Until the
ripening time no one shall know what is here contracted.
Mine is but a servant's part. I have spoken to Ilderim.
What sayest thou?"

Ben-Hur looked at the sheik.

"It is as he says, son of Hur," the Arab responded. "I
have given my word, and he is content with it; but
thou shalt have my oath, binding me, and the ready hands
of my tribe, and whatever serviceable thing I have."

The three—Simonides, Ilderim, Esther—gazed at Ben-
Hur fixedly.

"Every man," he answered, at first sadly, "has a cup of pleasure poured for him, and soon or late it comes to his hand, and he tastes and drinks—every man but me. I see, Simonides, and thou, O generous sheik!—I see whither the proposal tends. If I accept, and enter upon the course, farewell peace, and the hopes which cluster around it. The doors I might enter and the gates of quiet life will shut behind me, never to open again, for Rome keeps them all; and her outlawry will follow me, and her hunters; and in the tombs near cities and the dismal caverns of remotest hills, I must eat my crust and take my rest."

The speech was broken by a sob. All turned to Esther, who hid her face upon her father's shoulder.

"I did not think of you, Esther," said Simonides gently, for he was himself deeply moved.

"It is well enough, Simonides," said Ben-Hur. "A man bears a hard doom better, knowing there is pity for him. Let me go on."

They gave him ear again.

"I was about to say," he continued, "I have no choice, but take the part you assign me; and as remaining here is to meet an ignoble death, I will do the work at once."

"Shall we have writings?" asked Simonides, moved by his habit of business.

"I rest upon your word," said Ben-Hur.

"And I," Ilderim answered.

Thus simply was effected the treaty which was to alter Ben-Hur's life. And almost immediately the latter added:

"It is done, then."

"May the God of Abraham help us!" Simonides exclaimed.

"One word now, my friends," Ben-Hur said, more cheerfully. "By your leave, I will be my own until after the games. It is not probable Messala will set peril on foot for me until he has given the procurator time to answer him; and that cannot be in less than seven days from the dispatch of his letter. The meeting him in the Circus is a pleasure I would buy at whatever risk."

Ilderim, well pleased, assented readily.

"Let the horses be brought," said Ben-Hur. "I will return to the Orchard. The enemy will not discover me if I go now, and "—he glanced at Ilderim—"the four will be glad to see me."

As the day dawned, he and Malluch dismounted at the door of the tent.

CHAPTER VIII

THE day before the games, in the afternoon, all Ilderim's racing property was taken to the city, and put in quarters adjoining the Circus. Along with it the good man carried a great deal of property not of that class ; so with servants, retainers mounted and armed, horses in leading, cattle driven, camels laden with baggage, his outgoing from the Orchard was not unlike a tribal migration. Next morning the pageant would be far on the road to the desert, and going with it would be every movable thing of value belonging to the Orchard—everything save such as were essential to the success of his four. He was, in fact, started home ; his tents were all folded ; the dowar was no more ; in twelve hours all would be out of reach, pursue who might.

Neither he nor Ben-Hur over-estimated the influence of Messala ; it was their opinion, however, that he would not begin active measures against them until after the meeting in the Circus ; if defeated there, especially if defeated by Ben-Hur, they might instantly look for the worst he could do ; he might not even wait for advice from Gratus. With this view they shaped their course, and were prepared to betake themselves out of harm's way. They rode together now in good spirits, calmly confident of success on the morrow.

On the way, they came upon Malluch in waiting for them.

"To you, son of Arrius, my congratulations. There is nothing now to prevent your meeting Messala. Every condition preliminary to the race is complied with. I have the assurance from the editor himself."

"I thank you, Malluch," said Ben-Hur.

Malluch proceeded.

"Your colour is white, and Messala's mixed scarlet and gold. The good effects of the choice are visible already. Boys are now hawking white ribbons along the streets; to-morrow every Arab and Jew in the city will wear them. In the Circus you will see the white fairly divide the galleries with the red."

"The galleries—but not the tribunal over the Porta Pompæ."

"No; the scarlet and gold will rule there. But if we win"—Malluch chuckled with the pleasure of the thought—"if we win, how the dignitaries will tremble!"

And Malluch, greatly delighted, gave him parting salutation, and started to ride away, but returned presently.

"Your pardon," he said to Ben-Hur. "There was another matter. I could not get near Messala's chariot myself, but I had another measure it; and, from his report, its hub stands quite a palm higher from the ground than yours."

"A palm! So much?" cried Ben-Hur joyfully.

Then he leaned over to Malluch.

"As thou art a son of Judah, Malluch, and faithful to thy kin, get thee a seat in the gallery over the Gate of Triumph, down close to the balcony in front of the pillars, and watch well when we make the turns there; watch well, for if I have favour at all, I will—— Nay, Malluch, let it go unsaid! Only get thee there, and watch well."

At that moment a cry burst from Ilderim.

"Ha! By the splendour of God! what is this?"

He drew near Ben-Hur with a finger pointing on the face of the notice.

"Read," said Ben-Hur.

"No; better thou."

Ben-Hur took the paper, which, signed by the prefect of the province as editor, performed the office of a modern programme, giving particularly the several divertisements provided for the occasion. It informed the public that there would be first a procession of extraordinary splen-

dour ; that the procession would be succeeded by the
customary honours to the god Consus, whereupon the
games would begin ; running, leaping, wrestling, boxing,
each in the order stated. The names of the competitors
were given, with their several nationalities and schools
of training, the trials in which they had been engaged,
the prizes won, and the prizes now offered , under the
latter head the sums of money were stated in illuminated
letters, telling of the departure of the day when the simple
chaplet of pine or laurel was fully enough for the victor,
hungering for glory as something better than riches, and
content with it.

Over these parts of the programme Ben-Hur sped with
rapid eyes. At last he came to the announcement of the
race. He read it slowly. Attending lovers of the heroic
sports were assured they would certainly be gratified by
an Orestean struggle unparalleled in Antioch. The city
offered the spectacle in honour of the consul. One hundred
thousand sestertii and a crown of laurels were the prizes.
Then followed the particulars. The entries were six in
all—fours only permitted ; and, to further interest in the
performance, the competitors would be turned into the
course together. Each four then received description.

" I. A four of Lysippus the Corinthian—two greys, a bay, and
a black ; entered at Alexandria last year, and again at Corinth,
where they were winners. Lysippus, driver. Colour, yellow.

" II. A four of Messala of Rome—two white, two black ; victors
of the Circensian as exhibited in the Circus Maximus last year.
Messala, driver. Colours, scarlet and gold.

" III. A four of Cleanthes the Athenian—three grey, one bay ;
winners at the Isthmian last year. Cleanthes, driver. Colour,
green.

" IV. A four of Dicæus the Byzantine—two black, one grey, one
bay ; winners this year at Byzantine. Dicæus, driver. Colour,
black.

" V. A four of Admetus the Sidonian—all greys. Thrice entered
at Cæsarea, and thrice victors. Admetus, driver. Colour, blue.

" VI. A four of Ilderim, Sheik of the Desert. All bays ; first
race. Ben-Hur, a Jew, driver. Colour, white."

Ben-Hur, a Jew, driver !
Why that name instead of Arrius ?
Ben-Hur raised his eyes to Ilderim. He had found

the cause of the Arab's outcry.   Both rushed to the same conclusion.

The hand was the hand of Messala !

CHAPTER IX

LET us visit once more the palace on the island.

The five great chandeliers in the saloon are freshly lighted. The assemblage is much the same as that already noticed in connexion with the place.   The divan has its corps of sleepers and burden of garments, and the tables yet resound with the rattle and clash of dice.   Yet the greater part of the company are not doing anything.   They walk about, or yawn tremendously, or pause as they pass each other to exchange idle nothings.   Will the weather be fair to-morrow ?   Are the preparations for the games complete ?   Do the laws of the Circus in Antioch differ from the laws of the Circus in Rome ?   Truth is, the young fellows are suffering from ennui.   Their heavy work is done ;   that is, we would find their tablets, could we look at them, covered with memoranda of wagers— wagers on every contest ;   on the running, the wrestling, the boxing ;   on everything but the chariot-race.

And why not on that ?

Good reader, they cannot find anybody who will hazard so much as a denarius with them against Messala.

There are no colours in the saloon but his.

No one thinks of his defeat.

Why, they say, is he not perfect in his training ?   Did he not graduate from an imperial *lanista* ?   Were not his horses winners at the Circensian in the Circus Maximus ? And then—ah, yes ! he is a Roman !

In a corner, at ease on the divan, Messala himself may be seen.

Around him, sitting or standing, are his courtierly admirers, plying him with questions.   There is, of course, but one topic.

An outcry over about the door just then occasioned a rush to that quarter.

" A white ! A white ! "

" Let him come ! "

" This way, this way ! "

These and like exclamations filled the saloon, to the stoppage of other speech. The dice-players quit their games ; the sleepers awoke, rubbed their eyes, drew their tablets, and hurried to the common centre.

" I offer you——"

" And I——"

" I——"

The person so warmly received was the respectable Jew, Ben-Hur's fellow-voyager from Cyprus. He entered grave, quiet, observant. His robe was spotlessly white ; so was the cloth of his turban. Bowing and smiling at the welcome, he moved slowly towards the central table. Arrived there, he drew his robe about him in a stately manner, took seat, and waved his hand. The gleam of a jewel on a finger helped him not a little to the silence which ensued.

" Romans—most noble Romans—I salute you ! " he said.

" Easy, by Jupiter ! Who is he ? " asked Drusus.

" A dog of Israel—Sanballat by name—purveyor for the army ; residence, Rome ; vastly rich ; grown so as a contractor of furnishments which he never furnishes. He spins mischiefs, nevertheless, finer than spiders spin their webs. Come—by the girdle of Venus ! let us catch him ! "

Messala arose as he spoke, and, with Drusus, joined the mass crowded about the purveyor.

" It came to me on the street," said that person, producing his tablets, and opening them on the table with an impressive air of business, " that there was great discomfort in the palace because offers on Messala were going without takers. The gods, you know, must have sacrifices ; and here am I. You see my colour ; let us to the matter. Odds first, amounts next. What will you give me ? "

The audacity seemed to stun his hearers.

" Haste ! " he said. " I have an engagement with the consul."

The spur was effective.

"Two to one," cried half a dozen in a voice.

"What!" exclaimed the purveyor, astonished. "Only two to one, and yours a Roman!"

"Take three, then."

"Three say you—only three—and mine but a dog of a Jew! Give me four."

"Four it is," said a boy, stung by the taunt.

"Five—give me five," cried the purveyor instantly.

A profound stillness fell upon the assemblage.

"The consul—your master and mine—is waiting for me."

The inaction became awkward to the many.

"Give me five—for the honour of Rome, five."

"Five let it be," said one in answer.

There was a sharp cheer—a commotion—and Messala himself appeared.

"Five let it be," he said.

And Sanballat smiled, and made ready to write.

"If Cæsar die to-morrow," he said, "Rome will not be all bereft. There is at least one other with spirit to take his place. Give me six."

"Six be it," answered Messala.

There was another shout louder than the first.

"Six be it," repeated Messala. "Six to one—the difference between a Roman and a Jew. And, having found it, now, O redemptor of the flesh of swine, let us on. The amount—and quickly. The consul may send for thee, and I will then be bereft."

Sanballat took the laugh against him coolly, and wrote, and offered the writing to Messala.

"Read, read!" everybody demanded.

And Messala read:

"*Mem.*—Chariot-race. Messala of Rome, in wager with Sanballat, also of Rome, says he will beat Ben-Hur the Jew. Amount of wager, twenty talents. Odds to Sanballat, six to one.
    "Witnesses: SANBALLAT."

There was no noise, no motion. Each person seemed

held in the pose the reading found him. Messala stared
at the memorandum, while the eyes which had him in
view opened wide, and stared at him. He felt the gaze,
and thought rapidly. So lately he stood in the same
place, and in the same way hectored the countrymen
around him. They would remember it. If he refused
to sign, his hero-ship was lost. And sign he could not ;
he was not worth one hundred talents, nor the fifth part
of the sum. Suddenly his mind became a blank ; he stood
speechless ; the colour fled his face. An idea at last came
to his relief.

"Thou Jew !" he said, "where hast thou twenty
talents ? Show me."

Sanballat's provoking smile deepened.

"There," he replied, offering Messala a paper.

"Read, read !" arose all around.

Again Messala read :

> "AT ANTIOCH, *Tammuz* 16*th day*.
> "The bearer, Sanballat of Rome, hath now to his order with me
> fifty talents, coin of Cæsar.   SIMONIDES."

"Fifty talents, fifty talents !" echoed the throng in
amazement.

Then Drusus came to the rescue.

"By Hercules !" he shouted, "the paper lies, and the
Jew is a liar. Who but Cæsar hath fifty talents at order ?
Down with the insolent white !"

The cry was angry, and it was angrily repeated ; yet
Sanballat kept his seat, and his smile grew more exasperating the longer he waited. At length Messala spoke.

"Hush ! One to one, my countrymen—one to one,
for love of our ancient Roman name."

The timely action recovered him his ascendency.

"O thou circumcised dog !" he continued to Sanballat,
"I gave thee six to one, did I not ?"

"Yes," said the Jew, quietly.

"Well, give me now the fixing of the amount."

"With reserve, if the amount be trifling, have thy
will," answered Sanballat.

"Write, then, five in place of twenty."

" Hast thou so much ? "

" By the mother of the gods, I will show you receipts."

" Nay, the word of so brave a Roman must pass. Only make the sum even—six make it, and I will write."

" Write it so."

And forthwith they exchanged writings.

Sanballat immediately arose and looked around him, a sneer in place of his smile. No man better than he knew those with whom he was dealing.

" Romans," he said, " another wager, if you dare ! Five talents against five talents that the white will win. I challenge you collectively."

They were again surprised.

" What ! " he cried louder. " Shall it be said in the Circus to-morrow that a dog of Israel went into the saloon of the palace full of Roman nobles—among them the scion of a Cæsar—and laid five talents before them in challenge, and they had not the courage to take it up ? "

The sting was unendurable.

" Have done, O insolent ! " said Drusus, " write the challenge, and leave it on the table ; and to-morrow, if we find thou hast indeed so much money to put at such hopeless hazard, I, Drusus, promise it shall be taken."

Sanballat wrote again, and, rising, said, unmoved as ever, " See, Drusus, I leave the offer with you. When it is signed, send it to me any time before the race begins. I will be found with the consul in a seat over the Porta Pompæ. Peace to you ; peace to all."

He bowed, and departed, careless of the shout of derision with which they pursued him out of the door.

In the night the story of the prodigious wager flew along the streets and over the city ; and Ben-Hur, lying with his four, was told of it, and also that Messala's whole fortune was on the hazard.

And he slept never so soundly.

CHAPTER X

THE Circus at Antioch stood on the south bank of the river, nearly opposite the island, differing in no respect from the plan of such buildings in general.

In the purest sense, the games were a gift to the public ; consequently, everybody was free to attend ; and, vast as the holding capacity of the structure was, so fearful were the people, on this occasion, lest there should not be room for them, that, early the day before the opening of the exhibition, they took up all the vacant spaces in the vicinity, where their temporary shelter suggested an army in waiting.

At midnight the entrances were thrown wide, and the rabble, surging in, occupied the quarters assigned to them, from which nothing less than an earthquake or an army with spears could have dislodged them. They dozed the night away on the benches, and breakfasted there ; and there the close of the exercises found them, patient and sight-hungry as in the beginning.

The better people, their seats secured, began moving towards the Circus about the first hour of the morning, the noble and very rich among them distinguished by litters and retinues of liveried servants.

By the second hour, the efflux from the city was a stream unbroken and innumerable.

Exactly as the gnomon of the official dial up in the citadel pointed the second hour half gone, the legion, in full panoply and with all its standards on exhibit, descended from Mount Sulpius ; and when the rear of the last cohort disappeared in the bridge, Antioch was literally abandoned—not that the Circus could hold the multitude, but that a multitude was gone out to it, nevertheless.

A great concourse on the river shore witnessed the consul come over from the island in a barge of state. As the great man landed, and was received by the legion, the martial show for one brief moment transcended the attraction of the Circus.

At the third hour, the audience, if such it may be termed, was assembled ; at last, a flourish of trumpets called for silence, and instantly the gaze of over a hundred thousand persons was directed towards a pile forming the eastern section of the building.

There was a basement first, broken in the middle by a broad arched passage, called the Porta Pompæ, over which, on an elevated tribunal magnificently decorated with insignia and legionary standards, the consul sat in the place of honour.   On both sides of the passage the basement was divided into stalls termed *carceres*, each protected in front by massive gates swung to statuesque pilasters. Over the stalls next was a cornice crowned by a low balustrade ; back of which the seats arose in theatre arrangement, all occupied by a throng of dignitaries superbly attired. The pile extended the width of the Circus, and was flanked on both sides by towers which, besides helping the architects give grace to their work, served the *velaria*, or purple awnings, stretched between them so as to throw the whole quarter in a shade that became exceedingly grateful as the day advanced.

Looking across this sanded arena westwardly still, there is a pedestal of marble supporting three low conical pillars of grey stone, much carven.   Many an eye will hunt for those pillars before the day is done, for they are the first goal and mark the beginning and end of the racecourse. Behind the pedestal, leaving a passage-way and space for an altar, commences a wall ten or twelve feet in breadth and five or six in height, extending thence exactly two hundred yards, or one Olympic stadium.   At the farther or westward extremity of the wall there is another pedestal, surmounted with pillars which mark the second goal.

The racers will enter the course on the right of the first goal, and keep the wall at the time to their left.   The beginning and ending points of the contests lie, consequently, directly in front of the consul across the arena ; and for that reason his seat was admittedly the most desirable in the Circus.

Out of the Porta Pompæ over in the east rises a sound mixed of voices and instruments harmonized.   Presently, forth issues the chorus of the procession with which the celebration begins ;   the editor and civic authorities of

the city, givers of the games, follow in robes and garlands :
then the gods, some on platforms borne by men, others in
great four-wheel carriages gorgeously decorated; next
them, again, the contestants of the day, each in costumes
exactly as he will run, wrestle, leap, box, or drive.

Slowly crossing the arena, the procession proceeds to
make circuit of the course. The display is beautiful and
imposing. Approval runs before it in a shout, as the water
rises and swells in front of a boat in motion. If the dumb,
figured gods make no sign of appreciation of the welcome,
the editor and his associates are not so backward.

The reception of the athletes is even more demonstra-
tive, for there is not a man in the assemblage who has not
something to wager upon them, though but a mite or far-
thing. And it is noticeable, as the classes move by, that
the favourites among them are speedily singled out : either
their names are loudest in the uproar, or they are more
profusely showered with wreaths and garlands tossed
to them from the balcony.

If there is a question as to the popularity with the public
of the several games, it is now put to rest. To the splendour of the chariots and the superexcellent beauty of the
horses, the charioteers add the personality necessary to
perfect the charm of their display. Their tunics, short,
sleeveless, and of the finest woollen texture, are of the
assigned colours. A horseman accompanies each one of them
except Ben-Hur, who, for some reason—possibly distrust
—has chosen to go alone ; so, too, they are all helmeted
but him. As they approach, the spectators stand upon
the benches, and there is a sensible deepening of the
clamour, in which a sharp listener may detect the shrill
piping of women and children ; at the same time, the
things roseate flying from the balcony thicken into a
storm, and, striking the men, drop into the chariot-beds,
which are threatened with filling to the tops. Even the
horses have a share in the ovation ; nor may it be said
they are less conscious than their masters of the honours
they receive.

Very soon, as with the other contestants, it is made
apparent that some of the drivers are more in favour

than others ; and then the discovery follows that nearly every individual on the benches, women and children as well as men, wears a colour, most frequently a ribbon upon the breast, or in the hair : now it is green, now yellow, now blue ; but, searching the great body carefully, it is manifest that there is a preponderance of white, and scarlet and gold.

As the charioteers move on in the circuit, the excitement increases ; at the second goal, where, especially in the galleries, the white is the ruling colour, the people exhaust their flowers and rive the air with screams.

" Messala ! Messala ! "

" Ben-Hur ! Ben-Hur ! "

Such are the cries.

Upon the passage of the procession, the factionists take their seats and resume conversation.

" Ah, by Bacchus ! was he not handsome ? " exclaims a woman, whose Romanism is betrayed by the colours flying in her hair.

" And how splendid his chariot ! " replies a neighbour of the same proclivities. " It is all ivory and gold. Jupiter grant he wins ! "

The notes on the bench behind them were entirely different.

" A hundred shekels on the Jew ! "

The voice is high and shrill.

" Nay, be thou not rash," whispers a moderating friend to the speaker. " The children of Jacob are not much given to Gentile sports, which are too often accursed in the sight of the Lord."

" True, but saw you ever one more cool and assured ? And what an arm he has ! "

" And what horses ! " says a third.

" And for that," a fourth one adds, " they say he has all the tricks of the Romans."

A woman completes the eulogium.

" Yes, and he is even handsomer than the Roman."

Thus encouraged, the enthusiast shrieks again, " A hundred shekels on the Jew ! "

" Thou fool ! " answers an Antiochian, from a bench

well forward on the balcony. " Knowest thou not there are fifty talents laid against him, six to one, on Messala ? Put up thy shekels, lest Abraham rise and smite thee."

" Ha, ha ! thou ass of Antioch ! Cease thy bray. Knowest thou not it was Messala betting on himself ? "

Such the reply.

And so ran the controversy, not always good-natured. When at length the march was ended and the Porta Pompæ received back the procession, Ben-Hur knew he had his prayer.

The eyes of the East were upon his contest with Messala.

CHAPTER XI

ABOUT three o'clock, speaking in modern style, the programme was concluded except the chariot-race. The editor, wisely considerate of the comfort of the people, chose that time for a recess. At once the *vomitoria* were thrown open, and all who could hastened to the portico outside where the restaurateurs had their quarters. Those who remained, yawned, talked, gossiped, consulted their tablets, and, all distinctions else forgotten, merged into but two classes—the winners, who were happy, and the losers, who were grum and captious.

Now, however, a third class of spectators, composed of citizens who desired only to witness the chariot-race, availed themselves of the recess to come in and take their reserved seats ; by so doing they thought to attract the least attention and give the least offence. Among these were Simonides and his party, whose places were in the vicinity of the main entrance on the north side, opposite the consul. The women were Iras and Esther.

Upon being seated, the latter cast a frightened look over the Circus, and drew the veil closer about her face ; while the Egyptian, letting her veil fall upon her shoulders, gave herself to view, and gazed at the scene with the seeming unconsciousness of being stared at, which, in a woman, is usually the result of long social habitude.

The new-comers generally were yet making their first

examination of the great spectacle, beginning with the consul and his attendants, when some workmen ran in and commenced to stretch a chalked rope across the arena from balcony to balcony in front of the pillars of the first goal.

About the same time, also, six men came in through the Porta Pompæ and took post, one in front of each occupied stall; whereat there was a prolonged hum of voices in every quarter.

"See, see! The green goes to number four on the right; the Athenian is there."

"And Messala—yes, he is in number two."

"The Corinthian——"

"Watch the white! See, he crosses over, he stops; number one it is—number one on the left."

"No, the black stops there, and the white at number two."

"So it is."

These gate-keepers, it should be understood, were dressed in tunics coloured like those of the competing charioteers; so, when they took their stations, everybody knew the particular stall in which his favourite was that moment waiting.

"Did you ever see Messala?" the Egyptian asked Esther.

The Jewess shuddered as she answered no. If not her father's enemy, the Roman was Ben-Hur's.

"He is beautiful as Apollo."

As Iras spoke, her large eyes brightened and she shook her jewelled fan. Esther looked at her with the thought, "Is he then so much handsomer than Ben-Hur?" Next moment she heard Ilderim say to her father, "Yes, his stall is number two on the left of the Porta Pompæ"; and, thinking it was of Ben-Hur he spoke, her eyes turned that way. Taking but the briefest glance at the wattled face of the gate, she drew the veil close and muttered a little prayer.

Presently Sanballat came to the party.

"I am just from the stalls, O sheik," he said, bowing gravely to Ilderim, who began combing his beard, while his eyes glittered with eager inquiry. "The horses are in perfect condition."

Ilderim replied simply, "If they are beaten, I pray it be by some other than Messala."

Turning then to Simonides, Sanballat drew out a tablet, saying, "I bring you also something of interest. I reported, you will remember, the wager concluded with Messala last night, and stated that I left another which, if taken, was to be delivered to me in writing to-day before the race began. Here it is."

Simonides took the tablet and read the memorandum carefully.

"Yes," he said. "Their emissary came to ask me if you had so much money with me. Keep the tablet close. If you lose, you know where to come ; if you win "—his face knit hard—"if you win—ah, friend, see to it ! See the signers escape not ; hold them to the last shekel. That is what they would with us."

"Trust me," replied the purveyor.

"Will you not sit with us ? " asked Simonides.

"You are very good," the other returned ; "but if I leave the consul, young Rome yonder will boil over. Peace to you ; peace to all."

At length the recess came to an end.

The trumpeters blew a call at which the absentees rushed back to their places. At the same time, some attendants appeared in the arena, and, climbing upon the division wall, went to an entablature near the second goal at the west end, and placed upon it seven wooden balls ; then returning to the first goal, upon an entablature there they set up seven other pieces of wood hewn to represent dolphins.

"What shall they do with the balls and fishes, O sheik ? " asked Balthasar.

"Hast thou never attended a race ? "

"Never before ; and hardly know I why I am here."

"Well, they are to keep the count. At the end of each round run thou shalt see one ball and one fish taken down."

The preparations were now complete, and presently a trumpeter in gaudy uniform arose by the editor, ready to blow the signal of commencement promptly at his order. Straightway the stir of the people and the hum of their conversation died away. Every face near by, and every face in the lessening perspective, turned to the east, as all eyes settled upon the gates of the six stalls which shut in the competitors.

The unusual flush upon his face gave proof that even Simonides had caught the universal excitement. Ilderim pulled his beard fast and furious.

" Look now for the Roman," said the fair Egyptian to Esther, who did not hear her, for, with close-drawn veil and beating heart, she sat watching for Ben-Hur.

The trumpet sounded short and sharp ; whereupon the starters, one for each chariot, leaped down from behind the pillars of the goal, ready to give assistance if any of the fours proved unmanageable.

Again the trumpet blew, and simultaneously the gate-keepers threw the stalls open.

First appeared the mounted attendants of the charioteers, five in all, Ben-Hur having rejected the service. The chalked line was lowered to let them pass, then raised again. They were beautifully mounted, yet scarcely observed as they rode forward ; for all the time the trampling of eager horses, and the voices of drivers scarcely less eager, were heard behind in the stalls, so that one might not look away an instant from the gaping doors.

The chalked line up again, the gate-keepers called their men ; instantly the ushers on the balcony waved their hands, and shouted with all their strength, " Down ! down ! "

As well have whistled to stay a storm.

Forth from each stall like missiles in a volley from so many great guns, rushed the six fours ; and up the vast assemblage arose electrified and irrepressible, and, leaping upon the benches, filled the Circus and the air above it with yells and screams. This was the time for which they had so patiently waited !—this the moment of supreme interest treasured up in talk and dreams since the proclamation of the games !

" He is come—there—look ! " cried Iras, pointing to Messala.

" I see him," answered Esther, looking at Ben-Hur.

The veil was withdrawn. For an instant the little Jewess was brave. An idea of the joy there is in doing an heroic deed under the eyes of a multitude came to her, and she understood ever after how, at such times, the souls of men, in the frenzy of performance, laugh at death or forget it utterly.

The competitors were now under view from nearly every part of the Circus, yet the race was not begun ; they had first to make the chalked line successfully.

The line was stretched for the purpose of equalizing the start. If it were dashed upon, discomfiture of man and horses might be apprehended ; on the other hand, to approach it timidly was to incur the hazard of being thrown behind in the beginning of the race ; and that was certain forfeit of the great advantage always striven for —the position next the division wall on the inner line of the course.

The arena swam in a dazzle of light ; yet each driver looked first thing for the rope, then for the coveted inner line. So, all six aiming at the same point and speeding furiously, a collision seemed inevitable ; nor that merely. What if the editor, at the last moment, dissatisfied with the start, should withhold the signal to drop the rope ? Or if he should not give it in time ?

The crossing was about two hundred and fifty feet in width. Quick the eye, steady the hand, unerring the judgment required.

The divine last touch in perfecting the beautiful is animation. Can we accept the saying, then these latter days, so tame in pastime and dull in sports, have scarcely anything to compare to the spectacle offered by the six contestants. Let the reader try to fancy it ; let him first look down upon the arena, and see it glistening in its frame of dull-grey granite walls ; let him then, in this perfect field, see the chariots, light of wheel, very graceful, and ornate as paint and burnishing can make them—Messala's rich with ivory and gold ; let him see the drivers, erect and statuesque, undisturbed by the motion of the cars, their limbs naked, and fresh and ruddy with the healthful

polish of the baths—in their right hands goads, suggestive
of torture dreadful to the thought—in their left hands, held
in careful separation, and high, that they may not interfere with view of the steeds, the reins passing taut from the
fore ends of the carriage-poles; let him see the fours,
chosen for beauty as well as speed; let him see them
in magnificent action, their masters not more conscious
of the situation and all that is asked and hoped from
them—their heads tossing, nostrils in play, now distent,
now contracted—limbs too dainty for the sand which
they touch but to spurn—limbs slender, yet with impact
crushing as hammers—every muscle of the rounded bodies
instinct with glorious life, swelling, diminishing, justifying
the world in taking from them its ultimate measure of
force; finally, along with chariots, drivers, horses, let the
reader see the accompanying shadows fly; and, with such
distinctness as the picture comes, he may share the satisfaction and deeper pleasure of those to whom it was a
thrilling fact, not a feeble fancy. Every age has its plenty
of sorrows; heaven help where there are no pleasures!

The competitors having started each on the shortest
line for the position next the wall, yielding would be like
giving up the race; and who dared yield? It is not in
common nature to change a purpose in mid-career; and
the cries of encouragement from the balcony were indis-
tinguishable and indescribable; a roar which had the same
effect upon all the drivers.

The fours neared the rope together. Then the trumpeter
by the editor's side blew a signal vigorously. Twenty feet
away it was not heard. Seeing the action, however, the
judges dropped the rope, and not an instant too soon,
for the hoof of one of Messala's horses struck it as it fell.
Nothing daunted, the Roman shook out his long lash,
loosed the reins, leaned forward, and, with a triumphant
shout, took the wall.

"Jove with us! Jove with us!" yelled all the Roman
faction, in a frenzy of delight.

As Messala turned in, the bronze lion's head at the end
of his axle caught the fore-leg of the Athenian's right-
hand tracemate, flinging the brute over against its yoke-

fellow. Both staggered, struggled, and lost their headway. The ushers had their will at least in part. The thousands held their breath with horror ; only up where the consul sat was there shouting.

" Jove with us ! " screamed Drusus frantically.

" He wins ! Jove with us ! " answered his associates, seeing Messala speed on.

Tablet in hand, Sanballat turned to them ; a crash from the course below stopped his speech, and he could not but look that way.

Messala having passed, the Corinthian was the only contestant on the Athenian's right, and to that side the latter tried to turn his broken four ; and then, as ill-fortune would have it, the wheel of the Byzantine, who was next on the left, struck the tail-piece of his chariot, knocking his feet from under him. There was a crash, a scream of rage and fear, and the unfortunate Cleanthes fell under the hoofs of his own steeds ; a terrible sight, against which Esther covered her eyes.

On swept the Corinthian, on the Byzantine, on the Sidonian.

Sanballat looked for Ben-Hur, and turned again to Drusus and his coterie.

" A hundred sestertii on the Jew ! " he cried.

" Taken ! " answered Drusus.

" Another hundred on the Jew ! " shouted Sanballat.

Nobody appeared to hear him. He called again ; the situation below was too absorbing, and they were too busy shouting " Messala ! Messala ! Jove with us ! '

When the Jewess ventured to look again, a party of workmen were removing the horses and broken car ; another party were taking off the man himself ; and every bench upon which there was a Greek was vocal with execrations and prayers for vengeance. Suddenly she dropped her hands ; Ben-Hur, unhurt, was to the front, coursing freely forward along with the Roman ! Behind them, in a group, followed the Sidonian, the Corinthian, and the Byzantine.

The race was on ; the souls of the racers were in it ; over them bent the myriads.

CHAPTER XII

WHEN the dash for position began, Ben-Hur, as we have seen, was on the extreme left of the six. For a moment, like the others, he was half-blinded by the light in the arena ; yet he managed to catch sight of his antagonists and divine their purpose. At Messala, who was more than an antagonist to him, he gave one searching look. The air of passionless hauteur characteristic of the fine patrician face was there as of old, and so was the Italian beauty, which the helmet rather increased ; but more—it may have been a jealous fancy, or the effect of the brassy shadow in which the features were at the moment cast, still the Israelite thought he saw the soul of the man as through a glass, darkly : cruel, cunning, desperate ; not so excited as determined—a soul in a tension of watchfulness and fierce resolve.

In a time not longer than was required to turn to his four again, Ben-Hur felt his own resolution harden to a like temper. At whatever cost, at all hazards, he would humble his enemy ! Prize, friends, wagers, honour—everything that can be thought of as a possible interest in the race was lost in the one deliberate purpose. Regard for life even should not hold him back. Yet there was no passion on his part ; no blinding rush of heated blood from heart to brain, and back again ; no impulse to fling himself upon fortune : he did not believe in fortune ; far otherwise. He had his plan, and, confiding in himself, he settled to the task never more observant, never more capable. The air about him seemed aglow with a renewed and perfect transparency.

When not half-way across the arena, he saw that Messala's rush would, if there was no collision, and the rope fell, give him the wall ; that the rope would fall, he ceased as soon to doubt; and, further, it came to him, a sudden flash-light insight, that Messala knew it was to be let drop at the last moment (pre-arrangement with the editor could safely reach that point in 'the contest) ; and it suggested, what more Roman-like than for the official to lend himself to a countryman who, besides being so popular, had also so much at stake? There could be no other accounting for the confidence with which Messala pushed his four forward the instant his competitors were prudentially checking their fours in front of the obstruction—no other except madness.

It is one thing to see a necessity and another to act upon it. Ben-Hur yielded the wall for the time.

The rope fell, and all the four but his sprang into the course under urgency of voice and lash. He drew head to the right, and, with all the speed of his Arabs, darted across the trails of his opponents, the angle of movement being such as to lose the least time and gain the greatest possible advance. So, while the spectators were shivering at the Athenian's mishap, and the Sidonian, Byzantine, and Corinthian were striving, with such skill as they possessed, to avoid involvement in the ruin, Ben-Hur swept around and took the course neck and neck with Messala, though on the outside. The marvellous skill shown in making the change thus from the extreme left across to the right without appreciable loss did not fail the sharp eyes upon the benches: the Circus seemed to rock and rock again with prolonged applause. Then Esther clasped her hands in glad surprise; then Sanballat, smiling, offered his hundred sestertii a second time without a taker; and then the Romans began to doubt, thinking Messala might have found an equal, if not a master, and that in an Israelite!

And now, racing together side by side, a narrow interval between them, the two neared the second goal.

The pedestal of the three pillars there, viewed from the west, was a stone wall in the form of a half-circle, around which the course and opposite balcony were bent in exact parallelism. Making this turn was considered in all respects the most telling test of a charioteer; it was, in fact, the very feat in which Orestes failed. As an involuntary admission of interest on the part of the spectators, a hush fell over all the Circus, so that for the first time in the race the rattle and clang of the cars plunging after the tugging steeds were distinctly heard. Then, it would seem,

Messala observed Ben-Hur, and recognized him ; and at once the audacity of the man flamed out in an astonishing manner.

" Down Eros, up Mars ! " he shouted, whirling his lash with practised hand—" Down Eros, up Mars ! " he repeated, and caught the well-doing Arabs of Ben-Hur a cut the like of which they had never known.

The blow was seen in every quarter, and the amazement was universal. The silence deepened ; up on the benches behind the consul the boldest held his breath, waiting for the outcome. Only a moment thus : then, involuntarily, down from the balcony, as thunder falls, burst the indignant cry of the people.

The four sprang forward affrighted. No hand had ever been laid upon them except in love ; they had been nurtured ever so tenderly ; and, as they grew, their confidence in man became a lesson to men beautiful to see. What should such dainty natures do under such indignity but leap as from death ?

Forward they sprang as with one impulse, and forward leaped the car. Past question, every experience is serviceable to us. Where got Ben-Hur the large hand and mighty grip which helped him now so well ? Where but from the oar with which so long he fought the sea ? And what was this spring of the floor under his feet to the dizzy eccentric lurch with which in the old time the trembling ship yielded to the beat of staggering billows, drunk with their power ? So he kept his place, and gave the four free rein, and called to them in soothing voice, trying merely to guide them round the dangerous turn ; and before the fever of the people began to abate, he had back the mastery. Nor that only : on approaching the first goal, he was again side by side with Messala, bearing with him the sympathy and admiration of every one not a Roman. So clearly was the feeling shown, so vigorous its manifestation, that Messala, with all his boldness, felt it unsafe to trifle further.

As the cars whirled round the goal, Esther caught sight of Ben-Hur's face—a little pale, a little higher raised, otherwise calm, even placid.

Immediately a man climbed on the entablature at the
west end of the division wall, and took down one of the
conical wooden balls. A dolphin on the east entablature
was taken down at the same time.

In like manner, the second ball and second dolphin
disappeared.

And then the third ball and third dolphin.

Three rounds concluded : still Messala held the inside
position ; still Ben-Hur moved with him side by side ;
still the other competitors followed as before. The contest began to have the appearance of one of the double
races which became so popular in Rome during the later
Cæsarean period—Messala and Ben-Hur in the first, the
Corinthian, Sidonian and Byzantine in the second. Meantime the ushers succeeded in returning the multitude to
their seats, though the clamour continued to run the
rounds, keeping, as it were, even pace with the rivals in
the course below.

In the fifth round the Sidonian succeeded in getting a
place outside Ben-Hur, but lost it directly.

The sixth round was entered upon without change of
relative position.

Gradually the speed had been quickened—gradually the
blood of the competitors warmed with the work. Men and
beasts seemed to know alike that the final crisis was near,
bringing the time for the winner to assert himself.

The interest which from the beginning had centred
chiefly in the struggle between the Roman and the Jew,
with an intense and general sympathy for the latter, was
fast changing to anxiety on his account. On all the
benches the spectators bent forward motionless, except
as their faces turned following the contestants. Ilderim
quitted combing his beard, and Esther forgot her fears.

" A hundred sestertii on the Jew ! " cried Sanballat
to the Romans under the consul's awning.

There was no reply.

" A talent—or five talents, or ten ; choose ye ! "

He shook his tablets at them defiantly.

" I will take thy sestertii," answered a Roman youth,
preparing to write.

" Do not so," interposed a friend.

" Why ? "

" Messala hath reached his utmost speed. See him lean over his chariot-rim, the reins loose as flying ribbons. Look then at the Jew."

The first one looked.

" By Hercules ! " he replied, his countenance falling. " The dog throws all his weight on the bits. I see, I see ! If the gods help not our friend, he will be run away with by the Israelite. No, not yet. Look ! Jove with us ! Jove with us ! "

The cry, swelled by every Latin tongue, shook the *velaria* over the consul's head.

If it were true that Messala had attained his utmost speed, the effort was with effect ; slowly but certainly he was beginning to forge ahead. His horses were running with their heads low down ; from the balcony their bodies appeared actually to skim the earth ; their nostrils showed blood-red in expansion ; their eyes seemed straining in their sockets. Certainly the good steeds were doing their best ! How long could they keep the pace ? It was but the commencement of the sixth round. On they dashed. As they neared the second goal, Ben-Hur turned in behind the Roman's car.

The joy of the Messala faction reached its bound : they screamed and howled, and tossed their colours ; and Sanballat filled his tablets with wagers of their tendering.

Malluch, in the lower gallery over the Gate of Triumph, found it hard to keep his cheer. He had cherished the vague hint dropped to him by Ben-Hur of something to happen in the turning of the western pillars. It was the fifth round, yet the something had not come ; and he had said to himself, the sixth will bring it ; but, lo ! Ben-Hur was hardly holding a place at the tail of his enemy's car.

Over in the east end, Simonides' party held their peace. The merchant's head was bent low. Ilderim tugged at his beard, and dropped his brows till there was nothing of his eyes but an occasional sparkle of light. Esther scarcely breathed. Iras alone appeared glad.

Along the home-stretch—sixth round—Messala leading, next him Ben-Hur.

Thus to the first goal, and round it. Messala, fearful of losing his place, hugged the stony wall with perilous clasp ; a foot to the left, and he had been dashed to pieces ; yet when the turn was finished, no man, looking at the wheel-tracks of the two cars, could have said, here went Messala, there the Jew. They left but one trace behind them.

As they whirled by, Esther saw Ben-Hur's face again, and it was whiter than before.

Simonides, shrewder than Esther, said to Ilderim, the moment the rivals turned into the course, " I am no judge, good sheik, if Ben-Hur be not about to execute some design. His face hath that look."

To which Ilderim answered, " Saw you how clean they were and fresh ? By the splendour of God, friend, they have not been running ! But now watch ! "

One ball and one dolphin remained on the entablatures ; and all the people drew a long breath, for the beginning of the end was at hand.

First, the Sidonian gave the scourge to his four, and, smarting with fear and pain, they dashed desperately forward, promising for a brief time to go to the front. The effort ended in promise. Next, the Byzantine and Corinthian each made the trial with like result, after which they were practically out of the race. Thereupon, with a readiness perfectly explicable, all the factions except the Romans joined hope in Ben-Hur, and openly indulged their feeling.

" Ben-Hur ! Ben-Hur ! " they shouted, and the blent voices of the many rolled overwhelmingly against the consular stand.

From the benches above him as he passed, the favour descended in fierce injunctions.

" Speed thee, Jew ! "

" Take the wall now ! "

" On ! loose the Arabs ! Give them rein and scourge ! "

" Let him not have the turn on thee again. Now or never !"

Over the balustrade they stooped low, stretching their hands imploringly to him.

Either he did not hear, or could not do better, for half-way round the course and he was still following; at the second goal even still no change.

And now, to make the turn, Messala began to draw in his left-hand steed, an act which necessarily slackened their speed. His spirit was high; more than one altar was richer of his vows; the Roman genius was still president. On the three pillars only six hundred feet away were fame, increase of fortune, promotions, and a triumph ineffably sweetened by hate, all in store for him! That moment Malluch, in the gallery, saw Ben-Hur lean forward over his Arabs, and give them the reins. Out flew the many-folded lash in his hand; over the backs of the startled steeds it writhed and hissed, and hissed and writhed again and again; and though it fell not, there were both sting and menace in its quick report; and as the man passed thus from quiet to resistless action, his face suffused, his eyes gleaming, along the reins he seemed to flash his will; and instantly not one, but the four as one, answered with a leap that landed them alongside the Roman's car. Messala, on the perilous edge of the goal, heard, but dared not look to see what the awakening portended. From the people he received no sign. Above the noises of the race there was but one voice, and that was Ben-Hur's. In the old Aramaic, as the sheik himself, he called to the Arabs.

"On, Atair! On, Rigel! What, Antares! dost thou linger now? Good horse—oho, Aldebaran! I hear them singing in the tents. I hear the children singing and the women—singing of the stars, of Atair, Antares, Rigel, Aldebaran, victory!—and the song will never end. Well done! Home to-morrow, under the black tent—home! On, Antares! The tribe is waiting for us, and the master is waiting! 'Tis done! 'tis done! Ha, ha! We have overthrown the proud. The hand that smote us is in the dust. Ours the glory! Ha, ha!—steady! The work is done—soho! Rest!"

There had never been anything of the kind more simple; seldom anything so instantaneous.

At the moment chosen for the dash, Messala was moving in a circle round the goal. To pass him, Ben-Hur had to cross the track, and good strategy required the movement to be in a forward direction ; that is, on a like circle limited to the least possible increase. The thousands on the benches understood it all : they saw the signal given— the magnificent response ; the four close outside Messala's outer wheel ; Ben-Hur's inner wheel behind the other's car—all this they saw. Then they heard a crash loud enough to send a thrill through the Circus, and, quicker than thought, out over the course a spray of shining white and yellow flinders flew. Down on its right side toppled the bed of the Roman's chariot. There was a rebound as of the axle hitting the hard earth ; another and another ; then the car went to pieces ; and Messala, entangled in the reins, pitched forward headlong.

To increase the horror of the sight by making death certain, the Sidonian, who had the wall next behind, could not stop or turn out. Into the wreck full speed he drove ; then over the Roman, and into the latter's four, all mad with fear. Presently, out of the turmoil, the fighting of horses, the resound of blows, the murky cloud of dust and sand, he crawled, in time to see the Corinthian and Byzantine go on down the course after Ben-Hur, who had not been an instant delayed.

The people arose, and leaped upon the benches, and shouted and screamed. Those who looked that way caught glimpses of Messala, now under the trampling of the fours, now under the abandoned cars. He was still ; they thought him dead ; but far the greater number followed Ben-Hur in his career. They had not seen the cunning touch of the reins by which, turning a little to the left, he caught Messala's wheel with the iron-shod point of his axle, and crushed it ; but they had seen the transformation of the man, and themselves felt the heat and glow of his spirit, the heroic resolution, the maddening energy of action with which, by look, word and gesture, he so suddenly inspired his Arabs. And such running ! It was rather the long leaping of lions in harness ; but for the lumbering chariot, it seemed the four were flying. When the Byzantine and Corinthian were half-way down the course, Ben-Hur turned the first goal.

And the race was WON!

The consul arose; the people shouted themselves hoarse; the editor came down from his seat, and crowned the victors.

The young Jew looked up and beheld Simonides and his party on the balcony. They waved their hands to him. Esther kept her seat; but Iras arose, and gave him a smile and a wave of her fan—favours not the less intoxicating to him because we know, O reader, they would have fallen to Messala had he been the victor.

The procession was then formed, and midst the shouting of the multitude which had had its will, passed out of the Gate of Triumph.

And the day was over.

CHAPTER XIII

BEN-HUR tarried across the river with Ilderim; for at midnight, as previously determined, they would take the road which the caravan, then thirty hours out, had pursued.

The sheik was happy; his offers of gifts had been royal; but Ben-Hur had refused everything, insisting that he was satisfied with the humiliation of his enemy. The generous dispute was long continued.

In the midst of a controversy of the kind, two messengers arrived—Malluch and one unknown. The former was admitted first.

The good fellow did not attempt to hide his joy over the event of the day.

"But, coming to that with which I am charged," he said, "the master Simonides sends me to say that, upon the adjournment of the games, some of the Roman faction made haste to protest against payment of the money prize."

Ilderim started up, crying, in his shrillest tones:

"By the splendour of God! the East shall decide whether the race was fairly won."

"Nay, good sheik," said Malluch, "the editor has paid the money."

" 'Tis well."

" When they said Ben-Hur struck Messala's wheel, the editor laughed, and reminded them of the blow the Arabs had at the turn of the goal."

" And what of the Athenian ? "

" He is dead."

" Dead ! " cried Ben-Hur.

" Dead ! " echoed Ilderim. " What fortune these Roman monsters have ! Messala escaped ? "

" Escaped—yes, O sheik, with life ; but it shall be a burden to him. The physicians say he will live, but never walk again."

Ben-Hur looked silently up to heaven. He had a vision of Messala, chair-bound like Simonides, and, like him, going abroad on the shoulders of servants. The good man had abode well ; but what would this one with his pride and ambition ?

" Simonides bade me say, further," Malluch continued, " Sanballat is having trouble. Drusus, and those who signed with him, referred the question of paying the five talents they lost to the Consul Maxentius, and he has referred it to Cæsar. Messala also refused his losses, and Sanballat, in imitation of Drusus, went to the consul, where the matter is still in advisement. The better Romans say the protestants shall not be excused; and all the adverse factions join with them. The city rings with the scandal."

" What says Simonides ? " asked Ben-Hur.

" The master laughs, and is well pleased. If the Roman pays, he is ruined ; if he refuses to pay, he is dishonoured. The imperial policy will decide the matter. To offend the East would be a bad beginning with the Parthians ; to offend Sheik Ilderim would be to antagonize the desert, over which lie all Maxentius's lines of operation. Wherefore Simonides bade me tell you to have no disquiet ; Messala will pay."

Ilderim was at once restored to his good-humour.

" Let us be off now," he said, rubbing his hands. " The business will do well with Simonides. The glory is ours. I will order the horses."

"Stay," said Malluch. "I left a messenger outside. Will you see him?"

"By the splendour of God! I forgot him."

Malluch retired, and was succeeded by a lad of gentle manners and delicate appearance, who knelt upon one knee, and said, winningly, "Iras, the daughter of Balthasar, well known to good Sheik Ilderim, prays the good Sheik Ilderim to send word to the youth Ben-Hur that her father hath taken residence for a time in the palace of Idernee, where she will receive the youth after the fourth hour to-morrow."

The sheik looked at Ben-Hur, whose face was suffused with pleasure.

"What will you?" he asked.

"By your leave, O sheik, I will see the fair Egyptian."

Ilderim laughed, and said, "Shall not a man enjoy his youth?"

Then Ben-Hur answered the messenger:

"Say to her who sent you that I, Ben-Hur, will see her at the palace of Idernee, wherever that may be, to-morrow at noon."

The lad arose, and, with silent salute, departed.

At midnight Ilderim took the road, having arranged to leave a horse and a guide for Ben-Hur, who was to follow him.

CHAPTER XIV

GOING next day to fill his appointment with Iras, Ben-Hur turned from the Omphalus, which was in the heart of the city, into the Colonnade of Herod, and came shortly to the palace of Idernee.

Having passed through the vestibule he entered a passage which brought him to a closed door, in front of which he paused; and, as he did so, the broad leaves began to open of themselves, without creak or sound of lock or latch, or touch of foot or finger. The singularity was lost in the view that broke upon him.

Standing in the shade of the dull passage, and looking through the doorway, he beheld the atrium of a Roman house, roomy and rich to a fabulous degree of magnificence.

How large the chamber was cannot be stated, because of the deceit there is in exact proportions ; its depth was vista-like, something never to be said of an equal interior.

Ben-Hur sauntered about, charmed by all he beheld, and waiting. He did not mind a little delay ; when Iras was ready, she would come or send a servant. In every well-regulated Roman house the atrium was the reception chamber for visitors.

Twice, thrice, he made the round. He listened, but there was not a sound ; the palace was still as a tomb.

There might be a mistake. No, the messenger had come from the Egyptian, and this was the palace of Idernee. Then he remembered how mysteriously the door had opened, so soundlessly, so of itself. He would see !

He went to the same door. Though he walked ever so lightly, the sound of his stepping was loud and harsh, and he shrank from it. He was getting nervous. The cumbrous Roman lock resisted his first effort to raise it ; and the second—the blood chilled in his cheeks—he wrenched with all his might : in vain—the door was not even shaken. A sense of danger seized him, and for a moment he stood irresolute.

Who in Antioch had the motive to do him harm ?

Messala !

And this palace of Idernee ? He had seen Egypt in the vestibule, Athens in the snowy portico ; but here, in the atrium, was Rome ; everything about him betrayed Roman ownership.

There were many doors on the right and left of the atrium, leading, doubtless, to sleeping-chambers ; he tried them, but they were all firmly fastened. Knocking might bring response. Ashamed to make outcry, he betook himself to a couch, and, lying down, tried to reflect.

All too plainly he was a prisoner ; but for what purpose ? and by whom ?

Half an hour passed—a much longer period to Ben-Hur—when the door which had admitted him opened and closed noiselessly as before, and without attracting his attention.

The moment of the occurrence he was sitting at the farther end of the room. A footstep startled him.

"At last she has come!" he thought, with a throb of relief and pleasure, and arose.

The step was heavy, and accompanied with the gride and clang of coarse sandals. The gilded pillars were between him and the door; he advanced quietly, and leaned against one of them. Presently he heard voices—the voices of men —one of them rough and guttural. What was said he could not understand, as the language was not of the East or south of Europe.

After a general survey of the room the strangers crossed to their left, and were brought into Ben-Hur's view—two men, one very stout, both tall, and both in short tunics.

The mystery surrounding his own presence in the palace tended, as we have seen, to make Ben-Hur nervous; so now, when in the tall stout stranger he recognized the Northman whom he had known in Rome, and seen crowned in the Circus there as the winning pugilist; when he saw the man's face, scarred with the wounds of many battles, and imbruted by ferocious passions; when he surveyed the fellow's naked limbs, very marvels of exercise and training, and his shoulders of Herculean breadth, a thought of personal danger started a chill along every vein. A sure instinct warned him that the opportunity for murder was too perfect to have come by chance; and here now were the myrmidons, and their business was with him. He turned an anxious eye upon the Northman's comrade— young, black-eyed, black-haired, and altogether Jewish in appearance; he observed, also, that both the men were in costume exactly such as professionals of their class were in the habit of wearing in the arena. Putting the several circumstances together, Ben-Hur could not be longer in doubt; he had been lured into the palace with design. Out of reach of aid, in this splendid privacy, he was to die!

He undid the sash around his waist, and, baring his head and casting off his white Jewish gown, stood forth in an under-tunic not unlike those of the enemy, and was ready, body and mind. Folding his arms, he placed his back against the pillar, and calmly waited.

They advanced towards him.

"Hold!" said Ben-Hur, quitting the pillar. "One word."

They stopped.

"A word!" replied the Saxon, folding his immense arms across his breast, and relaxing the menace beginning to blacken his face. "A word! Speak."

"You came here to kill me."

"That is true."

"Then let this man fight me singly, and I will make the proof on his body."

A gleam of humour shone in the Northman's face. He spoke to his companion, who made answer; then he replied with the *naiveté* of a diverted child:

"Wait till I say begin."

By repeated touches of his foot, he pushed a couch out on the floor and proceeded leisurely to stretch his burly form upon it; when perfectly at ease, he said simply, "Now begin."

Without ado, Ben-Hur walked to his antagonist.

"Defend thyself," he said.

The man, nothing loth, put up his hands.

As the two thus confronted each other in approved position, there was no discernible inequality between them; on the contrary, they were as like as brothers. To the stranger's confident smile Ben-Hur opposed an earnestness which, had his skill been known, would have been accepted fair warning of danger. Both knew the combat was to be mortal.

Ben-Hur feinted with his right hand. The stranger warded, slightly advancing his left arm. Ere he could return to guard, Ben-Hur caught him by the wrist in a grip which years at the oar had made terrible as a vice. The surprise was complete, and no time given. To throw himself forward; to push the arm across the man's throat and over his right shoulder, and turn him left side front; to strike surely with the ready left hand; to strike the bare neck under the ear—were but petty divisions of the same act. No need of a second blow. The myrmidon fell heavily, and without a cry, and lay still.

Ben-Hur turned to the Northman, Thord by name.

"Ha! What! By the beard of Irmin!" the latter cried, in astonishment, rising to a sitting posture. Then he laughed.

"Ha, ha, ha! I could not have done it better myself."

He viewed Ben-Hur coolly from head to foot, and, rising, faced him with undisguised admiration.

"It was my trick—the trick I have practised for ten years in the schools of Rome. You are not a Jew. Who are you?"

"You knew Arrius the duumvir."

"Quintus Arrius? Yes, he was my patron."

"He had a son."

"Yes," said Thord, his battered features lighting dully, "I knew the boy; he would have made a king gladiator. Cæsar offered him his patronage. I taught him the very trick you played on this one here—a trick impossible except to a hand or arm like mine. It has won me many a crown."

"I am that son of Arrius."

Thord drew nearer, and viewed him carefully; then his eyes brightened with genuine pleasure, and, laughing, he held out his hand.

"Ha, ha, ha! He told me I would find a Jew here—a Jew—a dog of a Jew—killing whom was serving the gods."

"Who told you so?" asked Ben-Hur, taking the hand.

"He—Messala—ha, ha, ha!"

"When, Thord?"

"Last night."

"I thought he was hurt."

"He will never walk again. On his bed he told me between groans."

A light came to Ben-Hur, and he asked, "Thord, what was Messala to give you for killing me?"

"A thousand sestertii."

"You shall have them yet; and so you do now what I tell you, I will add three thousand more to the sum."

The giant reflected aloud.

"Give me four, good Arrius—four more—and I will stand firm for you, though old Thor, my namesake, strike me with his hammer. Make it four, and I will kill the

lying patrician if you say so. I have only to cover his
mouth with my hand—thus."

He illustrated the process by clapping his hand over his
own mouth.

" I will make it four thousand," Ben-Hur continued ;
" and in what you shall do for the money there will be no
blood on your hands, Thord. Hear me now. Did not
your friend here look like me ? "

" I would have said he was an apple from the same tree."

" Well, if I put on this tunic, and dress him in these
clothes of mine, and you and I go away together, leaving
him here, can you not get your sestertii from Messala all the
same ? You have only to make him believe it me that is
dead."

Thord laughed till the tears ran into his mouth.

" Ha, ha, ha ! five thousand sestertii were never won so
easily. And a wine-shop by the Great Circus !—all for a
lie without blood in it !—Ha, ha, ha ! Give me thy hand, O
son of Arrius. Get on now, and—ha, ha, ha !—if ever you
come to Rome, fail not to ask for the wine-shop of Thord
the Northman. By the beard of Irmin, I will give you the
best, though I borrow it from Cæsar ! "

They shook hands again ; after which the exchange of
clothes was effected. It was arranged then that a messenger
should go at night to Thord's lodging-place with the four
thousand sestertii. When they were done, the giant
knocked at the front door ; it opened to him ; and, passing
out of the atrium, he led Ben-Hur into a room adjoining,
where the latter completed his attire from the coarse garments of the dead pugilist. They separated directly in the
Omphalus.

" Fail not, O son of Arrius, fail not the wine-shop near
the Great Circus ! Ha, ha, ha ! By the beard of Irmin,
there was never fortune gained so cheap. The gods keep
you ! "

Upon leaving the atrium, Ben-Hur gave a last look at the
myrmidon as he lay in the Jewish vestments, and was
satisfied. The likeness was striking. If Thord kept faith,
the cheat was a secret to endure for ever.

*　　　*　　　*　　　*　　　*

At night, in the house of Simonides, Ben-Hur told the good man all that had taken place in the palace of Idernee; and it was agreed that, after a few days, public inquiry should be set afloat for the discovery of the whereabouts of the son of Arrius. Eventually the matter was to be carried boldly to Maxentius; then, if the mystery came not out, it was concluded that Messala and Gratus would be at rest and happy, and Ben-Hur free to betake himself to Jerusalem, to make search for his lost people.

At the leave-taking, Simonides sat in his chair out on the terrace overlooking the river, and gave his farewell and the peace of the Lord with the impressment of a father. Esther went with the young man to the head of the steps.

"If I find my mother, Esther, thou shalt go to her at Jerusalem, and be a sister to Tirzah."

And with the words he kissed her.

Was it only a kiss of peace?

He crossed the river next to the late quarters of Ilderim, where he found the Arab who was to serve him as guide. The horses were brought out.

"This one is thine," said the Arab.

Ben-Hur looked, and, lo! it was Aldebaran, the swiftest and brightest of the sons of Mira, and, next to Sirius, the beloved of the sheik; and he knew the old man's heart came to him along with the gift.

The corpse in the atrium was taken up and buried by night; and, as part of Messala's plan, a courier was sent off to Gratus to make him at rest by the announcement of Ben-Hur's death—this time past question.

Ere long a wine-shop was opened near the Circus Maximus, with inscription over the door:

THORD THE NORTHMAN.

BOOK SIXTH

CHAPTER I

OUR story moves forward now thirty days from the night Ben-Hur left Antioch to go out with Sheik Ilderim into the desert.

A great change has befallen—great at least as respects the fortunes of our hero. *Valerius Gratus has been succeeded by Pontius Pilate !*

The removal, it may be remarked, cost Simonides exactly five talents Roman money in hand paid to Sejanus, who was then in height of power as imperial favourite ; the object being to help Ben-Hur, by lessening his exposure while in and about Jerusalem attempting discovery of his people. To such pious use the faithful servant put the winnings from Drusus and his associates ; all of whom, having paid their wagers, became at once and naturally the enemies of Messala, whose repudiation was yet an unsettled question in Rome.

The worst of men do once in a while vary their wickednesses by good acts ; so with Pilate. He ordered an inspection of all the prisons in Judea, and a return of the names of the persons in custody, with a statement of the crimes for which they had been committed. The revelations were astonishing. Hundreds of persons were released against whom there were no accusations ; many others came to light who had long been accounted dead ; yet more amazing, there was opening of dungeons not merely unknown at the time by the people, but actually forgotten by the prison authorities. With one instance of the latter kind we have now to deal ; and, strange to say, it occurred in Jerusalem.

213

The Tower of Antonia, through the administration of Gratus, had been a garrisoned citadel and underground prison terrible to revolutionists. Woe when the cohorts poured from its gates to suppress disorder! Woe not less when a Jew passed the same gates going in under arrest!

With this explanation, we hasten to our story.

* * * * *

The order of the new procurator requiring a report of the persons in custody was received at the Tower of Antonia, and promptly executed; and two days have gone since the last unfortunate was brought up for examination. The tabulated statement, ready for forwarding, lies on the table of the tribune in command; in five minutes more it will be on the way to Pilate, sojourning in the palace upon Mount Zion.

A man appeared in a doorway leading to an adjoining apartment. He rattled a bunch of keys, each heavy as a hammer, and at once attracted the chief's attention.

"Ah, Gesius! come in," the tribune said.

As the new-comer approached the table behind which the chief sat in an easy-chair, everybody present looked at him, and, observing a certain expression of alarm and mortification on his face, became silent that they might hear what he had to say.

"O tribune!" he began. "It is now about eight years since Valerius Gratus selected me to be keeper of prisoners here in the Tower. I remember the morning I entered upon the duties of my office. There had been a riot the day before, and fighting in the streets. We slew many Jews, and suffered on our side. The affair came, it was said, of an attempt to assassinate Gratus, who had been knocked from his horse by a tile thrown from a roof. I found him sitting where you now sit, O tribune, his head swathed in bandages. He told me of my selection, and he gave me these keys, numbered to correspond with the numbers of the cells; they were the badges of my office, he said, and not to be parted with. There was a roll of parchment on the table. Calling me to him, he opened the roll. 'Here are maps of the cells,' said he. There were three of them. 'This one,' he went on, ' shows the arrangement of the upper floor ; this second one gives you the second floor ; and this last is of the lower floor. I give them to you in trust.'

" I saluted him, and turned to go away ; he called me back. ' Ah, I forgot,' he said. ' Give me the map of the third floor.' I gave it to him, and he spread it upon the table. ' Here, Gesius,' he said, ' see this cell.' He laid his finger on the one numbered V. ' There are three men confined in that cell, desperate characters, who by some means got hold of a state secret, and suffer for their curiosity, which '—he looked at me severely—' in such matters is worse than a crime. Accordingly, they are blind and tongueless, and are placed there for life. They shall have nothing but food and drink, to be given them through a hole, which you will find in the wall covered by a slide. Do you hear, Gesius ? ' I made him answer. ' It is well,' he continued. ' One thing more which you shall not forget, or——' He looked at me threateningly. ' The door of their cell— cell number V. on the same floor—this one, Gesius '— he put his finger on the particular cell to impress my memory —' shall never be opened for any purpose, neither to let one in nor out, not even yourself.' ' But if they die ? ' I asked. ' If they die,' he said, ' the cell shall be their tomb. They were put there to die, and be lost. The cell is leprous. Do you understand ? ' With that he let me go."

Gesius stopped, and from the breast of his tunic drew three parchments, all much yellowed by time and use ; selecting one of them, he spread it upon the table before the tribune, saying simply " This is the lower floor."

The whole company looked at

THE MAP.

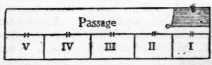

" This is exactly, O tribune, as I had it from Gratus. It is not a true map. It shows but five cells upon that floor, while there are six."

" Six, sayest thou ? "

" I will show you the floor as it is—or as I believe it to be."

Upon a page of his tablets, Gesius drew the following diagram, and gave it to the tribune:

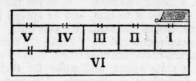

" Thou hast done well," said the tribune, examining the drawing, and thinking the narrative at an end. " I will have the map corrected, or, better, I will have a new one made, and given thee. Come for it in the morning."

So saying he arose.

" But hear me further, O tribune. Hear, and judge for yourself. I went to the door of number V. yesterday, curious to see the wretches who, against all expectation, had lived so long. The locks refused the key. We pulled a little, and the door fell down, rusted from its hinges. Going in, I found but one man, old, blind, tongueless and naked. His hair dropped in stiffened mats below his waist. His skin was like the parchment there. He held his hands out, and the finger-nails curled and twisted like the claws of a bird. I asked him where his companions were. He shook his head in denial. Thinking to find the others, we searched the cell. The floor was dry ; so were the walls. If three men had been shut in there, and two of them had died, at least their bones would have endured. The prisoner knew it, he caught my hand eagerly, and led me to a hole like that through which we were accustomed to pass him his food. Still holding my hand, he put his face to the hole and gave a beast-like cry. A sound came faintly back. I was astonished, and drew him away, and called out, ' Ho, here ! ' At first there was no answer. I called again, and received back these words, ' Be thou praised, O Lord ! ' Yet more astonishing, O tribune, the voice was a woman's. And I asked, ' Who are you ? ' and had reply, ' A woman of Israel, entombed here with her daughter. Help us quickly, or we die.' I told them to be of cheer, and hurried here to know your will."

The tribune arose hastily.

" Thou wert right, Gesius," he said, " and I see now. The map was a lie, and so was the tale of the three men. There have been better Romans than Valerius Gratus."

" Yes," said the keeper. " I gleaned from the prisoner that he had regularly given the women of the food and drink he had received."

" It is accounted for," replied the tribune, and observing the countenances of his friends, and reflecting how well it would be to have witnesses, he added, " Let us rescue the women. Come all."

Gesius was pleased.

" We will have to pierce the wall," he said. " I found where a door had been, but it was filled solidly with stones and mortar."

The tribune stayed to say to a clerk, " Send workmen after me with tools. Make haste ; but hold the report, for I see it will have to be corrected."

In a short time they were gone.

CHAPTER II

" A WOMAN of Israel, entombed here with her daughter. Help us quickly, or we die."

Such was the reply Gesius the keeper had from the cell which appears on his amended map as VI. The reader, when he observed the answer, knew who the unfortunates were, and, doubtless, said to himself, " At last the mother of Ben-Hur, and Tirzah his sister ! "

And so it was.

The morning of their seizure, eight years before, they had been carried to the Tower, where Gratus proposed to put them out of the way. He had chosen the Tower for the purpose as more immediately in his own keeping, and cell VI. because, first, it could be better lost than any other ; and, secondly, it was infected with leprosy ; for these prisoners were not merely to be put in a safe place, but in a place to die. They were, accordingly, taken down by slaves in the night-time, when there were no witnesses of the deed; then, in completion of the savage task, the same slaves walled up the door, after which they were themselves separated, and sent away never to be heard of more.

As the last step in the scheme, Gratus summarily removed the old keeper of the prisons; not because he knew what had been done—for he did not—but because, knowing the underground floor as he did, it would be next to impossible to keep the transaction from him. Then, with masterly ingenuity, the procurator had new maps drawn for delivery to a new keeper, with the omission, as we have seen, of cell VI. The instructions given the latter, taken with the omission on the map, accomplished the design—the cell and its unhappy tenants were all alike lost.

To form an adequate idea of the suffering endured by the mother of Ben-Hur, the reader must think of her spirit and its sensibilities as much as, if not more than, of the conditions of the immurement; the question being, not what the conditions were, but how she was affected by them.

In other words, let the serene, happy, luxurious life in the princely house be recalled and contrasted with this existence in the lower dungeon of the Tower of Antonia; then if the reader, in his effort to realize the misery of the woman, persists in mere reference to conditions physical, he cannot go amiss: as he is a lover of his kind, tender of heart, he will be melted with much sympathy. But will he go further; will he more than sympathize with her; will he share her agony of mind and spirit; will he at least try to measure it—let him recall her as she discoursed to her son of God and nations and heroes; one moment a philosopher, the next a teacher, and all the time a mother.

Would you hurt a man keenest, strike at his self-love; would you hurt a woman worst, aim at her affections.

With quickened remembrance of these unfortunates—remembrance of them as they were—let us go down and see them as they are.

The cell VI. was in form as Gesius drew it on his map. Of its dimensions but little idea can be had; enough that it was a roomy, roughened interior, with ledged and broken walls and floor.

The two women are grouped close by the aperture; one is seated, the other is half-reclining against her; there is nothing between them and the bare rock. The light, slanting upwards, strikes them with ghastly effect, and we cannot avoid seeing they are without vesture or covering. At the same time we are helped to the knowledge that love is there yet, for the two are in each other's arms. Riches take wings, comforts vanish, hope withers away, but love stays with us. Love is God.

Where the two are thus grouped the stony floor is polished shining-smooth. Who shall say how much of the eight years they have spent in that space there in front of the aperture, nursing their hope of rescue by that timid yet friendly ray of light? When the brightness came creeping in, they knew it was dawn; when it began to fade, they knew the world was hushing for the night, which could not be anywhere so long and utterly dark as with them.

Our recollections of them in former days enjoin us to be respectful; their sorrows clothe them with sanctity. Without going too near, across the dungeon, we see they have undergone a change of appearance not to be accounted for by time or long confinement. The mother was beautiful as a woman, the daughter beautiful as a child; not even love could say so much now. Their hair is long, unkempt, and strangely white; they make us shrink and shudder with an indefinable repulsion, though the effect may be from an illusory glozing of the light glimmering dismally through the unhealthy murk.

The mother thought she heard a sound over by the little trap in the partition-wall through which they held all their actual communication with the world. And she was not mistaken.

"Ho, there!" they heard next; and then, "Who are you?"

The voice was strange. What matter? Except from Tirzah, they were the first and only words the mother had heard in eight years. The revulsion was mighty—from death to life—and so instantly!

"A woman of Israel, entombed here with her daughter. Help us quickly, or we die."

"Be of cheer. I will return."

The women sobbed aloud. They were found; help was coming. From wish to wish hope flew as the twittering swallows fly. They were found; they would be released. And restoration would follow—restoration to all they had lost —home, society, property, son and brother! The scanty light glozed them with the glory of day, and, forgetful of pain and thirst and hunger, and of the menace of death, they sank upon the floor and cried, keeping fast hold of each other the while.

And this time they had not long to wait. Gesius, the keeper, told his tale methodically, but finished it at last. The tribune was prompt.

"Within there!" he shouted through the trap.

"Here!" said the mother, rising.

Directly she heard another sound in another place, as of blows on the wall—blows quick, ringing, and delivered with iron tools. She did not speak, nor did Tirzah, but they listened, well knowing the meaning of it all—that a way to liberty was being made for them. So men a long time buried in deep mines hear the coming of rescuers, heralded by thrust of bar and beat of pick, and answer gratefully with heart-throbs, their eyes fixed upon the spot whence the sounds proceed; and they cannot look away, lest the work should cease, and they be returned to despair.

The arms outside were strong, the hands skilful, the will good. Each instant the blows sounded more plainly; now and then a piece fell with a crash; and liberty came nearer and nearer. Presently the workmen could be heard speaking. Then—O happiness!—through a crevice flashed a red ray of torches. Into the darkness it cut incisive as diamond brilliance, beautiful as if from a spear of the morning.

"It is he, mother, it is he! He has found us at last!" cried Tirzah, with the quickened fancy of youth.

But the mother answered meekly, "God is good!"

A block fell inside, and another—then a great mass, and the door was open. A man grimed with mortar and stone-dust stepped in, and stopped, holding a torch over his head.

Two or three others followed with torches, and stood aside for the tribune to enter.

Respect for women is not all a conventionality, for it is the best proof of their proper nature. The tribune stopped, because they fled from him—not with fear, be it said, but shame; nor yet, O reader, from shame alone! From the obscurity of their partial hiding he heard these words, the saddest, most dreadful, most utterly despairing of the human tongue:

"Come not near us—unclean, unclean!"

So the widow and mother performed her duty, and in the moment realized that the freedom she had prayed for and dreamed of, fruit of scarlet and gold seen afar, was but an apple of Sodom in the hand.

She and Tirzah were—LEPERS!

Once—she might not tell the day or the year, for down in the haunted hell even time was lost—once the mother felt a dry scurf in the palm of her right hand, a trifle which she tried to wash away. It clung to the member pertinaciously; yet she thought but little of the sign till Tirzah complained that she, too, was attacked in the same way. The supply of water was scant, and they denied themselves drink that they might use it as a curative. At length the whole hand was attacked; the skin cracked open, the finger-nails loosened from the flesh. There was not much pain withal, chiefly a steadily increasing discomfort. Later their lips began to parch and seam. One day the mother, who was cleanly to godliness, and struggled against the impurities of the dungeon with all ingenuity, thinking the enemy was taking hold on Tirzah's face, led her to the light, and, looking with the inspiration of a terrible dread, lo! the young girl's eyebrows were white as snow.

Oh, the anguish of that assurance!

Slowly, steadily, with horrible certainty, the disease spread, after a while bleaching their heads white, eating holes in their lips and eyelids, and covering their bodies with scales; then it fell to their throats, shrilling their voices, and to their joints, hardening the tissues and cartilages—slowly, and, as the mother well knew, past remedy, it was affecting their lungs and arteries and bones, at each advance making the sufferers more and more loathsome ; and so it would continue till death, which might be years before them.

Another day of dread at length came—the day the mother, under impulsion of duty, at last told Tirzah the name of their ailment ; and the two, in agony of despair, prayed that the end might come quickly.

Still, as is the force of habit, these so afflicted grew in time not merely to speak composedly of their disease ; they beheld the hideous transformation of their persons as of course, and in despite clung to existence. One tie to earth remained to them ; unmindful of their own loneliness, they kept up a certain spirit by talking and dreaming of Ben-Hur. The mother promised reunion with him to the sister, and she to the mother, not doubting, either of them, that he was equally faithful to them, and would be equally happy of the meeting. And with the spinning and respinning of this slender thread they found pleasure, and excused their not dying. In such manner as we have seen, they were solacing themselves the moment Gesius called them, at the end of twelve hours' fasting and thirst.

The torches flashed redly through the dungeon, and liberty was come. " God is good," the widow cried—not for what had been, O reader, but for what was. In thankfulness for present mercy, nothing so becomes us as losing sight of past ills.

The tribune came directly; then in the corner to which she had fled, suddenly a sense of duty smote the elder of the women, and straightway the awful warning :

" Unclean, unclean ! "

The tribune heard it with a tremor, but kept his place.

" Give me thy story, woman—thy name, and when thou wert put here, and by whom, and for what."

" There was once in this city of Jerusalem a Prince Ben-Hur, the friend of all generous Romans, and who had Cæsar for his friend. I am his widow, and this one with me is his child. How may I tell you for what we were sunk here when I do not know, unless it was because we were rich ? Valerius Gratus can tell you who our enemy was, and when our imprisonment began. I cannot. See to what we have been reduced—oh, see, and have pity ! "

The air was heavy with the pest, and the smoke of the torches, yet the Roman called one of the torch-bearers to his side, and wrote the answer nearly word for word. It was terse and comprehensive, containing at once a history, an accusation, and a prayer. No common person could have made it, and he could not but pity and believe.

"Thou shalt have relief, woman," he said, closing the tablets. "I will send thee food and drink."

"And raiment, and purifying water, we pray you, O generous Roman ! "

"As thou wilt," he replied.

"God is good," said the widow, sobbing. "May His peace abide with you ! "

"And, further," he added, "I cannot see thee again. Make preparation, and to-night I will have thee taken to the gate of the Tower, and set free. Thou knowest the law. Farewell."

He spoke to the men, and went out the door.

Very shortly some slaves came to the cell with a large gurglet of water, a basin and napkins, a platter with bread and meat, and some garments of women's wear ; and, setting them down within reach of the prisoners, they ran away.

About the middle of the first watch, the two were conducted to the gate, and turned into the street. So the Roman quit himself of them, and in the city of their fathers they were once more free.

Up to the stars, twinkling merrily as of old, they looked ; then they asked themselves :

"What next ? and where to ? "

CHAPTER III

About the hour Gesius, the keeper, made his appearance before the tribune in the Tower of Antonia, a footman was climbing the eastern face of Mount Olivet. On the summit —to reach which he bent his steps somewhat right of the beaten path—he came to a dead stop, arrested as if by a strong hand. Then one might have seen his eyes dilate, his cheeks flush, his breath quicken, effects all of one bright sweeping glance at what lay before him.

The traveller, good reader, was no other than Ben-Hur; the spectacle, Jerusalem.

Not the Holy City of to-day, but the Holy City as left by Herod—the Holy City of the Christ. Beautiful yet, as seen from old Olivet, what must it have been then?

Ben-Hur betook him to a stone and sat down, and, stripping his head of the close white handkerchief which served it for covering, made the survey at leisure.

Probably no one has taken that view with sensations more keenly poignant, more sadly sweet, more proudly bitter, than Ben-Hur. He was stirred by recollections of his countrymen, their triumphs and vicissitudes, their history the history of God.

A country of hills changes but little; where the hills are, of rock, it changes not at all. The scene Ben-Hur beheld is the same now, except as respects the city. The failure is in the handiwork of man alone.

The sun dealt more kindly by the west side of Olivet than by the east, and men were certainly more loving towards it. The vines with which it was partially clad, and the sprinkling of trees, chiefly figs and old wild olives, were comparatively green. Down to the dry bed of the Kedron the verdure extended, a refreshment to the vision; there Olivet ceased and Moriah began—a wall of bluff boldness, white as snow, founded by Solomon, completed by Herod. Up, up the wall the eye climbed course by course of the ponderous rocks composing it—up to Solomon's Porch, which was as the pedestal of the monument, the hill being the plinth. Lingering there a moment, the eye resumed its climbing, going next to the Gentiles' Court, then to the Israelites' Court, then to the Women's Court, then to the Court of the Priests, each a pillared tier of white marble, one above the other in terraced retrocession; over them all a crown of crowns infinitely sacred, infinitely beautiful, majestic in proportions, effulgent with beaten gold—lo! the Tent, the Tabernacle, the Holy of Holies. The Ark was not there, but Jehovah was—in the faith of every child of Israel He was there a personal Presence. As a temple, as a monument, there was nowhere anything of man's building to approach that superlative apparition.

And still Ben-Hur's eyes climbed on and up—up over the roof of the Temple, to the hill Zion, consecrated to sacred memories, inseparable from the anointed kings. He knew the Cheesemonger's Valley dipped deep down between Moriah and Zion; that it was spanned by the Xystus; that there were gardens and palaces in its depths; but over them all his thoughts soared with his vision to the great grouping on the royal hill—the house of Caiaphas, the Central Synagogue, the Roman Prætorium, Hippicus the eternal, and the sad but mighty cenotaphs Phasælus and Mariamne—all relieved against Gareb, purpling in the distance. And when midst them he singled out the palace of Herod, what could he but think of the King who was coming, to whom he was himself devoted, whose path he had undertaken to smooth, whose empty hands he dreamed of filling? And forward ran his fancy to the day the new King should come to claim His own and take possession of it—of Moriah and its Temple; of Zion and its towers and palaces; of Antonia, frowning darkly there just to the right of the Temple; of the new unwalled city of Bezetha; of the millions of Israel to assemble with palm-branches and banners, to sing rejoicing because the Lord had conquered and given them the world.

The sun stooped low in its course. Awhile the flaring disc seemed to perch itself on the far summit of the mountains in the west, brazening all the sky above the city, and rimming the walls and towers with the brightness of gold. Then it disappeared as with a plunge. The quiet turned Ben-Hur's thought homeward. There was a point in the sky a little north of the peerless front of the Holy of Holies upon which he fixed his gaze; under it, straight as a lead-line would have dropped, lay his father's house, if yet the house endured.

Out in the desert while with Ilderim, looking for strong places and acquainting himself with it generally, as a soldier studies a country in which he has projected a campaign, a messenger came one evening with the news that Gratus was removed, and Pontius Pilate sent to take his place.

P

Messala was disabled and believed him dead; Gratus was powerless and gone; why should Ben-Hur longer defer the search for his mother and sister? There was nothing to fear now. If he could not himself see into the prisons of Judea, he could examine them with the eyes of others. If the lost were found, Pilate could have no motive in holding them in custody—none, at least, which could not be overcome by purchase. If found, he would carry them to a place of safety, and then, in calmer mind, his conscience at rest, this one first duty done, he could give himself more entirely to the King who was coming. He resolved at once. That night he counselled with Ilderim, and obtained his assent. Three Arabs came with him to Jericho, where he left them and the horses, and proceeded alone and on foot. Malluch was to meet him in Jerusalem.

Ben-Hur's scheme, be it observed, was as yet a generality.

In view of the future, it was advisable to keep himself in hiding from the authorities, particularly the Romans. Malluch was shrewd and trusty; the very man to charge with the conduct of the investigation.

Where to begin was the first point. He had no clear idea about it. His wish was to commence with the Tower of Antonia.

Under this inclination, moreover, there was a hope which he could not forego. From Simonides he knew Amrah, the Egyptian nurse, was living. It will be remembered, doubtless, that the faithful creature, the morning the calamity overtook the Hurs, broke from the guard and ran back into the palace, where, along with other chattels, she had been sealed up. During the years following, Simonides kept her supplied; so she was there now, sole occupant of the great house, which, with all his offers, Gratus had not been able to sell. The story of its rightful owners sufficed to secure the property from strangers, whether purchasers or mere occupants. People going to and fro passed it with whispers. Its reputation was that of a haunted house; derived probably from the infrequent glimpses of poor old Amrah, sometimes on the roof, sometimes in a latticed window. Certainly no more constant spirit ever abided than she; nor was there ever a tenement so shunned and fitted for ghostly habitation. Now, if he could get to her, Ben-Hur fancied she could help him to knowledge which, though faint, might yet be serviceable. Anyhow, sight of her in that place, so endeared by recollection, would be to him a pleasure next to finding the objects of his solicitude.

So, first of all things, he would go to the old house, and look for Amrah.

Thus resolved, he arose shortly after the going-down of the sun, and began descent of the Mount by the road which, from the summit, bends a little north of east. Down nearly at the foot, close by the bed of the Kedron, he came to the intersection with the road leading south to the village of Siloam and the pool of that name. There he fell in with a herdsman driving some sheep to market. He spoke to the man, and joined him, and in his company passed by Gethsemane on into the city through the Fish Gate.

CHAPTER IV

It was dark when, parting with the drover inside the gate, Ben-Hur turned into a narrow lane leading to the south.

Over in Bezetha he knew there was a khan, where it was his intention to seek lodging while in the city; but just now he could not resist the impulse to go home. His heart drew him that way.

The old formal salutation which he received from the few people who passed him had never sounded so pleasantly. Presently, all the eastern sky began to silver and shine, and objects before invisible in the west—chiefly the tall towers on Mount Zion—emerged as from a shadowy depth, and put on spectral distinctness, floating, as it were, above the yawning blackness of the valley below, very castles in the air.

He came, at length, to his father's house.

At the gate on the north side of the old house Ben-Hur stopped. In the corners the wax used in the sealing-up was still plainly seen, and across the valves was the board with the inscription—

" THIS IS THE PROPERTY OF
THE EMPEROR."

Nobody had gone in or out the gate since the dreadful day of the separation. Should he knock as of old ? It was useless, he knew ; yet he could not resist the temptation. Amrah might hear, and look out of one of the windows on that side. Taking a stone, he mounted the broad stone step, and tapped three times. A dull echo replied. He tried again, louder than before ; and again, pausing each time to listen. The silence was mocking. Retiring into the street, he watched the windows ; but they, too, were lifeless. The parapet on the roof was defined sharply against the brightening sky ; nothing could have stirred upon it unseen by him, and nothing did stir.

From the north side he passed to the west, where there were four windows which he watched long and anxiously, but with as little effect. At times his heart swelled with impotent wishes ; at others, he trembled at the deceptions of his own fancy. Amrah made no sign—not even a ghost stirred.

Silently, then, he stole round to the south. There, too, the gate was sealed and inscribed. The mellow splendour of the August moon, pouring over the crest of Olivet, since termed the Mount of Offence, brought the lettering boldly out ; and he read, and was filled with rage. All he could do was to wrench the board from its nailing, and hurl it into the ditch. Then he sat upon the step, and prayed for the New King, and that His coming might be hastened. As his blood cooled, insensibly he yielded to the fatigue of long travel in the summer heat, and sank down lower, and, at last, slept.

About that time two women came down the street from the direction of the Tower of Antonia, approaching the palace of the Hurs. They advanced stealthily, with timid steps, pausing often to listen. At the corner of the rugged pile, one said to the other, in a low voice :
" This is it, Tirzah ! "
And Tirzah, after a look, caught her mother's hand, and leaned upon her heavily, sobbing, but silent.

" Let us go on, my child, because "—the mother hesitated and trembled ; then, with an effort to be calm, continued—" because when morning comes they will put us
out of the gate of the city to—return no more."

She caught Tirzah's hand as she spoke, and hastened to
the west corner of the house, keeping close to the wall.   No
one being in sight there, they kept on to the next corner, and
shrank from the moonlight, which lay exceedingly bright
over the whole south front, and along a part of the street.
The mother's will was strong.   Casting one look back and
up to the windows on the west side, she stepped out into
the light, drawing Tirzah after her.

" Hist ! " said the mother.   " There is some one lying
upon the step—a man.   Let us go round him.   He is asleep,
Tirzah ! "

That moment the man sighed, and, turning restlessly,
shifted the handkerchief on his head in such manner that
the face was left upturned and fair in the broad moonlight.
She looked down at it and started ; then looked again, stooping a little, and arose and clasped her hands and raised her
eyes to heaven in mute appeal.   An instant so, and she
ran back to Tirzah.

" As the Lord liveth, the man is my son—thy brother ! "
she said, in an awe-inspiring whisper.

" My brother ?—Judah ? "

One of his hands was lying out upon the step palm up.
Tirzah fell upon her knees, and would have kissed it ; but
the mother drew her back.

" Not for thy life ; not for thy life !   Unclean, unclean ! "
she whispered.

Tirzah shrank from him, as if he were the leprous one.

Ben-Hur was handsome as the manly are.   His cheeks
and forehead were swarthy from exposure to the desert
sun and air ; yet under the light moustache the lips were
red, and the teeth shone white, and the soft beard did not
hide the full roundness of chin and throat.   How beautiful
he appeared to the mother's eyes !   How mightily she
yearned to put her arms about him, and take his head upon
her bosom and kiss him, as had been her wont in his happy
childhood !

Tirzah stared wistfully. The mother put her face in the dust, struggling to suppress a sob so deep and strong it seemed her heart was bursting. Almost she wished he might waken.

Presently the mother beckoned to Tirzah, and they arose, and taking one more look, as if to print his image past fading, hand in hand they recrossed the street. Back in the shade of the wall there, they retired and knelt, looking at him, waiting for him to wake—waiting some revelation, they knew not what. Nobody has yet given us a measure for the patience of a love like theirs.

By and by, the sleep being yet upon him, another woman, appeared at the corner of the palace. The two in the shade saw her plainly in the light: a small figure, much bent, dark-skinned, grey-haired, dressed neatly in servant's garb, and carrying a basket full of vegetables.

At sight of the man upon the step the new-comer stopped; then, as if decided, she walked on—very lightly as she drew near the sleeper. Passing round him, she went to the gate, slid the wicket latch easily to one side, and put her hand in the opening. One of the broad boards in the left valve swung ajar without noise. She put the basket through, and was about to follow, when, yielding to curiosity, she lingered to have one look at the stranger, whose face was below her in open view.

The spectators across the street heard a low exclamation, and saw the woman rub her eyes as if to renew their power, bend closer down, clasp her hands, gaze wildly around, look at the sleeper, stoop and raise the outlying hand, and kiss it fondly—that which they wished so mightily to do, but dared not.

Awakened by the action, Ben-Hur instinctively withdrew the hand; and as he did so, his eyes met the woman's.

"Amrah! O Amrah, is it thou?" he said.

The good heart made no answer in words, but fell upon his neck, crying for joy.

Gently he put her arms away, and lifting the dark face wet with tears, kissed it, his joy only a little less than hers. Then those across the way heard him say:

"Mother—Tirzah—O Amrah, tell me of them! Speak, speak, I pray thee!"

Amrah only cried afresh.

"Thou hast seen them, Amrah. Thou knowest where they are; tell me they are at home."

Tirzah moved, but the mother, divining her purpose, caught her and whispered, "Do not go—not for life. Unclean, unclean!"

Her love was in tyrannical mood. Though both their hearts broke, he should not become what they were; and she conquered.

Meantime Amrah, so entreated, only wept the more.

"Wert thou going in?" he asked presently, seeing the board swung back. "Come then. I will go with thee." He arose as he spoke. "The Romans—be the curse of the Lord upon them!—the Romans lied. The house is mine. Rise, Amrah, and let us go in."

A moment and they were gone, leaving the two in the shade to behold the gate staring blankly at them—the gate which they might not ever enter more. They nestled together in the dust.

They had done their duty.

Their love was proven.

Next morning they were found, and driven out the city with stones.

"Begone! Ye are of the dead; go to the dead!"

With the doom ringing in their ears, they went forth.

CHAPTER V

THE second morning after the incidents of the preceding chapter, Amrah drew near the well En-rogel, and seated herself upon a stone. One familiar with Jerusalem, looking at her, would have said she was a favourite servant of some well-to-do family. She brought with her a water-jar and a basket, the contents of the latter covered with a snow-white napkin. Placing them on the ground at her side, she loosened the shawl which fell from her head, knit her fingers together in her lap, and gazed demurely up to where the hill drops steeply down into Aceldama and the Potter's Field.

It was very early, and she was the first to arrive at the well.

The sun made its appearance, yet she sat watching and waiting ; and while she thus waits, let us see what her purpose is.

Her custom had been to go to market after nightfall. Stealing out unobserved, she would seek the shops in the Tyropœon, or those over by the Fish Gate in the east, make her purchases of meat and vegetables, and return and shut herself up again.

The next night, after her meeting with Ben-Hur, she stole out with her basket, and went over to the Fish Gate Market as usual. Wandering about, seeking the best honey, she chanced to hear a man telling a story.

What the story was the reader can arrive at with sufficient certainty when told that the narrator was one of the men who had held torches for the commandant of the tower of Antonia when, down in cell VI., the Hurs were found. The particulars of the finding were all told, and she heard them, with the names of the prisoners, and the widow's account of herself.

The feelings with which Amrah listened to the recital were such as became the devoted creature she was. She made her purchases, and returned home in a dream. What a happiness she had in store for her boy ! She had found his mother !

She put the basket away, now laughing, now crying. Suddenly she stopped and thought. It would kill him to be told that his mother and Tirzah were lepers. He would go through the awful city over on the Hill of Evil Counsel— into each infected tomb he would go without rest, asking for them, and the disease would catch him, and their fate would be his. She wrung her hands. What should she do ?

Like many a one before her, and many a one since, she derived inspiration, if not wisdom, from her affection, and came to a singular conclusion.

The lepers, she knew, were accustomed of mornings to come down from their sepulchral abodes in the hill, and

take a supply of water for the day from the well En-rogel.
Bringing their jars, they would set them on the ground and
wait, standing afar until they were filled. To that the
mistress and Tirzah must come ; for the law was inexor-
able, and admitted no distinction. A rich leper was no
better than a poor one.

So Amrah decided not to speak to Ben-Hur of the story
she had heard, but go alone to the well and wait. Hunger
and thirst would drive the unfortunates thither, and she
believed she could recognize them at sight ; if not, they
might recognize her.

Meantime Ben-Hur came, and they talked much. To-
morrow Malluch would arrive ; then the search should be
immediately begun. He was impatient to be about it. To
amuse himself he would visit the sacred places in the vicinity.

When he was gone she busied herself in the preparation
of things good to eat, applying her utmost skill to the work.
At the approach of day, as signalled by the stars, she filled
the basket, selected a jar, and took the road to En-rogel,
going out by the Fish Gate, which was earliest open, and
arriving as we have seen.

Shortly after sunrise, when business at the well was most
pressing, and the drawer of water most hurried ; when, in
fact, half a dozen buckets were in use at the same time,
everybody making haste to get away before the cool of the
morning melted into the heat of the day, the tenantry of
the hill began to appear and move about the doors of their
tombs. Somewhat later they were discernible in groups,
of which not a few were children so young that they suggested the holiest relation. Numbers came momentarily
around the turn of the bluff—women with jars upon their
shoulders, old and very feeble men hobbling along on staffs
and crutches. Some leaned upon the shoulders of others ;
a few—the utterly helpless—lay, like heaps of rags, upon
litters. Even that community of superlative sorrow had its
love-light to make life endurable and attractive. Distance
softened without entirely veiling the misery of the outcasts.

From her seat by the well Amrah kept watch upon the
spectral groups. She scarcely moved. More than once she
imagined she saw those she sought. That they were there

upon the hill she had no doubt; that they must come down and near she knew; when the people at the well were all served they would come.

Now, quite at the base of the bluff there was a tomb which had more than once attracted Amrah by its wide gaping. A stone of large dimensions stood near its mouth. The sun looked into it, through the hottest hours of the day, and altogether it seemed uninhabitable by anything living, unless, perchance, by some wild dogs returning from scavenger duty down in Gehenna. Thence, however, and greatly to her surprise, the patient Egyptian beheld two women come, one half-supporting, half-leading, the other. They were both white-haired; both looked old; but their garments were not rent, and they gazed about them as if the locality were new. The witness below thought she even saw them shrink terrified at the spectacle offered by the hideous assemblage of which they found themselves part. Slight reasons, certainly, to make her heart beat faster, and draw her attention to them exclusively; but so they did.

The two remained by the stone awhile; then they moved slowly, painfully, and with much fear towards the well, whereat several voices were raised to stop them; yet they kept on. The drawer of water picked up some pebbles, and made ready to drive them back. The company cursed them. The greater company on the hill shouted shrilly, "Unclean, unclean!"

"Surely," thought Amrah of the two, as they kept coming —"surely, they are strangers to the usage of lepers."

She arose, and went to meet them, taking the basket and jar. The alarm at the well immediately subsided.

"What a fool," said one, laughing, "what a fool to give good bread to the dead in that way!"

"And to think of her coming so far!" said another. "I would at least make them meet me at the gate."

Amrah, with better impulse, proceeded. If she should be mistaken! Her heart arose into her throat. And the farther she went the more doubtful and confused she became. Four or five yards from where they stood waiting for her she stopped.

"Amrah," said one of the lepers.

"Who are you?" she cried.

"We are they you are seeking."

Amrah fell upon her knees.

"O my mistress, my mistress! As I have made your God my God, be He praised that He has led me to you!"

And upon her knees the poor overwhelmed creature began moving forward.

"Stay, Amrah! Come not nearer. Unclean, unclean!"

The words sufficed. Amrah fell upon her face, sobbing so loud the people at the well heard her. Suddenly she arose upon her knees again.

"O my mistress, where is Tirzah?"

"Here I am, Amrah, here! Will you not bring me a little water?"

The habit of the servant renewed itself. Putting back the coarse hair fallen over her face, Amrah arose and went to the basket and uncovered it.

"See," she said, "here are bread and meat."

She would have spread the napkin upon the ground, but the mistress spoke again.

"Do not so, Amrah. Those yonder may stone you, and refuse us drink. Leave the basket with me. Take up the jar and fill it, and bring it here. We will carry them to the tomb with us. For this day you will then have rendered all the service that is lawful. Haste, Amrah."

The people under whose eyes all this had passed made way for the servant, and even helped her fill the jar, so piteous was the grief her countenance showed.

"Who are they?" a woman asked.

Amrah meekly answered, "They used to be good to me."

Raising the jar upon her shoulder, she hurried back. In forgetfulness, she would have gone to them, but the cry "Unclean, unclean! Beware!" arrested her. Placing the water by the basket, she stepped back, and stood off a little way.

"Thank you, Amrah," said the mistress, taking the articles into possession. "This is very good of you."

"Is there nothing more I can do?" asked Amrah. "I would die for you."

"Prove to me what you say, Amrah."

"I am ready."

"Then you shall not tell my son where we are or that you have seen us—only that, Amrah."

"But he is looking for you. He has come from afar to find you."

"He must not find us. He shall not become what we are. Hear, Amrah. You shall serve us as you have this day. You shall bring us the little we need—not long now—not long. You shall come every morning and evening thus, and—and "—the voice trembled, the strong will almost broke down—" and you shall tell us of him, Amrah ; but to him you shall say nothing of us. Hear you ? "

"The burden will be heavy, O my mistress, and hard to bear," said Amrah, falling upon her face.

"How much harder would it be to see him as we are," the mother answered as she gave the basket to Tirzah. "Come again this evening," she repeated, taking up the water, and starting for the tomb.

Amrah waited kneeling until they had disappeared ; then she took the road sorrowfully home.

In the evening she returned ; and thereafter it became her custom to serve them in the morning and evening, so that they wanted for nothing needful. The tomb, though ever so stony and desolate, was less cheerless than the cell in the Tower had been. Daylight gilded its door, and it was in the beautiful world. Then one can wait death with so much more faith out under the open sky.

CHAPTER VI

THE morning of the first day of the seventh month—Tishri in the Hebrew, October in English—Ben-Hur arose from his couch in the khan ill satisfied with the whole world.

Little time had been lost in consultation upon the arrival of Malluch. The latter began the search at the Tower of Antonia, and began it boldly, by a direct inquiry of the tribune commanding. He gave the officer a history of the Hurs, and all the particulars of the accident to Gratus, describing the affair as wholly without criminality. The object of the quest now, he said, was if any of the unhappy family were discovered alive to carry a petition to the feet of Cæsar, praying restitution of the estate and return to their civil rights. Such a petition, he had no doubt, would result in an investigation by the imperial order, a proceeding of which the friends of the family had no fear.

In reply the tribune stated circumstantially the discovery of the women in the Tower, and permitted a reading of the memorandum he had taken of their account of themselves ; when leave to copy it was prayed, he even permitted that.

Malluch thereupon hurried to Ben-Hur.

It were useless to attempt description of the effect the terrible story had upon the young man. The pain was not relieved by tears or passionate outcries; it was too deep for any expression.

At length he arose.

" I must look for them. They may be dying."

Malluch interposed, and finally prevailed so far as to have the management of the further attempt entrusted to him. The result was failure. And now, the morning of the first day of the seventh month, the extent of the additional information gained was that not long before two leprous women had been stoned from the Fish Gate by the authorities. A little pressing of the clue, together with some shrewd comparison of dates, led to the sad assurance that the sufferers were the Hurs, and left the old questions darker than ever. Where were they ? And what had become of them ?

Angry, hopeless, vengeful, Ben-Hur entered the court of the khan, and found it crowded with people come in during the night. While he ate his breakfast, he listened to some of them. To one party he was specially attracted. They were mostly young, stout, active, hardy men, in manner and speech provincial. In a short time he ascertained they were Galileans, in the city for various purposes, but chiefly to take part in the Feast of Trumpets, set for that day. They became to him at once objects of interest, as hailing from the region in which he hoped to find readiest support in the work he was shortly to set about.

While observing them, his mind running ahead in thought of achievements possible to a legion of such spirits disciplined after the severe Roman style, a man came into the court, his face much flushed, his eyes bright with excitement.

"They have discovered a conspiracy. Pilate's new aqueduct is to be paid for with money of the Temple."

"What, with the sacred treasure?"

They repeated the question to each other with flashing eyes.

"It is Corban—money of God. Let him touch a shekel of it if he dare!"

"Come," cried the messenger. "The procession to see Pilate is by this time across the bridge. The whole city is pouring after. We may be needed. Make haste!"

Lingering only to tighten their girdles, they said, "We are ready."

Then Ben-Hur spoke to them.

"Men of Galilee," he said, "I am a son of Judah. Will you take me in your company?"

"We may have to fight," they replied.

"Oh, then, I will not be first to run away!"

They took the retort in good humour, and the messenger said, "You seem stout enough. Come along."

Ben-Hur put off his outer garments.

When, at length, they reached the gate of the Prætorium the procession of elders and rabbis had passed in with a great following, leaving a greater crowd clamouring outside.

A centurion kept the entrance with a guard drawn up full armed under the beautiful marble battlements. The sun struck the soldiers fervidly on helm and shield; but they kept their ranks indifferent alike to its dazzle and to the mouthings of the rabble. Through the open bronze gates a current of citizens poured in, while a much lesser one poured out.

"What is going on?" one of the Galileans asked an outcomer.

"Nothing," was the reply. "The rabbis are before the door of the palace asking to see Pilate. He has refused to come out. They have sent one to tell him they will not go away till he has heard them. They are waiting."

Turning to the right, the party proceeded a short distance to a spacious square, on the west side of which stood the residence of the governor. An excited multitude filled the square. Every face was directed towards a portico built over a broad doorway which was closed. Under the portico there was another array of legionaries.

The throng was so close the friends could not well have advanced if such had been their desire; they remained therefore in the rear, observers of what was going on. About the portico they could see the high turbans of the rabbis, whose impatience communicated at times to the mass behind them; a cry was frequent to the effect, " Pilate, if thou be a governor, come forth, come forth ! "

An hour passed, and though Pilate deigned them no answer, the rabbis and crowd remained. Noon came, bringing a shower from the west, but no change in the situation, except that the multitude was larger and much noisier, and the feeling more decidedly angry.

And at last the end came. In the midst of the assemblage there was heard the sound of blows, succeeded instantly by yells of pain and rage, and a most furious commotion. The venerable men in front of the portico faced about aghast. The common people in the rear at first pushed forward; in the centre, the effort was to get out; and for a short time the pressure of opposing forces was terrible. A thousand voices made inquiry, raised all at once; as no one had time to answer, the surprise speedily became a panic.

Ben-Hur kept his senses.

" You cannot see," he said to one of the Galileans.

" No."

" I will raise you up."

He caught the man about the middle, and lifted him bodily.

" What is it ? "

" I see now," said the man. " There are some armed with clubs, and they are beating the people. They are dressed like Jews."

" Who are they ? "

" Romans, as the Lord liveth ! Romans in disguise.

Their clubs fly like flails! There, I saw a rabbi struck down—an old man! they spare nobody!"

Ben-Hur let the man down.

"Men of Galilee," he said, "it is a trick of Pilate's. Now, will you do what I say, to get even with the club-men?"

The Galilean spirit arose.

"Yes, yes!" they answered.

"Let us go back to the trees by the gate, and we may find the planting of Herod, though unlawful, has some good in it after all. Come!"

They ran back all of them fast as they could; and, by throwing their united weight upon the limbs, tore them from the trunks. In a brief time they, too, were armed. Returning, at the corner of the square they met the crowd rushing madly for the gate. Behind, the clamour continued —a medley of shrieks, groans and execrations.

"To the wall!" Ben-Hur shouted. "To the wall!— and let the herd go by!"

So, clinging to the masonry at their right hand, they escaped the might of the rush, and little by little made headway until, at last, the square was reached.

"Keep together now, and follow me!"

By this time Ben-Hur's leadership was perfect; and as he pushed into the seething mob his party closed after him in a body. And when the Romans, clubbing the people and making merry as they struck them down, came hand to hand with the Galileans, lithe of limb, eager for the fray, and equally armed, they were in turn surprised. Thus surprised and equally matched, the Romans at first retired, but finally turned their backs and fled to the portico. The impetuous Galileans would have pursued them to the steps, but Ben-Hur wisely restrained them.

"Stay, my men!" he said. "The centurion yonder is coming with the guard. They have swords and shields; we cannot fight them. We have done well; let us get back and out of the gate while we may."

They obeyed him, though slowly; for they had frequently to step over their countrymen lying where they had been felled; some writhing and groaning, some praying help, others mute as the dead. But the fallen were not all Jews. In that there was consolation.

The centurion shouted to them as they went off ; Ben-Hur laughed at him, and replied in his own tongue, " If we are dogs of Israel, you are jackals of Rome. Remain here, and we will come again."

The Galileans cheered, and laughing went on.

Outside the gate there was a multitude the like of which Ben-Hur had never seen, not even in the Circus at Antioch. The house-tops, the streets, the slope of the hill, appeared densely covered with people wailing and praying. The air was filled with their cries and imprecations.

The party were permitted to pass without challenge by the outer guard. But hardly were they out before the centurion in charge at the portico appeared, and in the gateway called to Ben-Hur.

" Ho, insolent ! Art thou a Roman or a Jew ? "

Ben-Hur answered, " I am a son of Judah, born here. What wouldst thou with me ? "

" Stay and fight."

" Singly ? "

" As thou wilt ! "

Ben-Hur laughed derisively.

" O brave Roman ! Worthy son of the bastard Roman Jove ! I have no arms."

" Thou shalt have mine," the centurion answered. " I will borrow of the guard here."

The people in hearing of the colloquy became silent ; and from them the hush spread afar. But lately Ben-Hur had beaten a Roman under the eyes of Antioch and the Farther East ; now, could he beat another one under the eyes of Jerusalem, the honour might be vastly profitable to the cause of the New King. He did not hesitate. Going frankly to the centurion, he said, " I am willing. Lend me thy sword and shield."

" And the helm and breastplate ? " asked the Roman.

" Keep them. They might not fit me."

The arms were as frankly delivered, and directly the centurion was ready. All this time the soldiers in rank close by the gate never moved ; they simply listened. As

Q

to the multitude, only when the combatants advanced to begin the fight the question sped from mouth to mouth, " Who is he ? " And no one knew.

Now the Roman supremacy in arms lay in three things— submission to discipline, the legionary formation of battle, and a peculiar use of the short sword. In combat, they never struck or cut ; from first to last they thrust—they advanced thrusting ; they retired thrusting ; and generally their aim was at the foeman's face. All this was well known to Ben-Hur. As they were about to engage he said :

" I told thee I was a son of Judah ; but I did not tell that I am lanista-taught. Defend thyself ! "

At the last word Ben-Hur closed with his antagonist. A moment, standing foot to foot, they glared at each other over the rims of their embossed shields ; then the Roman pushed forward and feinted an under-thrust. The Jew laughed at him. A thrust at the face followed. The Jew stepped lightly to the left ; quick as the thrust was, the step was quicker. Under the lifted arm of the foe he slid his shield, advancing it until the sword and sword-arm were both caught on its upper surface ; another step, this time forward and left, and the man's whole right side was offered to the point. The centurion fell heavily on his breast, clanging the pavement, and Ben-Hur had won. With his foot upon his enemy's back, he raised his shield overhead after a gladiatorial custom, and saluted the imperturbable soldiers by the gate.

When the people realized the victory they behaved like mad. On the house far as the Xystus, fast as the word could fly, they waved their shawls and handkerchiefs and shouted ; and if he had consented, the Galileans would have carried Ben-Hur off upon their shoulders.

To a petty officer who then advanced from the gate he said, " Thy comrade died like a soldier. I leave him unde-spoiled. Only his sword and shield are mine."

With that, he walked away. Off a little he spoke to the Galileans.

" Brethren, you have behaved well. Let us now separate, lest we be pursued. Meet me to-night at the khan in

Bethany. I have something to propose to you of great interest to Israel."

" Who are you ? " they asked him.

" A son of Judah," he answered simply.

A throng eager to see him surged around the party.

" Will you come to Bethany ? " he asked.

" Yes, we will come."

" Then bring with you this sword and shield that I may know you."

Pushing brusquely through the increasing crowd, he speedily disappeared.

At the instance of Pilate, the people went up from the city, and carried off their dead and wounded, and there was much mourning for them ; but the grief was greatly lightened by the victory of the unknown champion, who was everywhere sought, and by every one extolled. The fainting spirit of the nation was revived by the brave deed ; insomuch that in the streets and up in the Temple even, amidst the solemnities of the feast, old tales of the Maccabees were told again, and thousands shook their heads whispering wisely :

" A little longer, only a little longer, brethren, and Israel will come to her own. Let there be faith in the Lord, and patience."

In such manner Ben-Hur obtained hold on Galilee, and paved the way to greater services in the cause of the King who was coming.

And with what result we shall see.

BOOK SEVENTH

CHAPTER I

THE meeting took place in the khan of Bethany as appointed.
Thence Ben-Hur went with the Galileans into their country,
where his exploits up in the old Market-place gave him
fame and influence. Before the winter was gone he raised
three legions, and organized them after the Roman pattern.
He could have had as many more, for the martial spirit
of that gallant people never slept. The proceeding,
however, required careful guarding as against both Rome
and Herod Antipas. Contenting himself for the present
with the three, he strove to train and educate them for
systematic action. For that purpose he carried the officers
over into the lava-beds of Trachonitis, and taught them
the use of arms, particularly the javelin and sword, and
the manœuvring peculiar to the legionary formation ; after
which he sent them home as teachers. And soon the training became a pastime of the people. Yet withal he would
have failed but for the support he had from Simonides,
who furnished him arms and money, and from Ilderim,
who kept watch and brought him supplies. And still he
would have failed but for the genius of the Galileans.

Upon such a people, so quick, so proud, so brave, so
devoted, so imaginative, a tale like that of the coming of
the King was all-powerful. They asked Ben-Hur his
authority for the sayings, and he quoted the prophets, and
told them of Balthasar in waiting over in Antioch ; and
they were satisfied, for it was the old much-loved legend
of the Messiah, familiar to them almost as the name of the
Lord ; the long-cherished dream with a time fixed for its

realization. The King was not merely coming now; He was at hand.

So with Ben-Hur the winter months rolled by, and spring came, with gladdening showers blown over from the summering seas in the west; and by that time so earnestly and successfully had he toiled that he could say to himself and his followers, " Let the good King come. He has only to tell us where He will have His throne set up. We have the sword-hands to keep it for Him."

And in all his dealings with the many men they knew him only as a son of Judah, and by that name.

* * * * *

One evening, over in Trachonitis, Ben-Hur was sitting with some of his Galileans at the mouth of the cave in which he quartered, when an Arab courier rode to him, and delivered a letter. Breaking the package, he read:

" JERUSALEM, *Nisan IV*.

" A prophet has appeared who men say is Elias. He has been in the wilderness for years, and to our eyes he is a prophet; and such also is his speech, the burden of which is of one much greater than himself, Who, he says, is to come presently, and for whom he is now waiting on the eastern shore of the river Jordan. I have been to see and hear him, and the One he is waiting for is certainly the King you are awaiting. Come and judge for yourself.

" All Jerusalem is going out to the prophet, and with many people else; the shore on which he abides is like Mount Olivet in the last days of the Passover.

" MALLUCH."

Ben-Hur's face flushed with joy.

" By this word, O my friends," he said—" by this word, our waiting is at end. The herald of the King has appeared and announced Him."

Upon hearing the letter read, they also rejoiced at the promise it held out.

" Get ready now," he added, " and in the morning set your faces homeward; when arrived there, send word to those under you, and bid them be ready to assemble as I may direct. For myself and you, I will go see if the King be indeed at hand, and send you report. Let us, in the meantime, live in the pleasure of the promise."

Going into the cave, he addressed a letter to Ilderim, and another to Simonides, giving notice of the news received, and of his purpose to go up immediately to Jerusalem. The letters he dispatched by swift messengers. When night fell, and the stars of direction came out, he mounted, and with an Arab guide set out for the Jordan, intending to strike the track of the caravans between Rabbath-Ammon and Damascus.

The guide was sure, and Aldebaran swift ; so by midnight the two were out of the lava fastness speeding southward.

CHAPTER II

It was Ben-Hur's purpose to turn aside at the break of day, and find a safe place in which to rest ; but the dawn overtook him while out in the desert, and he kept on, the guide promising to bring him afterwhile to a vale shut in by great rocks, where there were a spring, some mulberry-trees, and herbage in plenty for the horses.

As he rode thinking of the wondrous events so soon to happen, and of the changes they were to bring about in the affairs of men and nations, the guide, ever on the alert, called attention to an appearance of strangers behind them.

" It is a camel with riders," the guide said, directly.

The long swinging stride of the camel brought its riders up to him. The tall brute stopped close by his horse, and Ben-Hur looking up, lo ! Iras herself under the raised curtain looking down at him, her great swimming eyes bright with astonishment and inquiry.

" The blessing of the true God upon you ! " said Balthasar, in his tremulous voice.

" And to thee and thine be the peace of the Lord," Ben-Hur replied.

" My eyes are weak with years," said Balthasar ; " but they approve you that son of Hur whom lately I knew an honoured guest in the tent of Ilderim the Generous."

Ben-Hur bowed.

" If you be, indeed, the Ben-Hur of whom my father has spoken, and whom it was my pleasure to have known as well, you will be happy, I am sure, to show us some near path to living water, that with its sparkle we may grace a morning's meal in the desert," said Iras with a smile.

Ben-Hur, nothing loath, hastened to answer :

" Fair Egyptian, I give you sympathy. Can you bear suffering a little longer, we will find the spring you ask for, and I promise that its draught shall be as sweet and cooling as that of the more famous Castalia. With leave, we will make haste."

So saying Ben-Hur rode forward with the guide, one of the inconveniences of travelling with camels being that it is necessarily an interdiction of polite conversation.

Afterwhile the party came to a shallow wady, down which, turning to the right hand, the guide led them. The bed of the cut was somewhat soft from recent rains, and quite bold in its descent. Momentarily, however, it widened; and ere long the sides became bluffs ribbed with rocks much scarred by floods rushing to lower depths ahead. Finally, from a narrow passage, the travellers entered a spreading vale which was very delightful ; but come upon suddenly from the yellow, unrelieved, verdureless plain, it had the effect of a freshly discovered Paradise. Under a leaning cliff over on the left the mulberry grove had planted itself, proclaiming the spring which the party were seeking. And thither the guide conducted them, careless of whistling partridges and lesser birds of brighter hues roused whirring from the reedy coverts.

The water started from a crack in the cliff which some loving hand had enlarged into an arched cavity. The horses were presently turned loose, and from the kneeling camel the Ethiopian assisted Balthasar and Iras ; whereupon the old man, turning his face to the east, crossed his hands reverently upon his breast and prayed.

" Bring me a cup," Iras said, with some impatience.

From the houdah the slave brought her a crystal goblet ; then she said to Ben-Hur :

" I will be your servant at the fountain."

They walked to the pool together. He would have

dipped the water for her, but she refused his offer, and kneeling held the cup to be filled by the stream itself.

She arose and said, holding the cup over the pool :

" O gods of Egypt ! I give thanks for a hero discovered —thanks that the victim in the palace of Idernee was not my king of men. And so, O holy gods, I pour and drink."

Part of the contents of the cup she returned to the stream, the rest she drank. When she took the crystal from her lips, she laughed at him.

" O son of Hur, is it a fashion of the very brave to be so easily overcome by a woman ? Take the cup now, and see if you cannot find a happy word in it for me ? "

He took the cup, and stooped to refill it.

" Most fair, were I an Egyptian or a Greek or a Roman, I would say "—he raised the goblet overhead as he spoke— " O ye better gods ! I give thanks that there are yet left to the world, despite its wrongs and sufferings, the charm of beauty and the solace of love, and I drink to her who best represents them—to Iras, loveliest of the daughters of the Nile ! "

She laid her hand softly upon his shoulder.

" You have offended against the law. The gods you have drunk to are false gods. Why shall I not tell the rabbis on you ? "

" Oh ! " he replied, laughing, " that is very little to tell for one who knows so much else that is really important."

" I will go further—I will go to the little Jewess who makes the roses grow and the shadows flame in the house of the great merchant over in Antioch. To the rabbis I will accuse you of impenitence ; to her——"

" Well, to her ? "

" I will repeat what you have said to me under the lifted cup, with the gods for witnesses."

He was still a moment, as if waiting for the Egyptian to go on. With quickened fancy he saw Esther at her father's side listening to the dispatches he had forwarded —sometimes reading them. In her presence he had told Simonides the story of the affair in the palace of Idernee. She and Iras were acquainted ; this one was shrewd and worldly ; the other was simple and affectionate, and therefore easily won. Simonides could not have broken faith—nor Ilderim—for if not held by honour, there was no one, unless it might be himself, to whom the consequences of exposure were more serious and certain. Could Esther have been the Egyptian's informant ? He did not accuse her ; yet a suspicion was sown with the thought, and suspicions, as we all know, are weeds of the mind which grow of themselves, and most rapidly when least wanted. Before he could answer the allusion to the little Jewess, Balthasar came to the pool.

" We are greatly indebted to you, son of Hur," he said, in his grave manner. " This vale is very beautiful ; the grass, the trees, the shade, invite us to stay and rest, and the spring here has the sparkle of diamonds in motion, and sings to me of a loving God.   It is not enough to thank you for the enjoyment we find ; come sit with us, and taste our bread."

" Suffer me first to serve you."

With that Ben-Hur filled the goblet, and gave it to Balthasar, who lifted his eyes in thanksgiving.

Immediately the slave brought napkins ; and after laving their hands and drying them, the three seated themselves in Eastern style under the tent which years before had served the Wise Men at the meeting in the desert. And they ate heartily of the good things taken from the camel's pack.

CHAPTER III

THE restfulness of the vale, the freshness of the air, the garden beauty, the Sabbath stillness, seemed to have affected the spirits of the elder Egyptian ; his voice, gestures, the whole manner were unusually gentle ; and often as he bent his eyes upon Ben-Hur conversing with Iras, they softened with pity.

" I am impatient," said Balthasar.   " Latterly my sleep has been visited by dreams—or rather by the same dream in repetition. A voice—it is nothing more—comes and tells me, ' Haste—arise ! He whom thou hast so long awaited is at hand.' "

"Then you have heard nothing of Him ? "

"Nothing, except the words of the voice in the dream."

"Here, then, are tidings to make you glad as they made me."

From his gown Ben-Hur drew the letter received from Malluch. The hand the Egyptian held out trembled violently. He read aloud, and as he read his feelings increased ; the limp veins in his neck swelled and throbbed. At the conclusion he raised his suffused eyes in thanksgiving and prayer. He asked no questions, yet had no doubts.

"Thou hast been very good to me, O God," he said. "Give me, I pray Thee, to see the Saviour again, and worship Him, and Thy servant will be ready to go in peace."

"Now that He has come, O Balthasar, you still think He is to be a Saviour, and not a king ? "

Balthasar gave him a look thoughtful as it was tender.

"How shall I understand you ? " he asked, in return.

"I will recall the difference between us," said Ben-Hur, with deference. "You were of opinion that He would be a king, but not as Cæsar is ; you thought His sovereignty would be spiritual, not of the world."

"Let me try, O son of Hur, and help you to a clear understanding of my belief ; then it may be, seeing how the spiritual kingdom I expect Him to set up can be more excellent in every sense than anything of mere Cæsarean splendour, you will better understand the reason of the interest I take in the mysterious Person we are going to welcome.

"I cannot tell you when the idea of a Soul in every man had its origin. Most likely the first parents brought it with them out of the garden in which they had their first dwelling. We all do know, however, that it has never perished entirely out of mind. By some peoples it was lost, but not by all ; in some ages it dulled and failed ; in others it was overwhelmed with doubts ! but, in great goodness, God kept sending us at intervals mighty intellects to argue it back to faith and hope.

"A word as to the pleasure there is in the thought of a Soul in each of us. In the first place, it robs death of its terrors by making dying a change for the better, and burial but the planting of a seed from which there will spring a new life. In the next place, behold me as I am—weak, weary, old, shrunken in body, and graceless ; look at my wrinkled face, think of my failing senses, listen to my shrilled voice. Ah ! what happiness to me in the promise that when the tomb opens, as soon it will, to receive the worn-out husk I call myself, the now viewless doors of the universe, which is but the palace of God, will swing wide ajar to receive me, a liberated immortal Soul !

" Consider first the excellence of the existence which was reserved for us after death, and give heed to the feelings and impulses the thought is sure to awaken in you—heed them, I say, because they are your own soul astir, doing what it can to urge you in the right way. Consider next, that the after-life has become so obscured as to justify calling it a lost light. If you find it, rejoice, O son of Hur —rejoice as I do, though in beggary of words. For then, besides the great gift which is to be saved to us, you will have found the need of a Saviour so infinitely greater than the need of a king ; and He we are going to meet will not longer hold place in your hope a warrior with a sword or a monarch with a crown.

" A practical question presents itself—How shall we know Him at sight ? If you continue in your belief as to His character—that He is to be a king as Herod was—of course you will keep on until you meet a man clothed in purple and with a sceptre. On the other hand, He I look for will be one poor, humble, undistinguished—a man in appearance as other men ; and the sign by which I will know Him will be never so simple. He will offer to show me and all mankind the way to the eternal life ; the beautiful pure Life of the Soul."

The company sat a moment in silence, which was broken by Balthasar.

" Let us arise now," he said—" let us arise and set forward again. What I have said has caused a return of impatience to see Him who is ever in my thought ; and if I seem to hurry you, O son of Hur—and you, my daughter —be that my excuse."

At his signal the slave brought them wine in a skin

bottle ; and they poured and drank, and shaking the lap-cloths out, arose.

While the slave restored the tent and wares to the box under the houdah, and the Arab brought up the horses, the three principals laved themselves in the pool.

In a little while they were retracing their steps back through the wady, intending to overtake the caravan if it had passed them by.

CHAPTER IV

THE caravan, stretched out upon the desert, was very picturesque ; in motion, however, it was like a lazy serpent. By and by its stubborn dragging became intolerably irksome to Balthasar, patient as he was ; so, at his suggestion, the party determined to go on by themselves.

If the reader be young, or if he has yet a sympathetic recollection of the romanticisms of his youth, he will relish the pleasure with which Ben-Hur, riding near the camel of the Egyptians, gave a last look at the head of the straggling column almost out of sight on the shimmering plain.

To be definite as may be, and perfectly confidential, Ben-Hur found a certain charm in Iras's presence. If she looked down upon him from her high place, he made haste to get near her ; if she spoke to him, his heart beat out of its usual time. The desire to be agreeable to her was a constant impulse. There were signs, too, that she well knew the influence she was exercising over him.

And so to them the nooning came, and the evening.

The sun at its going down behind a spur of the old Bashan, left the party halted by a pool of clear water of the rains out in the Abilene desert. There the tent was pitched, the supper eaten, and preparations made for the night.

The second watch was Ben-Hur's ; and he was standing, spear in hand, within arm-reach of the dozing camel, look-ing awhile at the stars, then over the veiled land, when a hand very fair even in the moonless gloaming was laid softly upon his shoulder. The touch thrilled him ; he started, turned—and she was there.

" I thought you asleep," he said presently.

" Sleep is for old people and little children, and I came out to look at my friends, the stars in the south—those now holding the curtains of midnight over the Nile. But confess yourself surprised ! "

He took the hand which had fallen from his shoulder, and said, " Well, was it by an enemy ? "

" Oh no ! To be an enemy is to hate, and hating is a sickness which Isis will not suffer to come near me. She kissed me, you should know, on the heart when I was a child."

" Your speech does not sound in the least like your father's. Are you not of his faith ? "

" I might have been "—and she laughed low—" I might have been had I seen what he has. I may be when I get old like him. There should be no religion for youth, only poetry and philosophy ; and no poetry except such as is the inspiration of wine and mirth and love ; and no philo- sophy that does not nod excuse for follies which cannot outlive a season. My father's God is too awful for me. I failed to find Him in the Grove of Daphne. He was never heard of as present in the atria of Rome. But, son of Hur, I have a wish."

" A wish ! Where is He who could say it no ? "

" Son of Hur ! "—she lowered her voice with singular dexterity, and, going nearer, spoke so her breath was warm upon his cheek—" son of Hur ! He thou art going to find is to be King of the Jews, is He not ? "

His heart beat fast and hard.

" A King of the Jews like Herod, only greater," she continued.

He looked away—into the night, up to the stars ; then his eyes met hers, and lingered there ; and her breath was on his lips, so near was she.

" Since morning," she said, further, " we have been having visions. Now if I tell you mine, will you serve me as well ? The vision which followed me was of magnificent war—war on land and sea—with clashing of arms and rush of armies, as if Cæsar and Pompey were come again, and Octavius and Antony. A cloud of dust and ashes

arose and covered the world, and Rome was not any more ;
all dominion returned to the East ; out of the cloud issued
another race of heroes ; and there were vaster satrapies
and brighter crowns for giving away than were ever known.
And, son of Hur, while the vision was passing, and after
it was gone, I kept asking myself, ' What shall he not have
who served the King earliest and best ? ' "

Again Ben-Hur recoiled. The question was the very
question which had been with him all day. Presently he
fancied he had the clue he wanted.

" So," he said, " I have you now. The satrapies and
crowns are the things to which you would help me. I see,
I see ! And there never was such queen as you would be,
so shrewd, so beautiful, so royal—never ! "

He carried the hand resting upon his neck to his lips.
" In love—in love ! " he said.

" You will find the King," she said, placing her other
hand caressingly upon his head. " You will go on and
find the King and serve Him. With your sword you
will earn His richest gifts ; and His best soldier will be
my hero."

He turned his face, and saw hers close above. In all
the sky there was that moment nothing so bright to him
as her eyes, enshadowed though they were. Presently he
sat up, and put his arms about her, and kissed her passionately, saying, " O Egypt, Egypt ! If the King has crowns
in gifts, one shall be mine ; and I will bring it and put it
here over the place my lips have marked. You shall be a
queen—my queen—no one more beautiful ! And we will
be ever, ever so happy ! "

" And you will tell me everything, and let me help you
in all ? " she said, kissing him in return.

The question chilled his fervour.

" Is it not enough that I love you ? " he asked.

" Perfect love means perfect faith," she replied. " But
never mind—you will know me better."

She took her hand from him and arose.

" You are cruel," he said.

Moving away, she stopped by the camel, and touched its
front face with her lips.

" O thou noblest of thy kind !—that, because there is no suspicion in thy love."

An instant, and she was gone.

CHAPTER V

THE third day of the journey the party nooned by the river Jabbok, where there were a hundred or more men, mostly of Peræa, resting themselves and their beasts. Hardly had they dismounted, before a man came to them with a pitcher of water and a bowl, and offered them drink ; as they received the attention with much courtesy, he said, looking at the camel, " I am returning from the Jordan, where just now there are many people from distant parts, travelling as you are, illustrious friend ; but they had none of them the equal of your servant here. A very noble animal. May I ask of what breed he is sprung ? "

Balthasar answered, and sought his rest ; but Ben-Hur, more curious, took up the remark.

" At what place on the river are the people ? " he asked.

" At Bethabara."

" It used to be a lonesome ford," said Ben-Hur. " I cannot understand how it can have become of such interest."

" I see," the stranger replied ; " you, too, are from abroad, and have not heard the good tidings."

" What tidings ? "

" Well, a man has appeared out of the wilderness—a very holy man—with his mouth full of strange words, which take hold of all who hear them. He calls himself John the Nazarite, son of Zacharias, and says he is the messenger sent before the Messiah."

Even Iras listened closely while the man continued :

" They say of this John that he has spent his life from childhood in a cave down by En-gedi, praying and living more strictly than the Essenes. Crowds go to hear him preach. I went to hear him with the rest."

" Have all these, your friends, been there ? "

" Most of them are going ; a few are coming away."

" What does he preach ? "

" A new doctrine—one never before taught in Israel, as all say. He calls it repentance and baptism. The rabbis do not know what to make of him ; nor do we. Some have asked him if he is the Christ, others if he is Elias ; but to them all he has the answer, ' I am the voice of one crying in the wilderness, Make straight the way of the Lord ! ' "

At this point the man was called away by his friends ; as he was going, Balthasar spoke.

" Good stranger ! " he said tremulously, " tell us if we shall find the preacher at the place you left him."

" Yes, at Bethabara."

" Let us make haste. I am not tired."

There was little conversation between the three at the stopping-place for the night west of Ramoth-Gilead.

" Let us arise early, son of Hur," said the old man. " The Saviour may come, and we not there."

" The King cannot be far behind His herald," Iras whispered, as she prepared to take her place on the camel.

" To-morrow we will see ! " Ben-Hur replied, kissing her hand.

Next day about the third hour, out of the pass through which, skirting the base of Mount Gilead, they had journeyed since leaving Ramoth, the party came upon the barren steppe east of the sacred river. Opposite them they saw the upper limit of the old palm lands of Jericho, stretching off to the hill-country of Judea. Ben-Hur's blood ran quickly, for he knew the ford was close at hand.

" Content you, good Balthasar," he said ; " we are almost there."

The driver quickened the camel's pace. Soon they caught sight of booths and tents and tethered animals ; and then of the river, and a multitude collected down close by the bank, and yet another multitude on the western shore. Knowing that the preacher was preaching, they made greater haste ; yet, as they were drawing near, suddenly there was a commotion in the mass, and it began to break up and disperse.

They were too late !

" Let us stay here," said Ben-Hur to Balthasar, who was wringing his hands. " The Nazarite may come this way."

The people were too intent upon what they had heard, and too busy in discussion, to notice the new-comers. When some hundreds were gone by, and it seemed the opportunity to so much as see the Nazarite was lost to the latter, up the river not far away they beheld a person coming towards them of such singular appearance they forgot all else.

Outwardly the man was rude and uncouth, even savage. Over a thin, gaunt visage of the hue of brown parchment, over his shoulders and down his back below the middle, in witch-like locks, fell a covering of sun-scorched hair. His eyes were burning-bright.   All his right side was naked, and of the colour of his face, and quite as meagre ; a shirt of the coarsest camel's-hair—coarse as Bedouin tent-cloth —clothed the rest of his person to the knees, being gathered at the waist by a broad girdle of untanned leather.   His feet were bare.   A scrip, also of untanned leather, was fastened to the girdle.   He used a knotted staff to help him forward.   His movement was quick, decided, and strangely watchful.   Every little while he tossed the unruly hair from his eyes, and peered round as if searching for somebody.

The fair Egyptian surveyed the son of the desert with surprise, not to say disgust.   Presently, raising the curtain of the houdah, she spoke to Ben-Hur, who sat his horse near by.

" Is that the herald of thy King ? "

" It is the Nazarite," he replied, without looking up.

In truth he was himself more than disappointed.

In this time of such interest to the new-comers, another man had been sitting by himself on a stone at the edge of the river, thinking yet, probably, of the sermon he had been hearing.   Now, however, he arose, and walked slowly up from the shore, in a course to take him across the line the Nazarite was pursuing and bring him near the camel.

And the two—the preacher and the stranger—kept on until they came, the former within twenty yards of the animal, the latter within ten feet.   Then the preacher stopped, and flung the hair from his eyes, looked at the stranger, threw his hands up as a signal to all the people

R

studying the face of the stranger, though with an interest
entirely different. He was not insensible to its purity of
feature, and its thoughtfulness, tenderness, humility and
holiness ; but just then there was room in his mind but
for one thought—Who is this man ? And what ? Messiah
or king ? Never was apparition more unroyal. Nay,
looking at that calm, benignant countenance, the very idea
of war and conquest, and lust of dominion, smote him like
a profanation. He said, as if speaking to his own heart,
Balthasar must be right and Simonides wrong. This man
has not come to rebuild the throne of Solomon ; he has
neither the nature nor the genius of Herod ; king he may
be, but not of another and greater than Rome.

It should be understood now that this was not a conclusion
with Ben-Hur, but an impression merely ; and while it
was forming, while yet he gazed at the wonderful countenance, his memory began to throe and struggle. " Surely,"
he said to himself, " I have seen the man ; but where and
when ? " Faintly at first, at last a clear light, a burst of
sunshine, the scene by the well at Nazareth what time the
Roman guard was dragging him to the galleys returned,
and all his being thrilled. Those hands had helped him
when he was perishing. The face was one of the pictures
he had carried in mind ever since. In the effusion of feeling
excited, the explanation of the preacher was lost by him,
all but the last words—words so marvellous that the world
yet rings with them :

"—this is the SON OF GOD ! "

Ben-Hur leaped from his horse to render homage to his
benefactor ; but Iras cried to him, " Help, son of Hur,
help, or my father will die ! "

He stopped, looked back, then hurried to her assistance.
She gave him a cup ; and leaving the slave to bring the
camel to its knees, he ran to the river for water. The
stranger was gone when he came back.

At last Balthasar was restored to consciousness. Stretching forth his hands, he asked feebly, " Where is he ? "

" Who ? " asked Iras.

An intense instant interest shone upon the good man's
face, as if a last wish had been gratified, and he answered :

" He—the Redeemer—the Son of God, whom I have seen again."

" Believest thou so ? " Iras asked, in a low voice, of Ben-Hur.

" The time is full of wonders ; let us wait," was all he said.

And next day while the three were listening to him, the Nazarite broke off in mid-speech, saying reverently, " Behold the Lamb of God ! "

Looking to where he pointed, they beheld the stranger again.   As Ben-Hur surveyed the slender figure, and holy beautiful countenance compassionate to sadness, a new idea broke upon him.

" Balthasar is right—so is Simonides.   May not the Redeemer be a king also ? "

And he asked one at his side, " Who is the man walking yonder ? "

The other laughed mockingly, and replied :

" He is the son of a carpenter over in Nazareth."

rose reddening her cheeks—the seal was Ben-Hur's. With quickened steps she hastened on.

Simonides held the package a moment while he also inspected the seal. Breaking it open, he gave her the roll it contained.

" Read," he said.

His eyes were upon her as he spoke, and instantly a troubled expression fell upon his own face.

" You know who it is from, I see, Esther."

" Yes—from—our master."

Though the manner was halting, she met his gaze with modest sincerity. Slowly his chin sank into the roll of flesh puffed out under it like a cushion.

" You love him, Esther," he said quietly.

" Yes," she answered.

" Let me, for your sake, my child, show you the worst. Seeing it with me may make it less terrible to you. His love, Esther, is all bestowed."

" I know it," she said calmly.

" The Egyptian has him in her net," he continued. " She has the cunning of her race, with beauty to help her—much beauty, great cunning ; but, like her race, again, no heart. The daughter who despises her father will bring her husband to grief."

" Does she that ? "

Simonides went on :

" When he has taken the Egyptian to wife, Esther, he will think of you with repentance and much calling of the spirit : for at last he will awake to find himself but the minister of her bad ambition. Rome is the centre of all her dreams. To her he is the son of Arrius the duumvir, not the son of Hur, Prince of Jerusalem."

Esther made no attempt to conceal the effect of these words.

" Save him, father ! It is not too late ! " she said entreatingly.

He answered, with a dubious smile, " A man drowning may be saved ; not so a man in love."

A blush burned Esther's whole face.

" I was concerned for him along—for his happiness, not

mine. Because I have dared love him, I shall keep myself
worthy his respect ; so only can I excuse my folly. Let
me read his letter now."

" Yes, read it."

She began at once, in haste to conclude the distasteful
subject.

"*Nisan, 8th day.*

" On the road from Galilee to Jerusalem.

" The Nazarene is on the way also. With Him, though without
His knowledge, I am bringing a full legion of mine. A second legion
follows. The passover will excuse the multitude. He said upon
setting out, ' We will go up to Jerusalem, and all things that are
written by the prophets concerning me shall be accomplished.'

" Our waiting draws to an end.

" In haste.

" Peace to thee, Simonides.   BEN-HUR."

Esther returned the letter to her father, while a choking
sensation gathered in her throat. There was not a word
in the missive for her—not even in the salutation had she a
share—and it would have been so easy to have written,
" and to thine, peace." For the first time in her life she
felt the smart of a jealous sting."

" The eighth day," said Simonides, " the eighth day ;
and this, Esther, this is the——"

" The ninth," she replied.

" Ah, then, they may be in Bethany now."

" And possibly we may see him to-night," she added,
pleased into momentary forgetfulness.

" It may be, it may be ! To-morrow is the Feast of
Unleavened Bread, and he may wish to celebrate it ; so
may the Nazarene ; and we may see Him—we may see
both of them, Esther."

At this point the servant appeared with the wine and
water. Esther helped her father, and in the midst of the
service Iras came upon the roof.

" Peace to you, Simonides, and to the pretty Esther
peace," said Iras, approaching the latter. " A man who
has millions in store, and fleets of ships at sea, cannot discern in what simple women like us find amusement. Let
us leave him. By the wall yonder we can talk."

They went to the parapet then, stopping at the place where, years before, Ben-Hur loosed the broken tile upon the head of Gratus. There she turned sharply upon the Jewess, and she said, " The King is coming."

Esther gazed at her in innocent surprise.

" The Nazarene," Iras continued, " He whom our fathers have been talking about so much, whom Ben-Hur has been serving and toiling for so long "—her voice dropped several tones lower—" the Nazarene will be here to-morrow, and Ben-Hur to-night."

Esther struggled to maintain her composure, but failed ; her eyes fell, the tell-tale blood surged to her cheek and forehead, and she was saved sight of the triumphant smile that passed, like a gleam, over the face of the Egyptian.

" See, here is his promise."

And from her girdle she took a roll.

" Rejoice with me, O my friend ! He will be here to-night ! On the Tiber there is a house, a royal property, which he has pledged to me ; and to be its mistress is to be——"

A sound of some one walking swiftly along the street below interrupted the speech, and she leaned over the parapet to see. Then she drew back, and cried, with hands clasped above her head, " Now blessed be Isis ! 'Tis he— Ben-Hur himself ! That he should appear while I had such thought of him ! There are no gods if it be not a good omen. Put your arms about me, Esther—and a kiss ! "

The Jewess looked up. Upon each cheek there was a glow ; her eyes sparkled with a light more nearly of anger than ever her nature emitted before.

" Dost thou love him so much, then, or Rome so much better ? "

The Egyptian drew back a step ; then she bent her haughty head quite near her questioner.

" What is he to thee, daughter of Simonides ? "

Esther, all thrilling, began, " He is my——"

A thought blasting as lightning stayed the words : she paled, trembled, recovered, and answered :

" He is my father's friend."

Her tongue had refused to admit her servile condition. Iras laughed more lightly than before.

" Not more than that ? " she said.   " Ah, by the lover-gods of Egypt, thou mayst keep thy kisses—keep them. Thou hast taught me but now that there are others vastly more estimable waiting me here in Judea ; and "—she turned away, looking back over her shoulder—" I will go get them.   Peace to thee."

Esther saw her disappear down the steps, when, putting her hands over her face, she burst into tears so they ran scalding through her fingers—tears of shame and choking passion.

CHAPTER II

AN hour or thereabouts after the scene upon the roof, Balthasar and Simonides, the latter attended by Esther met in the great chamber of the palace ; and while they were talking, Ben-Hur and Iras came in together.

The young Jew, advancing in front of his companion, walked first to Balthasar, and saluted him, and received his reply ; then he turned to Simonides, but paused in surprise at seeing Esther a woman now, and so beautiful ; and as he stood looking at her a still voice reminded him of broken vows and duties undone : almost his old self returned.

For an instant he was startled ; but recovering, he went to Esther, and said, " Peace to thee, sweet Esther—peace ; and thou, Simonides "—he looked to the merchant as he spoke—" the blessing of the Lord be thine, if only because thou hast been a good father to the fatherless."

Some one coming into the room interrupted him ; he turned, and arose with extended hands.

" Amrah !   Dear old Amrah ! " he cried.

She came forward ; and they, seeing the joy in her face, thought not once how wrinkled and tawny it was. She knelt at his feet, clasped his knees, and kissed his hands over and over ; and when he could he put the lank grey hair from her cheeks, and kissed them, saying, " Good

Amrah, have you nothing, nothing of them—not a word—not one little sign ? "

Then she broke into sobbing which made him answer plainer even than the spoken word.

" God's will has been done," he next said, solemnly, in a tone to make each listener know he had no hope more of finding his people. In his eyes there were tears which he would not have them see, because he was a man.

When he could again, he took seat, and said, " Come, sit by me, Amrah—here. No ? then at my feet : for I have much to say to these good friends of a wonderful man come into the world."

But she went off, and stooping with her back to the wall, joined her hands before her knees, content, they all thought, with seeing him. Then Ben-Hur, bowing to the old men, began again :

" I fear to speak about the Nazarene without first telling you some of the things I have seen Him do ; and to that I am the more inclined, my friends, because to-morrow He will come to the city, and go up into the Temple, which He calls His Father's house, where, it is further said, He will proclaim Himself. He brings twelve men with Him, fishermen, tillers of the soil, one a publican, all of the humbler class ; and He and they make their journeys on foot, careless of wind, cold, rain, or sun. Seeing them stop by the wayside at nightfall to break bread or lie down to sleep, I have been reminded of a party of shepherds going back to their flocks from market, not of nobles and kings. Only when He lifts the corners of His handkerchief to look at some one or shake the dust from His head, I am made know He is their teacher as well as their companion—their superior not less than their friend."

" The Greeks would call him a philosopher," said Iras.

" Nay, daughter," said Balthasar, " the philosophers had never the power to do such things."

" How know you this man has ? "

Ben-Hur answered quickly, " I saw Him turn water into wine."

" Very strange, very strange," said Simonides.

" What would you say," said Ben-Hur, with increased

earnestness—" what would you say to what I now tell
you ? A leper came to the Nazarene while I was with
Him down in Galilee, and said, ' Lord, if Thou wilt, Thou
canst make me clean.' He heard the cry, and touched the
outcast with His hand, saying, ' Be thou clean ' ; and forthwith the man was himself again, healthful as any of us
who beheld the cure, and we were a multitude."

" Such thing was never heard before—never in all
Israel ! " said Simonides, in undertone.

And then, while he was speaking, Amrah turned away,
and walked noiselessly to the door, and went out ; and none
of the company saw her go.

" The thoughts stirred by such things done under my
eyes I leave you to imagine," said Ben-Hur, continuing ;
" but my doubts, my misgivings, my amazement, were not
yet at the full. The people of Galilee are, as you know,
impetuous and rash ; after years of waiting their swords
burned their hands ; nothing would do them but action.
' He is slow to declare Himself ; let us force Him,' they
cried to me. And I too became impatient. If He is to be
king, why not now ? The legions are ready. So as He
was once teaching by the seaside we would have crowned
Him whether or not ; but He disappeared, and was next
seen on a ship departing from the shore. Good Simonides,
the desires that make other men mad—riches, power, even
kingships offered out of great love by a great people—
move this one not at all. What say you ? "

" God only is so great," said Balthasar to Simonides.

" Mark you," Ben-Hur proceeded, " I do but tell you
things of which I was a witness, together with a crowd of
other men. On the way hither I saw another act still
more mighty. In Bethany there was a man named Lazarus,
who died and was buried ; and after he had lain four days
in a tomb, shut in by a great stone, the Nazarene was shown
to the place. Upon rolling the stone away, we beheld the
man lying inside bound and rotting. There were many
people standing by, and we all heard what the Nazarene
said, for He spoke in a loud voice : ' Lazarus, come forth ! '
I cannot tell you my feelings when in answer, as it were,
the man arose and came out to us with all his cerements

about him. ' Loose him,' said the Nazarene next, ' Loose him, and let him go.' And when the napkin was taken from the face of the resurrected, lo, my friends ! the blood ran anew through the wasted body, and he was exactly as he had been in life before the sickness that took him off. He lives yet, and is hourly seen and spoken to. You may go see him to-morrow. And now, as nothing more is needed for the purpose, I ask you that which I came to ask, it being but a repetition of what you asked me, O Simonides, What more than a man is this Nazarene ? "

The question was put solemnly, and long after midnight the company sat and debated it ; Simonides being yet unwilling to give up his understanding of the sayings of the prophets, and Ben-Hur contending that the elder disputants were both right—that the Nazarene was the Redeemer, as claimed by Balthasar, and also the destined king the merchant would have.

" To-morrow we will see. Peace to you all."

So saying, Ben-Hur took his leave, intending to return to Bethany.

CHAPTER III

THE first person to go out of the city upon the opening of the Sheep's Gate next morning was Amrah, basket on arm.

As the reader must by this time have surmised, she was going to her mistress, whose tomb, it will be remembered, overlooked the well En-rogel.

Early as it was, the unhappy woman was up and sitting outside, leaving Tirzah asleep within. The course of the malady had been terribly swift in the three years. Conscious of her appearance, with the refined instincts of her nature, she kept her whole person habitually covered. Seldom as possible she permitted even Tirzah to see her.

While she sat there peopling the dusky solitude with thoughts even more cheerless, suddenly a woman came up the hill staggering and spent with exertion.

The widow arose hastily, and covering her head, cried, in a voice unnaturally harsh, " Unclean, unclean ! "

In a moment, heedless of the notice, Amrah was at her feet. All the long-pent love of the simple creature burst forth : with tears and passionate exclamations she kissed her mistress's garments, and for a while the latter strove to escape from her ; then seeing she could not, she waited till the violence of the paroxysm was over.

"What have you done, Amrah ? " she said. " Is it by such disobedience you prove your love for us ? Wicked woman ! You are lost ; and he—your master—you can never, never go back to him."

Amrah rose to her knees, and said, brokenly and with clasped hands, " O good mistress ! I am not wicked. I bring you good tidings."

" Of Judah ? " and as she spoke, the widow half withdrew the cloth from her head.

" There is a wonderful man," Amrah continued, " who has power to cure you. He speaks a word, and the sick are made well, and even the dead come to life. I have come to take you to him."

" Poor Amrah ! " said Tirzah compassionately.

" No," cried Amrah, detecting the doubt underlying the expression—" no, as the Lord lives, even the Lord of Israel, my God as well as yours, I speak the truth. Go with me, I pray, and lose no time. This morning he will pass by on his way to the city. See ! the day is at hand. Take the food here—eat, and let us go."

The mother listened eagerly. Not unlikely she had heard of the wonderful man, for by this time his fame had penetrated every nook in the land.

" Who is he ? " she asked.

" A Nazarene."

" Who told you about him ? "

" Judah."

" Judah told you ? Is he at home ? "

" He came last night."

The widow, trying to still the beating of her heart, was silent awhile.

" Did Judah send you to tell us this ? " she next asked.

" No. He believes you dead."

" There was a prophet once who cured a leper," the

mother said thoughtfully to Tirzah ; " but he had his power from God." Then addressing Amrah, she asked, " How does my son know this man so possessed ? "

" He was travelling with him, and heard the lepers call, and saw them go away well. First there was one man ; then there were ten ; and they were all made whole."

The elder listener was silent again. With her the hesitation was brief. To Tirzah she said :

" This must be the Messiah ! "

She spoke not coldly, like one reasoning a doubt away, but as a woman of Israel familiar with the promises of God to her race—a woman of understanding, ready to be glad over the least sign of the realization of the promises.

" There was a time when Jerusalem and all Judea were filled with a story that He was born. I remember it. By this time He should be a man. It must be—it is He. Yes," she said to Amrah, " we will go with you. Bring the water which you will find in the tomb in a jar, and set the food for us. We will eat and be gone."

The breakfast, partaken under excitement, was soon dispatched, and the three women set out on their extraordinary journey. As Tirzah had caught the confident spirit of the others, there was but one fear that troubled the party. Bethany, Amrah said, was the town the man was coming from ; now from that to Jerusalem there were three roads, or rather paths—one over the first summit of Olivet, a second at its base, a third between the second summit and the Mount of Offence. The three were not far apart ; far enough, however, to make it possible for the unfortunates to miss the Nazarene if they failed the one He chose to come by.

A little questioning satisfied the mother that Amrah knew nothing of the country beyond the Kedron, and even less of the intentions of the man they were going to see, if they could. She discerned, also, that both Amrah and Tirzah—the one from confirmed habits of servitude, the other from natural dependency—looked to her for guidance ; and she accepted the charge.

" We will go first to Bethphage," she said to them.

" There, if the Lord favour us, we may learn what else to do."

They descended the hill to Tophet and the King's Garden, and paused in the deep trail furrowed through them by centuries of wayfaring.

" I am afraid of the road," the matron said. " Better that we keep to the country among the rocks and trees. This is feast-day, and on the hill-side yonder I see signs of a great multitude in attendance. By going across the Mount of Offence here we may avoid them."

The face of the hill they essayed to cross was somewhat broken with pits, and ruins of old structures ; but when at last they stood upon the top to rest, and looked at the spectacle presented them over in the north-west—at the Temple and its courtly terraces, at Zion, at the enduring towers white beetling into the sky beyond—the mother was strengthened with a love of life for life's sake.

Though the good servant toiled faithfully to lighten the labour in descending the hill-side, not sparing herself in the least, the girl moaned at every step ; sometimes in extremity of anguish she cried out. Upon reaching the road—that is, the road between the Mount of Offence and the middle or second summit of Olivet—she fell down exhausted.

" Go on with Amrah, mother, and leave me here," she said faintly.

" No, no, Tirzah. What would the gain be to me if I were healed and you not ? When Judah asks for you, as he will, what would I have to say to him were I to leave you ? "

" Tell him I loved him."

The elder leper arose from bending over the fainting sufferer, and gazed about her with that sensation of hope perishing which is more nearly like annihilation of the soul than anything else. The supremest joy of the thought of cure was inseparable from Tirzah, who was not too old to forget, in the happiness of healthful life to come, the years of misery by which she had been so reduced in body and broken in spirit. Even as the brave woman was about leaving the venture they were engaged in to the deter-

s

mination of God, she saw a man on foot coming rapidly up the road from the east.

" Courage, Tirzah !   Be of cheer," she said.   " Yonder I know is one to tell us of the Nazarene."

Amrah helped the girl to a sitting posture, and supported her while the man advanced.

" In your goodness, mother, you forget what we are. The stranger will go around us ; his best gift to us will be a curse, if not a stone."

" We will see."

There was no other answer to be given, since the mother was too well and sadly acquainted with the treatment outcasts of the class to which she belonged were accustomed to at the hands of her countrymen.

As has been said, the road at the head of which the group was posted was little more than a worn path or trail, winding crookedly through tumuli of limestone.   If the stranger kept it, he must meet them face to face ; and he did so, until near enough to hear the cry she was bound to give. Then, uncovering her head, a further demand of the law, she shouted shrilly :

" Unclean, unclean ! "

To her surprise, the man came steadily on.

" What would you have ? " he asked, stopping opposite them not four yards off.

" Thou seest us.   Have a care," the mother said, with dignity.

" Woman, I am the courier of Him who speaketh but once to such as thou and they are healed.   I am not afraid."

" The Nazarene ? "

" The Messiah," he said.

" Is it true that He cometh to the city to-day ? "

"¡He is now at Bethphage."

" On what road, master ? "

" This one."

She clasped her hands, and looked up thankfully.

" For whom takest thou Him ? " the man asked, with pity.

" The Son of God," she replied.

" Stay thou here then ; or, as there is a multitude with

Him, take thy stand by the rock yonder, the white one under the tree ; and as He goeth by fail not to call to Him ; call, and fear not. If thy faith but equal thy knowledge, He will hear thee though all the heavens thunder. I go to tell Israel, assembled in and about the city, that He is at hand, and to make ready to receive Him. Peace to thee and thine, woman."

He went on, and they went slowly to the rock he had pointed out to them, high as their heads, and scarcely thirty yards from the road on the right. Standing in front of it, the mother satisfied herself they could be seen and heard plainly by passers-by whose notice they desired to attract. There they cast themselves under the tree in its shade. Ere long Tirzah slept, and fearing to disturb her, the others held their peace.

CHAPTER IV

DURING the third hour the road in front of the resting-place of the lepers became gradually more and more frequented by people going in the direction of Bethphage and Bethany ; now, however, about the commencement of the fourth hour, a great crowd appeared over the crest of Olivet, and as it defiled down the road thousands in number, the two watchers noticed with wonder that every one in it carried a palm-branch freshly cut. As they sat absorbed by the novelty, the noise of another multitude approaching from the east drew their eyes that way. Then the mother awoke Tirzah.

" What is the meaning of it all ? " the latter asked.

" He is coming," answered the mother. " These we see are from the city going to meet Him ; those we hear in the east are His friends bearing Him company ; and it will not be strange if the processions meet here before us."

Meantime the people in the east came up slowly. When at length the foremost of them were in sight, the gaze of the lepers fixed upon a man riding in the midst of what seemed a chosen company which sang and danced about Him in extravagance of joy. The rider was bareheaded and clad all in white. There was no need of any one to tell the lepers that this was He—the wonderful Nazarene!

"He is here, Tirzah," the mother said; "He is here. Come, my child."

As she spoke she glided in front of the white rock and fell upon her knees.

Directly the daughter and servant were by her side.

The moment of the meeting of the hosts was come, and with it the opportunity the sufferers were seeking; if not taken, it would be lost for ever, and they would be lost as well.

"Nearer, my child—let us get nearer. He cannot hear us," said the mother.

She arose, and staggered forward. Her ghastly hands were up, and she screamed with horrible shrillness. The people saw her—saw her hideous face, and stopped awe-struck—an effect for which extreme human misery, visible as in this instance, is as potent as majesty in purple and gold. Tirzah, behind her a little way, fell down, too faint and frightened to follow farther.

"The lepers! the lepers!"

"Stone them!"

"The accursed of God! Kill them!"

These, with other yells of like import, broke in upon the hosannas of the part of the multitude too far removed to see and understand the cause of the interruption. Some there were, however, near by, familiar with the nature of the man to whom the unfortunates were appealing—some who, by long intercourse with Him, had caught somewhat of His divine compassion: they gazed at Him, and were silent awhile, in fair view. He rode up and stopped in front of the woman. She also beheld His face—calm, pitiful, and of exceeding beauty, the large eyes tender with benignant purpose.

And this was the colloquy that ensued:

"O Master, Master! Thou seest our need; Thou canst make us clean. Have mercy upon us—mercy!"

"Believest thou I am able to do this?" He asked.

"Thou art He of whom the prophets spake—Thou art the Messiah!" she replied.

His eyes grew radiant, His manner confident.

"Woman," He said, "great is thy faith; be it unto thee even as thou wilt."

He lingered an instant after, apparently unconscious of the presence of the throng—an instant—then He rode away.

Immediately both the hosts, that from the city and that from Bethphage, closed around Him with their joyous demonstrations, with hosannas and waving of palms, and so He passed from the lepers for ever. Covering her head, the elder hastened to Tirzah, and folded her in her arms, crying, "Daughter, look up! I have His promise; He is indeed the Messiah. We are saved—saved!" And the two remained kneeling while the procession, slowly going, disappeared over the mount. When the noise of its singing afar was a sound scarcely heard the miracle began.

There was first in the hearts of the lepers a freshening of the blood; then it flowed faster and stronger, thrilling their wasted bodies with an infinitely sweet sense of painless healing. Each felt the scourge going from her; their strength revived; they were returning to be themselves. Directly, as if to make the purification complete, from body to spirit the quickening ran, exalting them to a very fervour of ecstasy. The power possessing them to this good end was most nearly that of a draught of swift and happy effect; yet it was unlike and superior in that its healing and cleansing was absolute, and not merely a delicious consciousness while in progress, but the planting, growing, and maturing all at once of a recollection so singular and so holy that the simple thought of it should be of itself ever after a formless yet perfect thanksgiving.

To this transformation—for such it may be called quite as properly as a cure—there was a witness other than Amrah. The reader will remember the constancy with which Ben-Hur had followed the Nazarene throughout His wanderings; and now, recalling the conversation of the night before, there will be little surprise at learning that the young Jew was present when the leprous woman appeared in the path of the pilgrims. At the close of the scene, consequently, Ben-Hur had withdrawn from the procession, and seated himself upon a stone to wait its passage.

From his place he nodded recognition to many of the people—Galileans in his league, carrying short swords under their long abbas. After a little a swarthy Arab came up leading two horses ; at a sign from Ben-Hur he also drew out.

"Stay here," the young master said, when all were gone by, even the laggards. "I wish to be at the city early, and Aldebaran must do me service."

He stroked the broad forehead of the horse, now in his prime of strength and beauty, then crossed the road towards the two women.

They were to him, it should be borne in mind, strangers in whom he felt interest only as they were subjects of a superhuman experiment, the result of which might possibly help him to solution of the mystery that had long engaged him. As he proceeded, he glanced casually at the figure of the little woman over by the white rock, standing there her face hidden in her hands.

"As the Lord liveth, it is Amrah !" he said to himself.

He hurried on, and passing by the mother and daughter, still without recognizing them, he stopped before the servant.

"Amrah," he said to her, "Amrah, what do you here ? "

She rushed forward, and fell upon her knees before him, blinded by her tears, nigh speechless with contending joy and fear.

"O master, master ! Thy God and mine, how good He is ! "

The woman he had seen before the Nazarene was standing with her hands clasped and eyes streaming, looking towards heaven. The mere transformation would have been a sufficient surprise ; but it was the least of the causes of his emotion. Could he be mistaken ? Never was there in life a stranger so like his mother. Scarcely believing his senses, he laid his hand upon the servant's head, and asked tremulously :

"Amrah, Amrah—my mother ! Tirzah ! tell me if I see aright."

" Speak to them, O master, speak to them ! " she said.

He waited no longer, but ran, with outstretched arms, crying, " Mother ! mother ! Tirzah ! Here I am ! "

Next moment the three, so long separated, were mingling their tears in each other's arms.

Naturally, the mother was the first to think of the cares of life.

" What shall we do now, my son ?   Where shall we go ? "

Then Ben-Hur, recalled to duty, observed how completely every trace of the scourge had disappeared from his restored people ; that each had back her perfection of person ; that, as with Naaman when he came up out of the water, their flesh had come again like unto the flesh of a little child ; and he took off his cloak, and threw it over Tirzah.

" Take it," he said, smiling ; " the eye of the stranger would have shunned you before, now it shall not offend you."

The act exposed a sword belted to his side.

" Is it a time of war ? " asked the mother anxiously.

" No."

" Why, then, are you armed ? "

" It may be necessary to defend the Nazarene."

Thus Ben-Hur evaded the whole truth.

" Has He enemies ?   Who are they ? "

" Alas, mother, they are not all Romans ! "

" Is He not of Israel, and a man of peace ? "

" There was never one more so ; but in the opinion of the rabbis and teachers He is guilty of a great crime."

" What crime ? "

" In His eyes the uncircumcised Gentile is as worthy favour as a Jew of the strictest habit.   He preaches a new dispensation."

The mother was silent, and they moved to the shade of the tree by the rock.   Calming his impatience to have them home again and hear their story, he showed them the necessity of obedience to the law governing in cases like theirs, and in conclusion called the Arab, bidding him take the horses to the gate by Bethesda and await him there ; whereupon they set out by the way of the Mount of Offence.   The return was very different from the coming ;

they walked rapidly and with ease, and in good time reached a tomb newly made near that of Absalom, over-looking the depths of Kedron. Finding it unoccupied, the women took possession, while he went on hastily to make the preparations required for their new condition.

CHAPTER V

BEN-HUR pitched two tents out on the Upper Kedron east a short space of the Tombs of the Kings, and furnished them with every comfort at his command ; and thither, without loss of time, he conducted his mother and sister, to remain until the examining priest could certify their perfect cleansing.

In course of the duty, the young man had subjected him-self to such serious defilement as to debar him from partici-pation in the ceremonies of the great feast, then near at hand. He could not enter the least sacred of the courts of the Temple. Of necessity, not less than choice, there-fore, he stayed at the tents with his beloved people. There was a great deal to hear from them, and a great deal to tell them of himself.

Stories such as theirs—sad experiences extending through a lapse of years, sufferings of body, acuter sufferings of mind—are usually long in the telling, the incidents seldom following each other in threaded connexion. He listened to the narrative and all they told him, with outward pati-ence masking inward feeling. In fact, his hatred of Rome and Romans reached a higher mark than ever ; his desire for vengeance became a thirst which attempts at reflec-tion only intensified. In the almost savage bitterness of his humour many mad impulses took hold of him. Each mental venture in reach of new expedients brought him back to the old conclusion—that there could be no sound success except in a war involving all Israel in solid union ; and all musing upon the subject, all inquiry, all hope ended where they began—in the Nazarene and His purposes.

At odd moments the excited schemer found a pleasure in fashioning a speech for that person.

" Hear, O Israel! I am He, the promised of God, born King of the Jews—come to you with the dominion spoken of by the prophets. Rise now, and lay hold on the world ! "

Would the Nazarene but speak these few words, what a tumult would follow ! How many mouths performing the office of trumpets would take them up and blow them abroad for the massing of armies !

Would He speak them ?

Meantime down the Kedron, and in towards Bezetha, especially on the roadsides quite up to the Damascus Gate, the country filled rapidly with all kinds of temporary shelters for pilgrims to the Passover. Ben-Hur visited the strangers, and talked with them ; and returning to his tents, he was each time more and more astonished at the vastness of their numbers. Might he not after all have misunderstood the Nazarene ? How much better this time for the movement than that other when, by Gennesaret, the Galileans would have forced assumption of the crown ! Then the support would have been limited to a few thousands ; now His proclamation would be responded to by millions—who could say how many ? Pursuing this theory to its conclusions, Ben-Hur moved amidst brilliant promises, and glowed with the thought that the melancholy man, under gentle seeming and wondrous self-denial, was in fact carrying in disguise the subtlety of a politician and the genius of a soldier.

Several times also, in the meanwhile, low-set, brawny men, bareheaded and black-bearded, came and asked for Ben-Hur at the tent ; his interviews with them were always apart ; and to his mother's question who they were he answered :

" Some good friends of mine from Galilee."

All these were incidents of occurrence between the twenty-first day of March—counting by the modern calendar—and the twenty-fifth. The evening of the latter day Ben-Hur yielded to his impatience, and rode to the city, leaving behind him a promise to return in the night.

CHAPTER VI

BEN-HUR alighted at the gate of the khan from which the three Wise Men more than thirty years before departed, going down to Bethlehem. There, in keeping of his Arab followers, he left the horse, and shortly after was at the wicket of his father's house, and in a yet briefer space in the great chamber. He called for Malluch first ; that worthy being out, he sent a salutation to his friends the merchant and the Egyptian. They were being carried abroad to see the celebration. The latter, he was informed, was very feeble, and in a state of deep dejection.

While the servant was answering for the elder, the curtain of the doorway was drawn aside, and the younger Egyptian came in, and walked—or floated, upborne in a white cloud of the gauzy raiment she so loved and lived in—to the centre of the chamber, where the light cast by lamps from the seven-armed brazen stick planted upon the floor was the strongest. With her, there was no fear of light.

The servant left the two alone.

Ben-Hur advanced to her eagerly, but stopped and gazed. Such a change he had never seen !

Theretofore she had been a lover studious to win him— in manner all warmth, each glance an admission, each action an avowal.

Such the Egyptian had been to Ben-Hur from the night of the boat-ride on the lake in the Orchard of Palms. But now !

It was not possible for her to have received a stranger with repulsion more incisive ; yet she was apparently as passionless as a statue, only the small head was a little tilted, the nostrils a little drawn, and the sensuous lower lip pushed the upper the least bit out of its natural curvature.

She was the first to speak.

" Your coming is timely, O son of Hur," she said, in a voice sharply distinct. " I wish to thank you for hospitality ; after to-morrow I may not have the opportunity to do so "

Ben-Hur bowed slightly without taking his eyes from her.

" Tell me," she continued, inclining her head, and permitting the sneer to become positive—" Tell me, O prince of Jerusalem, where is He, that Son of the carpenter of Nazareth, and Son not less of God, from whom so lately such mighty things were expected ? "

He waved his hand impatiently, and replied, " I am not His keeper."

The beautiful head sank forward yet lower.

" Has He broken Rome to pieces ? "

Again, but with anger, Ben-Hur raised his hand in deprecation.

" And how is it I see you in that garb ? Such is not the habit of governors in India or vice-kings elsewhere. I fear you have not entered upon your kingdom—the kingdom I was to share with you."

" The daughter of my wise guest is kinder than she imagines herself ; she is teaching me that Isis may kiss a heart without making it better."

Ben-Hur spoke with cold courtesy, and Iras, after playing with the pendant solitaire of her necklace of coins, rejoined, " For a Jew, the son of Hur is clever. I saw your dreaming Cæsar make His entry into Jerusalem. You told us He would that day proclaim himself King of the Jews from the steps of the Temple. I beheld the procession descend the mountain bringing Him. I heard their singing. They were beautiful with palms in motion. I looked everywhere among them for a figure with a promise of royalty—a horseman in purple, a chariot with a driver in shining brass, a stately warrior behind an orbed shield, rivalling his spear in stature. I looked for His guard. It would have been pleasant to have seen a prince of Jerusalem and a cohort of the legions of Galilee."

She flung her listener a glance of provoking disdain, then laughed heartily, as if the ludicrousness of the picture in her mind were too strong for contempt.

" Instead of a Sesostris returning in triumph, or a Cæsar helmed and sworded—ha, ha, ha !—I saw a man with a woman's face and hair, riding an ass's colt, and in tears.

The King ! the Son of God ! the Redeemer of the world—ha, ha, ha ! "

In spite of himself Ben-Hur winced.

"Daughter of Balthasar," he said, with dignity, "let us make an end of words. That you have a purpose I am sure. To it, I pray, and I will answer you ; then let us go our several ways, and forget we ever met. Say on ; I will listen, but not to more of that which you have given me."

The pink-stained fingers toyed daintily with the lustrous pendant at the throat, and her voice was exceeding low and soft ; only a tapping on the floor with her silken sandal admonished him to have a care.

"There was a Jew, an escaped galley-slave, who killed a man in the palace of Idernee," she began slowly.

Ben-Hur was startled.

"The same Jew slew a Roman soldier before the Market-place here in Jerusalem ; the same Jew has three trained legions from Galilee to seize the Roman Governor to-night ; the same Jew has alliances perfected for war upon Rome, and Ilderim the sheik is one of his partners."

Drawing nearer him, she almost whispered :

"You have lived in Rome. Suppose these things repeated in ears we know of. Ah ! you change colour."

He drew back from her with somewhat of the look which may be imagined upon the face of a man who, thinking to play with a kitten, has run upon a tiger ; and she proceeded :

"You are acquainted in the antechamber, and know the Lord Sejanus. Suppose it were told him with the proofs in hand—or without the proofs—that the same Jew is the richest man in the East—nay, in all the empire. The fishes of the Tiber would have fattening other than that they did out of its ooze, would they not ? "

"To give you pleasure, daughter of Egypt, I acknow-ledge your cunning, and that I am at your mercy. It may also please you to hear me acknowledge I have no hope of your favour. I could kill you, but you are a woman. The desert is open to receive me ; and though Rome is a good hunter of men, there she would follow long and far before she caught me, for in its heart there are wildernesses of spears as well as wildernesses of sand, and it is not unlovely to the unconquered Parthian.   In the toils as I am—dupe that I have been—yet there is one thing my due : who told you all you know about me ?   In flight or captivity, dying even, there will be consolation in leaving the traitor the curse of a man who has lived knowing nothing but wretchedness.   Who told you all you know about me ? "

"From this person I gathered a handful of little circumstances, and from that other yet another handful, and that afterwhile I put them together.   I had something from Sheik Ilderim as he lay with my father in a grove out in the desert.   The night was still, very still, and the walls of the tent, sooth to say, were poor ward against ears outside listening to—birds and beetles flying through the air."

She smiled at the conceit, but proceeded :

"Some other things I had from——"

"Whom ? "

"The son of Hur himself."

"Was there no other who contributed ? "

"No, not one."

Hur drew a breath of relief ; he had suspected that Esther had betrayed him, and said lightly, "Thanks.   It were not well to keep the Lord Sejanus waiting for you.   The desert is not so sensitive.   Again, O Egypt, peace ! "

To this time he had been standing uncovered ; now he took the handkerchief from his arm where it had been hanging, and adjusting it upon his head, turned to depart. But she arrested him ; in her eagerness, she even reached a hand to him.

"Stay ! " she said.

He looked back at her, but without taking the hand, though it was very noticeable for its sparkling of jewels ; and he knew by her manner that the reserved point of the scene which was so surprising to him was now to come.

"Stay, and do not distrust me.   If you but do what I say, I will save you.   That, also, I swear, by our holy Isis ! "

She spoke with animation ; indeed, she had never appeared to him so fascinating.

"You had once a friend," she continued.   " It was in your boyhood.   There was a quarrel, and you and he became enemies. He did you wrong. After many years you met him again in the Circus at Antioch."

" Messala ! "

" Yes, Messala. You are his creditor. Forgive the past ; admit him to friendship again ; restore the fortune he lost in the great wager ; rescue him. The six talents are as nothing to you ; not so much as a bud lost upon a tree already in full leaf ; but to him—— Ah, he must go about with a broken body ; wherever you meet him he must look up to you from the ground. O Ben-Hur, noble prince ! to a Roman descended as he is beggary is the other most odious name for death. Save him from beggary ! "

It seemed to Ben-Hur, when at last she paused to have his answer, that he could see Messala himself peering at him over her shoulder ; and in its expression the countenance of the Roman was not that of a mendicant or a friend ; the sneer was as patrician as ever, and the fine edge of the hauteur as flawless and irritating.

" The appeal has been decided then, and for once a Messala takes nothing. I must go and write it in my book of great occurrences—a judgment by a Roman against a Roman ! But did he—did Messala send you to me with this request, O Egypt ? "

" He has a noble nature, and judged you by it."

Ben-Hur took the hand upon his arm.

" As you know him in such friendly way, fair Egyptian, tell me, would he do for me, there being a reversal of the conditions, that he asks of me ? Answer, by Isis ! Answer for the truth's sake ! "

There was insistence in the touch of his hand, and in his look also.

" Oh ! " she began, " he is——"

" A Roman, you were about to say ; meaning that I, a Jew, must not determine dues from me to him by any measure of dues from him to me ; being a Jew, I must forgive him my winnings because he is a Roman. If you have more to tell me, daughter of Balthasar, speak quickly, quickly ; for, by the Lord God of Israel, when this heat of blood, hotter waxing, attains its highest, I may not be

able longer to see that you are a woman and beautiful! I
may see but the spy of a master the more hateful because
the master is a Roman. Say on, and quickly."

She threw his hand off and stepped back into the full
light, with all the evil of her nature collected in her eyes and
voice.

" Thou drinker of lees, feeder upon husks! To think I
could love thee, having seen Messala! Such as thou were
born to serve him. He would have been satisfied with
release of the six talents ; but I say to the six thou shalt add
twenty—twenty, dost thou hear ? The kissings of my
little finger which thou hast taken from him, though with
my consent, shall be paid for ; and that I have followed
thee with affectation of sympathy, and endured thee so
long, enter into the account not less because I was serving
him. The merchant here is thy keeper of moneys. If
by to-morrow at noon he has not thy order acted upon in
favour of my Messala for six-and-twenty talents—mark the
sum !—thou shalt settle with the Lord Sejanus. Be wise
and—farewell ! "

As she was going to the door, he put himself in her way.

" The old Egypt lives in you," he said. " Whether you
see Messala to-morrow or the next day, here or in Rome,
give him this message. Tell him I have back the money,
even the six talents, he robbed me of by robbing my father's
estate ; tell him I survived the galleys to which he had me
sent, and in my strength rejoice in his beggary and dishonour. O cunning incarnate, tell him that when the Lord
Sejanus comes to despoil me he will find nothing ; for the
inheritance I had from the duumvir, including the villa
by Misenum, has been sold, and the money from the sale is
out of reach, afloat in the marts of the world as bills of
exchange ; and that this house and the goods and mer-
chandise, and the ships and caravans with which Simonides plies his commerce with such princely profits are
covered by imperial safeguards. Tell him that along with
my defiance I do not send him a curse in words, but, as a
better expression of my undying hate, I send him one who
will prove to him the sum of all curses ; and when he looks
at you repeating this my message, daughter of Balthasar,

his Roman shrewdness will tell him all I mean.   Go now— and I will go."

He conducted her to the door, and, with ceremonious politeness, held back the curtain while she passed out.

" Peace to you ! " he said, as she disappeared.

CHAPTER VII

WHEN Ben-Hur left the guest-chamber, there was not nearly so much life in his action as when he entered it ; his steps were slower, and he went along with his head quite upon his breast.

The wound, it should be observed, was to his vanity ; and fortunately it is not often that people die of such hurts, or even continue a long time sick.   In Ben-Hur's case, moreover, there was a compensation ; for presently he exclaimed aloud, " Praised be the Lord God that the woman took not a more lasting hold on me !   I see I did not love her."

Then, as if he had already parted with not a little of the weight on his mind, he stepped forward more lightly ; and, coming to the place on the terrace where one stairway led down to the court-yard below, and another ascended to the roof, he took the latter and began to climb.   As he made the last step in the flight he stopped again.

" Can Balthasar have been her partner in the long mask she has been playing ?   No, no.   Hypocrisy seldom goes with wrinkled age like that.   Balthasar is a good man."

With this decided opinion he stepped upon the roof.

Ben-Hur permitted himself one glance over the parapet, then turned and walked mechanically towards the summer-house.

" Let them do their worst," he said, as he went slowly on. " I will not forgive the Roman.   I will not divide my fortune with him, nor will I fly from this city of my fathers.   I will call on Galilee first, and here make the fight.   By brave deeds I will bring the tribes to our side.   He who raised up Moses will find us a leader, if I fail.   If not the Nazarene, then some other of the many ready to die for freedom."

The interior of the summer-house, when Ben-Hur, slow sauntering, came to it, was murkily lighted. The faintest of shadows lay along the floor from the pillars on the north and west sides. Looking in, he saw the arm-chair usually occupied by Simonides drawn to a spot from which a view of the city over towards the Market-place could be best had.

" The good man is returned. I will speak with him, unless he be asleep."

He walked in, and with a quiet step approached the chair. Peering over the high back, he beheld Esther nestled in the seat asleep—a small figure snuggled away under her father's lap-robe. He put his arms upon the back of the chair, and thought :

" I will not wake her. I have nothing to tell her—nothing unless—unless it be my love. . . . She is a daughter of Judah, and beautiful, and so unlike the Egyptian ; for there it is all vanity, here all truth ; there ambition, here duty ; there selfishness, here self-sacrifice. . . . Nay, the question is not do I love her, but does she love me ? She was my friend from the beginning. I will go away, and wait another and a better time. I will wait. Fair Esther, dutiful child, daughter of Judah ! "

He retired silently as he came.

CHAPTER VIII

THE streets were full of people going and coming, or grouped about the fires roasting meat, and feasting and singing, and happy. The odour of scorching flesh mixed with the odour of cedar-wood aflame and smoking loaded the air ; and as this was the occasion when every son of Israel was full brother to every other son of Israel, and hospitality was without bounds, Ben-Hur was saluted at every step, while the groups by the fires insisted, " Stay and partake with us. We are brethren in the love of the Lord." But with thanks to them he hurried on, intending to take horse at the khan and return to the tents on the Kedron.

To make the place, it was necessary for him to cross the

T

thoroughfare so soon to receive sorrowful Christian perpetu-
ation.   There also the pious celebration was at its height.
Looking up the street, he noticed the flames of torches in
motion streaming out like pennons ; then he observed that
the singing ceased where the torches came.   His wonder rose
to its highest, however, when he became certain, that amid
the smoke and dancing sparks, he saw the keener sparkling of burnished spear-tips, arguing the presence of Roman
soldiers.   What were they, the scoffing legionaries, doing in
a Jewish religious procession ?   The circumstance was
unheard of, and he stayed to see the meaning of it.

Ben-Hur stepped into the street so close to the line of
march as to bring every one of the company under view
while passing.   The torches and the lanterns were being
borne by servants, each of whom was armed with a bludgeon
or a sharpened stave.   Their present duty seemed to be to
pick out the smoothest paths among the rocks in the streets
for certain dignitaries among them—elders and priests ;
rabbis with long beards, heavy brows, and beaked noses;
men of the class potential in the councils of Caiaphas and
Hannas.   Where could they be going ?   Not to the Temple,
certainly, for the route to the sacred house from Zion, whence
these appeared to be coming, was by the Xystus.   And
their business—if peaceful, why the soldiers ?

As the procession began to go by Ben-Hur, his attention
was particularly called to three persons walking together.
They were well towards the front, and the servants who
went before them with lanterns appeared unusually careful in the service.   In the person moving on the left of this
group he recognized a chief policeman of the Temple ; the
one on the right was a priest ; the middle man was not at
first so easily placed, as he walked leaning heavily upon
the arms of the others, and carried his head so low upon his
breast as to hide his face.   With great assurance, Ben-Hur
fell in on the right of the priest, and walked along with him.
Now if the man would lift his head !   And presently he
did so, letting the light of the lanterns strike full in his face,
pale, dazed, pinched with dread ; the beard roughed ;
the eyes filmy, sunken, and despairing.   In much going
about following the Nazarene, Ben-Hur had come to know

His disciples as well as the Master ; and now, at sight of the dismal countenance, he cried out :

" The 'Scariot ! "

Ben-Hur was carried passively along down the street, through the crowded lowlands between the hill Bezetha and the castle of Antonia, and on by the Bethesda reservoir to the Sheep Gate. There were people everywhere, and everywhere the people were engaged in sacred observances.

It being Passover night, the valves of the gate stood open. The keepers were off somewhere feasting. In front of the procession, as it passed out unchallenged, was the deep gorge of the Kedron with Olivet beyond, its dressing of cedar and olive trees darker of the moonlight silvering all the heavens. Two roads met and merged into the street at the gate—one from the north-east, the other from Bethany. Ere Ben-Hur could finish wondering whether he were to go farther, and if so, which road was to be taken, he was led off down into the gorge. And still no hint of the purpose of the midnight march.

Down the gorge and over the bridge at the bottom of it. There was a great clatter on the floor as the crowd, now a straggling rabble, passed over beating and pounding with their clubs and staves. A little further, and they turned off to the left in the direction of an olive orchard enclosed by a stone wall in view from the road. Presently they were all brought to a standstill. Voices called out excitedly in front ; a chill sensation ran from man to man ; there was a rapid falling-back, and a blind stumbling over each other. The soldiers alone kept their order.

It took Ben-Hur but a moment to disengage himself from the mob and run forward. There he found a gateway without a gate admitting to the orchard, and he halted to take in the scene.

A Man in white clothes, and bareheaded, was standing outside the entrance, His hands crossed before Him—a slender, stooping figure, with long hair and thin face—in an attitude of resignation and waiting.

It was the Nazarene !

Behind Him, next the gateway, were the disciples in a group ; they were excited, but no man was ever calmer than He. The torchlight beat redly upon Him, giving His hair a tint ruddier than was natural to it ; yet the expression of the countenance was as usual all gentleness and pity.

Presently the clear voice of the Christ arose.

" Whom seek ye ? "

" Jesus of Nazareth," the priest replied.

" I am He."

At these simplest of words, spoken without passion or alarm, the assailants fell back several steps ; the timid among them cowering to the ground ; and they might have let Him alone and gone away had not Judas walked over to Him.

" Hail, Master ! "

With this friendly speech he kissed Him.

" Judas," said the Nazarene mildly, " betrayest thou the Son of Man with a kiss ? Wherefore art thou come ? "

Receiving no reply, the Master spoke to the crowd again.

" Whom seek ye ? "

" Jesus of Nazareth."

" I have told you that I am He. If, therefore, you seek Me, let these go their way."

At these words of entreaty the rabbis advanced upon Him ; and seeing their intent, some of the disciples for whom He interceded drew nearer ; one of them cut off a man's ear, but without saving the Master from being taken. And yet Ben-Hur stood still ! Nay, while the officers were making ready with their ropes the Nazarene was doing His greatest charity—not the greatest in deed, but the very greatest in illustration of His forbearance, so far surpassing that of men.

" Suffer ye thus far," He said to the wounded man, and healed him with a touch.

Both friends and enemies were confounded—one side that He could do such a thing, the other that He would do it under the circumstances.

" Surely He will not allow them to bind Him ! "

Thus thought Ben-Hur.

" Put up thy sword into the sheath ; the cup which My Father hath given Me, shall I not drink it ? " From the offending follower, the Nazarene turned to His captors. "Are you come out as against a thief, with swords and staves to take Me? I was daily with you in the Temple, and you took Me not; but this is your hour, and the power of darkness."

The posse plucked up courage and closed about Him; and when Ben-Hur looked for the faithful they were gone—not one of them remained.

The crowd about the deserted Man seemed very busy with tongue, hand and foot. Over their heads, between the torch-sticks, through the smoke, sometimes in openings between restless men, Ben-Hur caught momentary glimpses of the Prisoner. Never had anything struck him as so piteous, so unfriended, so forsaken! Yet, he thought, the Man could have defended Himself—He could have slain His enemies with a breath, but He would not. What was the cup His Father had given Him to drink? And who was the Father to be so obeyed? Mystery upon mystery—not one, but many.

Directly the mob started in return to the city, the soldiers in the lead. Ben-Hur became anxious; he was not satisfied with himself. Where the torches were in the midst of the rabble he knew the Nazarene was to be found. Suddenly he resolved to see Him again. He would ask Him one question.

Taking off his long outer garment and the handkerchief from his head, he threw them upon the orchard wall, and started after the posse, which he boldly joined. Through the stragglers he made way, and by littles at length reached the man who carried the ends of the rope with which the Prisoner was bound.

The Nazarene was walking slowly, His head down, His hands bound behind Him; the hair fell thickly over His face, and He stooped more than usual; apparently He was oblivious to all going on around Him. In advance a few steps were priests and elders talking and occasionally looking back. When, at length, they were all near the bridge in the gorge, Ben-Hur took the rope from the servant who had it, and stepped past him.

"Master, Master!" he said hurriedly, speaking close

to the Nazarene's ear. "Dost Thou hear, Master? A word—one word. Tell me——"

The fellow from whom he had taken the rope now claimed it.

"Tell me," Ben-Hur continued, "goest Thou with these of Thine own accord?"

The people were come up now, and in his own ears asking angrily, "Who art thou, man?"

"O Master," Ben-Hur made haste to say, his voice sharp with anxiety, "I am Thy friend and lover. Tell me, I pray Thee, if I bring rescue, wilt Thou accept it?"

The Nazarene never so much as looked up or allowed the slightest sign of recognition; yet the something which when we are suffering is always telling it to such as look at us, though they be strangers, failed not now. "Let Him alone," it seemed to say; "He has been abandoned by His friends; the world has denied Him; in bitterness of spirit, He has taken farewell of men; He is going He knows not where, and He cares not. Let Him alone."

And to that Ben-Hur was now driven. A dozen hands were upon him, and from all sides there was shouting, "He is one of them. Bring him along; club him—kill him!"

With a gust of passion, which gave him many times his ordinary force, Ben-Hur raised himself, turned once about with his arms outstretched, shook the hands off, and rushed through the circle which was fast hemming him in. The hands snatching at him as he passed tore his garments from his back, so he ran off the road naked; and the gorge, in keeping of the friendly darkness, darker there than elsewhere, received him safe.

Reclaiming his handkerchief and outer garments from the orchard wall, he followed back to the city gate; thence he went to the khan, and on a good horse rode to the tents of his people out by the Tombs of the Kings.

As he rode, he promised himself to see the Nazarene on the morrow—promised it, not knowing that the unfriended Man was taken straightway to the house of Hannas to be tried that night.

CHAPTER IX

NEXT morning, about the second hour, two men rode full speed to the doors of Ben-Hur's tents, and dismounting, asked to see him. He was not yet risen, but gave directions for their admission.

"Peace to you, brethren," he said, for they were of his Galileans, and trusted officers. "Will you be seated ? "

"Nay," the senior replied, bluntly, "to sit and be at ease is to let the Nazarene die. Rise, son of Judah, and go with us. The judgment has been given. The tree of the cross is already at Golgotha."

Ben-Hur's face brightened with resolution, and he clapped his hands.

"The horses—and quickly ! " he said to the Arab who answered the signal. "And bid Amrah send me fresh garments, and bring my sword ! It is time to die for Israel, my friends. Tarry without till I come."

He ate a crust, drank a cup of wine, and was soon upon the road.

"Whither would you go first ? " asked the Galilean.

"To collect the legions."

"Alas ! " the man replied, throwing up his hands.

"Why alas ? "

"Master "—the man spoke with shame—" master, I and my friend here are all that are faithful. The rest do follow the priests."

"Seeking what ? " and Ben-Hur drew rein.

"To kill Him."

"Not the Nazarene ? "

"You have said it."

Ben-Hur saw the failure of the scheme he had built upon the fidelity of the Galileans ; their desertion, in fact, left nothing more of it. A dread seized him. It was possible his scheming, and labour, and expenditure of treasure might have been but blasphemous contention with God. When he picked up the reins and said, " Let us go, brethren," all before him was uncertainty. The faculty of resolving quickly, without which one cannot be a hero in the midst of stirring scenes, was numb within him.

"Let us go, brethren; let us to Golgotha."

They passed through excited crowds of people going south, like themselves. All the country north of the city seemed aroused and in motion.

Hearing that the procession with the condemned might be met with somewhere near the great white towers left by Herod, the three friends rode thither, passing round south-east of Akra. In the valley below the Pool of Hezekiah, passage-way against the multitude became impossible, and they were compelled to dismount, and take shelter behind the corner of a house and wait.

The waiting was as if they were on a river bank, watching a flood go by, for such the people seemed.

Half an hour—an hour—the flood surged by Ben-Hur and his companions, within arm's reach, incessant, undiminished. At the end of that time he could have said, "I have seen all the castes of Jerusalem, all the sects of Judea, all the tribes of Israel, and all the nationalities of earth represented by them."

Borne along with the stream were thousands not Jews—thousands hating and despising them—Greeks, Romans, Arabs, Syrians, Africans, Egyptians, Easterns. So that, studying the mass, it seemed the whole world was to be represented, and, in that sense, present at the crucifixion.

At length, from the direction of the great towers, Ben-Hur heard, at first faint in the distance, a shouting of many men.

"Hark! they are coming now," said one of his friends.

The shouting drew nearer each moment; and the air was already full of it and trembling, when Ben-Hur saw the servants of Simonides coming with their master in his chair, and Esther walking by his side; a covered litter was next behind them.

"Peace to you, O Simonides—and to you, Esther," said Ben-Hur, meeting them. "If you are for Golgotha, stay until the procession passes; I will then go with you. There is room to turn in by the house here."

The merchant's large head rested heavily upon his

breast ; rousing himself, he answered, " Speak to Balthasar ;
his pleasure will be mine. He is in the litter."

Ben-Hur hastened to draw aside the curtain. The
Egyptian was lying within, his wan face so pinched as to
appear like a dead man's. The proposal was submitted
to him.

" Can we see Him ? " he inquired faintly.

" The Nazarene ? Yes ; He must pass within a few feet
of us."

" Dear Lord ! " the old man cried fervently. " Once
more, once more ! Oh, it is a dreadful day for the world ! "

Shortly the whole party were in waiting under shelter of
the house. They said but little, afraid, probably, to trust
their thoughts to each other ; everything was uncertain,
and nothing so much so as opinions. Balthasar drew
himself feebly from the litter, and stood supported by a
servant ; Esther and Ben-Hur kept Simonides company.

Meantime the flood poured along, if anything, more
densely than before ; and the shouting came nearer, shrill
up in the air, hoarse along the earth, and cruel.

A band of legionaries fully armed followed next, marching
in sturdy indifference, the glory of burnished brass about
them the while.

Then came the NAZARENE !

He was nearly dead. Every few steps He staggered as
if He would fall. A stained gown badly torn hung from His
shoulders over a seamless under-tunic. His bare feet
left red splotches upon the stones. An inscription on a
board was tied to His neck. A crown of thorns had been
crushed hard down upon His head, making cruel wounds
from which streams of blood, now dry and blackened, had
run over His face and neck. The long hair, tangled in the
thorns, was clotted thick. The skin, where it could be seen,
was ghastly white. His hands were tied before Him.
Back somewhere in the city He had fallen exhausted under
the transverse beam of His cross, which, as a condemned
person, custom required Him to bear to the place of execution ; now a countryman carried the burden in His stead.
Four soldiers went with Him as a guard against the mob, who
sometimes, nevertheless, broke through, and struck Him

with sticks, and spat upon Him. Yet no sound escaped Him, neither remonstrance nor groan ; nor did He look up until He was nearly in front of the house sheltering Ben-Hur and his friends, all of whom were moved with quick compassion.   Esther clung to her father ; and he, strong of will as he was, trembled.   Balthasar fell down speechless.   Even Ben-Hur cried out, " O my God ! my God ! " Then as if He divined their feelings or heard the exclamation, the Nazarene turned His wan face towards the party and looked at them each one, so they carried the look in memory through life.   They could see He was thinking of them, not Himself, and the dying eyes gave them the blessing He was not permitted to speak.

" Where are thy legions, son of Hur ? " asked Simonides, aroused.

" Hannas can tell thee better than I."

" What, faithless ? "

" All but these two."

" Then all is lost, and this good Man must die ! "

The face of the merchant knit convulsively as he spoke, and his head sank upon his breast.   He had borne his part in Ben-Hur's labours well, and he had been inspired by the same hopes, now blown out never to be rekindled.

Two other men succeeded the Nazarene bearing cross-beams.

" Who are these ? " Ben-Hur asked of the Galileans.

" Thieves appointed to die with the Nazarene," they replied.

Next in the procession stalked a mitred figure clad all in the golden vestments of the high-priest.   Policemen from the Temple curtained him round about ; and after him, in order, strode the Sanhedrin, and a long array of priests, the latter in their plain white garments over-wrapped by abnets of many folds and gorgeous colours.

" The son-in-law of Hannas," said Ben-Hur, in a low voice.

" Caiaphas !   I have seen him," Simonides replied, adding, after a pause during which he thoughtfully watched the haughty pontiff, " And now am I convinced.   With such assurance as proceeds from clear enlightenment of the

spirit—with absolute assurance—now know I that He who
first goes yonder with the inscription about His neck
is what the inscription proclaims Him—KING OF THE JEWS.
A common man, an impostor, a felon, was never thus
waited upon.   For look! Here are the nations—Jerusalem, Israel.   Here is the ephod, here the blue robe with
its fringe, and purple pomegranates, and golden bells, not
seen in the street since the day Jaddua went out to meet
the Macedonian—proofs all that this Nazarene is King.
Would I could rise and go after Him ! "

Ben-Hur listened surprised ; and directly, as if himself
awakening to his unusual display of feeling, Simonides
said impatiently :

" Speak to Balthasar, I pray you, and let us begone.
The vomit of Jerusalem is coming."

Then Esther spoke.

" I see some women there, and they are weeping. Who
are they ? "

Following the pointing of her hand, the party beheld
four women in tears ; one of them leaned upon the arm of
a man of aspect not unlike the Nazarene's. Presently
Ben-Hur answered :

" The man is the disciple whom the Nazarene loves the
best of all ; she who leans upon his arm is Mary, the
Master's mother ; the others are friendly women of Galilee."

Esther pursued the mourners with glistening eyes until
the multitude received them out of sight.

It may be the reader will fancy the foregoing snatches
of conversation were had in quiet ; but it was not so.   The
talking was, for the most part, like that indulged by people
at the seaside under the sound of the surf ; for to nothing
else can the clamour of this division of the mob be so well
likened.

The demonstration was the forerunner of those in which,
scarce thirty years later, under rule of the factions, the
Holy City was torn to pieces ; it was quite as great in
numbers, as fanatical and bloodthirsty ; boiled and raved,
and had in it exactly the same elements—servants, camel-
drivers, marketmen, gate-keepers, gardeners, dealers in
fruits and wines, proselytes, and foreigners not proselytes.

watchmen and menials from the Temple, thieves, robbers, and the myriad not assignable to any class, but who, on such occasions as this, appeared no one could say whence, hungry and smelling of caves and old tombs—bareheaded wretches with naked arms and legs, hair and beard in uncombed mats, and each with one garment the colour of clay ; beasts with abysmal mouths, in outcry effective as lions calling each other across desert spaces. Some of them had swords ; a greater number flourished spears and javelins ; though the weapons of the many were staves and knotted clubs, and slings, for which latter selected stones were stored in scrips, and sometimes in sacks improvised from the foreskirt of their dirty tunics. Among the mass here and there appeared persons of high degree—scribes, elders, rabbis, Pharisees with broad fringing, Sadducees in fine cloaks—serving for the time as prompters and directors. If a throat tired of one cry, they invented another for it ; if brassy lungs showed signs of collapse, they set them going again ; and yet the clamour, loud and continuous as it was, could have been reduced to a few syllables—King of the Jews !—Room for the King of the Jews !—Defiler of the Temple !—Blasphemer of God !—Crucify Him, crucify Him ! And of these cries the last one seemed in greatest favour, because, doubtless, it was more directly expressive of the wish of the mob, and helped to better articulate its hatred of the Nazarene.

" Come," said Simonides, when Balthasar was ready to proceed—" come, let us forward."

Ben-Hur did not hear the call. The appearance of the part of the procession then passing, its brutality and hunger for life, were reminding him of the Nazarene. He remembered suddenly his own great indebtedness to the Man ; and with these recollections, the thought of his present powerlessness to give back help for help or make return in kind stung him keenly, and he accused himself. He had not done all he might ; he could have watched with the Galileans, and kept them true and ready ; and this—ah ! this was the moment to strike ! A blow well given now would not merely disperse the mob and set the Nazarene free ; it would be a trumpet call to Israel, and precipitate the long-dreamt-of war for freedom. The opportunity was going ; the minutes were bearing it away ; and if lost ! God of Abraham ! was there nothing to be done—nothing ?

That instant a party of Galileans caught his eye. He rushed through the press and overtook them.

" Follow me," he said. " I would have speech with you."

The men obeyed him, and when they were under shelter of the house, he spoke again :

" You are of those who took my swords, and agreed with me to strike for freedom and the King who was coming. You have the swords now, and now is the time to strike with them. Go, look everywhere, and find our brethren, and tell them to meet me at the tree of the cross making ready for the Nazarene. Haste all of you ! Nay, stand not so ! The Nazarene is the King, and freedom dies with Him."

They looked at him respectfully, but did not move.

" Hear you ? " he asked.

Then one of them replied :

" Son of Judah "—by that name they knew him—" son of Judah, it is you who are deceived, not we or our brethren who have your swords. The Nazarene is not the King ; neither has He the spirit of a king. We were with Him when He came into Jerusalem : we saw Him in the Temple ; He failed Himself, and us, and Israel ; at the Gate Beautiful He turned His back upon God and refused the throne of David. He is not King, and Galilee is not with Him. He shall die the death. But hear you, son of Judah. We have your swords, and we are ready now to draw them and strike for freedom ; and so is Galilee. Be it for freedom, O son of Judah, for freedom ! and we will meet you at the tree of the cross."

The sovereign moment of his life was upon Ben-Hur. Could he have taken the offer and said the word, history might have been other than it is ; but then it would have been history ordered by men, not God—something that never was, and never will be. A confusion fell upon him ; he knew not how, though afterwards he attributed it to the Nazarene ; for when the Nazarene was risen, he understood the death was necessary to faith in the resurrection, without which Christianity would be an empty husk. The confusion, as has been said, left him without the faculty of decision; he stood helpless—wordless even. Covering his face with his hand, he shook with the conflict between his wish, which was what he would have ordered, and the power that was upon him.

"Come; we are waiting for you," said Simonides, the fourth time.

Thereupon he walked mechanically after the chair and the litter. Esther walked with him. Like Balthasar and his friends, the Wise Men, the day they went to the meeting in the desert, he was being led along the way.

CHAPTER X

WHEN the party—Balthasar, Simonides, Ben-Hur, Esther, and the two faithful Galileans—reached the place of crucifixion, Ben-Hur was in advance leading them.

Ben-Hur came to a stop; those following him also stopped. As a curtain rises before an audience, the spell holding him in its sleep-awake rose, and he saw with a clear understanding.

There was a space upon the top of a low knoll rounded like a skull, and dry, dusty, and without vegetation, except some scrubby hyssop. The boundary of the space was a living wall of men, with men behind struggling, some to look over, others to look through it. An inner wall of Roman soldiery held the dense outer wall rigidly to its place. A centurion kept eye upon the soldiers. Up to the very line so vigilantly guarded Ben-Hur had been led; at the line he now stood, his face to the north-west. The knoll was the old Aramaic Golgotha—in Latin, Calvaria; anglicized, Calvary; translated, The Skull.

On its slopes, in the low places, on the swells and higher hills, the earth sparkled with a strange enamelling. Look where he would outside the walled space, he saw no patch of brown soil, no rock, no green thing; he saw only thousands of eyes in ruddy faces; off a little way in the perspective only ruddy faces without eyes ; off a little farther only a broad, broad circle, which the nearer view instructed him was also of faces. And this was the ensemble of three millions of people ; under it three millions of hearts throbbing with passionate interest in what was taking place upon the knoll ; indifferent as to the thieves, caring only for the Nazarene, and for Him only as He was an object of hate or fear or curiosity—He who loved them all, and was about to die for them.

Up on the knoll so high as to be above the living wall, and visible over the heads of an attending company of notables, conspicuous because of his mitre and vestments and his haughty air, stood the high-priest. Up the knoll still higher, up quite to the round summit, so as to be seen far and near, was the Nazarene, stooped and suffering, but silent. The wit among the guard had complemented the crown upon His head by putting a reed in His hand for a sceptre. Clamours blew upon Him like blasts—laughter —execrations—sometimes both together indistinguishably. A man—*only* a man, O reader, would have charged the blasts with the remainder of his love for the race, and let it go for ever.

All the eyes then looking were fixed upon the Nazarene. It may have been pity with which he was moved ; whatever the cause, Ben-Hur was conscious of a change in his feelings. A conception of something better than the best of this life— something so much better that it could serve a weak man with strength to endure agonies of spirit as well as of body ; something to make death welcome—perhaps another life purer than this one—perhaps the spirit-life which Balthasar held to so fast, began to dawn upon his mind clearer and clearer, bringing to him a certain sense that, after all, the mission of the Nazarene was that of guide across the boundary for such as loved Him ; across the boundary to where His kingdom was set up and waiting for Him. Then, as something borne through the air out of the almost forgotten, he heard again, or seemed to hear, the saying of the Nazarene :

" I AM THE RESURRECTION AND THE LIFE."

And the words repeated themselves over and over, and took form, and the dawn touched them with its light, and filled them with a new meaning. And as men repeat a question to grasp and fix the meaning, he asked, gazing at the figure on the hill fainting under its crown, Who the Resurrection ? and who the Life ?

" I AM,"

the figure seemed to say—and say it for him ; for instantly he was sensible of a peace such as he had never known—the peace which is the end of doubt and mystery, and the beginning of faith and love and clear understanding.

From this dreamy state Ben-Hur was aroused by the sound of hammering. On the summit of the knoll he observed then what had escaped him before—some soldiers and workmen preparing the crosses. The holes for planting the trees were ready, and now the transverse beams were being fitted to their places.

" Bid the men make haste," said the high-priest to the centurion. " These "—and he pointed to the Nazarene— " must be dead by the going-down of the sun, and buried that the land may not be defiled. Such is the Law."

With a better mind, a soldier went to the Nazarene and offered Him something to drink, but He refused the cup. Then another went to him and took from His neck the board with the inscription upon it, which he nailed to the tree of the cross—and the preparation was complete.

" The crosses are ready," said the centurion to the pontiff, who received the report with a wave of the hand and the reply :

" Let the blasphemer go first, the Son of God should be able to save Himself. We will see."

The people to whom the preparation in its several stages was visible, and who to this time had assailed the hill with incessant cries of impatience, permitted a lull which directly became a universal hush. The part of the infliction most shocking, at least to the thought, was reached—the men were to be nailed to their crosses. When for that purpose the soldiers laid their hands upon the Nazarene first, a shudder passed through the great concourse ; the most brutalized shrank with dread. Afterwards there were those who said the air suddenly chilled and made them shiver.

"How very still it is !" Esther said, as she put her arm about her father's neck.

And remembering the torture he himself had suffered, he drew her face down upon his breast, and sat trembling.

"Avoid it, Esther, avoid it !" he said. "I know not but all who stand and see it—the innocent as well as the guilty—may be cursed from this hour."

Balthasar sank upon his knees.

"Son of Hur," said Simonides, with increasing excitement—"Son of Hur, if Jehovah stretch not forth His hand, and quickly, Israel is lost—and we are lost."

Ben-Hur answered, calmly, "I have been in a dream, Simonides, and heard in it why all this should be, and why it should go on. It is the will of the Nazarene—it is God's will. Let us do as the Egyptian here—let us hold our peace and pray."

As he looked up on the knoll again, the words were wafted to him through the awful stillness—

"I AM THE RESURRECTION AND THE LIFE."

He bowed reverently as to a person speaking.

Up on the summit meantime the work went on. The guard took the Nazarene's clothes from Him ; so that He stood before the millions naked. The stripes of the scourging He had received in the early morning were still bloody upon His back ; yet He was laid pitilessly down, and stretched upon the cross—first, the arms upon the transverse beam ; the spikes were sharp—a few blows, and they were driven through the tender palms ; next, they drew His knees up until the soles of the feet rested flat upon the tree ; then they placed one foot upon the other, and one spike fixed both of them fast. The dulled sound of the hammering was heard outside the guarded space ; and such as could not hear, yet saw the hammer as it fell, shivered with fear. And withal not a groan, or cry, or word of remonstrance from the sufferer : nothing at which an enemy could laugh ; nothing a lover could regret.

"Which way wilt thou have Him faced ? " asked a soldier, bluntly.

"Towards the Temple," the pontiff replied. "In dying I would have Him see the holy house hath not suffered by Him."

The workmen put their hands to the cross, and carried it, burden and all, to the place of planting. At a word, they dropped the tree into the hole ; and the body of the Nazarene also dropped heavily and hung by the bleeding hands. Still no cry of pain—only the exclamation divinest of all recorded exclamations :

"Father, forgive them, for they know not what they do."

The cross, reared now above all other objects, and standing singly out against the sky, was greeted with a burst of delight ! and all who could see and read the writing upon the board over the Nazarene's head made haste to decipher it. Soon as read, the legend was adopted by them and communicated, and presently the whole mighty concourse was ringing the salutation from side to side, and repeating it with laughter and groans :

"King of the Jews ! Hail, King of the Jews ! "

The pontiff, with a clearer idea of the import of the inscription, protested against it, but in vain ; so the titled King, looking from the knoll with dying eyes, must have had the city of His fathers at rest below Him—she who had so ignominiously cast Him out.

The sun was rising rapidly to noon ; the hills bared their brown breasts lovingly to it ; the more distant mountains rejoiced in the purple with which it so regally dressed them. In the city, the temples, palaces, towers, pinnacles, and all points of beauty and prominence seemed to lift themselves into the unrivalled brilliance, as if they knew the pride they were giving the many who from time to time turned to look at them. Suddenly a dimness began to fill the sky and cover the earth—at first no more than a scarce perceptible fading of the day ; a twilight out of time ; an evening gliding in upon the splendours of noon. But it deepened, and directly drew attention ; whereat the noise of the shouting and laughter fell off, and men, doubting their senses, gazed at each other curiously : then they looked to the sun again ; then at the mountains, getting farther away ; at the sky and the near landscape, sinking in shadow ; at the hill upon which the tragedy was enacting ; and from all these they gazed at each other again, and turned pale, and held their peace

" It is only a mist or passing cloud,' Simonides said soothingly to Esther, who was alarmed   " It will brighter presently."

Ben-Hur did not think so.

" It is not a mist or a cloud," he said.   " The spirits who live in the air—the prophets and saints—are at work in mercy to themselves and nature. I say to you, O Simonides, truly as God lives, He who hangs yonder is the Son of God."

And leaving Simonides lost in wonder at such a speech from him, he went where Balthasar was kneeling near by, and laid his hand upon the good man's shoulder.

" O wise Egyptian, hearken ! Thou alone wert right— the Nazarene is indeed the Son of God."

Balthasar drew him down to him, and replied, feebly, " I saw Him a child in the manger where He was first laid ; it is not strange that I knew Him sooner than thou ; but oh that I should live to see this day ! Would I had died with my brethren ! Happy Melchior ! Happy, happy Gaspar ! "

" Comfort thee ! " said Ben-Hur.   " Doubtless they too are here."

The dimness went on deepening into obscurity, and that into positive darkness, but without deterring the bolder spirits upon the knoll. One after the other the thieves were raised on their crosses, and the crosses planted. The guard was then withdrawn, and the people set free closed in upon the height, and surged up it, like a converging wave. A man might take a look, when a new-comer would push him on, and take his place, to be in turn pushed on—and there were laughter and ribaldry and revilements, all for the Nazarene.

" Ha, ha ! If Thou be King of the Jews, save Thyself," a soldier shouted.

"Ay," said a priest, "if He will come down to us now, we will believe in Him."

Others wagged their heads wisely, saying, "He would destroy the Temple, and rebuild it in three days, but cannot save Himself."

Others still : "He called Himself the Son of God ; let us see if God will have Him."

The supernatural night, dropped thus from the heavens, affected Esther as it began to affect thousands of others braver and stronger.

"Let us go home," she prayed—twice, three times—saying, "It is the frown of God, father. What other dreadful things may happen, who can tell ? I am afraid."

Simonides was obstinate. He said little, but was plainly under great excitement. Observing, about the end of the first hour, that the violence of the crowding up on the knoll was somewhat abated, at his suggestion the party advanced to take position nearer the crosses. Ben-Hur gave his arm to Balthasar ; yet the Egyptian made the ascent with difficulty. From their new stand, the Nazarene was imperfectly visible, appearing to them not more than a dark suspended figure. They could hear Him, however—hear His sighing, which showed an endurance or exhaustion greater than that of His fellow-sufferers ; for they filled every lull in the noises with their groans and entreaties.

The second hour after the suspension passed like the first one. To the Nazarene they were hours of insult, provocation, and slow dying. He spoke but once in the time. Some women came and knelt at the foot of His cross. Among them He recognized His mother with the beloved disciple.

"Woman," He said, raising His voice, "behold thy son ! " And to the disciple, "Behold thy mother ! "

The third hour came, and still the people surged round the hill, held to it by some strange attraction, with which, in probability, the night in midday had much to do. They were quieter than in the preceding hour ; yet at intervals they could be heard off in the darkness shouting to each other, multitude calling unto multitude. It was noticeable, also, that coming now to the Nazarene, they approached

His cross in silence, took the look in silence, and so departed. This change extended even to the guard, who so shortly before had cast lots for the clothes of the Crucified ; they stood with their officers a little apart, more watchful of the one convict than of the throngs coming and going. If He but breathed heavily, or tossed His head in a paroxysm of pain, they were instantly on the alert. Most marvellous of all, however, was the altered behaviour of the high-priest and his following, the wise men who had assisted him in the trial in the night, and, in the Victim's face, kept place by him with zealous approval. When the darkness began to fall, they began to lose their confidence. There were among them many learned in astronomy, and familiar with the apparitions so terrible in those days to the masses ; much of the knowledge was descended to them from their fathers far back ; some of it had been brought away at the end of the Captivity; and the necessities of the Temple service kept it all bright. These closed together when the sun commenced to fade before their eyes, and the mountains and hills to recede ; they drew together in a group around their pontiff, and debated what they saw. " The moon is at its full," they said, with truth, " and this cannot be an eclipse." Then, as no one could answer the question common with them all—as no one could account for the darkness, or for its occurrence at that particular time, in their secret hearts they associated it with the Nazarene, and yielded to an alarm which the long continuance of the phenomenon steadily increased. In their place behind the soldiers, they noted every word and motion of the Nazarene, and hung with fear upon His sighs, and talked in whispers. The man might be the Messiah, and then—— But they would wait and see !

In the meantime Ben-Hur was not once visited by the old spirit. The perfect peace abode with him. He prayed simply that the end might be hastened. He knew the condition of Simonides' mind—that he was hesitating on the verge of belief. He could see the massive face weighed down by solemn reflection. He noticed him casting inquiring glances at the sun, as seeking the cause of the darkness. Nor did he fail to notice the solicitude with which Esther clung to him, smothering her fears to accommodate his wishes.

"Be not afraid," he heard him say to her; "but stay and watch with me. Thou mayst live twice the span of my life, and see nothing of human interest equal to this; and there may be revelations more. Let us stay to the close."

When the third hour was about half gone, some men of the rudest class—wretches from the tombs about the city—came and stopped in front of the centre cross.

"This is He, the new King of the Jews," said one of them.

The others cried, with laughter, "Hail, all hail, King of the Jews!"

Receiving no reply, they went closer.

"If Thou be King of the Jews, or Son of God, come down," they said loudly.

At this, one of the thieves quit groaning, and called to the Nazarene, "Yes, if Thou be Christ, save Thyself and us."

The people laughed and applauded; then, while they were listening for a reply, the other felon was heard to say to the first one, "Dost thou not fear God? We receive the due rewards of our deeds; but this Man hath done nothing amiss."

The bystanders were astonished; in the midst of the hush which ensued, the second felon spoke again, but this time to the Nazarene.

"Lord," he said, "remember me when Thou comest into Thy kingdom."

Simonides gave a great start. "When Thou comest into Thy kingdom!" It was the very point of doubt in his mind; the point he had so often debated with Balthasar.

"Didst thou hear?" said Ben-Hur to him. "The kingdom cannot be of this world. Yon witness saith the King is but going to His kingdom; and, in effect, I heard the same in my dream."

"Hush!" said Simonides, more imperiously than ever before in speech to Ben-Hur. "Hush, I pray thee! If the Nazarene should answer——"

And as he spoke the Nazarene did answer, in a clear voice, full of confidence :

" Verily I say unto thee, To-day thou shalt be with Me in Paradise ! "

Simonides waited to hear if that were all ; then he folded his hands and said, " No more, no more, Lord ! The darkness is gone ; I see with other eyes—even as Balthasar, I see with eyes of perfect faith."

The faithful servant had at last his fitting reward. His broken body might never be restored ; nor was there riddance of the recollection of his sufferings, or recall of the years embittered by them ; but suddenly a new life was shown him, with assurance that it was for him—a new life lying just beyond this one—and its name was Paradise. There he would find the Kingdom of which he had been dreaming, and the King. A perfect peace fell upon him.

Over the way, in front of the cross, however, there were surprise and consternation. The cunning casuists there put the assumption underlying the question and the admission underlying the answer together. For saying through the land that He was the Messiah, they had brought the Nazarene to the cross ; and lo ! on the cross, more confidently than ever, He had not only reasserted Himself, but promised enjoyment of His Paradise to a malefactor. They trembled at what they were doing. The pontiff, with all his pride, was afraid. Where got the Man His confidence except from Truth ? And what should the Truth be but God ? A very little now would put them all to flight.

The breathing of the Nazarene grew harder ; His sighs became great gasps. Only three hours upon the cross, and He was dying !

The intelligence was carried from man to man, until every one knew it ; and then everything hushed ; the breeze faltered and died ; a stifling vapour loaded the air ; heat was superadded to darkness ; nor might any one unknowing the fact have thought that off the hill, out under the overhanging pall, there were three millions of people waiting awestruck what should happen next—they were so still !

Then there went out through the gloom, over the heads

of such as were on the hill within hearing of the dying Man, a cry of despair, if not reproach :

"My God ! My God ! why hast Thou forsaken Me ? "

The voice startled all who heard it. One it touched uncontrollably.

The soldiers in coming had brought with them a vessel of wine and water, and set it down a little way from Ben-Hur. With a sponge dipped into the liquor, and put on the end of a stick, they could moisten the tongue of a sufferer at their pleasure. Ben-Hur thought of the draught he had had at the well near Nazareth ; an impulse seized him ; catching up the sponge, he dipped it into the vessel, and started for the cross.

" Let Him be ! " the people in the way shouted, angrily. " Let Him be ! "

Without minding them, he ran on, and put the sponge to the Nazarene's lips.

Too late, too late !

The face then plainly seen by Ben-Hur, bruised and black with blood and dust as it was, lighted nevertheless with a sudden glow : the eyes opened wide, and fixed upon some one visible to them alone in the far heavens ; and there were content and relief, even triumph, in the shout the Victim gave.

" It is finished ! It is finished ! "

So a hero, dying in the doing a great deed, celebrates his success with a last cheer.

The light in the eyes went out ; slowly the crowned head sank upon the labouring breast. Ben-Hur thought the struggle over ; but the fainting soul recollected itself, so that he and those around him caught the other and last words, spoken in a low voice, as if to one listening close by :

" Father, into Thy hands I commend My spirit."

A tremor shook the tortured body ; there was a scream of fiercest anguish, and the mission and the earthly life were over at once. The heart, with all its love, was broken ; for of that, O reader, the Man died !

Ben-Hur went back to his friends, saying simply, " It is over ; He is dead."

In a space incredibly short the multitude was informed

of the circumstance. No one repeated it aloud ; there was
a murmur which spread from the knoll in every direction ,
a murmur that was little more than a whispering, " He is
dead ! He is dead ! " and that was all. The people had
their wish ; the Nazarene was dead ; yet they stared at
each other aghast. His blood was upon them ! And
while they stood staring at each other, the ground commenced to shake ; each man took hold of his neighbour
to support himself ; in a twinkling the darkness disappeared, and the sun came out ; and everybody, as with
the same glance, beheld the crosses upon the hill all reeling
drunken-like in the earthquake. They beheld all three
of them ; but the One in the centre was arbitrary ; it
alone would be seen ; and for that it seemed to extend
itself upwards, and lift its burden, and swing it to and fro
higher and higher in the blue of the sky. And every man
among them who had jeered at the Nazarene ; every one
who had struck Him ; every one who had voted to crucify
Him ; every one who had marched in the procession
from the city ; every one who had in his heart wished
Him dead, and they were as ten to one, felt that he was in
some way individually singled out from the many, and that
if he would live he must get away quickly as possible from
that menace in the sky. They started to run ; they ran
with all their might ; on horseback, and camels, and in
chariots they ran, as well as on foot, but then, as if it were
mad at them for what they had done, and had taken
up the cause of the unoffending and friendless dead, the
earthquake pursued them, and tossed them about, and
flung them down, and terrified them yet more by the
horrible noise of great rocks grinding and rending beneath
them. They beat their breasts and shrieked with fear.
His blood was upon them ! The home-bred and the foreign,
priest and layman, beggar, Sadducee, Pharisee, were overtaken in the race, and tumbled about indiscriminately.
If they called on the Lord, the outraged earth answered
for Him in fury, and dealt them all alike. It did not
even known wherein the high-priest was better than his
guilty brethren ; overtaking him, it tripped him up also,
and smirched the fringing of his robe, and filled the golden

bells with sand, and his mouth with dust. He and his people were alike in the one thing at least—the blood of the Nazarene was upon them all.

When the sunlight broke upon the crucifixion, the mother of the Nazarene, the disciple, and the faithful women of Galilee, the centurion and his soldiers, and Ben-Hur and his party, were all who remained upon the hill. These had not time to observe the flight of the multitude ; they were too loudly called upon to take care of themselves.

" Seat thyself here," said Ben-Hur to Esther, making a place for her at her father's feet. " Now cover thine eyes, and look not up ; but put thy trust in God, and the spirit of yon just Man so foully slain."

" Nay," said Simonides reverently, " let us henceforth speak of Him as the Christ."

" Be it so," said Ben-Hur.

Presently a wave of the earthquake struck the hill. The shrieks of the thieves upon the reeling crosses were terrible to hear. Though giddy with the movements of the ground, Ben-Hur had time to look at Balthasar, and beheld him prostrate and still. He ran to him and called—there was no reply. The good man was dead ! Then Ben-Hur remembered to have heard a cry in answer, as it were, to the scream of the Nazarene in His last moment ; but he had not looked to see from whom it had proceeded ; and ever after he believed the spirit of the Egyptian accompanied that of his Master over the boundary into the Kingdom of Paradise. The idea rested not only upon the cry heard, but upon the exceeding fitness of the distinction. If faith were worthy reward in the person of Gaspar, and love in that of Melchior, surely he should have some special meed who through a long life had so excellently illustrated the three virtues in combination—Faith, Love and Good Works.

The servants of Balthasar had deserted their master ; but when all was over, the two Galileans bore the old man in his litter back to the city.

It was a sorrowful procession that entered the south gate of the palace of the Hurs about the set of sun that memorable day. About the same hour the body of the Christ was taken down from the cross.

The remains of Balthasar were carried to the guest-chamber. All the servants hastened weeping to see him ; for he had the love of every living thing with which he had in anywise to do ; but when they beheld his face, and the smile upon it, they dried their tears, saying, " It is well. He is happier this evening than when he went out in the morning."

Ben-Hur would not trust a servant to inform Iras what had befallen her father. He went himself to see her and bring her to the body. He imagined her grief ; she would now be alone in the world ; it was a time to forgive and pity her. He remembered he had not asked why she was not of the party in the morning, or where she was ; he remembered he had not thought of her ; and, from shame, he was ready to make any amends, the more so as he was about to plunge her into such acute grief.

He shook the curtains of her door ; and though he heard the ringing of the little bells echoing within, he had no response : he called her name, and again he called— still no answer. He drew the curtain aside and went into the room ; she was not there. He ascended hastily to the roof in search of her ; nor was she there. He questioned the servants ; none of them had seen her during the day. After a long quest everywhere through the house, Ben-Hur returned to the guest-chamber, and took the place by the dead which should have been hers ; and he bethought him there how merciful the Christ had been to His aged servant. At the gate of the kingdom of Paradise happily the afflictions of this life, even its desertions, are left behind and forgotten by those who go in and rest.

When the gloom of the burial was nigh gone, on the ninth day after the healing, the law being fulfilled, Ben-Hur brought his mother and Tirzah home ; and from that day, in that house the most sacred names possible of utter-ance by men were always coupled worshipfully togethe

GOD THE FATHER AND CHRIST THE SON.

———

About five years after the crucifixion, Esther, the wife of Ben-Hur, sat in her room in the beautiful villa by Misenum. It was noon, with a warm Italian sun making summer for the roses and vines outside. Everything in the apartment was Roman, except that Esther wore the garments of a Jewish matron. Tirzah and two children at play upon a lion's skin on the floor were her companions ; and one had only to observe how carefully she watched them to know that the little ones were hers.

Time had treated her generously. She was more than ever beautiful, and in becoming mistress of the villa she had realized one of her cherished dreams.

In the midst of this simple, home-like scene, a servant appeared in the doorway, and spoke to her.

"A woman in the atrium to speak with the mistress."

"Let her come. I will receive her here."

Presently the stranger entered. At sight of her the Jewess arose, and was about to speak ; then she hesitated, changed colour, and finally drew back, saying, " I have known you, good woman. You are——"

"I was Iras, the daughter of Balthasar."

Esther conquered her surprise, and bade the servant bring the Egyptian a seat.

"No," said Iras, coldly. " I will retire directly."

The two gazed at each other. We know what Esther presented—a beautiful woman, a happy mother, a contented wife. On the other side, it was very plain that fortune had not dealt so gently with her former rival. The tall figure remained with some of its grace ; but an evil life had tainted the whole person. The face was coarse ; the large eyes were red and pursed beneath the lower lids ; there was no colour in her cheeks. The lids were cynical and hard, and general neglect was leading rapidly to premature old age. Her attire was ill chosen and draggled. The mud of the road clung to her sandals. Iras broke the painful silence.

"These are thy children ? "

Esther looked at them and smiled.

"Yes. Will you not speak to them ? "

"I would scare them," Iras replied. Then she drew

closer to Esther, and seeing her shrink, said, " Be not afraid. Give thy husband a message for me. Tell him his enemy is dead, and that for the much misery he brought me I slew him."

" His enemy ! "

" The Messala. Further, tell thy husband that for the harm I sought to do him I have been punished until even he would pity me."

Tears arose in Esther's eyes, and she was about to speak.

" Nay," said Iras, " I do not want pity or tears. Tell him, finally, I have found that to be a Roman is to be a brute. Farewell."

She moved to go. Esther followed her.

" Stay, and see my husband. He has no feeling against you. He sought for you everywhere. He will be your friend. I will be your friend. We are Christians."

The other was firm.

" No ; I am what I am of choice. It will be over shortly."

" But "—Esther hesitated—" have we nothing you would wish ? nothing to—to—— ? "

The countenance of the Egyptian softened ; something like a smile played about her lips. She looked at the children upon the floor.

" There is something," she said.

Esther followed her eyes, and with quick perception answered, " It is yours."

Iras went to them, and knelt on the lion's skin, and kissed them both. Rising slowly, she looked at them ; then passed to the door and out of it without a parting word. She walked rapidly, and was gone before Esther could decide what to do.

Ben-Hur, when he was told of the visit, knew certainly what he had long surmised—that on the day of the cruci-fixion Iras had deserted her father for Messala. Neverthe-less, he set out immediately and hunted for her vainly ; they never saw her more, or heard of her. The blue bay, with all its laughing under the sun, has yet its dark secrets. Had it a tongue, it might tell us of the Egyptian.

Simonides lived to be a very old man. In the tenth year of Nero's reign, he gave up the business so long centred in the warehouse at Antioch. To the last he kept a clear head and a good heart, and was successful.

One evening, in the year named, he sat in his arm-chair on the terrace of the warehouse Ben-Hur and Esther and their three children were with him. The last of the ships swung at mooring in the current of the river; all the rest had been sold. In the long interval between this and the day of the crucifixion but one sorrow had befallen them : that was when the mother of Ben-Hur died; and then and now their grief would have been greater but for their Christian faith

The ship spoken of had arrived only the day before, bringing intelligence of the persecution of Christians begun by Nero in Rome, and the party on the terrace were talking of the news when Malluch, who was still in their service, approached and delivered a package to Ben-Hur.

"Who brings this?" the latter asked, after reading

"An Arab."

"Where is he?"

"He left immediately."

"Listen," said Ben-Hur to Simonides.

He read then the following letter :

"I, Ilderim, the son of Ilderim the Generous, and sheik of the tribe of Ilderim, to Judah, son of Hur.

"Know, O friend of my father's, how my father loved you. Read what is herewith sent, and you will know. His will is my will; therefore what he gave is thine.

"All the Parthians took from him in the great battle in which they slew him I have retaken—this writing, with other things, and vengeance, and all the brood of that Mira who in his time was mother of so many stars.

"Peace be to you and all yours.

"This voice out of the desert is the voice of

"ILDERIM, *Sheik.*'

Ben-Hur next unrolled a scrap of papyrus yellow as a withered mulberry leaf. It required the daintiest handling. Proceeding, he read :

"Ilderim, surnamed the Generous, sheik of the tribe of Ilderim, to the son who succeeds me.

" All I have, O son, shall be thine in the day of thy succession, except that property by Antioch known as the Orchard of Palms ; and it shall be to the son of Hur who brought us such glory in the Circus—to him and his for ever.

" Dishonour not thy father. ILDERIM THE GENEROUS, *Sheik*."

" What say you ? " asked Ben-Hur of Simonides.

Esther took the papers, pleased, and read them to herself. Simonides remained silent. His eyes were upon the ship ; but he was thinking. At length he spoke.

" Son of Hur," he said gravely, " the Lord has been good to you in these later years. You have much to be thankful for. Is it not time to decide finally the meaning of the gift of the great fortune now all in your hand, and growing ? "

" I decided that long ago. The fortune was meant for the service of the Giver ; not a part, Simonides, but all of it. The question with me has been, How can I make it most useful in His cause ? And of that tell me, I pray you."

Simonides answered :

" The great sums you have given to the Church here in Antioch, I am witness to. Now, instantly almost with this gift of the generous sheik's, comes the news of the persecution of the brethren in Rome. It is the opening of a new field. The light must not go out in the capital."

" Tell me how I can keep it alive."

" I will tell you. The Romans, even this Nero, hold two things sacred—I know of no others they so hold—they are the ashes of the dead and all places of burial. If you cannot build temples for the worship of the Lord above ground, then build them below the ground ; and to keep them from profanation, carry to them the bodies of all who die in the faith."

Ben-Hur arose excitedly.

" It is a great idea," he said. " I will not wait to begin it. Time forbids waiting. The ship that brought the news of the suffering of our brethren shall take me to Rome. I will sail to-morrow."

He turned to Malluch.

" Get the ship ready, Malluch, and be thou ready to go with me."

" It is well," said Simonides.

"And thou, Esther, what sayest thou?" asked Ben-Hur.

Esther came to his side, and put her hand on his arm, and answered:

"So wilt thou best serve the Christ. O my husband, let me not hinder, but go with thee and help."

* * * * *

If any of my readers, visiting Rome, will make the short journey to the Catacomb of San Calixto, which is more ancient than that of San Sebastiano, he will see what became of the fortune of Ben-Hur, and give him thanks. Out of that vast tomb Christianity issued to supersede the Cæsars.

THE END